The Dark That Binds

The Light of Darkness Book Three
Steve Pantazis

SP Books

Written by Steve Pantazis

Cover artwork by germancreative

Map design by Steve Pantazis

Interior artwork by Samsul Hidayat

Published by SP Books

To my wife, my love, my one and only
To my father, whose wisdom shaped my life
To my mother, who taught me to believe in myself

Contents

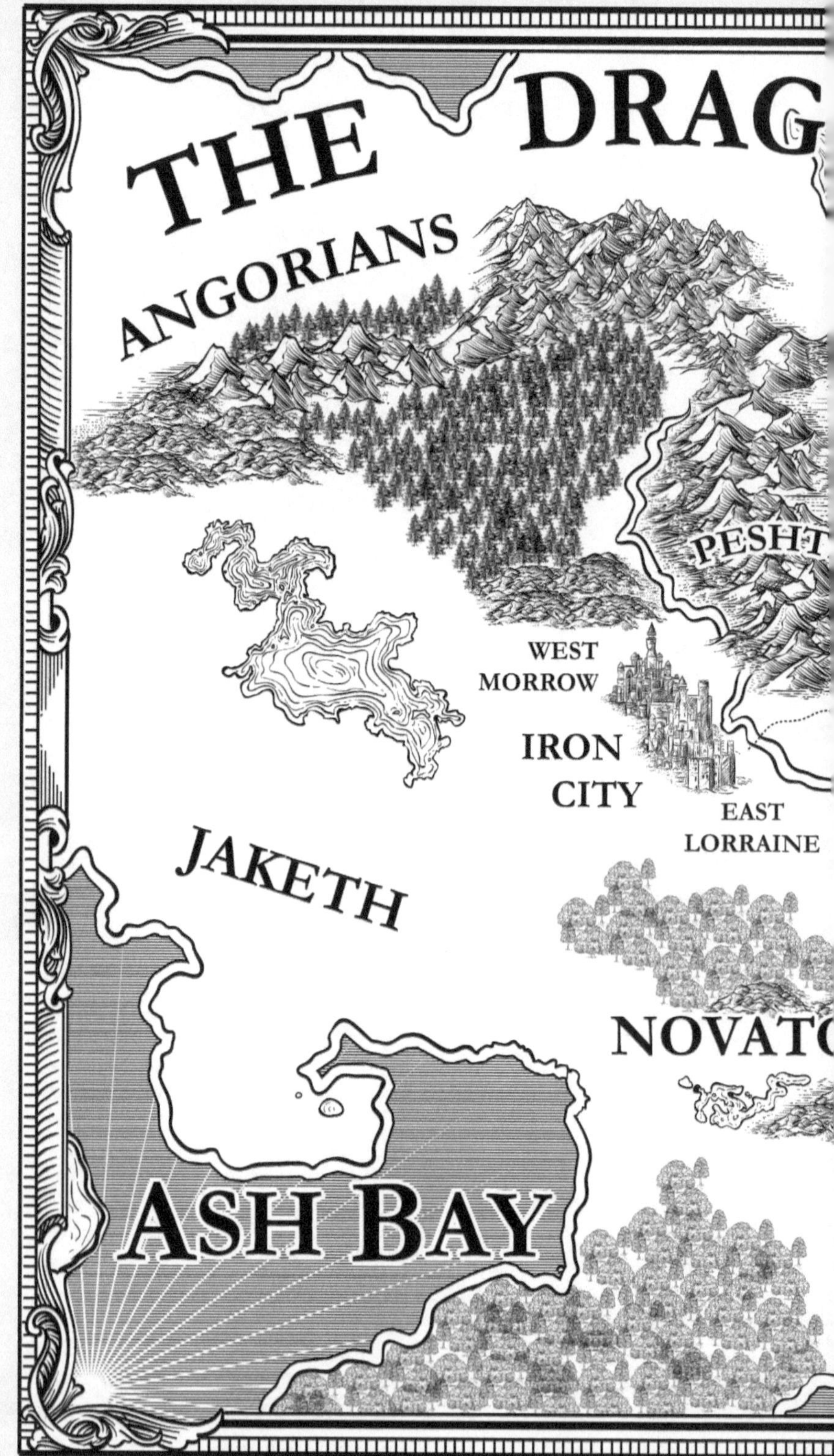

THE DRAG
ANGORIANS
PESHT
WEST MORROW
IRON CITY
EAST LORRAINE
JAKETH
NOVATO
ASH BAY

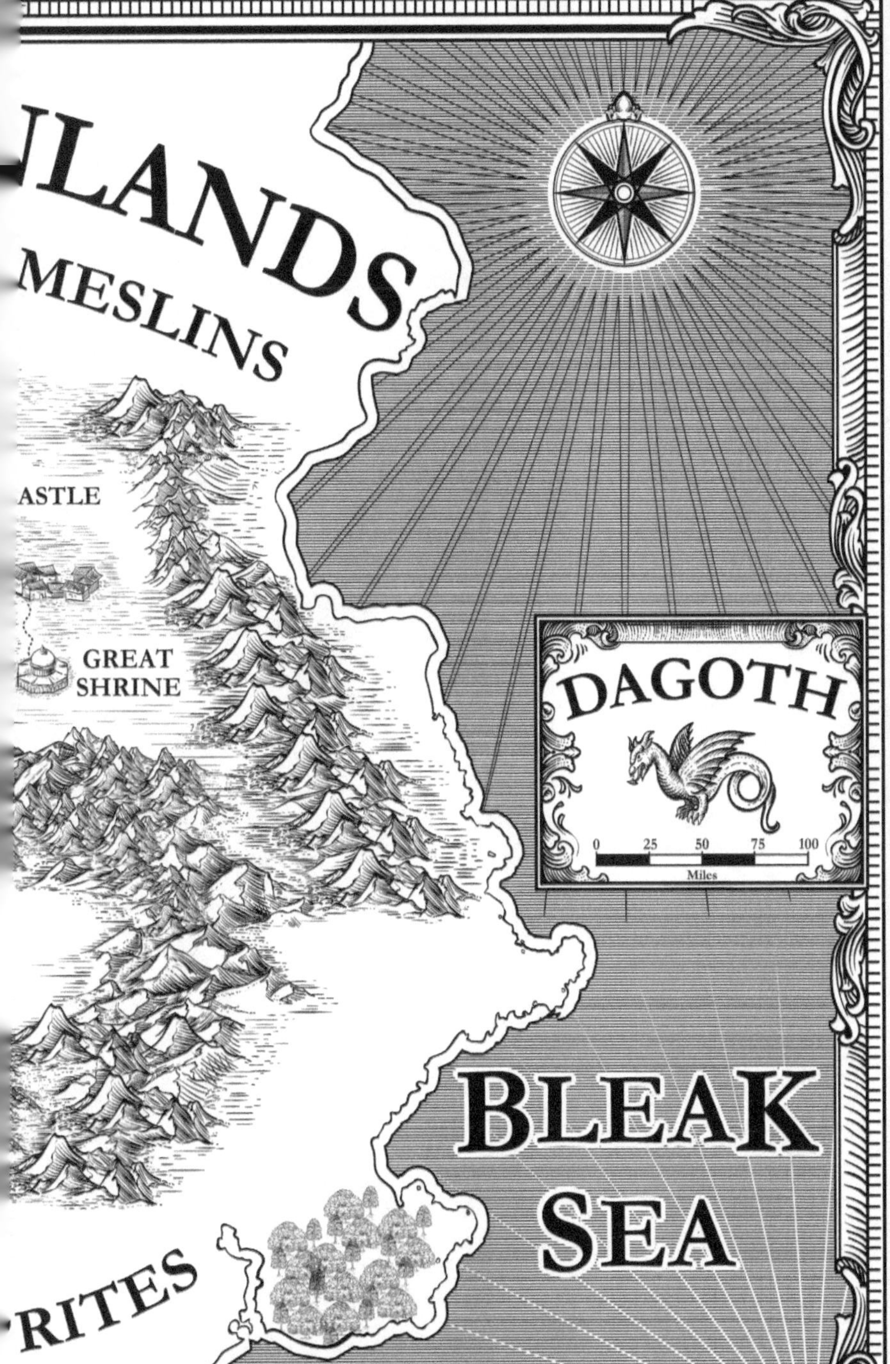
ILANDS
MESLINS
ASTLE
GREAT
SHRINE
RITES
DAGOTH
0 25 50 75 100
Miles
BLEAK
SEA

Chapter 1
The Plunge

KRUUSH PEEKED OVER THE beveled edge of the capstone's sloping roof and cursed under his breath.

The Watcher hadn't moved, not one inch since he had taken up his post by the stairway running down the length of the giant pyramid. How long had he stood with his back to the capstone, cowl drawn over his head, black fingernails dug into the shaft of his looped staff? Mere minutes? Longer? It was as if he'd turned to bronze.

He's become a blasted statue, Kruush thought, clenching his jaw.

Kruush scanned the flagstone-laden grounds around the pyramid far below. They were dotted with grass, brush, and palm trees, along with the ruins of several ancient buildings of worn stone. Sprawling jungle surrounded the complex, thick as the humid air that clung to his skin.

Where was Choola? The strange, little man was supposed to emerge from the jungle, make a ruckus, and draw the Watcher away from Petrah to give the young mage the chance to destroy the portal. Had Choola misunderstood the plan? Or had he lost his nerve and left Kruush and his companions to fend for themselves?

He's a coward, that's what he is.

Kruush ducked his head beneath the one-foot lip of stone that edged the capstone and wiggled his body backward, flat on his belly. Tan and Sooka looked at him expectantly, also on their bellies.

"The Watcher's still there, same spot," Kruush whispered. "No sign of Choola, either."

Sooka, irascible to begin with, scowled so hard his eyebrows knitted together like a long caterpillar. "I told you that depending on him was a bad idea. Did you listen to me? Of course not."

"Did you now? And what glorious plan did you come up with instead?" The heavy stench of the jungle was getting to Kruush, a mix of moist earth, decaying leaves, and tropical gloom.

Sooka slicked back his ragged mop of reddish-brown hair, exposing the sheen on his forehead. "You hired me to take you this far, and I did. Is it my fault we're stuck up here? I'm a guide, not a magician."

Kruush swatted a mosquito. If he never stepped foot in this wretched place again, it would be a blessing. "Petrah needs us. We can't wait here indefinitely. What if the Watcher stays the rest of the day and through the night? We need a distraction to force him to leave."

Tan flicked sweat from his brow with his thumb. "We can't depend on Choola to distract him, now that he vanished."

"I know that," Kruush said, trying to keep his frustration from getting the better of him, as it had Sooka. "It's that confounded Watcher. He's—" Kruush didn't know how to describe him. "Inhuman."

Never had Kruush seen the likes of such a man: tall beyond conception and skin as smooth as a river rock, with a robe that matched the drab, gray patina of his complexion. There was no rise or fall of his chest, no shift of his fingers or feet, nothing but absolute stillness and an unnatural aura that made Kruush's blood run cold.

He's not a man at all.

If he wasn't a man, what was he?

"We can be stealthy," Tan said. "We climb down, nice and quiet, and sneak into the passage below us undetected. Twenty feet of passageway, and we're through the portal. As long as the Watcher keeps his back to us, we can make it."

"And if he turns around?" Kruush asked. "You've not seen how he moves. He's quick as the wind, like nothing you've witnessed. And he wields that staff of his like it's made of bamboo." Kruush shivered, remembering how swift and nimble the Watcher had been and how he'd pushed Petrah through the portal with the tip of his staff before Petrah had the opportunity to destroy it.

"Even so," Tan said. "We should take the chance."

A rumble of thunder cracked from the east as the wind picked up. It smelled like rain. Hiding on a slope of stone was no place to be if a deluge hit them.

Kruush swore, pulling on his matted beard. "Fine, let's take our *chance*. Sooka, you agree?"

The scowl remained on the guide's face. "I'm not going first, if that's what you think."

"Did anyone ask you to go first?"

Tan volunteered. "I'll do it."

"No," Kruush said, twisting his beard into a knot. "It should be me. Then you, then Sooka. And then we—"

A shout broke from the distance, distinctly human. Choola?

Kruush and his companions crawled to the edge of the roof. Kruush peered over the stone lip.

Choola appeared from the jungle, a tiny shape hopping across the field on all fours and waving his arms wildly like a baboon. He yelled up to the Watcher. "*Chakata!*"

The Watcher, still standing at the top of the long stairway running to the base of the pyramid, swiveled his cowl toward the Machoon intruder.

"*Hoomeni da chakata ma!*" Choola called.

The Watcher replied in the same language, his voice ringing out as if striking a temple bell. "*Na Hoomeni!*"

Choola beckoned the Watcher with excited hoops of his arms. "*Chakata ma!*"

The Watcher stepped down the first few steps.

That's it! Kruush thought. *Keep going.*

"*Chakata!*" Choola insisted.

The Watcher took several more steps, then stopped. Only the top of his cowl was visible from Kruush's vantage point.

Go on! Just a few more stairs.

But the Watcher remained where he was, even with Choola taunting him.

"Let's go," Kruush whispered to the others.

Carefully, he slid down the angular stone. Kruush dangled his legs over the eave and dropped as quietly as possible to the landing just below. He backed against the flat face of the tetrahedral capstone and waited for Tan.

Tan wasn't as graceful. His boots thudded the stone loudly.

You idiot! Kruush wanted to yell.

The Watcher climbed several steps and snapped his head toward them. Inky, gleaming eyes peeked out from his cowl.

Kruush froze, breath caught in his throat.

Then he shoved Tan through the narrow passageway. "Move!" He followed right after him. The blackened tunnel ended in a wall with a shimmering oval that floated in front of it.

The portal between worlds.

The oval emitted hazy daylight from the other side—an impossible illusion, considering there should have been a solid wall behind it. The shimmering reminded Kruush of swimming under the surface of a river and looking up through blurry, water-filled eyes. He could make out trees and sticklike towers beyond the rippling face of the wall.

Kruush pushed Tan forward. "Go!"

Tan stumbled and reached out with his hands. A second later, he disappeared.

Kruush turned. Where was Sooka? Just then, the wiry guide appeared at the mouth of the passageway. But as Sooka headed inside, he was flung backward as if he had been caught in a fisherman's net. A horrified look crossed the guide's face, followed by a piercing wail.

And then he was gone.

Gods help us!

Kruush plunged through the portal as if chased by a demon.

Chapter 2
New World

THE FIRST THING PETRAH noticed after stumbling across the portal was the hazy sky—wisps of clouds strewn above, masking the afternoon sun—and that he was alone atop a hill with withered, brown grass, and not a soul in sight. Then the cold hit him, the thick jungle heat replaced by a gust of chilled air filled with the scent of tree sap that made his eyes water. With hands tucked into his armpits, he took in the downward-sloping hillside that led to a valley and a strange city beyond, or what remained of one. The jutting towers of metal and stone clustered together like a band of tall shadows. He could barely make out the shapes through the blur and sting of his tears.

This was the new world.

Dagoth.

His homeland and the wintry domain from his dreams.

And it was freezing.

He'd used his first few minutes on the unfamiliar landscape to search for a spot to shield himself from the unforgiving wind. A minute's walk from where the portal hovered unaffected by the drafts over the short, brown grass, he came upon the edge of a forest of birch and oak, stripped of their leaves. The branches shuddered in the wind and the boughs creaked hauntingly. Petrah found an oak with a wide trunk to block the gusts from scraping his face. Leaning against the sturdy tree, he slipped into a trance using Copper Still, the mantra he'd practiced as a mage journeyman. The world stilled, becoming quiet and distant. Drawing from his channeling skills, he summoned an invisible shield to block the crosswind that nipped at him. It was similar to the one he'd formed to protect against the sandstorm in the great Agobo Desert months earlier.

His teeth stopped chattering long enough for him to blink away the wetness in his eyes and take stock of his situation. He was woefully underdressed in his body-length saba, whose thin fabric did little to protect him. His heavier clothing had been lost when the Machoon hunters had pursued him and his friends in Darkforth. The saba had been plenty warm in the heat of Âhn. But here . . .

Here, it's frigid.

How could the Watcher allow him to come here so unprepared? He hugged his arms to his chest, still deathly cold.

"Allow" was the wrong word.

He pushed me.

The Watcher had shoved him through the portal, and Petrah's opportunity to destroy it from the Acian side was lost.

Petrah shook his head as an upshot of wind dug under his shield, drawing fresh tears. Could he have destroyed the portal, if given more time? When he'd finally made it to the portal, after so much agonizing effort, he'd realized his arcane skills were no match for the powerful magics that had created it. He might have studied the portal for centuries and still lacked the knowledge to undo it.

Petrah peered past the forest's edge, past the grassy slope and valley, to the ruined city of crumbling iron buildings far in the distance. Now that the wind wasn't blinding him, he saw the city was as large as Meerjurmeh's capital of Hōvar and was bordered by a wide river. If he left now, he might find shelter for the night inside the city. But from his vantage point, with trees in the way, he couldn't take in the details well enough to decide how to approach the enormous city. He needed to return to the clearing, to the top of the hill where the portal hung, suspended impossibly off the ground, an oval shape that reminded Petrah of a mirror he had seen in Mokan-lee's manor.

Comforting warmth lay behind the barrier, nagging at him, begging him to return to it, to cast aside caution and step through.

No, he couldn't chance it.

He'd seen what happened when he touched the portal's surface from the Dagothan side in his dreams. It had given Aman clear entry to Acia. Would touching it now, from this side, break the seal between worlds? Or had he already done so when the Watcher had shoved him through?

The right thing to do—the *only* thing to do—was to destroy the portal. But how?

Petrah projected mental feelers to probe the portal's shimmering surface.

He couldn't grasp the edges or find purchase. Was he too far away?

His invisible shield faltered, letting in more cold air. Numbness crept back into his toes, fingertips, and face.

Bracing against the biting chill, he reinforced his shield and strode toward the portal. The gateway between worlds defied the wind that swept across the brown, dead grass.

A few paces short of the shimmering oval, he stopped. The portal swirled at the edges, darkening at the center, hinting at the dark-gray stone of the pyramid passageway on the other side.

Not quite confident his shield would hold, he slipped back into a trance. Again, he extended his mental feelers, sending out tendrils of thought to probe the portal. The portal produced no surface tension, no resistance, nothing to latch on to. At least if he could grasp the edges using a tethering technique, he might be able to manipulate the shape of it, maybe collapse it. Was the portal more like smoke or mist rather than liquid or some type of membrane? If it was, why did the wind have no effect on it?

Petrah's shield faded again. He was losing precious strength—and energy. He gave up on the portal. The shield was more important. So was finding shelter.

Petrah turned his attention back to the city. Without the trees in the way, he was able to discern more details. Dozens of buildings spanned the skyline, taller than any he'd seen in Acia. Windswept clouds cast them in swaths of bronze and gray.

The structures appeared as a twisted system of chewed metal scaffolding, the same as he'd observed in his dreams. Many were stripped of their facades, leaving behind exposed latticework of beams, girders, struts, and columns. It was as if the gods had come down and battled among them. They were all different heights, the tallest higher even than the great stone pyramid, Hachaqua.

In his world of Acia, metal was rarely used in construction. The Ter-jurah and Con-jurah used stone, the Korinians too. The Prallites used lumber to erect their homes, and stone and timber to make fortifications. The artisans of the Provinces of the South, rich with forests, also crafted their abodes from wood.

It appeared the ancients of this world had used metal instead, and they'd clad their structures with stone and precious rectangles of glass. Petrah counted twenty rows of glass running up one of the taller towers. Twelve on another. Sixteen on a third. All the glassblowers of the Provinces in Acia, combined, couldn't produce glass on this scale.

Outside the city limits stood two bridges, also in shambles, spanning a river to an arid stretch of land that was as bleak as the Derel Wastelands in North Terjurmeh. A road carved through the desert, leading to a range of mountains beyond. As Petrah squinted to see down the distant road, he spotted what looked like settlements comprising a handful of smaller dwellings of stone, gray and beige in the light. They were too far away to tell whether people lived there or if they were abandoned by time.

The Watcher had called this place "the Dragonlands," the desolate remnants of a once-flourishing civilization, now laid to waste, as if a dragon had scoured and scorched everything.

But no dragon had done this. This was the result of time and decay. Dagoth was named for its emptiness, and emptiness Petrah felt.

He pulled his saba around him. He needed to find refuge from the wind. The woods offered none. The city was the obvious choice. If Petrah sought soldiers loyal to his brother's cause, he could show them the gold necklace with the medallion the Watcher had given him. They might grant him shelter. The necklace was oppressive in the way it stuck to his chest, like a lodestone against iron.

As Petrah battled to keep his shield intact, questions flooded his mind.

Why hadn't the Watcher warned him the weather would be so harsh? Why hadn't he provided Petrah with a cloak? Why hadn't he set the portal in the city itself?

Which begged another question: where was Petrah's brother?

Petrah had expected Aman to be waiting for him astride his coal-colored horse, surrounded by soldiers on horseback, like the ones in his dreams.

I'm all alone.

Not that he wanted to see his brother. That would just make Petrah his prisoner, and Aman would force Petrah to take him back through the portal.

Petrah trembled as the frost seeped into his skin. He was losing sensation in his cheeks, earlobes, the tip of his nose, toes, and fingertips. He wiggled his toes and flexed his fingers.

With his dwindling reserve of energy, he willed himself into a trance. Projecting his mental feelers once again, he felt outward, toward the city.

Find someone . . . anyone.

He did. Not just one person, but many.

He sensed human heartbeats, faint but present. From what he could tell, the majority of heartbeats were congregated in a tight knot along the eastern and western fringes of the city. Scattered throughout the rest of the city were pockets of people, some on the move.

He widened his search in all directions and noticed a strange shift behind him. Something was happening with the portal. His shield fell away as he lost his concentration. Petrah turned just in time to see two men stumble through the shimmering gateway, one after another.

"Tan! Kruush!"

Kruush ran over to him and grabbed his arm. "The Watcher's coming! Run!"

Tan veered in the forest's direction as if he hadn't seen Petrah, and Kruush ran after him. Petrah chased his friends, shouting, "Stop!" He pushed ahead, overtaking Kruush and then reaching Tan in time to grasp a handful of Tan's saba and yank him to a halt, colliding with him.

Tan tripped, then wheeled, wild-eyed, before recognizing Petrah. "Petrah!"

Petrah drew in hurtful swallows of cold air. He gave Tan a hug, then Kruush. "How did you find me?"

Tan spoke first, drawing his arms close to his body for warmth. "Kruush did. Tell him."

"It doesn't matter," Kruush said crossly, sucking in a mouthful of air. "Gods, it's freezing. Why is it freezing?"

"It's winter here," Petrah said. The brief chase had warmed him, but now he was shaking again, slurring his words from the numbness in his cheeks.

Tan darted his eyes through the trees and toward the portal. "You think the Watcher's coming?"

"I don't know," Petrah said, rubbing his hands together furiously. "But I think the more pressing concern is freezing to death."

"But he saw us!" Tan said.

"And he got Sooka, poor bastard," Kruush added. "But I agree. We'll freeze to death standing here."

Tan looked around, briskly running his hands over his arms. "Where do we go then?"

Icy wind stung Petrah's eyes. He pointed behind him, toward the city. "There. It's our best chance."

Kruush shook his head. "I heard what that Watcher said. He *wants* you to go to your brother. If we stumble into the wrong people—"

"I know that," Petrah said sharply, getting more annoyed by the frigid breath, which burst out in foggy plumes. "What choice do we have?"

"I thought the plan was to destroy the portal," Tan said between chattering teeth.

"I—I can't," Petrah said. "I tried."

"We're on the wrong side, anyway," Kruush said, shivering.

"Coming here was a mistake," Tan said. "We need to go back—" He stopped, looking at the portal. "Wait, something's happening."

The portal's surface rippled as if a storm raged across the surface of a lake. Then it began to dissolve. And shrink. Its edges collapsed in on the center. A few heartbeats later, the portal was gone.

Tan ran over and swiped his hand through the air where the portal was standing a moment earlier. "Where is it?"

Petrah's breathing turned shallow as dread stole the breath from his lungs. He'd intended to destroy the portal. But now that it was gone . . .

Tan raised his voice in alarm. "Where is it, Petrah?"

"I—" Petrah started. "I don't know."

"What do you mean, you don't know? How do we get back home?"

Petrah's jaw ached from his teeth rattling, and his eyes were a watery mess. His neck hurt from shivering so hard. "We have to find shelter before it gets dark." He pointed at the city. "We go there. Agreed?"

Tan, now a quivering, cold mess like Petrah, nodded reluctantly.

Kruush's face blanched as if he'd realized he might never see his wife again. He nodded as well. "Aye, let's get away from this wicked place."

Chapter 3
Strangers

T HE GRAVEYARD THAT WAS once a thriving metropolis resolved itself into stark clarity.

Petrah and his friends clutched arms to chest and trudged quietly as the brunt of the icy wind bore savagely down on them. It wasn't just cold. It was bone-chilling, joint-freezing, teeth-shattering cold.

They traveled the dry, packed ground, devoid of any greenery, to a cracked road made of a dark, charcoal-like gravel pressed flat, perhaps by giant stone rollers like the Korinians used. The roads carved avenues between the disintegrating buildings like black rivers. Wreckage completely blocked some roads, others buckled to where they disappeared into crevasses belowground. Walkways capped either side of the avenues, most broken apart or littered with rubble. Some of the lower buildings had stone or brick facades, cornices, and gables, while those that rose many stories upward were only iron or steel in construction, with entire matrixes of rusting girders, trusses, and beams. Petrah spotted missing floors and partial stairways. The windowpanes that were intact were rectangular, fitted into metal frames in repeating patterns that ran horizontally.

With a shaky finger, Tan pointed at a dilapidated tower that had caved in. "What a mad city. Why would anyone build these things?"

Kruush cupped his hands and blew into them. "Why would the Machoo build pyramids to sacrifice people? None of it makes sense. They're all mad."

"I've been to five cities between Terjurmeh and Meerjurmeh," Tan said, shivering as he spoke. "None have buildings half the height of these, even in Elmar, with their tall minarets. Do you suppose Korin has buildings like these? I've never been there, but I know of the scale of their Grand Pyramids."

Kruush rubbed his arms, then crossed them tightly against his wide chest. "At the rate we're going, none of us will see Korin. Let's stay focused."

Petrah couldn't feel his toes anymore. Nor parts of his face. He'd long since fought the trembling that racked his shoulders and strained his neck. How could anyone stand this place, even with proper attire?

Chilled to the core as he was, he remained vigilant and used his channeling skills to cast a wide net of mental feelers to detect the faintest approach of anything human or animal. Along one avenue, buttressed by slender, metal towers on either side, he picked up movement from behind. "Quick! Someone's approaching."

The three scurried behind a jumble of stone blocks that had been part of a building's exterior, now a slope of jagged rock. Petrah peeked between a chunk of chipped stone that was split like a fishtail, using the slit to peer up the avenue. Eleven horsemen comprising armed male and female riders made their way at a casual pace. They traveled in pairs, save for the rider in front, a woman with steel wingtips upon her helm. She set the tempo, leading her steed with a confident but relaxed posture that told Petrah she was in command. The horses were barded with blankets for warmth, and the riders wore fur-lined woolen cloaks over breastplates, knee guards, and greaves. They had on leather-padded helms and muffs over their ears. Some were equipped with daggers and swords, others with short bows, most with spears. As they passed, Petrah saw the insignia of a coiled serpent embroidered on the backs of their cloaks—Aman's soldiers. All he had to do was show the leader the Watcher's talisman and demand she bring him to see his brother.

I can't do that.

The Watcher wanted Petrah to find his brother. Petrah didn't. With the one portal gone, Aman might know of a second, one that required the Key—Petrah—to unlock. Then Aman would have what he wanted: a way into Acia. Petrah couldn't allow that. But it put him in a difficult spot: not having a way home.

When the riders were well enough along, and the clop of their horses' shod hooves receded, Petrah turned to his friends. "All clear."

"At least they didn't stop," Tan said. "Gods, my chest feels tight, like it's caught in a vise."

"I can't feel my face, and my legs are frozen," Kruush said. "Help me up."

Petrah could hardly feel his friend's hand to help him stand. They needed to find some place warm. But where? With twilight upon them, they were running out of daylight. Petrah's throat was dry and scratchy, his lips chaffed, his limbs quivering, and his nose, ears, and cheeks in pain from the cold. He flexed his fingers to keep his blood circulating. He had heard stories of an affliction that affected unprepared travelers who visited the upper reaches of Acia, where the wind blew cold and snow covered the land. Their skin would turn red and cold, then hard, numb, and pale. The toes were most at risk, sometimes turning black and gangrenous, which would require amputation to save the person's life.

They hurried along, Petrah leading them.

"What do you make of this?" Tan's speech slurred as he pointed at a rusted pole leaning at a steep angle from an intersection of roads. A narrow metal placard was mounted on top. It had faded green paint and foreign symbols stamped on its surface.

Petrah's speech came out just as slurred, his cheek muscles deadened by the cold. "A guidepost maybe. I saw similar ones in my dreams."

Kruush covered his eyes as a headwind battered them. "Who cares what purpose they served? Petrah, where's our blasted shelter already?"

Petrah felt along the avenue with his mind. "Next street over."

They trudged on, feet like blocks of stone, passing a plaza with a cracked stone fountain and heading toward a short building with large, granite squares along the base. "There," Petrah said.

A fire glowed through empty metal window frames, their panes of glass gone, exposing the interior to the elements. The stone facing that once covered the lowest stories of the outside lay in piles of rubble. Petrah caught the scent of charbroiled meat through the open windows.

"I'm sensing four people inside, three adults and a child. I don't know if any of them are armed or part of Aman's army."

"I thought we said we were going to avoid people," Tan said.

Kruush kneaded his shaking hands. "The devil may care if they're soldiers or squatters. I can't stand this damned wind a moment longer."

"Then we agree to approach these people?" Petrah asked. "Tan?"

Tan, stiff as if his lower body had frozen solid, nodded curtly.

Petrah could see the people plainly through the window frames, huddled around a campfire set upon a tiled floor. The two men were square-jawed with curly, almost frizzy beards—the older one with gray, thinning hair, and the younger one with dark, wavy hair. The woman was considerably heavier than the men and fair-complected. The girl had brown skin and was maybe five or six years old. They wore pants, shoes, shirts, and coats, with scarves around them—styles unfamiliar to Petrah. The shearing wind didn't seem to penetrate the glassless windows, and their campfire burned with no sputter. A V-shaped gap in the wall offered the only way in without having to climb over a windowsill.

Petrah squeezed through the gap, trailed by his friends. "Hello?"

The older male jumped up in an instant and drew a short sword from the scabbard by his feet. The younger male drew a knife. The heavyset woman pulled the young girl behind her.

Petrah held up neutral hands as the man with the sword approached him. He was tall, like Petrah. His narrow blade differed from the heartier blades of Terjurmeh. This was a crude weapon meant for piercing, not hacking, making it a poor choice for the battlefield. But here, facing three unarmed men who were cold and weakened, it carried a mighty advantage.

"We mean no harm," Petrah said, teeth chattering. "We just need warmth." He rubbed his hands together to display his intent.

The man with the sword spoke to him. It sounded like gibberish at first, although the tempo and cadence had a familiar quality. It was the same dialect as the riders used. It made Petrah think of his mother.

"He doesn't speak Jurmehan," Tan said, holding his palms out submissively as well.

The man with the sword uttered something else, this time more aggressively, taking another step toward Petrah.

"I think I understand him," Petrah said. He spoke a couple of choppy words he thought the man might understand.

The man shook his head, not comprehending.

Petrah tried again, pointing to himself as he stressed the first word. "Meeee." Then the second. "Frennn."

"Me fren?"

No, that wasn't it. *Think. You know this.* Wasn't this the language Petrah's mother spoke? The language Petrah spoke as a child? He strained to remember what she said to him in her dreams. He pointed at himself again. "Me."

The man pointed at him. "You."

Petrah gave a conservative nod, pantaining his excitement. He tried the second word. "Fren."

The man blinked. "Friend?"

Petrah cracked a smile. He was getting somewhere. "Yes." Petrah placed a hand on his chest. "Me friend."

The man looked at Petrah strangely and asked a question. Petrah rolled the unusual-but-familiar syllables around in his head. When Petrah bumbled his response, the man asked again, slower and clearer.

The words fit like a belt and buckle, coming together cohesively. *"Who are you?"*

"Walker," Petrah said, chastising himself for not knowing the word "traveler." It caused as much confusion as he imagined it would. He pretended his mother had asked the question. *Who are you, son?* In his dreams, they spoke easily to each other. Were they speaking Jurmehan? He couldn't recall. "Come from," he started, as if answering his mother. "Come from," he repeated. *You come from far away*, his mother said. *But you're here now, home where you belong.* "From far away." That seemed to communicate the point.

The man lowered his sword a little. "From where?"

Petrah made a circle with one hand and stuck his finger through. Again, he played the conversation in his mind as if talking with his mother. "Another land," he said. It was ambiguous, but the man got the meaning.

"What do you want from us?"

You want to warm yourself, Petrah imagined his mother saying to him in her native tongue. *And you're thirsty. Tell the nice man.* "Heat." Petrah tapped his lips. "Water." He wanted to say food, too, but that would be pushing it. *Ask him if it's acceptable.* "Is all right?"

The older man glanced at the younger one, who looked like he might be his son, but then shook his head and said, "You're strangers. We don't know you. You should go elsewhere."

But there's nowhere for us to go.

Petrah rummaged through his memories, his dreams, anything that could help him conjure the right thing to say. The word he most desperately needed came to his lips. "Please."

The woman said, "You're dressed oddly. What is your purpose here?"

Tan butted in. "What's she saying?"

"Hush," Petrah told him. His thoughts were still coalescing, becoming more coherent now that the wind wasn't knifing his face. *Tell him you're looking for me*, his mother said in his mind. "Find mother," he said to the woman. *And that you've come a long way and have far to go.* He could barely pantomime the motion with his still-thawing fingers. "Have to walk far."

She pressed him with another question. "Don't you have somewhere else you can go?"

If Petrah and his companions were turned away, they might freeze to death. "No." He gave her a pleading look. "Please."

The woman considered his response, tapping a finger against her chin. The girl remained behind her, and the men kept their defensive postures. At last, the woman said, "You can share our fire." She gave the older man a meaningful look. "Right?"

The older man dropped his sword by his side and shrugged. The younger one motioned for Petrah and his friends to join them.

"Thank you," Petrah said, relieved as much as he was grateful.

The fire produced a pleasant blaze, although it had an unnatural smell. When Petrah peered into the small metal tub that produced the flame, he saw no firewood.

The girl poked her head out from the woman's hip. "What's your name?" She had green eyes, like the woman.

"Petrah."

She giggled. "That's a funny name."

"What your name?"

"You mean, '*What's* your name.'"

"Yes, sorry. *What's* your name?"

The girl pointed proudly to herself. "Mila!"

"Pleased to meet you, Mila." Petrah smiled, and the girl returned the smile. The words they exchanged tickled his ears with strange comfort, like bringing water to parched lips. This was the language of his childhood. He had forgotten how to speak it, but understood everything he heard. With his mother's help—and encouragement—he'd speak it again.

You're doing great, his mother said in his thoughts. *See how the words are coming back to you? It'll get easier.*

The others introduced themselves. The older man was Sammus, the younger his son, Yunior, and the woman was Teenuh, who was also Mila's mother. Petrah introduced his friends. Kruush and Tan bowed their heads, giving thanks in Jurmehan.

Sammus passed around a metal canteen. Petrah took his fill of water and passed it on to his friends. The water eased his frost-scraped throat. The heat from the fire helped return the circulation to his face and fingers. The thaw left painful, needle-like tingles in his feet and hands.

Yunior asked, "Where does your mother live?"

Petrah made a motion with his hands. "In city, I think." The man gave a confused look and Petrah corrected himself. "I believe"—he willed the words to his lips—"she lives in the city."

"What's her name? Maybe we've met her."

Petrah didn't know his mother's name. Not once had it been uttered in his dreams. In fact, he had never thought of what her real name might be. He knew only one name: "I call her Mama."

Yunior laughed and Sammus joined in. Even Teenuh cracked a smile. "That's funny," Yunior said. "*Mama*," he said to the others, still laughing.

Mila spoke up. "You don't know your mama's name? I know mine!"

The woman tsked. "Mila, don't be rude!" Then to Petrah, she said, "Forgive my daughter. She can be brash at times."

"I understand," Petrah said. "But I think the word is"—he searched his memory—"*bold*." *Good*, Petrah's mother said. *You were bold, too. And brash. And many other good things.*

"Bold perhaps, but she needs to learn her place among strangers." Teenuh gave her daughter a chastising look, then carried on. "When was the last time you saw your mother?"

"I not seen her since—" Petrah started over. "I *have* not seen her since I was little, maybe Mila's age. I've been looking for her for many years."

"That's much too long to not see one's mother. I hope you find her."

Sammus looked Petrah over suspiciously. "Why are you dressed like that? This is winter. Always winter here."

"What's he asking?" Kruush said.

"About our lack of clothing." To Sammus, Petrah said, "It's"—Petrah wished he remembered how to say "complicated" in his native tongue—"a long story." It didn't dilute the man's suspicion, but he gave a look of understanding.

It was almost dark outside. There was no way Petrah or his friends could survive the night without proper heat or clothing. *Ask them if you can stay the night,* Petrah's mother said to him. *You know the words now.* He did, and they flowed seamlessly from his lips. "May we stay here tonight? We promise to leave first thing in the morning."

In a surprise move, Sammus grabbed Petrah by the wrist, turning it over. "Where's your mark?"

Petrah pulled free. "What mark?" He was shaken by the man's aggression.

Sammus held up his left wrist so Petrah and his companions could see. It was scarred as if branded by a hot iron. Petrah made out the shape of a serpent wreathed in flame with a ring around it. The others had identical brands, even the girl.

Petrah tugged down on the collar of his saba to show Sammus the medallion resting against his chest. This time, he could pull it away from his skin. He showed the serak on the front, the triangle with the lidless eye of San in the center that served as the religious symbol for the Ter-jurah and An-jurah. He flipped it over to reveal the relief of a serpent uncoiling from the center on the other side, nearly identical to the brands these people had on their flesh.

Sammus backed away as if struck by a draft of wind. "Holy Father!" He moved his fingers up and down three times in rapid succession. "Look!" he said to the others.

The adults took their turns looking, but their reactions were similarly fearful. They all made the same up-and-down motions with their hands.

"Are you an enforcer?" Sammus asked.

Petrah had never heard of the term. "Enforcer?"

"An anointed one." When Petrah didn't respond, Sammus said, "A servant of the Shrine whose duty is to enforce the faith."

"No, I'm not an enforcer," Petrah said. "Neither are they." He gestured to his friends, who were taking in the conversation with reservation.

Sammus's brown eyes reflected a mix of relief and disappointment. He sheathed his sword and motioned for Yunior to put his dagger away. "There's power in the device you wear. I can feel it. Maybe you're from the spirit world. Maybe you're here to test us, to see if we're worthy, sent by the Holy Father himself." He moved his fingers up and down three times, as before.

Petrah let the man toil with the thought. Better to give in to his superstition than to bare the truth. "Where did you get your marking?"

Sammus frowned. "The Shrine, of course. Where else? Everyone has them, except the Unbelievers." He spat on the ground. "Are your friends Unbelievers?"

Teenuh smacked Sammus on the shoulder. "Don't be rude." Then she repeated the question to Petrah. "Are they Unbelievers?"

"Of course not," Petrah said. "They're just like me."

"What's happening?" Kruush asked warily.

"They're pointing out how dangerous it is for us as foreigners." Petrah pushed the subject of their stay, directing the question to Teenuh. "May we rest here tonight?"

"Your companions, they're not thieves, are they, or cutthroats?" she asked.

"Look at them," Petrah said. "They're not even armed."

"They speak differently from you."

"We all speak *Jurmehan*. Please. It's just one night."

Teenuh gave it some thought, then said, "Very well, you can stay." Sammus protested, but she shushed him. "They're not sleeping out in the cold. We have food and spare blankets." She pointed to the folded wool blankets and bulging backpacks in the corner. "We might have something warmer for you to wear."

"Thank you." Petrah looked around the room. There were broken tiles and porcelain, debris, and sections of collapsed ceiling revealing rusting steel trusses. The masonry wall at the back of the foyer had stress fractures spidering across. A dim passageway lay beyond. "Is this your home?"

Teenuh's face fell. "Our home is gone. This is temporary."

"I'm sorry, I didn't—"

"The mountain raiders destroyed our home. We're lucky to have our lives." Her expression turned more hopeful. "We're pilgrims, on our way to the Great Shrine. Father protect us, but we should get there in a few days. You're welcome to join us." Sammus gave her a dark look, but she whisked her hand at him and went on. "The Grand Marshall's army will look after us. They despise the raiders. Show them your amulet, and they will let you pass."

Petrah had no interest in going near any shrine or army, so he simply thanked her.

Yunior served Petrah and his friends helpings of roasted meat and unleavened bread baked into crunchy rectangles. The meat was gamey, like lope, but there wasn't much to share.

Petrah gave his appreciation, but could tell Sammus wanted them out as soon as possible. He had every intention of granting the man his wish.

"How well do you know the city?" Teenuh asked.

"Not well at all," Petrah said. "This is my first time here since I was . . ." He pondered it. "Since I was a boy." The words of his native tongue came easier to him now.

"You said you want to find your mother, yes?"

"Yes."

"And you believe she's in the city?"

Petrah couldn't recall from his dreams a specific place, but with the ruination he'd seen, it had to be the city. "Yes."

"Then your best bet to find her is to go to East Lorraine or West Morrow. They're on opposite ends of the city. The Grand Marshall has a garrison in East Lorraine, so if you head there, be careful. They're a rough-and-tumble lot."

"Where's the Great Shrine?" Petrah asked.

"Out in the desert. If you travel far enough, you'll encounter settlements along the way." Petrah noted the word "travel" for future reference. "Strange that you don't know these things, considering the amulet you wear. It was given to you, wasn't it?" Her question prompted a dubious look from Sammus.

"It was given to me, yes."

Yunior said, "If the cleric's men catch you lying, they'll cut out your tongue. They have no tolerance for Unbelievers."

"We're true believers," Petrah said, signing the air up and down three times as Sammus had done.

Sammus's expression remained sour. "So you say." He buttoned his jacket and went outside.

Teenuh said, "Don't mind Sammus. He means well. He just wants to protect us."

"Thank you for letting us stay with you," Petrah said, realizing how poorly equipped the Watcher had left him.

"The cold is cruel, the wind is worse. You'll have neither this night."

Teenuh doled out blankets to her guests—scraps of wool patched together and worn with use. Petrah draped a blanket over his shoulders and let the thick material trap his body heat. It smelled of tallow. After that, Teenuh and Mila bedded down while Sammus and Yunior made small talk. Kruush, Tan, and Petrah found a spot near the corner, away from the others. They sat facing each other on the hard floor. Petrah filled his friends in on his exchange with their benefactors.

Tan gave Petrah a friendly pat on the leg. "Nicely done. I thought for a moment they would send us off to fend for ourselves. But you negotiated like a master trader, and in their language, no less. Impressive."

"Agreed," Kruush said, eyes puffy from fatigue. "I'm proud of you. Mokan-lee would be too. And that's saying a lot."

The mention of Mokan-lee stirred up an image of the mogul's daughter smiling at Petrah, her large, brown eyes lifting at the corners to match her shapely lips.

Mina would be proud as well, Petrah thought. His hand went to the breast pocket of his saba, where Mina's lock of hair was safely stowed. To know that part of her was with him—and had traveled across worlds—eased the tension in his shoulders and stilled his racing heart.

Kruush's cheeks drooped, and his demeanor turned melancholy. "What are we doing here, Petrah? Not this building, but here, in this dreadful land? The portal is gone. Wasn't our aim to destroy it? What else was there for us to do?"

"We don't know that it's gone," Petrah said. "It disappeared, yes. But I didn't make it vanish. It did so on its own." *Or the Watcher did it.*

"Then we should return to the hilltop on the morrow," Tan said. "If it's not there, then we can assume it's gone for good."

Kruush furrowed his brow. "With what provisions, exactly? We have no food, no water, no warm clothes of our own. And if the portal is still gone, what do we do, wander the countryside? Leave and come back yet again? Or light a fire and sing songs while we wait for it to magically reappear?"

Tan's face pinched in annoyance. "If you have a better idea, let's hear it."

Kruush wrung his hands. "I don't have ideas, just questions. How do I get back to my wife? How do we go home? How do we depart this horrid place and never come back?"

We've just arrived, Petrah wanted to tell him. But his purpose—*their* purpose—had been singular: to stop Aman from crossing into Acia. Was the portal gone for good, or would it return? Was there another somewhere in the city? Or perhaps on an open field like in his dream?

The Watcher had sent Petrah to Dagoth to find his brother, insisting Petrah was the Key and that he was integral to Aman's plans to bring a great and terrible prophecy to fruition. If Petrah refused his destiny, if he avoided his brother, could he keep Aman from achieving his goal and entering Acia? How else could Petrah stop him?

"Petrah?" Tan asked.

Petrah looked at his friends. They were weary, but their eyes revealed more than mere exhaustion. There was a feverish brightness, a desperation in how they waited for him to answer and assure them he could find a way home.

"Let me think," Petrah said.

Kruush sniffed with disapproval and looked away. Tan offered a tight-lipped smile of encouragement.

Petrah watched the dwindling fire, pondering, pondering, yet coming up with no answers. The flames danced orange and blue. His thoughts drifted off, lost in the memories of his dreams. Although he couldn't remember the details of his childhood, he could remember his mother's embrace, hear her voice, and see her face. She was his one connection to the past . . . and to this place.

She abandoned me.

The thought stirred up dark feelings. A mother would never do that to a child, someone she loved and cared about, would she?

No, she hid me from my brother to protect me.

That made more sense. A mother might let her child go if it meant saving his life.

But she could have followed me.

That part stung. Why hadn't she gone with him to Acia? Was that also to protect him, or to rid herself of a burden? It got him thinking about how he got to Acia in the first place. If his mother had found a portal, that meant . . .

She must know where one is!

That was it! Petrah turned to Tan and Kruush. "I have an idea for how we can find a portal home."

Kruush arched a curious brow. "Don't you mean *the* portal?"

"That's the thing," Petrah said. "The Watcher indicated there might be more than one. I've seen several in my dreams, none quite the same."

Kruush folded his arms across his chest. "What are you saying?"

"I'm saying we need to find someone who can either create one or find one for us."

"And who would that be?"

Petrah's voice cracked with emotion. "My mother."

Chapter 4
Trapped

PETRAH STIRRED BEFORE FIRST light, muscles cold and stiff from having slept the night on the hard floor. The scent of meat from the evening before was gone, replaced by wintry nothingness.

Petrah had shared a blanket with Tan, small but thick enough to keep them warm. Sammus and Yunior were already up, packing their belongings next to a lantern that was partially shuttered, attending to the task with care to not make any noise. Teenuh was still asleep with Mila cradled against her, the pair wrapped in an animal skin of dark fur. Mila had her thumb tucked into her mouth. Petrah marveled at Teenuh and her daughter, at the love they had for each other. It made Petrah's heart ache to see his mother again.

She's here, somewhere.

But where? And how would he find her?

Petrah sat up. His bladder was full, and he had an oily taste in his mouth, like rancid fat. Although the flame was out from the kettle that produced their fire, Petrah felt its residual heat, as if there were coals inside, still aglow.

He had dreamed of his mother, of her crying alone by a campfire. In his dream, he had seen her face, her pale blue eyes and sunken cheeks, and her brown hair that was turning gray. She had worn a beaded necklace with a silver pendant and fish stamped on it.

The necklace gave Petrah an idea.

He roused Tan, then Kruush, who had curled up covered with a shirt that Teenuh had lent him. They collected themselves, looking weary and wrung out, and sat up.

"Good morning," Petrah said, trying to sound cheery.

"Is it now?" Kruush rubbed his temples. "Gods, my head feels like a gonatan stomped all over it."

"It looks like it too," Tan said, peeling back his half of the crumpled blanket to massage his calves. "Yes, quite a stomping, I'd say."

Kruush snorted and pointed at Tan's hair, which was sticking up at an angle. "You're a fine one to talk. And if you care to know, I was dreaming of bacon. Lovely, lovely bacon. A thick slab cooked in a skillet over a fire, served with a nice helping of pujin to mop up the grease. Oh, and cha to sip and ponder how I might spend my day with my wife. Not wake up here to see your ugly face."

"I think the word you're looking for is handsome." Tan licked his palm and smoothed back his hair. "But bacon does sound good. Do you suppose they have any in Dagoth?"

"By San's teeth, they better." Kruush glanced over at Sammus, who gave him a dark look. "Or perhaps not. There's no telling what these people eat. But I have a feeling—"

Petrah cleared his throat. "Gentlemen, if I might interrupt?" When he had their attention, he continued. "I have an idea to propose."

Tan asked, "Does it have anything to do with bacon?"

"Sadly, no. But it has to do with finding my mother." Petrah paused as Junior walked past them to fetch a small travel pack of worn burlap propped up by the back wall. "I can't say that she's alive, but in my heart, I believe she is. Nor can I say where she might live, only that I believe she's here, somewhere in this city. Or, if not in the city, then perhaps one of the settlements outside the city limits."

"Searching for her could take months," Kruush said.

"It could." Petrah had waited years to find her. "Or it could take a lifetime . . . or just one day." Kruush arched a brow. "I know it seems impossible. But consider this. After I got separated from you, Sooka, and Choola in Darkforth, what happened to me? I was lost. I couldn't find you. I couldn't get back to the top of the waterfall I had tumbled over, and I didn't know where to go. At one point, with fever raging from the dog bite and endless dizziness, I thought I might lie down and never wake up. But I couldn't do that. I had to locate Hachaqua." He folded the corner of the blanket draped over his knee into a triangle, recreating the step pyramid. He tapped it with a finger. "I had seen it in my dream with the Watcher, but I didn't know where it was or if it existed."

"But you found it," Tan said. "Just like Kruush found it."

Kruush nodded. "He had put a picture of it in my mind, somehow. Different from how he got there, I suppose."

"Yes," Petrah said. "I got there because I'd visualized the pyramid and let it manifest its location for me. I *felt* it. The same with Kushan, if you recall."

Kruush grinned. "I remember. You were drawn to that woeful place like a lodestone. Sooka thought it ridiculous." He chuckled, then lost his smile. "I hope the Watcher let the poor sap go. Sooka was testy, but he was a decent man."

Petrah doubted the Watcher would let Sooka go. He'd seen the giant cave in a man's skull without hesitation. "In my dream last night, I saw my mother. She was wearing a necklace with a silver pendant. I have a faint memory of that necklace. If she still has it . . ."

Tan beamed. "Then you might locate it. Find the necklace and you find your mother."

"Exactly." Petrah returned a wide grin of his own. Teenuh was awake now. Mila continued to sleep as her mother unlatched her arms from her daughter and stood. Soon, everyone would be up. "I'm going to close my eyes. This should only take a few minutes."

Petrah shut his eyes and quieted his mind. He concentrated on his mother's necklace—the shape of it, the way it glinted in the light, how he imagined it in his palm, the weight of it. He placed his fingers on the cold floor and let them move back and forth, searching for a warmth in the center of his forehead, as he'd done in the jungle when searching for the pyramid.

When he opened his eyes, his fingers faced east, toward the empty window frames in the front of the building. "That way," he said.

Kruush bobbed his head. "Then east it is."

After Mila finally roused, Teenuh invited Petrah and his friends to share a breakfast of oat bars that smacked of butter and honey. A few mouthfuls of water washed down the gritty, dense oats. The food quelled Petrah's hunger and gave him a burst of energy.

"Thank you for sharing your food and drink with us," Petrah said. "And for letting us stay the night."

Teenuh smiled. "You're quite welcome."

Mila leaned her head against her mother's shoulder, and Teenuh rubbed her arm.

"Have you decided where you will go?" Teenuh asked.

"East Lorraine."

"Remember what I told you. There's a garrison stationed there. But—" She looked Petrah over, top to bottom. "You can't travel like that. You have no possessions, no weapons, nothing to barter with except for the device around your throat, and nothing to keep you warm. That won't do."

She searched through her packs and pulled out a thin jacket of treated leather, along with a gray wool sweater, and a crocheted scarf of faded brown. She handed the items to Petrah. "It's the best we can offer." The wool and leather had mingled with the scents of each other.

Yunior got up. "What are you doing? Those are ours."

"Not anymore," Teenuh said. Before Yunior could raise his voice, she cut him off. "Those weren't ours to begin with, remember? They were taken, not earned."

"Those people were dead," Yunior countered. "If we hadn't taken their clothing, someone else would have."

"And now the dead serve the living yet again. I won't see these men freeze, Yunior."

"Let them have the clothes and be on their way," Sammus told his son. He gave Petrah a look that teetered between sympathy and disdain. Petrah nodded kindly, and this time Sammus reciprocated.

Petrah let Tan have the jacket. Kruush couldn't fit his boxy body into the sweater, so Petrah wore it and gave Kruush the scarf, which unfolded to be more of a shawl. Petrah ran his hands over the knit sweater. The wool was surprisingly soft, swaddling his body with much-needed warmth.

Teenuh provided Petrah with directions for finding East Lorraine. "Travel the avenue north, then cut east. You'll know you're there when you see the barricade: a fortified wall that runs north to south across several blocks. Behind the wall lies the Grand Marshall's war camp. His men guard the barricade and patrol the perimeter. There are two gates for the common folk, one leading in, the other out. The guards will question you, and if they see fit, they will detain you, and you don't want that. The better option is to hang back a couple of blocks and walk due east to the water's edge. That's where the fishermen go. Follow the bank south along the river and you'll pass a gap between the river and the barricade. Keep going and you'll enter East Lorraine. It's the longer, more roundabout route, but it'll get you in without being hassled."

"What about soldiers?" Petrah asked. "Don't they guard the gap?"

"They don't have to," she said. "There's a seawall. It's difficult to scale, although I've heard there are stairs that climb up from the shore. But there are plenty of soldiers around. Keep your head down, mind your business, and avoid eye contact. Most important: don't let them see that you're not marked. Hide your wrists."

Petrah said his goodbyes and thanked Teenuh profusely for her advice and generosity. She even gave him a canteen of water and some of the oat bars, enough for a meal among them. Petrah handed the bars to Tan, who stuffed them into the clever pockets stitched on the inside of his jacket. The canteen had an adjustable leather strap attached to a pair of small metal rings on top of the canteen, creating a loop. He pulled the strap over his head to let the canteen rest crosswise against his chest.

"One deed deserves another," she said. "If you carry it forward to someone in need, then you repay the debt."

"We won't forget that," Petrah said. "How will you get to your shrine?"

"There's a caravan leaving by the west bridge. We'll gather there, resupply, and head across the river. Are you sure about going to East Lorraine? It's not a kind place."

"I understand, but it's our best chance."

"Then blessed be the Father. May his shadow keep you safe." She signed the air.

"Thank you, Teenuh, for everything."

Mila waved her fingers at Petrah as he prepared to head out. "I hope you find your mama," she said, smiling up at him.

Petrah smiled back. "I hope so too."

O UTSIDE, SUNLIGHT FILTERED BETWEEN the clouds, lighting up the avenue. Even with their new attire, the headwind was ruthless in how it clawed their exposed faces and hands and penetrated the gaps in their clothing. Petrah blinked fresh tears.

"The wind snatches your breath away," Tan said, shielding his mouth against a sudden gust.

Kruush used his scarf to protect the lower part of his face. "Is it like this all year long? Surely, there must be a warm season."

"I've never seen it," Petrah said. "Not once in my dreams."

Kruush shook his head. "Dreams are meant to escape reality. You can be warm or wealthy or at a tavern with friends, surrounded by casks of ale and feasting on piping-hot manja stuffed with sweet figs while listening to a minstrel sing a song for your beloved. And you can dream of summer too. Even in a place such as this."

Petrah's dreams painted the worst aspects of reality. How wonderful it would be to dream as Kruush did.

"When we return home," Petrah said, wishing he had something warm to cover his head, "I'll take us to the finest tavern in Hōvar. Ahleen and Mina will join us, and we'll dine like kings and queens and drink until we're deep in our cups and the sun rises. And maybe we'll find Tan a respectable woman."

Tan flashed a grin. He had the collar of his jacket flipped up to guard his neck from the wind. "Or just a woman. She doesn't have to be respectable. But I appreciate the gesture."

They wended around rubble and down avenues that could easily fit a dozen horsemen side by side. Petrah remained vigilant, sending out mental feelers to detect threats. They encountered a smattering of people—one or two at a time—bundled up with heavy coats and walking briskly, with nary a glance their way. No militia or riders. Tall buildings lined the streets, their once-gleaming glass windows dulled, cracked, or broken—the few that still sat in their steel casings. Grass and shrubs sprouted randomly from the split roads and sidewalks, the grass browned and the shrubs leafless.

During their short breaks, Petrah would concentrate on his mother's voice. It drew him northeast. The wind died down for a time, giving him and his companions respite from the dreadful chill.

"Look at these," Kruush said as they passed a fenced-in area with rows of hip-high granite stones of varying shapes, many bearing faded inscriptions. A few had accompanying figurines, also weathered. Yellowed weeds grew between them. "Odd form of decoration, wouldn't you say?"

"I think they mark and honor the dead," Petrah said. The strap from Teenuh's canteen dug into his neck. He repositioned it to rest over his sweater. "I believe the deceased are entombed below."

"Why wouldn't they just bury them out in the desert or in a catacomb?"

Petrah didn't have an answer. "I would ask their ancestors."

Kruush harrumphed. "Strange world you come from."

Once they passed the display of stones, Tan pointed up the avenue. "We're close."

Several hundred feet ahead was the barricade Teenuh had mentioned: a wall built across the road, constructed of sheets of metal cascading over one another. Petrah estimated the wall to be twenty to twenty-five feet in height. It connected two buildings occupying opposing sides of the road with a double-hinged gate in the center. Twin pennants with red dragons were mounted on either end. The gate was open to a line of drays and wagons pulled by horses or donkeys and a few people on foot shouldering baskets stuffed with belongings. Petrah counted four soldiers, two inspecting the first wagon and another two talking among themselves.

"I think we've gone too far," Petrah said, looking in the direction of the river, which was blocked by a building that had collapsed and left a skeleton of rusted metal and a cascade of shattered glass and slabs of broken stone. Teenuh had suggested hanging back a couple of blocks from the barrier and heading due east.

They backtracked to the nearest intersection and turned east. Morning gave way to afternoon, and they came upon the river. The wind was especially brutal out in the open, with no buildings to shield its wrath. It sheared the surface of the water, creating a slight chop. The water rolled in lightly against a rocky shoreline below a seawall that rose thirty feet to street level. Petrah tucked his hands under his sweater, but the cold was so severe, he could hardly feel them. A short distance north, the seawall had collapsed, leaving a landslide of broken bedrock along the shore's edge. This river was nothing like the ones in Terjurmeh and Meerjurmeh. It stretched far across to the other side and was more turbulent.

"We can climb down there," Petrah said, noting the broken bedrock. He wiped his runny nose with the back of one hand and wiped the tears from his eyes with the other. His earlobes hurt from the scaling chill, and he could see his friends suffering just the same as they hugged their arms to their chests and turned their heads away from the wind to breathe, lest it snatch their breath away.

They picked their way down the chunks of the roadside to the rock-strewn shoreline. As Teenuh had said, this was where the fishermen went. They were spread out into ones, twos, or threes along the rocky shore, bundled with heavy jackets and hoods, and equipped with buckets, nets, and wood or metal rods used for fishing. They mostly ignored the newcomers as Petrah and his friends strode across pebbles and rocks. Petrah was thankful for his garb. Besides protecting him from the hateful wind, it helped him and his friends not appear as obvious foreigners.

As they navigated the shoreline, they passed a pair of women whose faces were tattooed with bright, swirling patterns that reminded Petrah of the way the Machoo decorated their faces. The women stared with intent interest, one even gripping a paring knife in her hand. Petrah offered a polite smile and moved past them. The fishermen didn't say anything or block Petrah's passage.

"I see a way up," Tan said, pointing out a stairwell with a rusted metal banister made of pipes and built into the wall. There was increasing commotion from above the seawall: the sound of movement . . . and people.

They halted at the base of the stairwell and looked at the top. The sheer wall and stairs protected them from the wind. Petrah picked up familiar smells: hay, wood smoke, and iron being worked over a fire. He concentrated on the presence above.

"What do you think?" Tan asked.

"I'm detecting a lot of people up there, animals too," Petrah said. "I suggest we blend in like we belong here. We need to remember to keep our wrists hidden. We don't want to attract any unwanted attention."

Kruush looked at his scarf, then down at his saba. "Blend in? I look like a gonatan herder."

"You know what I mean," Petrah said.

"Do you know where we're going?"

"Approximately."

Kruush grunted. "That doesn't sound reassuring."

"If you must know," Petrah said, "I need a quiet space to focus, sheltered from the cold. I can hardly feel my face." It was a poor excuse. A mage should be able to set aside his discomfort and channel his energies in a practiced fashion, like a swordsman gauging his stance and footing atop a windy bluff before engaging an opponent. "I'll go first."

Petrah started up the stairs, cautious but doing his best not to let his uncertainty show. He poked his head above the landing and paused, one hand flat against the wall, the other on his canteen.

Before him was a large square, set against a backdrop of buildings in remarkably good shape. People bustled about with purpose. There was a massive wood stable where riders attended to their horses; a forge that housed a kiln and workstations for workers to fashion steel into parts for weapons and armor; several silos; boxlike structures with metal roofs, perhaps for storage; and level ground where men, women, and children carried materials and supplies to and from different locations.

One thing was clear: everyone served a function, regardless of age.

There were no stragglers, no idlers. That meant Petrah and his friends needed to head topside and not dawdle.

Kruush and Tan joined Petrah up top, and the trio moved through the maze of people and structures, including hovels and shanties bunched together that looked to be living quarters for families. The air stank of smelted ore and fish, then meat being cut at a slaughterhouse they passed by. Petrah marveled at the quantity of steel—strips, sheets, blocks, entire beams— reclaimed from the city, stacked inside an open storehouse.

There was a fenced-off area containing an outbuilding, perhaps an armory, where workers were handing off spears to others standing inside. Steps away was a stone building with a wide entrance. A throng of people slowly shuffled inside into what appeared to be a temple with wood benches where the devout could gather and pray. Clouds of incense filtered out, overpowering the rank odors with smoldering resin. The worshippers waiting in line murmured to themselves and raised their hands to the heavens every so often. Petrah noted they did this with their branded wrists. He expected their foreheads to be anointed with Sercula, the oil and blood mix used by priests in Terjurmeh, but they were bare.

Their customs differ from ours, yet they pray to the same dark god.

He tried not to think that San, the god they were praying to, was his father.

Petrah and his companions walked to the left of the worshipers, moving quickly and quietly. People hurried across the square in all directions. Petrah led his friends around workers lifting and stacking heavy sacks while a woman yelled at a pair of young children, a boy and a girl, standing by a sack that had torn open to shed its kernels of grain onto the ground. He stopped when the woman grabbed the boy's left wrist and shook it. The boy was branded. He couldn't have been more than nine or ten. The boy sniffled, red-faced, while the girl stood next to him, eyes damp as if she were about to cry.

Tan spoke into Petrah's ear. "We should keep moving."

Petrah turned to go, but the image of the boy remained. It reminded him of the incident on Hah'xallah, when he'd used a word of power to toss a cruel father into a crowd of spectators. Why had it bothered him so? Why did it bother him now?

Petrah walked faster, maneuvering around stands and people, shaking off the memory. A stiff hand on his shoulder halted him. Kruush. His friend nudged with his chin, and Petrah turned to see a column of men-at-arms on horseback on approach, eight total. The crowd parted as the horsemen guided their barded horses through the square. The riders wore animal furs or leathers over shirts of chain mail and were armed with a variety of weapons, their shields strapped to the flanks of their horses or their backs. Embossed in red on the shields were clawing, winged dragons with looped, barbed tails. Petrah noted similar insignia on several pennants he had seen mounted atop buildings: red dragons against fields of black.

One soldier, a thick man with a stiff, red beard, caught Petrah's gaze and held it. He broke formation and urged his horse forward, toward Petrah and his companions, never losing eye contact. Petrah held his breath, forgetting the crowd and the cold. People moved out of the rider's way. Petrah pressed his wrists to his sides. Had the man seen he was unbranded? Was it the sweater that drew him? Or did Petrah stick out as a foreigner who didn't belong here? But as Petrah braced for an encounter, another rider called over, and the red-bearded man wheeled his horse. He glanced back once, then spurred his steed and caught up with his column, falling back in place with the other horsemen.

When they cleared the main square and hit a quiet street, Petrah let out a breath he'd kept bottled up in his lungs.

"That was intense," Kruush said, echoing Petrah's sentiment. "He singled you out for no reason. You'd think he was a Draad from back home."

"Great. More soldiers." Tan gestured with a nod.

Soldiers entered a tall, metal building on the other side of the street. A barracks perhaps.

"We should get going," Petrah said.

As they headed up the street, Petrah couldn't help but look up at the dizzyingly tall building. It had to be at least twice the size of Hachaqua. Canvas billowed over blown-out windows on the ground level. How did anyone get up top? Were there spiral stairs, a lift operated by winches and cables, or were the heights unobtainable, save by birds looking to roost?

The next street over was mostly deserted. They traveled a particularly long block filled with rundown, adjoining brick buildings with boarded-up windows. Petrah made them stop at the next intersection. He was shivering again as a crosswind raged, tossing his hair and needling his skin.

Tan bobbed up and down on his feet as if the action might keep him warm. "I can't feel my face anymore."

"Nor can I," Kruush said, squeezing his cheeks. "Petrah, how much farther?"

Petrah visualized his mother's necklace in his mind and felt the warm sensation in his forehead leading him due north along the avenue—the only part of him that was warm. The feeling had grown in intensity over the past few minutes. His excitement swelled, filling him with anticipation. Could she really be here?

"Two or three blocks."

They turned down a street of ramshackle buildings, some collapsed into rubble, the rest decorated with deteriorating brick facades. Petrah saw a hodgepodge of coverings—canvas, wood, metal—that would otherwise be gaping holes in the construction. He detected many heartbeats.

People lived inside these dwellings. He even caught faces peeking out, watching their procession.

"Gives me the shivers," Kruush said, looking about.

Petrah gestured to the half-ruined brick building on the corner. "Over there."

Rotting wood planking boarded up the front of the building, warped along the fringes. The boards gaped just enough for a body to squeeze through if one were to give a careful tug. Too much, and it might fall away. A fusty smell was mixed with something foul, like stagnant sewer water. Another block over, a column of horsemen was making its way slowly up the street.

"Are you sure this is it?" Tan asked, screwing up his face at the obvious stench.

Petrah's forehead tingled as it had when he came to the clearing at Hachaqua. "This is it, I'm certain." With cheeks flushed from anxious expectation, he placed his numb fingers over the edge of the boarding.

Here goes nothing.

He pulled. The wood creaked but gave slightly.

He stuffed his body sideways, pressing his canteen snugly against his chest, and slipped inside. The stench hit him like diving headfirst into a lake from a cliff. His eyes adjusted to the dim, taking in details: sagging walls with rust stains, piles of loose bricks, gaps in the floors above, a decomposing stone staircase, and garbage scattered across the paved floor. Daylight spilled into a hallway on the right, along with the steady drip of water. On the other side of a wall with exposed lathing, he detected the heartbeat of a solitary individual. The heartbeat sped up as Kruush wormed his way in behind Petrah, making a scraping noise as the boarding scuffed the floor.

"Who's there?" It was a woman's voice, gruff and aged by the sound of it—different from the voice in Petrah's dream. She spoke the native language with a lisp.

Petrah stepped around a sizable chunk of fallen ceiling. He used his birth name. "Immael."

"I don't know any Immael," she said. "I'll whistle if you don't stop where you are."

Petrah stopped and motioned for Kruush to do the same. Tan was already standing still, hand clamped over his nose and mouth to block the smell.

Petrah called to the woman. "Will you come out?"

An elderly woman stepped into the hallway carrying a long knife. Petrah's excitement dissolved into disappointment. She was not what he'd envisioned. She was short, five feet at the most, thin as a bundle of branches, with layers of filthy rags draping off her body. Her face was pinched and smudged with grime, her hair gray and thinning, with bits of scalp poking through. Around her throat, though, was the necklace from his dream, identical in every way, down to the shiny pendant stamped with the double fish insignia.

The word *Mama* caught on his tongue as he tried to conjure it.

"What do you want?" the woman asked.

"I came here to find my—" He couldn't bring himself to say "mother." This woman was someone else. His shoulders sagged. If she wasn't his mother, then what was she doing with her necklace? He pointed at it. "Where did you get that?"

The woman touched the pendant reflexively, then held up her knife. She was marked on the wrist, like Sammus and Teenuh. "This is mine. Try to take it and see what happens."

Maybe it was the squeal in her voice or the fact he had wasted valuable time pursuing the wrong path, but cold anger welled up within him. This woman was some slattern, with clothes and stench to match. "I don't want to take your necklace. I want to know where you got it."

"It's mine, and I don't have to tell you." She reached beneath her rags and pulled out what looked like a reed pipe with a tapered end. It wasn't any longer than four fingers across. "Now get out of here!"

Petrah stepped toward her. He felt the space around the woman's throat, the beaded necklace resting against it. If he wanted, he could rip it off her. "Where did you get that? It's not yours!"

"Step any closer and you'll regret it." She lifted the reed pipe as a threat.

"Blazes, what's going on?" Kruush asked.

"Not now." Petrah pressed the woman for an answer. "That necklace belonged to my mother. How did you come across it?"

"I told you, it's mine," she said. "How I got it is none of your business. Now leave."

"No. I don't believe you. You found it or you"—he tried to think of the word—"*stole* it. You stole it from my mother, didn't you? Where is she? Where's my mother?" He clamped invisible fingers around her throat. He would squeeze if he had to in order to get an answer out of her.

The woman pulled at her necklace as if she suddenly had trouble breathing. "You demon! Get out. Get out, get out, get out!"

"Tell me where my mother is!" Petrah pressed into the hollow of her throat ever so slightly. He was prepared to choke the truth from her.

She clawed at her throat, like the red-horned warrior, scraping with long, curling fingernails. "You're"—she fought for breath—"a demon!"

Oma had called him a demon too. Being accused made him angrier. "I'm going to crush the life out of you if you don't tell me where my mother is, so help me!"

"Petrah, what are you doing to her?" Tan asked.

Petrah lost his concentration on the woman. A shrill sound filled the air. The woman blew into her reed pipe, retreating quickly into the building. There was a second whistle a moment later, this one coming from somewhere outside.

Kruush stepped back. "Gods, what's happening?"

"We have to get out of here," Petrah said. "Go!"

Tan, Kruush, and Petrah pushed through the boarded gap into daylight. Outside, many whistles sounded, coming from different buildings. People's faces appeared through various openings—ugly, unwelcome faces. They blew their reed pipes in concert at the strangers.

"Run!" Petrah said, pointing east. "Head toward the water!"

They ran down the middle of the street as the whistles chased after them like the wind. If they could get away from this street, could they find a temporary place to hide and wait for any trouble to pass? Petrah's hopes rose. Across the avenue was a tumbledown of rubble, with large, slanted slabs perfect for hiding behind.

The whistles receded by the time they hit the midway mark down the street. Petrah skidded to a halt. "Horsemen!" He picked up on a congregation of heartbeats heading south on the avenue toward their intersection. The thunder of galloping followed.

Tan waved them to an alley between brick buildings. "Over there!" The tops of two buildings had collapsed against each other, forming a precarious archway. They ran into the alley. Partway through, they had to clamber over loose bricks. The alleyway cut through to an adjacent street from there. Petrah tripped and scuffed his palm against the jutting brick as he caught his fall. He got up and pressed on.

That damned woman! That thief!

The alley dipped, then rose sharply, ending in a leaning wood fence of vertical slats that seemed to create a dead end at first. Petrah grabbed the slats, pulled, and pushed. He found a pair of loose slats. Kruush helped Petrah yank them free. They squeezed through the tight gap, but the strap from Petrah's canteen snagged on a stray nail poking out from the wood. The forward motion and weight of his body caused the strap to yank free from its metal loop. The canteen slipped and fell to the ground. Petrah picked it up and clutched it under one arm, strap dangling.

"Which way?" Tan asked in a most desperate voice.

This street contained rows of attached brick buildings, but they were in terrible shape, almost all caved in. The street collapsed into a giant sinkhole in front of them, leaving a thin strip of walkway running left and right, making it impossible to cross. They could either head toward the water or the opposite way. Already, Petrah noticed the horses change direction. They were converging on the new street. Soldiers were also coming through the alley toward them. They couldn't backtrack or hide among the wreckage around them or run away from their pursuers.

They couldn't go anywhere.

We're trapped!

"Petrah?"

Petrah tried to breathe. He found it nigh impossible to make his lungs work. "We're—" he fought to say it, as if the word were poison on his chapped lips. "We're finished."

"What do you mean, 'finished'? We have to run!"

"Look." He pointed east to where the street met the avenue.

The first rider rounded the corner toward them, a female with long, black hair peeking out from a metal helm bearing spikes that looked like the quills of a river beast. Her pauldrons bore scarlet ribbons that fluttered in the wind. The riders who trailed her bore no ribbons.

She pointed her spear toward her quarry. "Stay where you are!" A soldier appeared from the alley behind Petrah, followed by three more. The first carried a studded mace, the others wielded swords.

"Don't show them your—" Petrah started, but it was too late. Kruush and Tan had already raised their hands in surrender. The soldiers would see their unbranded wrists.

The female rider reined in her destrier along the narrow pathway, coming within a body length of Petrah. The warhorse snorted and steamed its breath into the air. "Are there any more?" she asked the soldiers on foot.

"No, Lieutenant," the one with the mace said. "Just these three."

"Look," another said, "they're unmarked."

Petrah tried to free his medallion from where it clung stubbornly to the hollow of his throat. He dropped the canteen and used both hands. "I have this. See?"

The lieutenant ignored him. "Bind them."

One soldier grabbed Kruush by the arm and forced it behind his back, while another grabbed Tan's. A third reached for Petrah, but he pulled away. "Wait, you don't understand. I'm marked. I'm one of you! Look at my—" The soldier snatched his hand before he could figure out the word for "medallion."

"You're under arrest," the lieutenant said, staring at Petrah with her harsh, green eyes. She was young, perhaps a couple of years older than him, but she exhibited firm command over those around her. "You are hereby charged with attempted infiltration as an unmarked, as governed by the Law. If found guilty by the Lord Magistrate for your crime, you will be put to death. Do you understand?"

"You're making a mistake!" Petrah yelled. "Take a look. Please!"

"There are no mistakes." She signaled to the soldiers. "Take them to the Stacks."

Chapter 5
Hands of Justice

THE STACKS WERE LOCATED beneath a crumbling trio of tubular, brick towers that might have stretched to the sky in their day but now reached maybe three stories. They were attached to a building whose interior was dank, empty, and open to a loft where pigeons roosted. Bird droppings stained the stonework inside, trailing down to the subbasement where Petrah, Tan, and Kruush awaited judgment.

Petrah and his friends occupied a pen lined with straw, barricaded from the pigs in their neighboring pen, but not their squeals, grunts, or odor. Their captors had removed their manacles, but there wasn't anywhere for them to go. They were sealed in. Now they sat with their backs to a wall, Petrah between them, sharing a ragged, fleece blanket they had found next to a tin bucket that also bore the stench of swine. Loose straw was scattered on the floor around them.

Petrah had spent the frigid night with his head leaned against the pockmarked stone wall contemplating his actions from the previous day. That thief . . .

She wasn't my mother. I should have left as soon as I realized it.

His anger had gotten him and his friends captured and confined here. If he would have just heeded the old woman's warning. She'd given him ample chance to leave.

But I didn't leave. I was stubborn. And now we're here.

"I'll get us out of this," Petrah said for the third time. *I just need to—* What did he need to do?

The dryness in his mouth sucked up the thought from his mind, like a strip of rawhide set out too long in the sun. His throat was abraded from having walked a mile in the cold behind the lieutenant and the soldiers who apprehended him and his friends. He licked his chapped lips, wishing for a sip of water. The soldiers had kept their canteen and left them with little more than a ladle-worth apiece in a metal pot. They'd drank it all before bedding down for the night.

"Aye, you keep saying that," Kruush said in a voice as chafed as Petrah's. "And I keep thinking I'm going to wake up in my wife's loving arms and rid myself of this nightmare."

"I know it's my fault we're here," Petrah said, "and I'm sorry. I was so blinded by wanting to find my mother that I couldn't see."

"Aye," Kruush said. "Like Qufah and Qufay. The 'blind and the bli nded.'"

"Exactly like that." When he was a mage apprentice, Petrah had passed the statues of Qufah and Qufay each day at school. The pair had guarded the student hall as a reminder to all who entered that the blind might see the truth, but not the blinded.

Kruush tutted. "I hope at least the judgment against us will be swift. I'd hate to think their executioner would use a dull blade."

Tan pinched a piece of straw between his fingers. "Terjurmehan executioners love to dull their instruments, especially for use in front of a crowd, where the *oohs* and *ahs* stretch hack after hack after—"

"I got it," Petrah said, irritation soaking into his bones, like the chilled, damp air around him. Above, the pigeons cooed and fluttered their wings. Ventilated slats let in the morning light. It brought in the outside air but did little to carry away the horrid stink.

Tan flicked the straw. "Are you at least thinking of a way out? You've had all night."

"I already told you I was," Petrah said, annoyed at Tan and even more at his inability to find a solution. It was like being a prisoner again in the

Machoo village in Darkforth. Except this time there was no Choola to free them. "Once I get to the right person, I'll show them my medallion, and we'll be gone from this place."

"And who might that lovely person be?" Tan asked. "Certainly not that pretty lass with the ribbons on her shoulder armor."

Petrah rolled his eyes. "Leave it to you to notice how pretty she was. Where was your charm when you needed it?"

"Bring her back here, and I'll show you," Tan said, baring a smile.

Petrah snorted a laugh. The swine perked their ears, which made Petrah laugh even harder. "Our audience agrees. I'm sure they're looking forward to your show. On the off chance it doesn't work, may our deaths be quick and clean."

Tan obliged a nod. "If there's such a thing as the afterlife, you're buying the first round of ale."

Petrah thought how nice it would be to have one swallow of the golden drink. "As many pints as you want."

Kruush changed the subject. "I see why these people want to come to Acia. This frozen place is falling apart. There's gloom and desperation everywhere you look. It's as if their world is dying."

"It *is* dying," Petrah said, resting his head against the wall. "I sensed it when I first arrived. There's a sickness of some kind that has affected Dagoth. I felt it in the forest, on the hilltop, and by the water. It's as if a poison has seeped into the world and taken root. Something terrible happened here ages ago. The Watcher alluded to it when we spoke in Âhn."

"For a dying land," Tan said, "these people have done remarkably well, given the cruel environment. They're tough. Something keeps them going. Something more than the need to survive."

"It's their faith," Petrah said. "You've seen their branding. It unites them together and gives them purpose. They serve their dark god and those who preach his ways."

Kruush smiled tenuously. "Their one true god."

"Exactly."

"Which is?" Tan asked.

"Which one do you think, moron?" Kruush said, frowning. "*Our* god."

Tan tossed the bit of straw over his worn boots. "Then if that's the case, we shouldn't be in"—he looked around him—"this sty. We should be welcomed."

Kruush arched a brow. "You mean, just like the Machoo and the An-jurah did for us? That kind of welcome?"

"We're strangers," Petrah said. "Think about Sammus, for example. He would have ousted us, if not for Teenuh's compassion. We're outsiders here as much as we were in Darkforth."

Tan threw up his hands. "But the An-jurah and Ter-jurah are working together, aren't they? They consider each other outsiders, don't they? What about the Machoo and Idarians? Seems to me they're all one big happy family these days."

"They came together, bound by something far stronger than their differences," Petrah said. "Hatred. Hatred of those who don't share their faith."

Kruush nodded. "Aye, they're coming together to defeat their enemies once and for all."

"Not just to defeat them," Petrah said, thinking back to his dreams. "But to crush them and wipe them out of existence. The key lies in numbers. If Acia divides itself evenly, you need to tip the balance in your favor if you're plotting a worldwide coup. If my brother leads these people into Acia, the An-jurah and their allies will have the numbers they need."

"Without you, he can't cross over," Kruush said. "You're the Key, remember?"

"I remember, but that was assuming I could avoid my brother. Look where we are." Petrah stretched his arms to emphasize their imprisonment. "We have no choice now. We're unmarked. That's bad news for us. They're going to take us before a magistrate, and that person is going to decide our fate. You understand what happens if we're found guilty, don't you? But if I show this"—Petrah pulled down on his sweater to reveal the medallion sucked against the hollow of his throat—"we have a chance."

Tan picked up a clump of straw and let it fall between his fingers. "From the frying pan into the fire, eh?"

Kruush tugged on his unkempt beard. "I'm for staying alive. That medallion might be our only chance. If you show it, the magistrate will want to know where you got it."

"More important than saying where I got it is telling the magistrate who it's for," Petrah said, dreading the idea of mentioning his brother's name.

Kruush looked at Tan, who seemed just as put off by the idea. But Tan nodded, and Kruush turned back to Petrah. "Do what you must. We're with you on this."

"I will," Petrah said. "If there was any other way . . ."

Kruush rested a hand on his shoulder. "I know. We'll get through this."

The iron door on the balcony above them squealed open, and they looked up. A soldier entered, followed by the lieutenant who had charged Petrah and his friends as infiltrators. The soldier slid a ladder down to the subbasement.

The lieutenant addressed the prisoners in her native tongue. "Rise and follow me. The Lord Magistrate awaits."

THE JUDITARIUM, AS THE green-eyed lieutenant called it, was a separate building that served as East Lorraine's justice hall. With her helmet off, the lieutenant was as pretty as Tan boasted, with skin pale as cream and eyebrows that curved delicately, although her heavy-heeled gait indicated absolute authority.

A grand entryway led through brass double doors to a corridor at least a hundred feet in length. The building's interior was clear of debris, with a well-trodden floor of gray-and-white marble dulled by time. Paintings hung on the walls, depicting various figures in robes. It smelled of dust and stone and ages long gone.

The hall ended in a doorway that led to a large room with benches facing a dais and an imposing table with clawed feet that looked like falcon talons grasping balls of wood. Behind the table sat a man in black robes, like the figures in the paintings. His skin was as dark as a Mumooni tribesman, and he had tightly curled hair atop his head that poked out from beneath a stiff-fabric headdress whose peak came together in an exaggerated curve. His frizzy, salt-and-pepper beard jutted from his chin like a spearhead.

To his right side stood an older woman, also in robes, with eyes round as an owl's. Seated to his left at a low desk was a greasy-haired man with parchment, pen, and ink, perhaps the court's scribe. The room was otherwise empty, although it could have held eighty, maybe a hundred people.

The lieutenant went before the dais and had Petrah, Kruush, and Tan stand side by side in front of the magistrate while two soldiers posted guard by the door. Sconces bore lanterns that lit the room against the dying light. With the approach of evening, a chill fell upon the city, and even here, Petrah noticed his breath fog.

Don't these people ever tire of the cold?

He would have expected at least a brazier to warm the magistrate, but the only flame came from a pillar candle burning on the scribe's desk.

"These are the accused, Lord Magistrate," the lieutenant said, presenting her prisoners. "The tall one speaks Glesh, but they all speak the priest's tongue." She acknowledged the woman in the robes with a tip of her head.

The Lord Magistrate looked at Petrah and his companions shrewdly. "Where are they from?"

"We don't know, Your Honorable," the lieutenant said. "They perpetrated the crime of infiltration as an unmarked. We believe they serve the mountaineers in their plot to sabotage us."

The magistrate wove his fingers together and shifted his attention to Petrah. "They don't look like mountain men. I'm curious about this one. Bilingual, you said?"

"Yes, Your Honorable."

"Come. Approach the bench."

The lieutenant shoved Petrah forward until he was right up to the high table. Spidery hairs rose up the magistrate's cheeks, forming muttonchops beneath his headdress. "Where did you get that scar above your brow?" He motioned to the sickle-shaped scar on Petrah's forehead.

"I was born with it, Your Honorable."

"You speak Glesh well enough. Usually, scars are earned, not made in the womb. A child born with a scar is 'touched,' as the priests say. The question is, touched by the one true god, or his impostor?"

Petrah was quick to answer the magistrate's question. "The true one, Your Honorable."

"And which god is that?"

"San."

"The accepted name is Sag-ahn, sometimes Shay-tan if you're Meslin. Although I've heard the priests, even the Grand Marshall himself, use the name you mentioned. Isn't that right, Your Holiness?"

The robed woman in the priest's robes gave a curt nod. Petrah didn't like how she studied him with her owl eyes, as if he were a field mouse.

The magistrate continued. "You claim to be touched by Sag-ahn, yet you do not wear the brand of true faith. See this?" He raised his left wrist. "This is the allegiance of faith. This is the devotion to the one true god, a seal of profession made through the union of flesh, fire, and iron. It is absolute, irrevocable, and everlasting." He dropped his hand. "Lieutenant Tirra says you speak the priest's tongue. Let's have it."

"We call it Jurmehan, Your Honorable," Petrah said, speaking the favored language of his homeworld, Acia.

Kruush and Tan both looked at Petrah at once, as if awoken from a stupor.

"Do you know why it's called the priest's tongue?"

"No, Your Honorable."

"Because it's sacred, commissioned by the Grand Marshall himself as the tongue of tongues. The question now becomes: how did you learn such a language? Our priests teach it to a select few—only the most devout among their congregations—and we school our military in its usage. The mountain men don't speak it, except for their spies. Isn't that right, Lieutenant?"

"Yes, Your Honorable." She spoke Jurmehan with an accent like the magistrate's. Petrah wondered if his accent sounded similar to hers. Glesh was his native tongue. As a slave, Petrah had learned Jurmehan, but he'd never quite gotten his vowels to have the same smoothness as the Ter-jurah, even with years of practice.

The magistrate, sticking with Jurmehan, said, "You are neither clergy nor military. Nor are you one of us." The magistrate's eyes hardened. "Who sent you, and what is your purpose?"

Petrah glanced at Kruush, who nodded his encouragement. "I can't say who sent me, only that I was told to find the Great One, Your Honorable. He goes by the name Aman, but we call him San-Jahad where I'm from. He is the Great One and the Great Son, blood of his father, the one true god."

The magistrate's eyes widened at first, as did the lieutenant's, then narrowed. He continued in Jurmehan. "Yes, we know who that is. You speak of the Grand Marshall. If you were sent to find him, then why all this skulking about? You should have knocked on the front gate and presented yourself if you were truly sent here for a noble purpose. You do realize how unconvincing you sound, don't you? I also find your declaration about hiding the identity of your sender unacceptable."

Petrah pressed on, trying to sound sure of himself, although he suspected his voice wobbled. "We are expected by the Grand Marshall, Your Honorable. That is a true statement, and all that I can say."

The magistrate's doubtful expression deepened. "For what purpose?"

"For this." Petrah tugged the medallion nestled in the jugular notch of his throat. It pulled away from his skin, still tethered to its chain. When he let go, it hung suspended, floating in midair. The chain rested against the back of his neck.

The magistrate glanced at Lieutenant Tirra and back to Petrah. "What manner of device is that?"

"Proof, Your Honorable, that I am who I say I am. It's a sigil the Grand Marshall would recognize."

"What business do you have with the Grand Marshall?"

"That business is our own. I tried to explain it to the lieutenant before she arrested us. This is just a big misunderstanding, Your Honorable."

The magistrate tugged on his pointy beard. "Very well." He tipped his head toward the lieutenant. "Remove the device and bring it to me so I might inspect it."

Lieutenant Tirra cautiously reached for the medallion. As soon as she touched it, she recoiled. She tried again, but her hand snapped back as if swatted away. "I can't," she said in Jurmehan, her voice laced with fear. "It's . . . it's too cold."

"Preposterous!" The magistrate grabbed a dip pen from a wooden cup on top of his table and stepped down from the dais. He was shorter than he appeared on the bench. With an irritated swish of the hand, he waved the lieutenant aside and snapped his fingers at the nearest guard. "Bring the lamp here."

The soldier grabbed the lamp from the table and brought it close, illuminating the magistrate's dark skin in the yellow light. His skin smelled of garlic as if he'd subsisted on whole bulbs of the aromatic plant. The magistrate beckoned to the woman in the black robes. "Your Holiness, if you would take a look with me?"

The Lord Magistrate used the nib from his pen to move the floating chain around Petrah's neck in the lamplight's direction. "Interesting. Yes, interesting indeed. What do you think, Your Holiness?"

"This is the syriak with the all-seeing eye in the center, and"—she took hold of the fountain pen and twisted the chain ever so slightly. The medallion flipped about its vertical axis as if fixed in place like a weathervane—"this is the nautilus serpent on the back, born of flame, reaching out from its genesis toward oblivion."

"It resembles the moodra burned into our flesh," the magistrate said. "I can feel the cold just inches from it. It's unnatural, and"—he stepped back—"I can't stare at it too long without getting dizzy. Strange."

"Its properties are quite strange, I agree," the priest said. "It's drawing heat to it." She tugged at the chain with her pen. The medallion moved perhaps a half-inch. "It resists, as if heavy, yet it's weightless."

"What manner of metal does that?"

"Nether metal," she said. "Metallurgists use names like erlatum and negated irinium. I've never seen such a material with my own eyes before, but I've read about it. They're said to originate from the Netherworld. It's also said that ancient amulets of great power were forged or cast with them. If this were genuinely of such origin, then the accused should not be able to stand it pressing against his skin. It should burn him. But he's unscathed, see? That means it's not a nether metal."

"What would the alternative be?"

"A charm imbued with levitation properties. A magus with the right skill set could do it." She turned her owl-like eyes toward Petrah. "Is that what this is—an illusion?"

"It's not an illusion," Petrah said, offended by the very notion. "Touch it."

"I don't have to touch it," she said sharply. "It's a fake." She handed the magistrate his dip pen.

"But the cold, the dizziness—" the magistrate started. "A fake, you say?"

"The charm is a fraud. Its wearer speaks with a false tongue, like the mountain men."

"I'm not tricking you," Petrah said, his face growing warm with his words. "The medallion is real!"

She pointed at him with a rigid, accusatory finger. "You're an infiltrator, along with your coconspirators here, dispatched to East Lorraine to trick us into believing you were sent to meet with the Grand Marshall. What is your real purpose? Is it to glean our secrets, to assassinate one of our officials, to go after the Grand Marshall himself?" Her round eyes flared threateningly. "As the Lord Magistrate said before, you should have presented yourself at the front gate. Only an impostor would sneak in. The same goes for your accomplices."

"He's *not* an impostor, just as we're not accomplices," Kruush said defiantly. Tan gave a firm nod in Petrah's defense.

The Lord Magistrate scowled and climbed up the dais to his seat. Once seated, he straightened his back and spoke. "This is a grave accusation, Your Holiness. The original charge is infiltrating as an unmarked. The sentence for such a crime is branding or death. I was leaning toward branding, but now . . ." His eyes bore down on the accused. "Now we add charges of falsification and deception. There is only one punishment for such crimes. But this device he wears . . ."

"I stand by my testimony," the priest said, folding her arms. Her thin lips pulled taut across her crooked teeth. "He's using a ruse to distract you, Your Honorable. Let it not deter you from leveling your judgment."

"It's not a ruse!" Petrah insisted.

The magistrate sighed, apparently frustrated, perhaps conflicted, but definitely disappointed with the situation. "Then this court has no choice but to find the accused guilty on all counts. I hereby render punishment in the form of death by public hanging."

"This is real!" Petrah said, raising the medallion as far out in front of him as the chain would allow. "If the Grand Marshall learns you've harmed us, he will kill you, all of you!" His words echoed in the large chamber, surprising not only himself but the rest of the court.

There were a few seconds of stunned silence before the priest in the black robes spoke. "Lord Magistrate, are you going to allow this charlatan to speak to you like that?"

The magistrate glared at her. "I'm thinking. Give me a moment."

"They must be put to death. The Law demands it!"

The magistrate slapped his hand on the high table. "And I said I need a moment!" His deep voice turned shrill. He turned his attention to Petrah, then Kruush and Tan, his gaze as venomous as a scorpion's sting. Petrah held his breath as the magistrate continued to cycle back and forth between him and his companions before settling on his medallion again. It lasted maybe three seconds before the magistrate shook his head with a scowl. "Curses and anathemas! I will not let that"—he pointed at Petrah's medallion, still floating in front of him—"that *thing* sway my judgment."

He straightened his posture.

"The Grand Marshall arrives on the morrow. You three will be brought before his procession as it passes the gallows in the town square. If he so pleases, he will allow the lieutenant and the steward of the gallows to present you, fully chained and on display for all to see. Let it be known that if he fails to acknowledge you, the execution will commence immediately afterward, and you will cease breath and sight of this world. I, Lord Magistrate of East Lorraine, do proclaim this for the court record. Do the accused understand my judgment?"

All three nodded.

"Court dismissed!"

THE STACKS WERE FREEZING cold that night.

High above, snow blew in through the vents, landing on the straw. It melted at first, but by midnight there was a powder coating an inch thick. The swine in the adjacent pen snorted, then quieted down. They roused again at dawn, just as the darkness melted away to gray light.

Neither Petrah nor his friends had slept a wink, nor did they speak to each other. Troubling thoughts kept Petrah to himself. He rubbed the breast pocket with Mina's lock of hair to comfort himself. The Watcher had promised his medallion would save him, but it had only succeeded in remaining saddled around his neck like an albatross of lead. He had hoped to avoid any encounters with his brother. Doing so was a last resort, but now . . .

It was still early morning when Lieutenant Tirra arrived, wearing her battle armor beneath an animal skin cloak. An accompanying soldier let down the metal ladder again for Petrah and the others to climb. A second soldier held woolen cloaks in his arms. When Petrah made it topside, the soldier gave him a cloak, along with a drink from his waterskin. Petrah was thankful for the added warmth. The water took away the desert in his throat, and he was even given jerked meat to eat quickly as two more soldiers readied shackles, manacles, and chains.

After the meat was consumed, the soldiers put the three in irons. Petrah took the front, Kruush the middle, and Tan the rear.

"Just so you know," Lieutenant Tirra said in Jurmehan to them, "if you must die today, I will make sure the steward of the gallows makes it quick."

Petrah hadn't expected the lieutenant to offer any mercy, let alone compassion. He remembered Aggren's drawn-out misery at the hands of Meska and his cronies.

Petrah wanted no part in swaying by a rope tied around his throat, choking as his life slowly left him. "Thank you."

The air was shockingly still outside, the streets and buildings covered in a half-foot of snow, with drifts piled up against corners and walls. Above, clouds blanketed the skies in swirls of gray, promising more snow. Petrah had seen snow only in his dreams and from a distance atop the mountains of the Eastern Gates, leading into Darkforth.

The snow didn't have a smell to it, but the air seemed cleaner, even quieter; if only Petrah could have a moment free of the jangle of chains to listen. He glanced behind him and noticed the strange looks on his companion's faces as they trudged through the snow. Petrah was grateful they were here with him.

For the last time, perhaps.

Ahleen would never know Kruush's fate, nor Tan's or Petrah's. Even now she might presume them lost or dead.

I'm sorry, Ahleen. I hadn't meant for this to happen.

Then there was Mina, who had not only captured Petrah's heart but caged it for all of eternity.

Ahleen would mourn her husband, but would Mina remember Petrah, or would he fade from memory?

There will be others, men her father will approve of. They will clamor for her heart, and she will choose one.

Or her father would choose for her.

If only Petrah could return to Montabijon for a few minutes to visit Mina. He'd recite the poem he had penned for her in the wilderness, tell her how much he loved her, and say his goodbye.

Her spirit will be with me until my final breath.

Gallows Corner, as the lieutenant called it, was a clearing set between two streets that branched out into a Y from the main avenue. A permanent wood scaffold stood several feet off the ground with two posts mounted up top, positioned at either end, joined by a wood transom. A worker standing on a short ladder was knotting a third hang noose over the crossbeam. Below him was a trapdoor that spanned the width of the stage.

Petrah slowed.

He reeled at the thought of swaying in the cold, rope creaking as the life was choked out of him.

This is no way for a man to die. A sword to the neck would be more merciful. This is cruelty beyond reason.

The soldier holding the chain to his manacles cursed and yanked him forward.

Several soldiers were waiting for them, along with a tall man with gray hair and a crooked nose wearing a brown burnoose and leather riding boots over his breeches.

The steward, no doubt.

Hundreds of people had gathered along the sidewalks of the main avenue, citizens and soldiers alike. At the north end of the avenue, the main gate remained closed. A handful of bowmen posted up top.

The steward walked up to the lieutenant.

People congregating by Gallows Corner turned their attention to the procession of prisoners. Several catcalled or threw rocks or trash at the condemned. Petrah ducked his head as one rock flew by. A second struck him in the ear. It smarted, but at least it didn't draw blood.

The lieutenant greeted the steward in their native tongue. "Where do you want them?"

The man with the burnoose gestured behind him. "Stand them by the gibbet for all to see. I have the writ of execution up already." He pointed at the parchment nailed to the closest post.

"The Lord Magistrate asked that we seek the favor of His Greatness to recognize the tallest of the three prisoners before proceeding with the hanging."

"Yes, I've heard. Quite the unusual request. I was hoping to be done with this business early. The crowd is restless, as you can see."

"We'll execute them if they fail to gain the favor of His Greatness."

The steward looked Petrah over and then spit on the ground. "Fair enough. The spectacle will have to wait then. But take off their cloaks. They look too comfortable."

Lieutenant Tirra ordered her men to comply. Her green eyes reflected command, but her voice carried a tinge of reluctance, as if a small corner of her soul harbored pity for the condemned. Or was Petrah imagining it?

It doesn't matter. She's not here to keep us from freezing. She has a job to do.

One soldier collected the cloaks while a second removed the chains and ankle cuffs, leaving the prisoners bound only at the wrists and shivering. The catcalling intensified as Petrah took to the stage in his filthy saba. A barrier of soldiers formed a protective wall against the swelling mob.

They were a despondent lot, with dirty faces, skinny bodies, and haunted eyes—starvelings, all of them. That didn't deter them from jeering at the condemned.

Petrah shook from the cold on the wood platform, taking his designated place to the right of Kruush. The Terjurmehan looked like a ghost of his former self, his head drooped forward and shoulders hunched. Tan didn't fare any better.

"I'm sorry," Petrah said to them.

"No talking!" a soldier snapped.

Minutes after taking to the stage, the crowd's attention shifted away from the condemned, toward the north. A horn blast sounded in the distance, matched by one closer, and the throng cheered with left arms pumping the air, each person's wrist branded by the moodra, as the magistrate had called it. Petrah could see partway down the avenue, but not to the main gate.

It was at that moment the back of Petrah's neck tingled. It began as a bead of fear, then progressed to the feeling he would sometimes get after an exhausting night of dreams, settling into a pressure in his temples and a warmth on the left side of his forehead that centered the closer he faced north. He was picking up a presence.

Not just any presence.

It's him.

The medallion at the base of his throat became lighter. It lifted on its own accord and hovered in front of him. No one paid him any attention or noticed the levitating medallion. The crowd, the soldiers below the gallows, the lieutenant, and the steward—they were all focused on the approach of the Grand Marshall, oblivious to the prisoners.

Petrah mentally prepared himself for an unsatisfactory outcome. He had no god to pray to, certainly not San.

At least I have my friends with me. Aggren, you left too soon. You too, Jow. We should all be here, the five of us, to meet the afterlife together. What a sight that would be.

A cheer went up, and people started chanting discordantly, then in unison.

Mahdi! Mahdi!

It was reminiscent of the pulsing of the spectators at Hah'xallah and the way they called for the hammers to be used to slaughter the Con-ju-rah.

Horns blasted, and the cries of the crowd went wild.

Petrah saw a column of horsemen approach. He immediately recognized the man at the head of the column.

Aman!

The Great One rode at the vanguard of the column astride a black charger larger than any horse Petrah had ever seen. Its coat was as dark as coal, caparisoned over the flank by a rich fabric the color of blood, trimmed in black, and bearing the crest of a dragon with spread talons. Aman wore a light helm with decorative alar on either side, with wings of gold. He had no nose or cheek guards, nothing to hide a face that was by all accounts handsome, with pronounced cheekbones, a nose with a high bridge. The closer he came, the more striking his appearance. Petrah noted a complexion of light skin free of blemishes or facial hair. His black, curly locks spilled out from his helm to the sides and back. Closer still, Petrah noticed the brightness of his eyes—blue like Petrah's—and how alert they were, surveying left and right as he waved at the cheering crowd. No detail was lost on Aman.

The steward and the lieutenant pushed through the spectators to the edge of the avenue. They kneeled and bowed their heads. Aman slowed his horse and steered slightly toward them, an amused expression on his face.

The center of Petrah's forehead was burning now. Despite the cold air, he perspired. Aman beckoned the kneelers, and they approached.

The steward spoke quickly and motioned toward the gallows. As soon as Aman caught Petrah looking at him, he smiled. Aman's eyes were of the fiercest blue, as radiant as glittering jewels under the sun. His gaze lingered—much like in the dream where Petrah had huddled between the ruins of a sandstone building that had collapsed.

Here, Aman's silent stare was filled with the same three words as in the dream: *I. See. You.*

Petrah shivered, gripped by the throat and unable to draw breath. Aman turned to the steward to say something to him, and the choke-hold released. He guided his horse back into formation, glancing at Petrah once more before resuming to wave at the enthralled crowd. The people cheered and cried his name. As soon as he faded from view, the heat on Petrah's forehead left him and his medallion fell back into place. He shuddered as the cold air evaporated the sweat from his brow and hair.

After the rest of the horsemen passed, the nearby crowd stopped their chanting and returned their attention to the display on stage.

The steward ripped down the writ of execution. People booed and catcalled from the crowd. A few threw rocks.

The steward turned on them summarily and tore the writ in twain. He spoke loudly. "By decree of the Grand Marshall, the execution of the convicted is hereby annulled." There were shouts of condemnation, but the steward raised his voice over the rabble. "Oppose his decree, and you'll find yourself with a noose about your neck. Now go home!" He whistled to the line of soldiers in front of the stage, and they moved forward as a phalanx to instill order.

The unruly crowd quieted down and disbanded, murmuring in discontent among themselves but obeying the edict nonetheless.

The steward deferred to the lieutenant. "All yours."

Lieutenant Tirra turned to Petrah and his comrades and spoke in Jurmehan. Her lifted eyes reflected satisfaction from Aman's verdict. "You have gained the Grand Marshall's favor, a most fortunate turn of events. You are to be bathed and fed."

Kruush and Tan exhaled, the pressure of impending death releasing in long, foggy plumes. Petrah felt it too: relief from the tightness in his chest, the tension in his neck and shoulders, and the knot in his gut. But the image of his brother staring at him remained, and with it, a chill that wouldn't let go.

The lieutenant motioned to Petrah. "You are to have a private audience with His Greatness at sundown." This time she smiled. "The one true god favors you this day."

Chapter 6
Great One

"**G**ODS ABOVE AND BELOW," Kruush said in a singsong voice, "this feels good."

He soaked in a tub heated by a coal-fed boiler outside their tent while Petrah and Tan leaned back in wicker chairs. They were dressed in fresh clothes: breeches, boots, long-sleeved wool shirts, and overcoats made of ruddy animal furs, fox perhaps. Petrah had transferred Mina's lock to the pocket in his breeches. They'd already eaten: hot soup filled with hearty potatoes, onions, and a meat Petrah guessed as chicken. Outside the tent, Petrah heard soldiers walking by in their boots.

"Anything is good compared to where we'd be right now," Tan said, molded to his seat like a piece of flatbread cooking on the inside of a clay oven. "We'd be a feast for crows, having our eyes dined upon. Now look at us."

"We're lavishing like kings in here," Kruush said. "'Forget the past, enjoy the present,' my grandfather used to say." Kruush whistled an old Terjurmehan drinking song Petrah recognized from his days living in Elmar.

Tan ran a hand through the shaggy fur of his coat. "What do you suppose they're going to do with us?"

"We're warm and free of stink," Petrah said, marveling at how clean his skin felt. Even bathing by the falls in Darkforth didn't compare with having honest-to-goodness soap and a scrubbing stone. "I can't think of anything else right now."

"Well, we'd better start thinking," Tan said, turning sour-faced. "Last I recall, we were in the frying pan about to be tossed into the fire. It seems to be a theme with us. Darkforth, the portal, then this morning. We're either in trouble, about to get into trouble, or have trouble looming around the corner. Yet here we are, lounging like royals, as if all is well."

Kruush splashed water over the rim of the tub. "Leave it to you to foul the mood. I'm with Petrah for taking a moment to appreciate being alive. But you won't let it happen. Do you think Petrah and I are fools, expecting riches and a life of leisure to follow?"

"I never claimed you were fools. I'm just saying that I'm tired of almost dying." Tan tapped his new boots on the permafrost-covered ground.

"All right, Your Cleverness," Kruush said, "what's your grandiose plan? What should we do next to avoid dying? Come on, let's hear it."

Tan folded his arms.

"Hah," Kruush said. "Looks like they noosed your tongue!" He dunked his head.

Petrah watched the tub water swill. "What's the use of planning, anyway? I'm to have a private audience with my brother. Do I have a choice? No. Choice is an illusion. The Watcher was right."

Tan scraped the ground with the heel of his boot. "If you believe those sorts of things,"

"I don't want to," Petrah said, as the cold slowly seeped back in. "But unfortunately, I must."

Lieutenant Tirra escorted Petrah in the late afternoon to the only tower in East Loraine that was still intact from top to bottom. It stood monstrously tall, with glass windows on each floor.

The inside was gutted, a wireframe representation of what it once was. A horse-driven pulley system operated an elevator running up the length of a rectangular shaft in the center. The elevator car comprised a cage affixed to cables and flywheels. The lieutenant closed the cage door, securing Petrah inside. There was a small window with a view of the outside.

"Aren't you going with me?"

"I'm not permitted." Her helm was off, leaving her black, flowing hair to cascade like a waterfall behind her shoulders. She was a lot comelier without her helm, but nowhere near as beautiful as Mina.

"Then I'm to go alone?" Petrah glanced uneasily above at the seemingly endless quadrangular channel.

"Not alone, not if our god is in your heart." She signaled to the lift operator, an old man with hunched shoulders who got his horses moving in a circle. "Good luck to you."

Slowly, the winch kicked in, and the lift groaned as it creaked upwards. Petrah gripped a metal handhold to steady himself within the tight confines of the wooden cage, which rattled as it climbed. The lieutenant disappeared from view.

Petrah looked out the small windowpane as the car rose. The ascension made him giddy. As the ground shrank away, he could see more of the city: neighboring buildings, a stone tower collapsed into a heap of rubble, an encampment of shanties, then rooftops, and in the distance, the glint of water from the river. Had anyone in Acia ever ascended a manmade structure so tall?

A wave of gooseflesh swept over Petrah's skin, leaving a trail of tiny raised bumps in its wake.

He was no longer alone.

A presence above him—heavy and oppressive—penetrated the ceiling of his cage. It bore down on him, pushing, pushing. He clutched the handhold with both hands and gripped it tight, squeezing until his knuckles hurt. His vision darkened, and the river blended in with the landscape and the giant, iron towers of the city, melding into an indistinct gray. The pressure in the small car swelled and contracted with an unsteady rhythm that echoed in his skull. *What is happening to me?* It was like the palpitations of a heart, twisted and poisoned, suffused with shadows. His own heart echoed the sinister rhythm, pounding a dread-filled drumbeat against his ribs. A sheen of sweat grazed his brow, and his palms turned clammy, slick against the metal he clutched so desperately.

Don't panic. Don't you dare.

The creak of the winching mechanism vibrated in his ears—grinding, grating, clanking. Then the car lurched as if the cable might snap and send him into freefall. Petrah lost his grip with his right hand for a precious second before clamping down on the handhold. Pain surged in his wrist from having twisted it to support his weight.

How much farther? His fingers grew numb. *How much higher?*

The air became heavier still, tainted with an energy he'd felt only among the most powerful clergy of Terjurmeh. The taste of iron bloomed on his tongue, as if he'd bitten his cheek and drawn blood, but it was the air itself, charged as if a storm was about to break.

There was only one being capable of such a crushing presence, of weaving darkness into the very air.

A demigod. A brother. His brother.

Aman.

Petrah's breath hitched as the lift shuddered to a halt.

He let go of the handhold and turned away from the window to face the retractable wall at the rear of the car. Circulation was restored to his hands, producing a throbbing. Behind the wooden barrier lay the presence he'd felt during his climb, the mountain of ancient power waiting to sweep him away.

The hairs on the back of Petrah's neck came to full attention. Instead of a warmth in the center of his forehead, his entire head bathed in a heat that pricked like pins and needles. Petrah held his breath and waited.

The rear wall lifted on a pulley, scraping as it drew upward. Beyond the car's threshold was a short corridor opening up to an enormous room filled with gray daylight.

At first, Petrah's eyes couldn't focus. Everything was hazy. He picked out a silhouette against the backdrop of dismal gray, a spectral figure carved of ink and shadow.

Then he saw bright azure blue in the shape of eyes and heard a voice, deep and strong and as soothing as it was authoritative. "Come, Immael."

As if released from shackles, Petrah stepped forward, off the lift, and into the short corridor. Every nerve tingled in warning, every instinct screamed for him to turn back. But he didn't. He couldn't.

The figure, nebulous a moment earlier, resolved into the distinct form of a man. Yet the outline of his brother's body played tricks on him, blurring with the dim surroundings, distorting the air, and curving unnaturally, as if an artist had painted the figure and purposely smudged the edges.

The skin on Petrah's nape prickled. He tamped down his welling panic, forcing his attention away from the shifting aura to the man himself.

Breathe. It's important to breathe.

Petrah expected to see his brother dressed as a warrior, but instead of battle armor, Aman wore black leather beneath a light, quilted jacket chased with silver thread. The Grand Marshall of Dagoth was immaculately clean and civilized, without a snag, mar, or wrinkle, as was his hair, now brushed behind him like a plunging, gleaming current, the hue of raven's feathers. He was about Petrah's height and build, physically toned and healthy, as compared to Petrah's emaciated state.

Petrah guessed his age to be somewhere in his thirties, although Aman carried himself with the grace and deportment of someone who had been around for the better part of a century.

Aman stood in front of Petrah, as calm as he was regal. He was both mortal and something greater. As his head shifted to take in his younger brother, the distorted space around him moved. Petrah drew in a staccato breath as the aura swelled, then shrank again.

"Brother," Aman greeted in Jurmehan, smiling while holding his arms outward in open welcome.

Petrah bowed his head, compelled to heed Aman's invitation, as if fingers pushed down on his crown to make him do it. "Brother," he replied in kind.

He stepped into the man's embrace, cringing as Aman drew him close and cloaked him in his dreadful, asphyxiating aura. It not only constricted him but swaddled him like a frigid blanket.

I can't breathe. I can't—

Petrah fought the urge to squirm out of his brother's grip.

Don't do it. Stay put.

Petrah listened to his gut, hard that it was. He even wrapped his hands around Aman's back and gave a brief squeeze, hoping it would prove he wasn't afraid, wasn't at all repelled.

Aman drew back and smiled his approval. The icy sensation clung to Petrah like hoarfrost, but he resisted the desire to shake it off.

Aman appraised Petrah from head to foot. "This day is long overdue. How many years has it been since you left your homeland? Three, four years?"

To Petrah, it had been a lifetime. "Five years."

"Much too long, then." Aman touched the necklace around Petrah's throat with his fingertip. There was no adverse effect, no negative reaction—unlike the people who had tried to touch it before. "You wear our family crest. It signifies your divine right." Aman lifted the medallion and flipped it over. "I saw this in a dream. Our mutual friend has done well in giving it to you. But now"—he tugged, and the chain broke free—"you are burdened no longer." Aman pocketed the medallion as if it were an ordinary object.

Petrah's hand went to his throat. He could breathe freely again, the albatross gone. "It was supposed to guide me straight to you."

"Obviously, there were complications. I would have thought the people under my command were better educated as to its significance. I'm deeply disappointed with my subjects. I must apologize for their poor judgment."

"They didn't know," Petrah said, thinking about the lieutenant, the magistrate, even the owl-eyed priestess.

"That doesn't excuse their behavior," Aman said with an undertone of authority. "Worry not. This won't happen again." The way he said it assured Petrah of consequences, which made Petrah feel even worse about opening his mouth. Aman swept his hand to his left and lightened his voice. "Come, allow me to give you a breathtaking view of our world."

Aman led them across a hallway, past a partition, to a second room ringed with panes of glass that ran floor to ceiling, each about twelve feet in height.

"Behold the Iron City as few ever have," he said.

Vertigo overtook Petrah for a moment before he realized the glass was fixed in place and not going anywhere. He gingerly extended his fingertips to the clear pane. It rebuffed the push he gave. He peered at the streets fifty stories below, then the river in the distance and desert behind it, followed by a road leading from the collapsed metal bridge through the hinterlands beyond and toward the mountains where it disappeared. The mountains themselves were rocky, with sparse woodland and brush among the crags. Dozens, maybe hundreds, of campfires dotted the landscape.

"The mountaineers find refuge there. It's become their home. They call themselves the Peshte." Aman bore the same accent as the magistrate and lieutenant, although his Jurmehan was impeccable. "They quarrel with us, as you might have heard."

"I have," Petrah said, taking in the whole of the land beneath the fading light of day. It was serene as it was austere. If the cold in the city was harsh, Petrah could only imagine how brutal it was in the mountains. "What do you call yourselves?"

"We are a patchwork of peoples from different regions: Angorians from the forests, Novatoa from the hills, Meslins from the desert, Jaketh from the prairie lands, Ska'rites from the sea, and dozens more. What unites us is our faith. Together, we are the Marked of Sag-ahn. He is the All Father, Truthforger, Darkwreather, and he has many more names of devotion to those who believe."

"But the Peshte are different," Petrah said.

"The Peshte believe in Jovah, the false god. He hides behind the mask of creation, oblivious to the truth of the one true god. As long as they believe in falsehoods, the Peshte are our enemy. But if they wish to submit, who are we to turn them away?" He smiled diplomatically, and Petrah noticed how clean and straight his teeth were. "I have generously offered them subjugation, yet they declined. Now they hang onto their mountainous reaches, their feet cut out from them, and slowly their legs, and soon their torso. The stubborn head will come last, but by then, we will rid ourselves of this place, won't we?" Aman's aura expanded as he said "we," raking Petrah's skin with ice, before contracting again.

Petrah held firm against the chill of nether energy. *There is no "we,"* he thought, digging into his resolve. *There is only you, Aman.* But he responded in a measured tone, careful to frame the appropriate response. "And when will that be?"

"It depends, really. We consolidate our hold here, strengthen our numbers, and bide our time. Eventually, I will marshal my forces and call upon my allies to march."

Which meant Aman didn't have a strict timeline. But how long was "eventually"? A month, a year, a decade? Petrah had been here a few days. Every fiber of his being wanted to be rid of this place. To take his friends and flee. But where could they go? How could they get away? Petrah scanned the city and its environs. Everywhere he looked, he saw desolation. "What happened to this world?"

Aman laid a palm against the glass. "A great civilization once ruled here. Now it lies in ruins. How, you ask? Through treachery, warfare, and misguided beliefs. The ancients of this world lost everything they had at their height through the desertion of faith, through profligacy and stupidity and intemperance. Because of their treachery, the waters are filled with poison, the fields are dead or withering, and the cold is everlasting. The eternal winter will win eventually, and anyone left behind will meet their end. This world is sick, Immael, doomed to end up a tomb. We must leave it while we can."

Aman turned toward Petrah. A wash of cold swept Petrah's face, as if a cold breeze had blown in through a gap in the glass. "Your world is healthy and teeming with life. The only problem, as we both know, is the people; or, more pointedly, those people who embrace the same ideals as the mountaineers do here. But once we bridge the gap to your world, we will remedy that problem." There was that "we" again.

Did Aman know where to find a portal? Was it the same one Petrah and his friends had entered through? Was it a different one? Did it exist yet, or would the Watcher create it when the time came?

Aman brought them around to the north side of the room, where more windows peered out onto the Iron City. It was a fitting name, considering the sheer quantity of iron and steel: metal towers, metal sculptures, homes made of metal scraps, ramps, bridges, and elevated walkways, all metal, with stone and glass to dress their starkness. Petrah saw a plethora of pennons and buntings, fields of black with coiled dragons in red.

Hundreds of people occupied the streets below, going about their business. A large forge billowed smoke from exhaust stacks in the distance. The people were tiny from up here, as if Petrah could pinch them between his fingers and pick them up.

"Look at them," Aman said. "Look at all the people down there. Just specks to us. Who's the father, the mother, the child? The bricklayer, the soldier, the cobbler? You couldn't tell from this height. From here they look identical, like ants beneath your feet. Yet they lack the harmony or the purpose of the ant or bee. One kills a fellow man for a cut of cloth; another repents for stealing food from a babe; a third visits a lover and then returns to her ignorant husband; a baby dies from an untreatable disease. It's chaos out there. One might think the world is spinning out of control." He paused, pressing his fingertips against the glass. "What do you think, Immael? Is the world spinning out of control?"

The question caught Petrah off guard. Was Aman testing him to understand how his mind worked? How he reasoned? "I guess it depends. There is chaos, but there is also order. If you're asking about people, they're capable of both. Maybe they should be more like the ants—more predictable."

Aman quirked up an unsettling grin, a flash of teeth hinting at the predator behind the smile. "People are all ordered in their own way, part of a threadwork of living bodies serving a common purpose. What is that purpose, you ask? What drives the spokes and gears of the machine? It's a commonality, a single-mindedness experienced through the spirit that washes away the borders of their origins, dialects, and cultures." Aman turned away from the window. His irises gleamed like blue gemstones in the dying light. "Maybe the ants are onto something."

Petrah met his eyes. Brilliant, blue, wicked. So clever, so devious. How could anyone trust him? Yet he commanded attention. No, he demanded it. Petrah couldn't break the stare. He remained transfixed, lured in by the intense fire of Aman's presence, glamored by it.

"You see, the spirit is stronger than the body. Torch the flesh, tear the man limb from limb, cut him up into little pieces, and what are you left with? The spirit! No matter what you do to the body, that cavity of meat has a soul inside, and it's the soul that connects us to our divine beginnings. Without a soul, we're nothing more than a pack of dogs on the hunt." Aman paused, lifting a finger. Petrah followed the movement of his hand, inexplicably drawn to it. "With a soul, we're much, much more. We can achieve greatness." He leaned close with his suffocating aura. Petrah tried to pull back but was unable.

"That is our purpose, Immael. We are not on this earth to mate, masticate, and worm the ground. We are here to govern the elements, to exercise authority over all living creatures, and to rule with sovereignty. We are here to connect to the heavens, to the spiritual beings that watch over us and succor us through invisible influence, to the ruling class of the spirit world; and, of course, to our father. For some of us, we have closer ties to the Father than others. You and I share a direct lineage that elevates us above the rest of these walking monkeys. To think that my own people nearly hanged you today . . ." Aman shook his head. "But fate is an interesting thing. It tends to make things happen in a certain fashion, wouldn't you agree?"

It was the Watcher's words, materializing from a dream.

"I do," Petrah said, not daring to miss a beat, even though his thoughts were more sluggish, as if sleep beckoned. Was it exhaustion? Or was it his brother's aura that sapped him of his strength? Petrah recalled the auras of formidable channelers like Uhtah-Pei and Baaka. Theirs paled in comparison to the fell power Aman exuded. If that was any indication of Aman's channeling abilities, how could anyone defeat him? *How can*

I *defeat him?* Could a word of power send his brother crashing through the window behind him? Or was it folly to believe such an attempt would succeed? The only sure way to stop his brother was to keep him here, in this world. To do that, Petrah needed to find a portal Aman didn't know existed, and escape through it with his friends.

Petrah's thoughts turned to his mother, the one person who might know the whereabouts of a portal. *Kruush, Tan, and I must get to it first, enter it, and then destroy it.* But Petrah still didn't understand how a portal worked, what it was made of, or how to control or destroy it. It remained an enigma to him. If he couldn't understand it, then all he would accomplish by reentering Acia would be to open the way for Aman. *I can't let that happen. I can't!*

Aman placed a brotherly hand on Petrah's shoulder, perhaps reading the shift in Petrah's mien. Petrah resisted the impulse to flinch and recoil from his touch. "I see trouble under the surface, Immael. What ails you?"

Petrah didn't hold back. "I've been wondering if our mother is still alive. I was so sure I would find her. But after coming here . . ."

Aman nodded. "Yes, I see how that would be troubling. Unfortunately, we do not share the same mother." Petrah frowned, not expecting that. "You don't know, do you?"

"I assumed—"

"You assumed since we share the same father, the same would hold true of our mother. Rest assured, it isn't so. My mother died birthing me. Your mother, however, is alive."

A welling of hope fought its way through the ice encasing Petrah's optimism. He didn't want to let it get the best of him, though. "How do you know she's alive?"

"I sought her out long ago." Petrah's mind immediately went to a dream where Aman and his horsemen hunted after him and his mother. Reading his concern, Aman said, "I did so with good intentions. After all, we share a common bond: you. By the time I found her, you were already gone. She hid you well, though, didn't she? So well, in fact, that I doubted you and I would ever meet. Yet, here we are, brother, standing side by side."

Petrah reeled from the revelation. In his dreams, Petrah's mother had done everything in her power to prevent Aman from finding Petrah. "She told you she sent me away?"

"She did," Aman said. "I know it's hard to believe, but guilt and grief are powerful motivators to confessing the truth."

Chills rose up Petrah's neck. "You're positive she's alive?"

"I am."

Petrah's heart pounded from the staggering news. Conflicting emotions surged within him, torn between hope and skepticism. Could he trust Aman's words? It was difficult to ignore the nagging doubt, the persistent voice whispering that this revelation might be a ploy, a manipulative attempt to draw him closer to Aman and under his control. Petrah yearned to believe that his mother had truly protected him by sending him away, but the uncertainty entangled his thoughts.

"Do you know where she is?"

"I do," Aman said. "In fact, I will take you to her."

"When do we go?" Petrah was eager to leave. He had tried to find his mother and failed. He would not allow this opportunity to pass. He *had* to see her.

"Tomorrow, we will travel across the desert and mountains to my castle, where my forces gather and train, readying themselves for the crossover to your world."

"Across the mountains?" It sounded impossibly far away.

"It's a fair distance by caravan. But"—Aman raised his finger—"one doesn't need to travel on foot or by horse to reach a destination. People with our abilities have another way, a way I will show you."

"What about my companions? I want them with me when we go."

"They will travel separately."

Petrah didn't like that idea. "I want them with us."

"I assure you, they will not be harmed or spoiled when they arrive. They'll be a day behind at the latest." Aman fixed him with a gaze that told Petrah not to challenge the decision.

Petrah's concern for his mother's well-being bled into his voice. "Is my mother safe?"

"Quite. I have to tell you, dear brother, she disappointed me by hiding you. But that is all in the past now."

Petrah looked at Aman. Same blue eyes as he had, but that's where the similarities ended. Nothing else about their physiques was alike. They had nothing in common, except . . .

"What of our father?"

"We share his blood in our veins," Aman said with an air of pride. "We are demigods, you and I. Who can boast of such lineage? The mountain men? Definitely not."

"But we bleed the same as any mortal," Petrah said. "I don't *feel* any different from anyone else."

"That's because you have yet to realize your potential. You are not like any other mortal. You are more—much more. If you are slain, you will not die a normal death. You will be reborn. Ask your mother. She will tell you."

A terrible thought dawned on Petrah, a thought so devastating, it sent ice-cold tingles up his neck.

"Yes," Aman said, nodding at Petrah's understanding. "You know, don't you?"

He did, and it burned his innards as if he had swallowed a goblet of molten lead. "My mother didn't just push me through a portal, did she?"

"No, dear brother. She certainly did not."

Chapter 7
Monster of Men

P ETRAH SAT ALONE IN his guest quarters, a corner room two stories below where he had met Aman, with a nighttime view of both the river and the city proper. The plain room was lacking as far as accommodations went—nothing more than a space of glass, steel, and stone with a small oil lamp and a mattress stuffed with feathers lying in the corner. There was another room with a hole in the floor for bodily waste. It stunk of old excrement. Petrah doubted the bucket of water next to it could rinse away the filth.

The smell was the least of his problems. His primary concern was the runaway thoughts about his mother and what she had done to him.

He saw it now in vivid detail. It had been cloaked in dreams, torn from his memories, although it dwelled in the depths of his mind like a terrifying creature lurking at the bottom of a lake, always there, always waiting to surface.

She betrayed me.

No, it wasn't betrayal. She had done it to protect him. Or, more importantly, to protect him from his brother—or perhaps the world from Aman.

Petrah pulled up his shirt and looked at the skin on his belly. Just below the breastbone lay the familiar vertical scar from childhood. He'd first seen it when he was eleven, when the scar was a fresh line of angry pink. All these years and he'd not known the cause.

Until his brother opened his eyes.

So it's true.

The squeal of the lift sounded, heralding the approach of its car. Petrah detected the presence of one person, but it wasn't his brother. The lift stopped on his floor, and the wooden door raised.

A skinny young boy with bright copper eyes and a dirty thin face stepped out. The boy carried a food tray in one hand with a mug balanced on top and a jug in his other hand. The aroma of cooked fish followed.

"Here, let me help you," Petrah said in Glesh, taking the tray. He set it down on the floor while the boy placed the jug beside it.

The boy pointed to the tray. "I've brought you your evening meal, compliments of my master: smoked eel, root vegetables, nuts, fruit, thick slices of bread and butter, and an assortment of cheeses, along with ale and water."

Petrah had seen the starving faces of children, and this boy was no different. He reminded Petrah of the beggar's daughter from Kanmar. Petrah had tried to help her, to feed her a few morsels of bread, only to fail. How could Aman give Petrah such a grand meal when there were hungry people in his city, like this boy?

"Are you hungry?"

The boy glanced at the food and licked his lips. It was obvious he was famished. "I'm fine, sir."

Petrah looked the boy up and down. He was anything but *fine*. His pants and shirt were threadbare, his shoes had holes, and his face was smudged with soot. "Sit with me. There's plenty for the both of us."

"I can't do that, sir. The food is for you. I should go." The boy turned to leave.

"Wait." The boy looked at him. "What's your name?"

"Asha, sir."

"How old are you?"

"Ten, sir."

He was but a child. Petrah grabbed the lamp and set it on the floor beside the tray, then sat cross-legged and patted the space beside him. "Sit, Asha." The boy stared at the tray, conflicted but hungry. "Please."

The boy took a seat. He folded his hands in his lap and set his back straight. His collarbones protruded sharply, and his arms were bony.

"I want you to eat as much as you want," Petrah said. "Anything you like."

"But I—"

"Anything, Asha. I insist. All right?"

The boy nodded, then helped himself to the buttered bread and cheese. He ate like a tempest, stuffing his mouth and chewing voraciously. When was the last time he had a square meal?

Petrah wrapped a piece of eel with a slice of bread. The salty, smoky flavor was heavenly. He washed it down with ale. "Have some eel. It's good."

"I can't let my master smell it on my breath," the boy said as he stuffed a handful of nuts in his mouth and chomped noisily.

"Then have some grapes." There were two clusters of plump grapes, green and purple. Petrah couldn't fathom how grapes could grow in this climate. The boy accepted a cluster and stuffed a grape in his mouth.

Petrah ate slowly, more interested in making sure the boy had his fill. "Do you have a family, Asha? Parents? Brothers or sisters, perhaps?"

The boy shrugged, then plucked a purple grape and devoured it, along with a few more nuts.

"Where are you from?"

The boy pointed to the window, chewing quickly. "The mountains."

"You're Peshte?"

Asha nodded, tearing off one more piece of bread. Aman had spoken poorly about the Peshte. Was this boy a slave, perhaps the property of the Marked? Had he been taken from his family when he was a baby?

The boy wiped his face and stood. "I must go back to my master. Thank you for the food, sir. That was"—the boy blinked as if having trouble finding the right words—"kind of you."

Petrah rose to his feet. He wanted to offer the boy the rest of the bread to take with him, but the boy bowed his head quickly and dashed off. In seconds, he was gone.

At least he won't go hungry tonight.

Petrah sat on the edge of his bed, feeling a little more himself. He finished the remaining food and even dabbed the breadcrumbs with moist fingers. It took a few minutes for the hunger to subside and the feeling of fullness to take hold.

Petrah dragged his bed over to the window so he could gaze out. His mind reeled when he looked straight down at the city. It wasn't natural to be so high off the ground. Which ancient civilization had built these towers, and for what purpose? That led to more troubling thoughts, like what he was doing here, and more urgently, what he needed to do. It bled over into fretting over Tan and Kruush. He prayed they had been treated as guests, not prisoners.

Petrah's thoughts returned to the boy as he watched the campfires in the mountains. Asha didn't know if he had any family. Perhaps his parents were sitting at a campfire right now, wondering if their son was alive and well. Was Petrah's mother thinking about him at the moment, wondering the same?

He fell asleep picturing her sorrowful, pale-blue eyes.

P ETRAH AWOKE TO THE sound of thunder. Outside, the sky was still dark, the Iron City drenched in rain. Whatever snow there was had turned to slush. He had dreamed very little and remembered nothing except for a sense of loss. His hand went instinctively in search of Mina's lock of hair in his breast pocket. He panicked, not feeling any pocket at all, only to realize he had changed clothes and transferred the lock to the pocket in his breeches. The lock had fared poorly. It was more of a clump now than anything else, and purely symbolic of the one thing that kept his despair at bay: his sweet Mina.

If you don't get back to her, she'll become someone else's Mina.

But if Aman somehow made it to Acia, losing Mina to the son of a politician or wealthy aristocrat would be the least of Petrah's worries. His brother would not allow the good people of Meerjurmeh to survive.

The thought further blackened his mood, which was already trampled upon by the fact he was alone, separated from his friends.

Water streaked the panes of glass, blurring the still-burning fires in the mountains. Petrah sat with his back against the window, which rattled against his spine with each thunder peal. Closing his eyes, he clutched the lock of hair against his cheek, imagining Mina nestling against his shoulder, listening to the rain together. He smiled to himself, soothed as he envisioned her expression of wonderment as she looked at the landscape far below.

She was his muse, his inspiration. Words formed in his thoughts, lines that might become a verse, perhaps a poem. He whispered them as the rain pelted the glass.

"Though the skies are dark, though the clouds weep, I can't help but cherish the tears they cast. For they remind me of you. And you remind me of—"

A thunderclap rumbled, shaking the glass. It severed his concentration and brought him back to the moment—to what was at stake and the threat Aman posed.

Petrah pocketed Mina's lock of hair. The words of his poem washed away with the rain.

He got up and walked to the center of the wall of glass windows, where he could view the entire mountain range. If Aman came through on his promise to take Petrah to see his mother, the next step would be to find a way back to Acia. Assuming Petrah could find another portal, how could he and his friends escape from Aman and return to Acia but also stop Aman from crossing over? Could the mountaineers help? If the Peshte were the enemies of the Marked, could Petrah go to them?

Petrah was out of his depth. He needed his friends. Together, they could figure out their next move. They could plan—

The hairs on Petrah's arms and neck came to attention. He was no longer by himself.

He spun to find Aman standing beside his bed, a fur coat draped over his beige robe, and looking out the window to his city. How did he get into the room? Why hadn't Petrah heard the lift approach?

Petrah's heart raced as he observed the unnatural curvature of space around the outline of his brother's body. Did other people see the same thing?

"We're leaving," Aman said without turning around. He pointed behind him to the bed, where a similar robe to the one he wore was folded neatly. "Put that on."

Petrah stayed his place. "What about my companions? Where are they?"

"I already told you, they are traveling separately. Now, put the robe on. We have to leave."

Petrah didn't like Aman's sharp tone, nor the fact his friends were already traveling. He donned the robe. The fabric was thin, lightweight, and soft, like fleece, but warm. He joined Aman by the window. The rain had stopped, and the sky was just lightening in the east beneath a pall of heavy cloud cover. The wind, however, was relentless, snapping the many black-and-red pennons and banners throughout the city below, even shaking the windows.

"I've seen your country in my visions," Aman said, continuing to look out the window. "The climate is warm, even hot and arid in places. Here"—he presented the landscape with a sweep of the hand—"the cold is perpetual, and the lands barely produce the crops needed to sustain my people, their steeds, and their livestock. They know famine and disease all too well." He stared past the glass, arms bent behind his back, hands grasping forearms. His voice grew distant.

"A long time ago, this world thrived. There were seasons, the water was clean, the fields bountiful, and the population plentiful. The peoples of these lands created grand cities, like the one before us, marvels of industry and ingenuity. Now look at it. It lies in shambles, a shadow of what was." He stabbed the glass with a finger. It wobbled. "Such a shame, really."

"Then why stay here?" Petrah asked. "In the city, I mean."

"Quite simple: the steel. Look around you; it's everywhere. Control the steel, and you control the economy of this land. Control the economy, and you unite the disparate peoples into a single body, like a spider's web held together by strands, nearly invisible and nearly unbreakable. Bring them faith, and you control their hearts."

Petrah pictured a web in his mind, and the various races of men Aman had described the evening before as intersecting points on the web. By themselves, they were nothing. But bound together . . .

"See that plant there yonder with the smokestack?"

Petrah saw the stack belching smoke into the morning air.

"The forge beneath it works day and night off of coal mined from the east," Aman said. "Workers toil ceaselessly, feeding it the remains of these metal giants to make armor, weapons, shields, and machinery. Then, with wood stripped from the forests, they build carts, wagons, and catapults."

"But the people are hungry," Petrah said. There was the boy who had brought him dinner, grateful for a single crumb, and the downhearted children in the streets, desperate for a warm meal. "I've seen their faces, the young in particular." *They're only children. How can you not see that?*

"They do with what they have," Aman said, the surface of his eyes glittering like the ripple of water at sundown. "I provide for my people and protect them, and I expect much in return. Some of these towers around us have been converted into terraces where we can trap the heat for growing wheat, barley, and vegetables. Then there are the fields beyond West Morrow where our horses and livestock graze. It's a delicate balance to keep our people and animals from starving and to keep them producing."

So there it was. *He gives them just enough so they can survive and be useful.* Petrah looked out at the city. Even at this hour, it was alive with activity: people at work or on the move, cavalry patrolling the avenues, carts being loaded or unloaded.

"No one remembers what it was like before the downfall of the old civilizations," Aman said, his voice far away. "Not their fathers or great-grandfathers, nor their great-grandfathers before them."

Aman turned to Petrah, the shimmer in his eyes taking on a radiant blue in the predawn. "Dagoth fell at the hands of those who believed in the false god, the same scourges that hide in the mountains. They have wrecked its beauty, its bounty, and its worth. Your world still holds promise, although the false god influences a great many people. They have become blinded by the light of falsehood. We will change that, won't we?"

The question left a bitter ringing in Petrah's ears. He kept saying "we," as if Petrah would willingly take part in his plot to harm the good people of Acia.

Aman stepped away from the window. He tossed his fur on the bed. "We are leaving. Take my hand, Immael."

Petrah regarded his brother's outstretched hand, the flat palm and smooth fingers stretched toward him in invitation. He sensed a field of energy flowing into his brother's fingertips. "What for?"

"You asked how we can traverse the mountains. Take my hand, and I will show you." Aman nodded his assurance. "Trust me, it won't hurt."

Trust. Petrah trusted nothing about Aman. But he lifted his left arm anyway and reached with his hand toward his brother's . . . and took it. Aman's hand was not only warm to the touch but surged with a static charge that ran up Petrah's arm and spread throughout his body.

And then he was falling.

Petrah clenched his eyes shut. Vertigo and darkness took him, the same as when he had stepped through the Watcher's portal.

The sensation was gone in an instant.

The darkness disappeared when he opened his eyes, replaced by the cool, clear light of dawn.

Petrah snatched his hand away, stunned. His breath was shallow, the air growing thin, and queasiness churned his stomach. His head throbbed as he steadied his feet.

They were no longer fifty stories up in a building overlooking a ruined city. They were on the side of a dirt road in the middle of a settlement with single-story adobe structures, surrounded by desert. The mountains were behind them, the city was nowhere in sight. There were shacks, stands, and kiosks where merchants set up their wares. Petrah saw kiln-fired pottery, baskets, dried fruits and nuts, desiccated scorpions and beetles for sale, and a variety of odd jerkies and vegetables with withered shoots and leaves. The scent of sandalwood and pepper gave the dawn spicy tones, like those of Hōvar's markets.

Around them walked men dressed similarly to Aman, with long robes of different colors. Women wore ankle-length, loose-fitted garments under robes, many with headscarves or with faces completely veiled except for their eyes. The air was warmer here, although it was still cold, compared to Acia.

"How—?" Petrah began, his words cut short by his disbelief.

"Astounding, isn't it?" Aman said, chin high and shoulders back, pride in his voice.

Until this moment, Petrah had only guessed at Aman's potential as a channeler. His aura, his presence, and his confidence hinted at his abilities. But to travel miles in seconds, and to do so effortlessly and with such precision?

Petrah shook the dizziness from his head. "The magi of my world speak of such means of travel, but I never thought it possible." If Aman possessed this command of travel, did he even need a portal?

"There are many mysteries in the universe. If angels can traverse impossible distances in a blink, then why can't we?" Aman beckoned north with a wave of his hand. "Come. I'm taking you to my castle."

Petrah followed Aman through the winding, unpaved streets. Most of the buildings were simple in construction, made entirely of earthen bricks, and a few were erected with sandstone or limestone blocks. Men and women bowed their heads at Aman's passing or raised their marked wrists and ululated in jubilation. Aman smiled and waved at all of them.

A group of young boys and girls ran up to him.

"Mahdi! Mahdi!" they cheered. Some called him "Uncle." They were dressed in tatters, dirty in the faces and arms, and many underweight, but they were all smiling, all excited to see Aman.

Aman laughed. He touched the tightly knotted hair of one boy and tousled the hair of a girl with long, straight blonde hair. They giggled and held out their hands. Had Petrah misjudged his brother, thinking of him as a ruthless, cold tyrant and nothing more? These children adored him. How could so many of his dreams paint Aman as a villain, yet here he was, the kindhearted "Uncle"?

"Have you been kind to your mothers and fathers?" Aman asked in Glesh.

They bobbed their heads, smiling and laughing.

"Good, good." Aman reached into one of his robe's pockets, and like a magician, pulled out a handful of what looked like translucent red gemstones. He held his palm open for the children to see. "Cherry candies. Who deserves one?"

"Me, me, me," they said over each other, clapping their hands or bobbling up and down on their tiptoes.

"I think each of you deserves a candy. Except maybe for you." Aman playfully poked one girl on the nose.

At first, she looked as if the world had fallen out from under her. Then she smiled, reflecting Aman's playful grin.

"It's settled then. You all get one." They cheered as only children could. "In fact"—he jiggled the contents in his hand—"I think I might have enough for two apiece." The eyes of the children grew large. "Do you think you might like that?"

"Yes," they cried out gleefully.

"I don't know," Aman said teasingly, withdrawing his hand. "I think you're just trying to take advantage of me. You're not taking advantage of Uncle, are you?"

"No, no," they said in unison.

He opened one eye more than the other, like a father deciding whether to scold or reward his children. "Very well."

Aman held out his palm in offering. For an impoverished child, the candies were a gift of the ages. "Go ahead, but do it nicely, or I'll cuff you behind the ear."

"Yes, Uncle," they said eagerly.

They each took two candies and skittered off, laughing.

"They love you," Petrah said, raising his eyebrows in surprise as he spoke the words. "Everyone does." It was as if these people saw in Aman a charitable, humble, and giving person who reigned through kindness and generosity. Did they not feel his aura, the dark power drawn straight from the Netherworld?

"And I love them equally," Aman said, leading them toward a large building with a domed cap and a quad of minarets surrounding it. "It's an important lesson to heed for any ruler. If you love your people, they will love you back."

Petrah considered his brother's comment. Maybe he spoke the truth and cared for these people. Maybe they were more than mules or servants to him. But Petrah couldn't dismiss his brother's view of those who believed in the "false god." For them, he had only blind hate and a desire to remove them from the cosmos. Petrah reminded himself of what he'd witnessed in his dreams, of the senseless murder and bloodshed. No, a single act of kindness couldn't wipe away Aman's crimes in Petrah's nightmares.

A line of worshippers, at least a hundred deep, waited to enter the domed building, most rocking back and forth on their heels and babbling to themselves, as if in prayer. They all wore wood masks over their faces, painted gold, with black eyes, hollow mouths, and dribbles of red on the cheeks, as if the masks were crying blood.

"They wait to recite their pledges at the shrine," Aman explained. "The masks block out distractions so they can whisper holy devotions as they wait. It lifts my heart each time I see them. Do they not do the same where you're from?"

"They don't use masks in Terjurmeh," Petrah said. "But the priests draw triangles on the foreheads of the devout. It's an anointing oil mixed with blood."

"Blood is sacred," Aman said. "Your people are pious, like ours."

Petrah no longer considered the Ter-jurah *his* people, but he kept that to himself.

They continued until the streets opened to the desert. Hundreds of tents occupied the stretch of empty land, the larger tents mounted with poles up top bearing the Grand Marshall's black banners, fields of black with a lick of fire escaping the gaping, fierce jaws of the red dragon.

This was a city, not just a village.

They turned west toward a monstrous castle that rose from the desert beyond the outskirts of the settlement. It reminded Petrah of the stories he'd heard of the castles in Prall. This one had ashlar facing on the outer walls, which climbed fifty feet and easily stretched a mile. Turrets were mounted at the beginning, middle, and end of the wall. Battlements traversed the top, forming a toothy smile against the clear sky.

A group of soldiers waited by the open portcullis, dressed in chain mail under damascened plate armor with spiraled serpents embossed on their breastplates. They wore helms with decorative, arching snakes. Red horsehair plumes ridged the backs of the snakes like manes.

They raised mailed fists and cheered as Aman and Petrah approached. A young soldier in scaled armor ran over to Aman, dropped to the ground, and kissed his feet. He spoke rapidly in Glesh. Aman placed a gentle hand upon his head, and the youth backed away, bowing and praising him.

Aman and Petrah walked over to the biggest man Petrah had ever seen. He towered at least seven feet and was broad like a bull. His helm had webbed wings, rather than plumes, with hinged cheek guards that exposed his iron-hard face, deep gray eyes, and large mustachio. His freakishly huge body was made even more massive by his plate armor. Even with such bulk, he bent a knee and bowed his head. The other soldiers mirrored his action.

The giant's voice pealed like thunder. "Grand Marshall."

"Lord Verek," Aman said in greeting. "You may rise." The man rose to his full height. From this close, he blocked nearly all of Petrah's view of the gate behind him. "What news do you have?"

"The Peshte sent a raiding party last night. We sent them back with their tails between their legs."

"How many casualties?"

"We lost five. They lost four times as many. About a dozen rode off. Three of them were seriously wounded."

Aman looked the mountain of a man directly in the eyes. He spoke with steel in his voice. "Next time, no survivors."

The giant inclined his head. "Your will, Your Greatness." The other soldiers kept their heads bowed, as if to lift them might earn them punishment.

Aman introduced Petrah. "This is my brother, Immael. Immael, this is Lord Verek, captain of my guard. He holds the noble title of Grand Insept and has land to the east and a mighty stable of horses, don't you?"

The giant offered a firm nod, his winged helmet stiff with the motion.

"He protects the territory from mountain scum. Isn't that right, Lord Verek?"

"Yes, Your Greatness."

Aman gave Petrah a chilly smile. "Better to have this one at your back than your front."

The idea of meeting Lord Verek on the battlefield gave Petrah gooseflesh all over.

Then, to Verek and his men, Aman said, "Peace be with you."

"And with you, Your Greatness," they replied.

Petrah followed Aman through the gatehouse and then past a portico into the keep. They walked along a marble gallery that faced an open courtyard.

"This is my home," Aman said, switching to Jurmehan and stretching out his arms in presentation. "It belonged to a powerful oligarch back before the Amerans that built it fell, along with the rest of civilization. It was left in ruins from their war. My people rebuilt her one stone at a time. She will continue to stand proudly, well after we have deserted this world."

"It's an impressive fortification," Petrah said, taking in the thick walls and cloistered feeling. "An army would be hard-pressed to get through the front gate, let alone into the castle itself."

"No fastness is unassailable. You must always remember that," Aman said. "Gates can be breached, walls scaled, and grounds sapped. The original castle was overrun by raiders." Aman's irises took on a vitreous gleam. "But the ruler escaped unscathed and was able to round up a small force to retake his keep, then the rest of the castle. While the raiders looked outward, they failed to look inward and note the hidden tunnel that ran to the field on the west side. Can you believe a secret passage turned the tide against the raiders? It's a cautionary tale: we must pay heed to the minutest details, lest we fall victim to our own blindness."

They passed an area with a high, vaulted ceiling and then into a long, torch-lit hallway. They paused at the end, where a curved marble banister wound down a flight of stairs, the bottom hidden from view. The air smelled of cold stone.

"Tomorrow, I will take you to see your mother. But today, we celebrate." Aman put a brotherly hand on Petrah's shoulders. "I have a surprise for you."

A shiver rose up Petrah's spine at the mention of "surprise," sending a prickling sensation across the back of his neck. He eyed the stairway, searching the shadows as if something sinister waited below. "Down there?"

Aman picked up on his trepidation. "Yes, down there. It's a good surprise, I promise."

Aman descended, and Petrah followed reluctantly. He didn't like the puckish look on his brother's face. They went down another set of steps and stopped in front of a pair of doors guarded by two burly men with black turbans, scarves, and naked scimitars hanging from their belts. A triangular device was grooved into the stone lintel above with a lidless eye in the center. The magistrate had called it a syriak, similar to the serak of the Ter-jurah.

A guard depressed a lever, and the doors slowly swung inward.

The blood drained immediately from Petrah's face.

A large, candlelit chamber revealed a dozen men and women on their knees, chained to metal hitching posts like pack animals. The women wore body-length, outer garments, exposing only their eyes. The men were bare-chested and barefoot, dressed only in dirty linen pants corded at the waists, with soiled, tanned skin and matted hair and beards. Desperate faces regarded Aman, eyes wide with fear.

One woman called out to Aman. She sounded young, her voice high-pitched and nearly hysterical. "Please forgive me, Lord. I want to repent. Please, let me repent!"

A man to her left begged, "We will do anything, Lord. Please. Whatever you ask! We will all repent, won't we?" The others nodded with fervent up and down motions.

Aman raised his hand calmly. "And you will. But repenting means one has done something wrong. You didn't do anything wrong in my absence, did you?"

The prisoners looked from person to person and shook their heads. The room stunk of sweat, urine, and days-old blood.

"Is your sister telling the truth?" Aman asked of the women huddled next to the young one who had called out. "That she did nothing wrong?"

The women nodded rapidly, sniffling.

"Say it!"

"She did nothing wrong," the woman said, voice breaking. "Please don't hurt her. Please don't!" She sobbed as the man next to her clutched the other girl.

Cold crept down Petrah's neck. His throat tightened. He couldn't process what he was seeing in front of him. Nor could he understand his brother's sudden transformation from Uncle to hideous jailor. Was this the same man who, earlier, had earned the laughter—and trust—of children?

He keeps these people as prisoners. And he tortures them!

Petrah looked at his brother with horror and revulsion.

Aman said to Petrah, "Look at them, brother. Sinners, all of them. Don't believe anything they say. They are liars, thieves, and deceivers. They are all criminals."

Petrah turned to his brother, trembling as he spoke. "Criminals? What crimes did these poor people commit?"

"Poor people?" Aman's expression hardened. His nostrils flared. Spittle flew as he said, "These are heathens! Peshte scum! Mountaineers who would see my people dead! Would you rather they roam free? Would you let them go so they could slit your throat in the middle of the night? Don't let the chains fool you. They are murderers! They would claw your eyes out for the joy of it. But here"—he gestured at the holding cell—"here they are where they belong."

Petrah shivered. Was it fear? Rage? Repulsion? The boy who had served him last night was Peshte. Any of these people could be his mother, his father, his uncle, or his aunt. Yet they were penned in like swine waiting to be slaughtered.

Aman snapped his fingers at one of the big guards. The man drew a knife from his belt and handed it to Aman. The handle was wrapped in leather, the foot-long blade sharpened on one side, curving sinisterly to a pointed tip. Aman offered it to Petrah, handle first. "It's time for you to prove yourself. It's time to prove whose son you are. Take this. Then choose one of them, any of them, and take their life."

Petrah stared at the leather handle, mouth open.

"Take it!"

Petrah shook his head, mind numb, eyes fixed on the handle and the deadly blade. "I won't do it."

"Won't or can't? These people spit at our father. They curse his name. They hate him just as they hate us. Hand any of them this blade and they'll gladly gut you. They are the enemy. The enemy!"

Petrah's shaking was so bad he couldn't see straight. "You have no right."

Aman narrowed his eyes. "What did you say?"

Petrah spoke louder, bolder. "I said you have no right."

Aman's expression became feral, uncaged, something inhuman. "No right?" Aman rasped. He tossed the knife aside. It clattered on the stone floor. He smacked his hands together, and the air crackled. Darkness swelled from his person, a bloom of black ink, spreading, spreading.

Petrah shrank back. The prisoners cried out and huddled together. They pleaded, murmured prayers, and begged for forgiveness.

"No right?" Aman repeated, baring teeth bright like krell fangs. His eyes flared, turning to blue fire. Burning, burning, glowing against the growing dark. "I have every right!"

Petrah fumbled with his hands. He tried to think of a Kantaka pose, anything to use on his brother. But as he curled his fingers into claws, one of the oversized guards grabbed him from behind and yanked his arm behind his back, and pushed up. Petrah yelped in pain.

Aman stepped up to him, eyes afire, a furnace of divine power. His voice was venom and malice. "Do you think yourself so pure? Do you think yourself innocent?" He backhanded Petrah across the face. It stung sharply. "You're not innocent. You're a killer!" Needles of pain stabbed Petrah's skin. "Oh, yes, I know. I know what you've done. I know what you're capable of. Now you will see what *I* am capable of."

He spoke to the guard holding Petrah in place. "Make him watch."

The guard pushed up on the arm wedged behind Petrah's back, so hard Petrah thought his arm might rip out of his shoulder socket. Then, with his other meaty hand, the guard pinched Petrah just below the eyes so they were forced to remain open and clamped Petrah's jaw, immobilizing his head.

Darkness spilled into the prison cell as Aman stalked toward the cowering Peshte. It drank the light, shrinking it to a visible horizontal band across the middle of their faces. It drenched their mouths and foreheads in shadow and the rest of their bodies in total darkness, hiding all but their terror-stricken eyes.

Then, one by one, they began to scream.

Chapter 8
Prophet

K RUUSH AND TAN SAT in the back of a horse-drawn cart, along with eight soldiers, all squished together. They knocked around as the cart drove over the desert highway, feeling every bump and dip in the road. Thankfully, the rivets sewn into the soldiers' leather armor didn't chafe or cuff the two Ter-jurah men bunched up next to them. A dozen men-at-arms on horseback formed the vanguard of the procession.

"I don't know how much more of this thumping I can take," Kruush said.

"It was your idea to get in the back," Tan said. "Not mine, remember?"

"Don't think I don't regret it. And here I thought we were 'guests.'" Kruush scowled. "Last I checked, guests were supposed to ride in comfort, not like swine on the way to a ranch."

"Maybe they don't know much about hospitality. Different culture, different way of thinking."

"Or lack of thinking. These bastards speak Jurmehan worse than those Darkforth pigs, and they smell funny, too." The woman to his left—with the unibrow—narrowed her eyes at him but didn't say anything. "See what we're dealing with?"

"I'd watch your words," Tan said. "These people aren't deaf."

Kruush huffed. "You mean this braindead lot? Please! I hope Petrah's enjoying his luxury coach with His Royal Highness. Sure was nice of him to leave us with the likes of these brutes."

"It wasn't like he had a choice. And neither do we. Who knows how long we'll be in this cart? Complaining's not going to do us very good."

"It might not do much, but it makes me feel better. Speaking of which, take a look." Kruush pointed his finger to the side of the desert highway.

There was a gathering of mudbrick buildings and a larger stone one in the center, with a cupola bearing hammered copper tiles. The horse-drawn cart turned off the road. Several people stood outside the stone building's entrance, dressed in thick, wool robes with chains made of heavy links crossed diagonally over their chests, as if they stored treasure inside their bodies.

Tan craned his neck. "Who do you suppose they are?"

"Not sure, but they don't look too friendly."

"I was hoping for a bathhouse. Or a brothel."

Kruush shook his head. "You're always thinking with your little pinky. Someday it's going to fall off."

The cart stopped right in front of the stone building. The horsemen dismounted, and a man with red tassels on his pauldrons waved the soldiers off the back of the cart, Kruush and Tan included.

"You two," he said in stilted Jurmehan. "Come." He beckoned the pair to follow him. The man spoke to one of the robed figures in Glesh. He pointed at the open doors. "Inside."

Kruush gave the building with the cupola a second look. "What is this place?"

"Shrine," the man said tersely. "In!"

Kruush noticed the entire procession of soldiers looking at him. He shrugged. "Fine."

Inside the building, large pillar candles lit up the underside of the cupola, which depicted a mural of winged angels in tunics pointing their spears down at a groveling host of hideous-looking men, women, and children.

Lovely, Kruush thought. *Everyone thinks they're an artist.*

Pews lined the main chamber, split up the middle by an aisle leading to a dais with a brass brazier where a man in a robe with crisscrossed chains tended to smoldering coals with a poker. Several more pokers rested against the inside of the brazier's rim. The air stunk of melting tallow.

The horseman with the red tassels led Kruush and Tan up the center aisle.

"I don't like the look of this," Kruush whispered.

A woman with a shaved scalp stepped onto the dais. She also wore a robe with chains crossed over her torso. She said something to the red-tasseled man in her native tongue, then spoke to the newcomers in Jurmehan. Even though her accent was strong, her words came through intelligibly.

"I thank you for coming to our shrine. Are you both penitent men in the eyes of the one true god?"

Kruush looked at Tan and then said, "If you mean San, then yes."

"Only the penitent may be blessed in his name. It means you have a chance at salvation."

"That's a relief," Kruush muttered under his breath.

The woman priest didn't take kindly to the lightness of his comment. "This is a holy shrine. Your words are being measured from above as well as below. You would do well to remember that." Then, in a more formal tone, she said, "Are you remorseful, apologetic, and repentant in the Father's name?"

Kruush noticed the swordsmen gathering around him and how they all had their hands on the hilts of their weapons. *This doesn't look good.*

"Aye," he said warily, "I am."

"Do you confess your sins, the sins of the unmarked?"

Kruush thought they had already been exonerated. "Now, see here, there's no need—"

The chained woman shouted over him. "Do you confess, or do you not?" Her eyes gave off heat like the hot coals beside her.

The swordsmen tightened their knot around the newcomers. They were restless, as if waiting for the wrong answer to be spoken so they could unsheathe their weapons. Kruush had a sinking feeling about what was happening. He saw it in Tan's fearful eyes, too.

Damn. Just when things were looking up.

There was only one way to answer the woman's question and make it out of this place alive.

"Aye, we do," Kruush said with a heavy heart. He had never considered himself a religious person, not even as a boy when his parents would take him to Temple every San's Day. For Kruush, his faith had become a stranger to him. And with Petrah's revelation of his lineage to the dark god, Kruush's trust in San had faltered. Now, in this place, and trapped by these people, there was nothing left of him to give to the god of his homeland. He was at their mercy, saying what they wanted to hear, but feeling none of it in his heart.

The woman smiled coldly. "Then all is forgiven." She nodded to the soldiers.

Hands quickly grabbed Kruush and Tan. Kruush bucked against the seizure.

It was futile.

The soldiers overpowered them and dragged them to a pair of chairs behind the dais. The chairs were constructed of heavy timber, their legs and backs bolted to stone. Each chair was fitted with restraints: straps for the forearms, upper arms, necks, and ankles. The soldiers strapped Kruush and Tan in, wrists facing up. Lastly, they clamped their hands in a fashion where their arms were completely immobilized.

The woman with the shaved scalp took one of the hot pokers from the brazier.

Except it wasn't a poker.

The hot end of the shaft bore a circle of iron with a familiar device on it. The woman stepped toward the strapped-in foreigners, her face etched with unwavering devotion. She radiated an eerie serenity, a blend of purpose and chilling calm. Kruush's wide eyes met the priestess's gaze. In that helpless moment, he glimpsed the depth of her conviction, written as a creased smile that told him she believed she could save his tormented soul.

"This will hurt for only a moment."

PETRAH PACED IN THE late afternoon, blowing hot air out through pursed lips to counter his rage.

He walked back and forth in the second-story apartment facing the courtyard of Aman's keep, barefoot on the terracotta tile floor. The single room was huge and appointed with furnishings fit for a king, but he could have been in a dungeon for all he cared. What Aman had done was unforgivable. And what Petrah had seen—

What he'd heard—

The screams. *The screams!*

He covered his ears with his hands and pressed against them until they hurt, but the screaming continued.

He kept hearing the one girl pleading, crying, begging Aman not to hurt her, and the woman he'd named as her sister doing the same. Petrah had frozen at that moment, unable to stop his brother, unable to intervene. The darkness had been unlike anything Petrah had seen or felt—so absolute, so wrong—infecting the very air as if had been laced with poison.

He had no right, yet he said he did. What kind of monster believes that?

A knock on the door jarred him.

Petrah clutched his chest, heart thumping. He sensed a presence outside his door. Was his brother on the other side? He searched for an aura, but felt none. No, this wasn't his brother. This was someone else.

Petrah's heart slowed, and his goosebumps went away.

He cleared his throat. "Come in."

A veiled young woman entered and bowed her head. She spoke to him in Glesh. "The Grand Marshall bids you join him for supper. He will send someone shortly to fetch you."

How could Petrah dine with his brother after what had happened? He needed to be alone, away from the man. He needed time to think and soothe his nerves. "Tell him I'm not hungry."

She looked down at the slippers covering her small feet. "But he insisted," she said meekly.

Petrah watched as she pressed her palms together and squeezed her elbows against her belly. After what his brother had done earlier, Petrah couldn't allow Aman to harm another soul. "Do I need to change clothes?" Two ankle-length robes with long, flaring sleeves lay stretched across the top of his luxurious bed. He'd found them in his apartment when he first entered.

The young lady looked up, hesitant. "He didn't say, but I can ask."

"No need," Petrah said, offering her a reassuring smile. "I will change and attend supper. Thank you."

The woman bowed and backed out the door.

A MILITARY OFFICER UNDER Lord Verek's command dressed in a long, red cape escorted Petrah to the dining hall. Petrah wore a beige robe trimmed in black with a brass-buttoned collar that cinched around his throat. His escort's face was a patchwork of scars, and his demeanor was rough, like his voice. He led them at a brisk pace down a curved staircase with worn marble treads.

"You will sit near the head of the table, near His Greatness," the man instructed in Glesh that had an accent different from the people Petrah had interacted with. Was he from a distant part of Dagoth, a Ska'rite from the coast perhaps, or a Novatoan from the hills?

"Must I sit so close?" Petrah asked, brushing his fingertips along the stone blocks of the stairwell's wall. It was a foolish question. Petrah regretted it as soon as he asked.

The man with the scarred face snorted. "Fifty guests will be dining this evening. You should be honored to be so close." They reached the bottom of the stairs and entered a loggia with a wall on one side and arches facing an open courtyard on the other.

Petrah ventured a second question, one more appropriate. "Who will be there?"

"Important guests and allies," the scarred man said. "High-ranking officials, Insepts from strategic regions, influential friends of His Greatness's. They are the power that binds the realm."

Petrah hoped Kruush and Tan would be there. He desperately needed to see them. "I have two companions traveling here from the Iron City. Do you know if they've arrived and if they will be at supper?"

"No."

Petrah expected something more, but the man offered no further explanation. Weren't his friends set to arrive today? Or was it tomorrow?

The officer led Petrah along several more corridors, up a level, then down again. Petrah heard voices ahead, the buzz of lively conversation and merriment. This would be his first glimpse of the Grand Marshall's inner circle. Were they any different from the rough types he's seen so far, men like his escort and the giant Lord Verek?

The dining hall was a grand room with high ceilings and hanging chandeliers bedecked with jeweled oil lamps. The lamps scattered light across a mighty table whose top was a single, thick slab of wood. On top sat platters of cheeses, breads, and grapes, and a variety of creamy dips in silvered dishes. Petrah searched for his friends but saw only strangers.

"Wait here." Petrah's escort left him standing by himself as he went over to Aman, who was surrounded by an enthralled handful of guests laughing at something he said. The officer spoke in Aman's ear. Aman waved him off and turned his blue eyes toward Petrah. The skin on Petrah's face crawled, turning warm. He bottled up his breath and held it while his brother peered at him.

Aman was a fount of tranquility—no hint of the predator Petrah had witnessed earlier, no sign of the monster. Gone, too, was his aura, as if he could hide it at will. As soon as Aman returned his attention to his guests, Petrah shuddered. He released the air from his lungs and waited for his escort to walk back to him. How could his brother be so calm, so unbothered? To kill so easily and then entertain as a statesman?

He has no soul, Petrah thought. But that wasn't true. The Great One was flesh and blood. His soul was his connection to the Netherworld, his conduit to the vast well of power he had summoned earlier. Petrah shuddered again. He tried to block his memory of the Peshte prisoners and shut out their wails, shrieks, and screams.

The officer with the scarred face returned. "His Greatness is pleased you are here. I will show you your assigned seat, and then you are free to mingle until suppertime."

Petrah kept to himself after his escort left the room. He had no desire to mingle. He stayed away from Aman and away from his coterie, choosing to observe and remain quiet. He picked out officers from Aman's army. They dressed formally in robes like Petrah's, buttoned at the throat, wearing ribbons upon their shoulders like the lieutenant who had arrested Petrah and his friends. The other guests wore robes or tunics of fine fabric, with bright sashes, tassels, and brass accouterments fixed to their outfits in various shapes of animals and mystic symbols. Some women wore see-through scarves over their faces and decorative henna tattoos on top of their hands. They conversed in small groups, laughing and carrying on, barely paying attention to the sixteen-year-old who was left to fend for himself.

When supper was announced, a servant in a stiff, black jacket escorted Petrah to his seat, three chairs away from Aman who sat at the head of the table. Petrah avoided eye contact with his brother, remaining small and quiet, and as invisible as he could. Aman didn't seem to care. He enjoyed the company of the guests seated closest to him. They fawned at his feet with unabashed obsequiousness, vying for his approval with revolting flattery. Their smiles disguised an undercurrent of fear which Petrah picked up from their quickened heartbeats and tiny darts of the eyes at their neighbors. If one didn't outshine the other, would they fall out of favor?

They bow and scrape. They would stab each other in the back if it meant gaining position.

At one point, Aman raised his cup and had the entire table salute Petrah as his honored guest. It was as if the atrocity from earlier had never happened. Petrah shrank in his seat as Aman lavished him with attention and praise in Glesh.

"Tonight, we hold a special celebration. Tonight, I share this feast with my younger brother, Immael. He is the blood of my blood, the blood of the Father. I have dreamed of this night for years, to sit at the same table, to be as a family, as brothers. You see before you a gifted young man. A man who has traveled worlds to be here with me on this auspicious night. A man who will help me fulfill my destiny, help me liberate our people, and bring us greatness. And, yes, he is the more handsome of us. Just look at those dazzling blue eyes." A few chuckles escaped the gathering. "So raise your cups, and say it with me: to Immael."

"To Immael," they repeated. They drank while Petrah looked on, drained of color, wishing he could run from the room. The heavyset man next to Petrah clapped him on the shoulder. Then, thankfully, servants arrived with steaming platters of food, and everyone's interest shifted to the aroma of roasted meats and fish.

Petrah exhaled, grateful to be rid of the attention. He would rather have crawled into a hole and vanished.

A servant offered Petrah a helping of kabobs, flatbread, and dip. He numbly accepted, allowing the young man to load up his plate. Petrah nibbled a triangle of toasted bread while his neighbors tucked in. He wasn't hungry. Where were Kruush and Tan?

Petrah should have insisted they accompany him and Aman. Surely, a channeler of Aman's prowess could have transported all of them from the Iron City.

No, Aman wanted me to himself. He wanted to see if I was as vile as he was. Now he knows how different we are.

After supper, the guests retired to a drawing room where they drank spiced tea and smoked from water pipes that looked like the jalibis the Ter-jurah used. Petrah pardoned himself. He asked a servant where the courtyard was and slipped quietly out of the dining room.

Petrah had no intention of finding the courtyard. He wanted to search for his friends. He had every intention of leaving the castle this evening, although he didn't know where to go. There was a part of him that wanted to see if his brother would fulfill his promise and bring Petrah to his mother. The other part shouted at him to grab his friends and flee.

Where are they?

A shiver ran down Petrah's neck. He was afraid for his friends' safety. Who knew what Aman had ordered his soldiers to do? He put nothing past his heartless brother.

Petrah got lost on the third turn.

He assumed he was going down the stairs to another landing, but it kept going. He paused at the bottom and saw a tunnel that sloped downward and curved to the right. The hewn walls here were rougher than in other parts of the castle, the scent of stone more apparent. A single torch lit the length of the corridor.

Petrah was about to turn around when he thought he heard a faraway voice.

"Hello?" he called.

No response.

He felt outward with his palm. There was a presence beyond, and the faint beating of a human heart. A soldier? No, why would a soldier be down here—and all alone? Someone in distress, perhaps? Or just a lone soul, like him, who wanted to get away from everyone else?

Curious, Petrah started down the corridor.

He navigated the tunnel as it bent slightly to the right. The ground was marred where picks had chipped away at the bedrock. It took him several minutes to reach the end. A torch lit up a heavy metal door with rusting rivets and a barred window.

Petrah peeked inside and saw a small cell with a single occupant: a girl dressed in a ratty tunic, sitting upright in the middle of a bed of straw. She hummed a soft melody that a mother might hum to her child at bedtime and rocked back and forth while hugging her knees. Her left ankle was fettered with a shackle and secured to a metal rod hammered into the ground. She was young, maybe eight or nine. Stark, white hair draped over her dirtied dress. There was something familiar about her face . . .

Have I seen her before? But where?

He couldn't recall.

Petrah spoke to her in Glesh through the bars, trying his best not to startle her. "Hello?"

She looked up, neither startled nor surprised. "Hello." Her accent was different from the other natives, with a strong pronunciation of her syllables.

"What are you doing locked up in there?"

"Just waiting for my master," she said matter-of-factly. "What are you doing standing out there?"

"I got lost." Petrah noticed three sliding bolts mounted on the door, two slid into the wall, and one into the ground. "Do you speak the priest's tongue, by any chance?"

She nodded, turning around in her seat to face him. Her irises were gray like storm clouds, as different from the people of Dagoth as Petrah's was from the people of Acia. The torchlight danced in her eyes, capturing his attention with their stormy brilliance.

"Is it all right if I open this door and come in?"

She shrugged as if Petrah were one of many guests who came to visit. "The door is noisy."

Petrah slid back the bolts and pulled open the door. Sure enough, it squealed terribly. He froze for a moment and listened. He heard nothing other than his own rapid breathing. Musty hay filtered out of the cell, along with fouler odors.

The girl was a slight thing, with blanched, pale skin and freckles about her smallish nose. Her arms and legs were slender and delicate. She was . . . *fragile.* That was the word. Fragile like the shell of an egg or the petals of a flower. Her hair was her most remarkable feature, white as the snow he'd seen in the Iron City, long and straight, running to the middle of her back. Unlike the rest of her, which was filthy, her hair seemed uncharacteristically free of grease and tangles.

"May I sit with you?"

"If you like." She scooted to her right, making space for him. He sat by her side and mirrored her posture, drawing his legs up to his chest.

She studied him like a grownup might, with careful attention to his features, as if processing the details of his face—his blue eyes, the scar above his brow, the frown lines on his forehead.

"Why are you locked up?" he asked.

"My master says I have to stay here."

There was a bruise under her left cheek and more bruising on her leg and upper arm.

"I'm going to get you out of here," Petrah said. He examined the fetter. It was a simple metal cuff with a small keyhole.

"Where would we go?" she asked. "You said so yourself you got lost coming here."

Petrah had forgotten that small detail. The girl was as clever as she was young. "It's true. You wouldn't happen to know where we are, would you?"

She curved her pale, chapped lips into a smile. "I do. I even know where my master sleeps. Did you know he had an altar put into his bedchamber so he can perform rituals?"

Petrah's stomach soured at the thought. He was deeply impressed with the girl's command over Jurmehan. He'd known many adults in Terjurmeh who spoke with less grace.

"No, I had no idea." He tapped the shackle around her ankle. "Give me a moment to concentrate on the lock."

"It won't work, not even if you had the key. My master did something to it. Only he can unlock it."

"We'll see about that."

Petrah quickly figured out the locking mechanism, using his mind alone to probe the tumbler and pins, like a blind person feeling an object with their hands to build a mental picture. He had freed himself aboard the slave galley in Elmar; he could free this girl. The pins on this lock were a little tricky, but he had gotten good at manipulating small objects with his thoughts. Surely, with a little finesse, he could move the pins into the right positions.

He tried the first one . . . and recoiled.

A pressure clamped around his throat as if someone were attempting to strangle him. It cut off his airway.

He clawed at his throat as if still wearing the medallion, making a choking sound as he struggled. After a few scary attempts at inhaling, the pressure released.

He gulped air. He saw phantom flashes of light, but they went away as his breathing returned to normal.

"Told you," the girl said, hardly surprised or concerned. "Only my master can unlock it."

Petrah collapsed onto a bale of hay next to her. He massaged the cartilage in his throat. "What's your name?"

"Sametha. You can call me Sam if you like."

"That's a very pretty name."

"It's Peshten."

"You're from the mountains?" *Not this girl, too!* How many captives did Aman have?

"I was born there, but I don't remember it, really. My master tells me stories about my people. He doesn't like them very much. Where are you from?"

"From the Iron City originally. I don't remember it either." She smiled at that. "I'm Petrah by the way."

Sametha giggled. "That's not your real name."

Petrah frowned. "How do you know it's not my real name?"

"I know lots of things. I even knew you would come here tonight."

"How's that?"

Sametha shrugged. "I can see the future. My master says I'm a prophet. He says I'm the last one."

Aman had also claimed to be the last of a long line of prophets. A lie, Petrah was sure. "Sam, you really knew I was coming here to visit you?"

"Uh-huh."

"But how?"

"I just see things," she said. Her gray eyes reminded him of the winter sky.

"Did you see anything else?"

Sametha looked down. "Bad things. Lots of them. My master's not a good man. He's going to hurt a lot of people. I don't want him to, but Jovah tells me that's his purpose."

"Jovah speaks to you?"

"Sometimes. But only when I'm alone. Or afraid."

"Listen, I'm going to get you out of here. That's a promise. Do you understand?"

"No, I have to stay here. My master won't let me go. I see things for him. But he didn't know you were coming to see me." She whispered, "I never told him."

Petrah smiled delicately. "I'm glad you didn't. But I can't leave you here, Sam."

"I want to change my future," she said sadly. "I don't want to grow up with my master."

"Then let me help you."

"You already did."

"I'm changing your future by coming here?"

"Uh-huh," she said excitedly. "And I'm changing yours."

"I don't understand," Petrah said.

"My master told me we can change our destiny. Mine is to serve him for the rest of my life. Yours is to do something really important, but bad."

"Bad?" All sorts of terrible thoughts crept into Petrah's head. Was she referring to him opening the portal for his brother, or something else? "So what am I changing by coming here? What is different?"

"Timing." Sametha twisted a handful of her white hair.

"Timing?"

"Yes. When things will happen."

Petrah studied her for a long moment. She sat with her hands cupped, one over the other, calves folded beneath her legs, large, pretty eyes thoughtfully watching him. She needed a bath, a change of clothes, and some salve where the fetter rubbed the skin raw on her ankle. If Ahleen were here, she'd tend to the girl. Even though Sametha seemed to accept her role as a slave, the slight tremble in her bottom lip said she was truly frightened and that she desperately wanted to leave.

Looking at the way she twisted her hair, Petrah realized where he had seen her before. Not in person, but in his dreams—dreams that didn't end well for either of them.

Sametha's eyes widened. She clutched Petrah's hand. "You have to go. Hurry!"

Petrah placed a hand over hers. "I'm coming back, you know."

Sametha took a deep breath and forced a smile. "I know."

Chapter 9
Twist of Fate

PETRAH SEQUESTERED HIMSELF IN his apartment for the evening.

The plan had changed.

He was no longer leaving the castle by himself. He was taking Sametha with him.

The first challenge was to free her from her cell without being seen. He had failed to unlock the shackle, but that didn't mean he couldn't break the chain. He just needed the right implement.

The second challenge was deciding where to go. He wasn't familiar with the countryside. His missing friends further complicated things.

Where were they? The sooner they arrived, the sooner they could leave. Having Kruush and Tan with him meant they could work together to devise an escape route. Petrah needed a lookout while he worked to free Sametha, and they required a clear egress from the castle without alerting the watch. That meant learning the layout of the castle and its grounds and finding a means of transportation. Horses were the swiftest mode of travel, and Sametha could double up with Petrah on one mount. But how would Petrah and his friends secure three steeds?

That's why I need them with me. To figure these things out.

The longer Sametha stayed a prisoner, the longer she would suffer at the hands of her master. No child should be locked away like an animal. Even the swine at the Stacks in the Iron City had a better life than poor Sam. If Petrah didn't get her out, who would? She'd be stuck in this insufferable stronghold, serving the whim of his ruthless brother.

I have to free her. I must!

The hour was late, and drowsiness settled in. Petrah was too weary from the long day to tie up the loose ends. He'd meditate on it first thing in the morning. Then he'd research their escape.

He laid back against his pillow, lids growing heavier by the breath. *I'll find a way, Sam, I promise.*

P ETRAH WAS STARTLED WHEN he opened his eyes.

Aman stood by his bed, watching over him the same way the krell had looked at him in the desert—curiosity mixed with predator instinct. His dark aura was back, blurring his black hair with the early morning light, and his irises scorched blue against the starkness of his white sclera.

For a moment, Petrah could not move or breathe. He lay frozen, watching his brother, feeling the icy fringes of the aura rake over his skin.

Did his brother know about Petrah's visit with Sametha?

Aman beckoned with a hand. "Get dressed. I'm taking you to see your mother."

With that, Aman left Petrah alone in his apartment.

Petrah waited until the door locked before he could breathe again. He shivered, but the chill from having seen his brother standing over him remained like a cold shadow. He rubbed the goosebumps from his arms and—

Petrah was about to swing his feet over the side of his bed when his brother's startling announcement echoed in his mind. *I'm taking you to see your mother.*

Petrah sat for a long moment, staring at the terracotta floor, collecting his thoughts.

My mother. I'm going to see my mother.

His stomach twisted into anxious knots. Was it the lingering effect from his brother's surprise visit, or was it nerves—the anticipation of finally reuniting with the woman who had brought him into this world? She was both a mother and a stranger to him. What did he know about her?

Petrah searched his memories, catching small glimpses of her face—of her brow always wrinkled in worry, her eyes perpetually creased at the corners in sadness—and fragments of time spent together. Of him climbing a gnarled tree stripped of its leaves while she begged for him to be careful. Hiding between broken heaps of stone as soldiers patrolled the streets. And a precious moment where she cradled him in front of a crackling fire and sang him a lullaby. Were they inventions from his dreams, or were they real?

I don't know.

Would he know once he saw her and looked into her pale blue eyes? Would he remember his childhood, not just pieces, but all of it?

Petrah donned his clothes in a hurry, hopping across the tiled floor on one foot as he squeezed into his moleskin boot. When he finished dressing, he opened the door, where a soldier with a forked beard was waiting for him. The soldier led him to a horse-drawn coach just beyond the castle gate. Bands of clouds congregated above—gray, like Sam's eyes—although there was a small, clear stretch of sky to the east where the sun had risen in an orange fury.

Petrah joined his brother in the coach. The interior smelled of pipe smoke, reminiscent of Mokan-lee's tea room back at Bokania. The seat cushions were made of worn leather the color of rust, and the floor was paneled in scuffed wood. Small curtains were tied back from the windows set into the doors on each side of the carriage.

Aman said nothing but peered out the coach's window as if his younger brother weren't there. He thumped the door, and the trio of armed horsemen at the van of their procession started forward.

They rode in silence through unpaved streets, a patchwork of criss-crosses through a desert city with one and two-story sandstone and mudbrick buildings. The jostle of the coach reminded Petrah of his ride to the Great Council with Master Joriah. It seemed a thousand years ago, back when he wore the White and imagined a day when he would become a full-fledged mage for the Green Flame. What folly!

You will never step foot in the Canteem again, never listen to another lecture from Master Nole, never watch Master Maglo's jowls shake in laughter, never lead another class, never be anything more than an aban-doner. You are on your own now, so stop thinking of what could have been and focus on what must be.

As they traveled, Petrah kept playing out in his mind what he wanted to say to his mother. What could he say? It was silly to think that anything rehearsed would come out the way he intended. Part of him still believed this was all a ruse, a trick of Aman's to get his hopes up. But to what end?

He tried to let it go and focused on meditating instead.

The procession turned onto a filthy street with litter in the gutter and the stench of rancid lard, slowing and then coming to a stop in front of a row of single-story, dilapidated homes made of adobe. They looked more like books on a shelf than dwellings, bunched tightly together, with doors made of different materials, none in good repair. Petrah glimpsed curious passersby through the window who paused to look at the coach. As soon as the driver came around to open the door, they scurried off.

Petrah stepped down from the carriage and waited for his brother to do the same, but Aman remained in the coach, and the soldier shut the door. Through the window, Aman pointed at the home with the wood door whose green paint had all but peeled off. "She's in there."

"You're not coming with me?"

"No. I'll fetch you at high noon." Aman thumped the door. The carriage rolled off, rattling over the uneven street, harnesses jingling and hooves clopping.

One of his horsemen remained behind, a young, steely-eyed soldier in chain mail. He tied off his horse to a hitching post up the block, then jogged back to stand watch. His black cloak bore the insignia of the coiled dragon. It was enough for people rounding the block to cross the street and hurry past.

Petrah went to knock on the door but stopped himself. What if his mother didn't recognize him? What if she didn't believe him? What if she wasn't even there? Or worse, what if she didn't want to see him, like the slattern who had blown the reed whistle?

Knock already!

Petrah knocked once on the misshapen wood door. His heart galloped in his chest like a herd of chargers.

An older man with a deep stoop and bulge in the back of his neck opened the door. He eyed the soldier suspiciously and Petrah even more so. The aroma of cooked garlic and onions wafted from inside. "What do you want?"

"I'm here to see the lady of the house," Petrah said in Glesh.

The man gave him a queer look, then started laughing, revealing missing and yellowed teeth. "Lady of the house? Hah, that's a new one. You mean Alis?"

Was that his mother's name? "I believe so."

"Either you mean to see her or you don't. Which is it?"

"I do."

"And who are you?"

"I'd rather tell her myself."

The man wiggled his jaw back and forth as if thinking it through. His grimace told Petrah the intrusion annoyed him, but he glanced again at the soldier and said, "Stay here." He shut the door.

When he returned, he gestured gruffly. "Come in."

The inside of the one-room abode was saturated with the fumes of cooked aromatics, but Petrah detected the smell of damp stone and old clothes too. There were no furnishings other than a simple table, upon which rested dirty ceramic cups and bowls, and below it, a pair of discolored cushions for sitting.

A woman squatted by an open hearth with a few coals smoldering on andirons amid a heap of ash. She was checking on a kettle supported by a chimney crane. The woman was needle-thin in the arms and legs and wore a mangy, brown-and-beige animal skin over her hunched shoulders. She was barefoot, despite the cold in the room.

As soon as she turned her head, Petrah's heart leaped into his mouth. "Mama!"

It was the only thing he could say, the only thing that sounded right to say.

She blinked her blue eyes several times and reached over for a poker hanging from a metal hook. She used it to pull herself up with both hands, wincing and grunting from the exertion, then looked at him again. "Immael?"

Her cheeks were sunken, her teeth stained and crooked. Her lips curled into a half-smile momentarily, then dipped sadly.

To Petrah, she was beautiful.

"No, it can't be. He's—" She left it unfinished.

"No—I'm not," Petrah said firmly.

"But—" She looked at him doubtfully and shook her head. "You must be someone else."

"I'm him, Mama."

"You're, you're—" She stopped herself again, and covered her mouth. "Oh, my god!"

Petrah walked over to her, arms stretched outward, tears in his eyes. Nothing from the past mattered at that moment.

His mother cried. She knew! She knew it was him.

He hugged her, weeping and holding onto her fragile form, not wanting to let go, lest she disappear. She smelled of wood and stone and cold iron, but her hair smelled fresh, as if she'd rolled through a meadow filled with wildflowers. The old man watched them, but Petrah barely noticed.

"All these years," his mother said between sobs. "All these years of torment. And now. . . and now . . ." She pulled back, wiped the tears, and took in all of him. "My sweet Immael. It's you, isn't it?"

"It is, Mama."

She clasped a hand over her mouth and cried. Her voice broke apart like brittle leaves in the wind. "My Immael, it really is you." She touched his brow and ran a thin finger over his scar. She laughed between sobs. "Your angel's kiss. Of course, it's you."

She fanned her face. "I'm dizzy. I have to sit down."

Petrah went to help her, but she shooed him away. "None of that now. I'll be all right. I'll make us tea, and we'll sit. Jerald, this is my son, Immael," she said.

The older man granted the tiniest of nods, suspicion still played out on his face, although his eyes showed surprise. "I'll be outside. Holler if you need anything." He left them alone.

Alis grabbed a couple of cups and poured tea from the kettle. "Jerald means well. He's not been the same since he lost his wife. He took ill after she passed. Jerald's kind enough to let me stay here. I look after him the best I can. He looks after me too." There was affection in her words.

Petrah was glad she had someone in her life. In his dreams, she was always alone.

They sat across from each other at the stone table. The tea smelled earthy and yeasty, but unlike sprushah, which was bitter, this decoction had a mellow, zesty sweet flavor, like the rind of a Terjurmehan prot.

For a long minute, Petrah's mother studied him, and he her. Her face was careworn, ravaged by time and life's hard choices, with skin that cracked above her cheeks and around blue eyes that were as pale as in his dreams. She had the same angular narrowing toward the chin as he did, the same arch to her laugh lines, and, Petrah imagined, the same smile, although his was vacant now.

Concern branded itself onto his mother's face. Bony clavicles and thin arms portrayed a frailty that made him think of his old cellmate, Jow-quu. *You've suffered, Mama. You've suffered greatly.*

Although her body showed wear, her voice came through light and resilient. "You're all grown up. How old are you now, I forget?" She counted on her lean fingers. "Fifteen. No, sixteen! You would have just turned sixteen midyear. I was a few years older than you when I had you. Now look at me. I'm old!"

"You're not old," he lied. He would have guessed her twice her age when she gave birth to him.

"Worn, then. You're young and sturdy. When you were a boy, we lived in the Iron City. You loved to climb. You'd climb the scaffoldings and walk the steel beams like an acrobat. It always made me nervous, but up you'd go. Up, up, my little climber. Do you remember?"

Petrah did—glimpses of the past he'd hoped he would discover in his mother's presence—and it made him laugh. He had loved to climb. Trees, walls, terraces—anything he could grab a hold of. The gnarled tree with the missing leaves had been one of his favorites because it was in a park where he could play with other children. He remembered taking turns chasing or being chased. Sometimes, when his mother wasn't looking, he would jump up and catch the thick bough of the gnarled tree and haul himself up. Then he would see how far he could climb, careful to find branches that would support his weight, while his mother begged him to be careful or demanded he climb down. Other memories, just as clear, worked their way up from their slumbering depths. "I fell once or twice."

"And nearly broke your neck. You were a reckless boy—but smart and clever, much more so than your friends. So very clever, my little Immael." She beamed, tiny wrinkles bunched up around her eyes. "How about your friend? Sharif, was it? Do you remember him? He had that funny laugh."

Petrah pictured a boy his age with curly hair the color of sand and a laugh that came out of one side of his mouth. "I think so."

"You two were thick as thieves, always getting in trouble together. You both would bother that old man with the bad hip, only because he made that sticky, sweet candy you liked. I forget what it was."

Petrah chuckled. "Taffy."

"That's it. You would entertain him with jokes, trying to make him laugh, but really, you wanted that taffy. He liked you boys. Even if you acted silly, he would always reward you. He was a good man."

The memories came to Petrah like dribbles from a cracked jug of water, slowly but steadily. "Do you know what happened to Sharif?"

His mother looked down at her hands as if searching for the answer between the creases of her knuckles. "I don't know. After you left—" She shook her head, then smiled, but Petrah could feel the hole in her spirit, the part of her that had lost something precious, something dear. "And now here you are. I still can't believe it." She smacked her cheeks as if waking from a dream. "Tell me everything about yourself. I want to hear it all!"

He caught her up on his life in Terjurmeh and his pursuit of magehood. He spoke fondly of his friends, his classmates at Maseah, his friendship with Ajoon, and his love for Mina.

His mother smiled at times and teared up at others, but she let him speak. He told her of his adventure into Darkforth and of the Watcher who guided him back to this world. He omitted mentioning his time with his brother. Petrah didn't have the heart to tell her he was now in Aman's charge—if he could call it that—when it was the very thing she had wanted Petrah to avoid. He kept any mention of Aman out of the conversation.

"Mina sounds quite enchanting. Her father is wealthy, you say?"

"He is," Petrah said. "He owns a huge plantation and has servants. It's a bit intimidating. He's very protective of his daughter. So are her two brothers, Milio and Mikano. My friend Kruush believes if I can improve my worth in their eyes, I might win their approval. I don't know if it's possible. I'm not an aristocrat or anything special." Petrah found his Glesh came naturally now. He plucked words he didn't even realize he knew from the recesses of his mind.

"I beg to differ," his mother said. "You *are* special. Look at how you came back to me. Look at all you've achieved. They should be lucky to have you in their lives."

If only Mokan-lee could see it that way. Petrah didn't want to brood in front of his mother, so he changed the subject to her. "And what about you, Mama? I know nothing about you."

"There's nothing much to say, really," she said.

"Then tell me about my father."

She grew quiet. Petrah resisted slurping his tea, as he would have done in Meerjurmeh, but sipped it, waiting for his mother to say something. He needed her to tell him the truth.

"There's little to tell," she said, smoothing her dress down her sides, contemplative as a person about to enter a deep cave. Her eyes drifted to the corner of the room, and she spoke in a distant voice. "For me, life wasn't easy. My parents died at an early age, and I had no siblings, no aunts or uncles, no cousins or blood relatives. I was an orphan. But a kindly stable master named Jarvin took pity on me and welcomed me into his home. With him, his wife, and two boys, we were a family. Jarvin taught me how to shoe horses, repair saddles and stirrups, and even ride."

Her wistful eyes returned to Petrah, then went to her lap. "I loved to ride horses. It brought me joy and escape. But I was alone, so very alone. I don't know why. My new family was good to me." She swallowed, took a breath, and composed herself. Petrah didn't dare interrupt her. He could feel the pain in her strained voice.

"I had these dark thoughts—" She breathed in, then out. In, then out. "I won't burden you with the details. It's not for you to know." She paused and rubbed her left wrist with her right thumb. "But I'll say this: your father saved me when I needed him the most, when my prayers turned desperate." She dropped to a whisper. "When I thought I couldn't take it anymore."

Petrah remained utterly still. *I'm sorry, Mama,* he wanted to tell her. But his duty was to listen and not speak. If she wanted to say more on the matter, she would.

Alis took a long swallow of tea. "But you asked about your father." Her tone returned to normal, the subject from a moment earlier forgotten. "I might say your father was handsome, almost beautiful, like a statue crafted by an artisan, but I'd be lying. I don't recall his likeness, nor the shape of his face. I do remember his voice—deep as a rumble in the earth, but soothing too, like a breeze stirring up leaves in the morning. And his eyes—like watching the stars in the night sky. In all honesty, it's but a glimpse of how I imagined him. It was enough, though, enough to know he looked like you."

Petrah fumbled with his hands. There was more to the story, much more. It prompted questions. *Did you love my father? Was he kind to you?* He stopped himself, folded his hands, and waited for his mother to continue.

Her eyes brimmed with tears. "Your father and I were a moment in time, son. When I found out I was with child, I—" She drew in a couple of shallow breaths. "I was scared. No, petrified. I worried about the child I carried. Would he be sick? Would he be cursed? A monster? I ran away, ran to the big city, and hid from the world. But then you were born." She smiled lovingly. "When I saw your face, I knew. I knew it was an angel who kissed your brow, and that you were good and whole. I knew then that you would be all right."

His mother looked off into the shadows for a moment. "I tried to provide for you, for us. To clothe you, feed you, and protect you. To keep my child, my beautiful child, safe. I found a man to take care of us for a while when you were young. But he was—" Her cup shook in her hand. "He was unkind. I'm sorry for what he did to you."

A faint memory of a man with a beard and hard eyes came to Petrah, murky at best. But it was his fists that seemed clear as daylight: scarred skin, large knuckles, a mottling on one hand—his dominant hand. Fists that became hammers that Petrah felt now upon his face and temples.

His mother paused and drew slow circles over the rim of her cup with her thumb, changing the conversation to Aman. "I found out about your half-brother in a chance meeting. He was a young man, ambitious and powerful. I could tell at first glance there was something familiar about him, something that I saw in you. But what could it be? Then the answer struck me like a bolt of lightning: you both shared the same father. A mother knows these things." She smiled mirthlessly. "And he asked about you. He asked like he had been seeking me out." She clenched her cup, as if afraid to let it go. "I knew then I had to hide you from him." She looked up at Petrah with pleading eyes.

"You have to realize, I only tried to protect you. I wanted to keep you safe. I knew that if I let him see you, he would steal you from me, and that terrible things would happen to you. Awful, horrible things.

"Then, on the morning your brother came for you, it occurred to me what I had to do. I had to choose. I had to choose to let him take you, or—" She sucked down a shuddering breath. "You understand, don't you?"

Petrah found his hand drifting to his stomach where he imagined his mother's blade had pierced his gut. Her eyes followed.

She put her cup down and began crying, reaching out with her hands. "I never meant to hurt you! I never meant to—" She shook her head and cried. "My sweet Immael! What have I done to you? What have I done!"

Petrah watched her with pity, not anger. His mind denied him the memory of his death, and he was grateful for that. Not that he wanted to remember. His mother sobbed, her entire body shaking. No matter how much he wanted to be angry with her, he couldn't. This was his mother. A son only had one mother. He couldn't hate her. Not now.

Not ever.

Thinking through his past, he had a revelation: his mother had never opened a portal, nor had she pushed him through one, nor did she have any idea where to find one. He had bridged the gateway between worlds on his own merit, through his death. As the Watcher claimed, he was the Key. It meant he could unlock the doorway between worlds . . . and cross from one to the other.

But he didn't die.

He had drifted in the void between the living and the dead. He awoke in a field in an unfamiliar land, stripped of his memories, of the trauma that led him to the foreign world. His only tie to the past lay in dreams and, eventually, the Watcher.

The words came out unbidden. "I forgive you." His voice was hoarse as grit. He held his breath and waited for her to say something, but she just looked at him with deep shame running the course of her tear-streaked face. "Mama, do you hear me?"

She nodded as tears ran down her cheeks. "Come here." She opened her arms and beckoned with her hands.

They embraced each other and cried. Petrah held on as if letting go would make him awaken from this dream, this second chance. She was so light in his arms, almost weightless, but her hold was strong and full of life. Their tears mingled in a watery torrent, liberating years of held-in emotions. All the hurt and disappointment Petrah harbored toward his mother melted away at that moment, released with a long, necessary cleansing of tears. This was what he wanted more than anything—not an excuse or an apology, but love; the selfless love only a mother could give.

They wiped their eyes, and Alis had him sit down next to her. "Now listen to me. Listen closely, Immael, because this is the hardest thing I will ever say to you, my darling son." She composed herself, took in a few breaths, and looked him in the eye.

"I want you to leave this place and forget about your mother." He protested, but she stilled him with a hand. "I said to listen, didn't I?" He gave in and she continued. "You have to leave here. This isn't your home anymore. There is nothing here but trouble. I want you to forget about this world and return to your own. Take your friends with you and never look back. And when you get home, I want you to go to your Mina and hug her and tell her how much you love her. Will you do that for me? Will you do that for your mother?"

Petrah gave her a bittersweet smile and tried not to release the floodgate of emotions, especially at the mention of his Mina. "I will, Mama."

"Good." She smiled and took his hand in hers. "You've made me whole again, even if I wake up tomorrow and believe this was all a dream." She brought his hand to her face. "I love you, sweet child. I love you so much. You have given me a spark of life and a chance at redemption I never would have imagined possible. No matter what happens from this day forth, it will keep my spirit alive. Now say goodbye to your Mama. We will see each other again, I promise, in this life or the hereafter."

Petrah wanted to stay. He'd searched all his life, and he had only just found his mother. Maybe he could take her with him, and when the moment was right, Sam too—and his friends. Now that he knew he was the Key, truly the Key, he would find his way home. The unanswered question was *how*.

"Mama, I won't leave you here. You're coming with me."

She shook her finger at him. "No, I'm not. I'm staying right here. I have Jerald to look after me. I'm not alone. You go on and live your life."

"But—"

"I said I'm staying. And that's that."

Petrah would have objected, but his mother fixed him with a stalwart stare. She wasn't going anywhere.

"Tell me you understand."

He relented. "I understand, Mama."

"Here." She reached beneath her animal skin and pulled out a simple necklace of corded leather. She lifted it over her head. A small pendant hung suspended from it, round and made of deep-blue glass. It had a white disk in the middle and a black dot in the center of that.

"The ancients call this the matia, the all-seeing eye. I've worn it ever since you were little. Do you remember?"

Petrah vaguely recalled his mother wearing it.

"Some say it's silly because it's supposed to bring the wearer good fortune. But I believe it. After all, it brought me you." She offered it to him. "Take it, my child. Wear it and remember me."

Petrah reluctantly took it from her. He adjusted the knot on the cord and slid the leather twine over his head. With his thumb, he traced the smooth curve of the glass. A comforting warmth spread through him. He had a tough time holding back the tears. "Thank you, Mama. I'll wear it, I promise."

"That's it, my Immael, my sweet, sweet Immael." Her face brightened. "You know what your name means, don't you?"

He had often wondered, but assumed it was a name passed down from her father or her father's father.

"It means 'God with us.' As in Jovah, the one true god. Jovah is with you, son."

"Jovah?" He was surprised to hear the name of the god of the mountain people. "Jovah couldn't possibly be with me."

Not once had Petrah thought of Jovah—Jah to the people of Acia—as being a part of him. Nor had he felt it. Could he have missed an integral part of himself all these years, something hidden within him, within his soul?

"But he is, son. From the moment you were born, from the moment I saw your angel's kiss, I knew. Jovah is most certainly with you, even if the blood of Sag-ahn flows through your veins. That's why you have that beautiful name. Don't forget. And don't forget your Mama, either."

Petrah kissed her hand. The tears followed. "I won't forget, Mama, I promise."

Chapter 10
Prophecy

THE RIDE BACK TO the castle was uncomfortably quiet, except for the jostle over the uneven streets, the creak of the wheels, and Aman's one question to Petrah: "Did you get what you wanted?"

Petrah didn't appreciate the coldness of his brother's question. Aman was being callous on purpose. But why? Was it because his own mother was dead and he was envious of Petrah? Or was it because Aman enjoyed making Petrah feel small?

Petrah responded with kindness. Wasn't that what miserable people hated the most? "Yes. Thank you for taking me to her."

Aman didn't ask any follow-on questions. Maybe the guard had overheard Petrah's conversation with his mother and reported every word.

Maybe Aman doesn't care.

Perhaps "care" was the wrong word. Aman watched Petrah like a krell watching an unwary gonatan. He might have noticed the corded necklace Petrah's mother had given him, but he didn't mention it. Yet he never took his eyes off Petrah.

Petrah spent the time processing his visit with his mother. So many feelings tugged at him, but mostly he was left with unasked questions. He'd meant to ask her more of his childhood, to tease out the details still missing from his memory. Were there other friends besides Sharif? What did they do in the Iron City?

The more important question—the most important perhaps—was: why didn't they leave? Why didn't they get out of the city before Aman came for Petrah, before it was too late?

It would have been a different life. We could have hidden, maybe in the mountains. Would the Peshte have accepted them? Looked after them? Protected them? Petrah knew almost nothing of the people, other than the cruelty they'd suffered at Aman's hands.

But there was no going back, no changing the past, no entertaining what could have been. Decisions were made, and consequences were wrought from those decisions. It was better to look forward, not backward.

"I've been informed your companions will arrive first thing in the morning," Aman said at one point during their ride.

"They are?" It was the only response Petrah could come up with. He was eager to get out of the coach, away from his brother and his predatory gaze. He changed to a different topic, one he knew would break Aman's spell over him. "I've been thinking about when you might leave for Acia." This earned a look of intrigue. "How will your"—he tried to find the right word—"*allies* know to receive you?"

"Our mutual friend, of course."

"The Watcher."

"That's his title. Did he ever tell you his name?"

"I've heard Gatekeeper."

"That's just another title. His name is Azazel. He's one of the angels that was sent to watch over mankind. You know their story, don't you?"

Petrah had never considered whether the Watcher had a name. *All this time I didn't think once to ask, not even in my dreams.* "I know he was once an angel and that he was here, in Dagoth."

"Dagoth was called Aerth back then, in the beginning. The Watchers were indeed angels. Jovah entrusted Azazel and his brothers to look after mankind. They were gods among mortals, but not so infallible as to resist temptation. They mated with mortal women and gave rise to a race of giants called the Nephilim. This angered Jovah greatly, and he flooded the world, killing the giants, along with all the men, women, and children of the world, save for the Chosen, whom Jovah found uncorrupted by the wiles of his brethren. As punishment, Azazel and his kind were bound in chains and forced to witness the destruction of their children and the people they taught and looked after. It's a cautionary tale for all of us to remember."

"The Watcher told me about his punishment. He said he was put in chains, and that San freed him."

"Our father knows mercy as well as he knows the truth of things. Jovah acted out of wrath . . . and cruelty. What kind of god kills off his creation? All those people gone, just because Jovah wanted his angels to suffer unto him. Cynical, don't you think?"

Like the Watcher's name, Petrah hadn't given it any thought. He didn't pretend to know the mind of gods or angels. "I suppose."

"You suppose?" Before Petrah could get an earful of backlash, Aman changed course in their conversation. "*Illiam senua wisa té nallia.* Do you know the meaning of the phrase?"

The words had a smoothness to them, like running water in Petrah's mind, yet there was an authoritative inflection that invoked an image of fire. "Something about burning, I believe."

Aman nodded, impressed. "It's angelic speak, our birth tongue. It means, 'Woe, for how my eyes burn.' If you ever saw an angel mourn, you would understand the true depth of its meaning. The tongue of angels is many-layered, like ripples in a pond. One could study a phrase for a lifetime and never understand its connotation. Don't doubt for a moment the pain Jovah had caused his Watchers. They still mourn their children, and they should! But as you see, Aerth is no more. That age passed long ago. Dagoth is all that remains, and the successors of the first man and woman of this world live on."

"But," Petrah said, thinking of all the deaths caused by this wrathful god, Jovah, the one his mother said was with him from the moment he was born, "how did anyone survive the flood?"

"The waters of the world receded, and the Chosen began anew. Their descendants prospered and begat a multitude of children, and their descendants forgot the Nephilim, the Watchers, and the near destruction of mankind, as if history had erased itself. If people are immortal through their children, then this is the greatest travesty of humanity: they forget, and history is doomed to repeat itself."

"Did they build the Iron City?"

"No. A new civilization, more advanced than any of its predecessors, was responsible for the Iron City, as it was for other cities of equal stature throughout the world. My people are their offspring, as are the vile mountain men."

Sametha was from the mountains. So was Asha, the boy who had served Petrah supper. Did Aman consider them vile too? It brought out a bitterness in Petrah's throat. "Why do you hate them so?"

Aman seemed surprised, if not put off by the question. "They burn offerings to their god. They praise Jovah and worship the sun from their pinnacles. They raid and fight and whore, and yet they martyr themselves in his name and shed our blood in his name and rape and kill our women in *his* name. They claim to be pious and pure, like their forefathers. Pah! Mark my words: if Jovah hadn't vowed to never flood this world again, he'd smite the entire lot of them."

"The Watcher said Jovah already started over by creating man in Acia."

"Yes, I've heard the story: he created a new race of man from the bones of the Chosen. And so the world has become unclean, not so different from this one. The Peshte would fit in with the hypocrites of your world."

Of course, Aman would say that of the Peshte. He hated them with every part of his being. Yet he was the worst hypocrite of all, pretending to be "Uncle" to the children while committing unspeakable acts whenever it pleased him.

"But back to your original question. Azazel brokers the way for us. He is the conduit between worlds. I've seen your Ter-jurah and An-jurah in my dreams, heard the prayers of the Sacred Nine and the high priests, felt the undulation of their divine power channeling to the Father, beckoning me to unleash my Dragon upon the lands." Aman's face took on a dangerous twist of glee. "Worry not, little brother. You've not been forgotten." The glee turned vicious, like that of a krell before the kill. "Father has a special place for you."

Petrah looked away, and the coach fell silent, save for the groan of wood and clop of hooves. Dark thoughts swirled through Petrah's mind, accompanied by the Watcher's tinny voice and the promise of doom.

When they arrived at the front gate of the castle, the mammoth captain of the guard was waiting for them, along with a squad of soldiers.

"I have business to attend to," Aman told Petrah as they stepped out of the coach. "No need to wait up for me." They headed toward the soldiers. "Lord Verek will show you around the grounds." Then, with a knowing look, he added, "Make sure you stay out of places where you don't belong."

LORD VEREK WAS ANYTHING but satisfactory company. His armor creaked, his footsteps were heavy, and he smelled like he'd slept in the pens with the cattle. He spoke tersely, pointing out things using one or two words, his thunderous voice harsh on Petrah's ears. The webbed wings of his gigantic helm appeared so high up that they could have passed for a bird in flight.

He's a mountain with his peak in the clouds. One misstep, and he'll topple and crash.

Petrah liked the idea of that, but the Grand Insept was sure-footed, stamping the ground with a heavy beat that vibrated up his plate armor into Petrah's ears.

The more Petrah saw of the castle grounds, the more enormous it seemed.

Besides the keep and crenelated protective wall on the outside, there was a bailey in the center where soldiers trained and bowmen practiced their archery. Verek pointed out various buildings, including the armory, buttery, mess hall, and garrison.

An outdoor kennel caged hunting hounds who barked and scratched at their enclosures as Petrah and the captain passed. They reeked of feral musk.

Petrah noted doorways, passages, and means of ingress and egress. Whenever they came upon soldiers or workers, the men and women would bow their heads and touch their fingers to their foreheads as a sign of greeting. Verek grunted in reply, annoyed at the constant attention. All the while, Petrah fretted over his friends, then his mother, then Sametha, and back again.

I should be with Kruush and Tan, not stuck with this oaf of a tree.

He wanted to be rid of Verek, but at the same time, he needed to familiarize himself with the castle grounds to procure an escape route.

"I don't see any horses," Petrah said as they traversed the final ward around the keep, on their way back toward the gatehouse.

"The stables lie without the castle walls," Verek said.

"Show them to me."

Verek grimaced under his winged helm. "We should stay here."

"I don't want to stay here. I want to see the stables."

The captain looked down at Petrah, bat wings following the tilt of his colossal head. Petrah glared up at him. Verek said nothing, instead leading them through the gatehouse, out the portcullis, and around to the north side where a fenced corral stood attached to the castle wall.

Horses ran freely or were attended to by groomers and trainers. At the far end was a massive length of wooden stables that could easily house several hundred horses for Aman's cavalry. Stable hands worked furiously, pitching hay and mucking. Above, the sky had turned a sleet gray. Flurries fell, pushed east by the rising wind.

Verek pointed. "The stables."

"I want to see the horses," Petrah said. "I want to see my brother's stallion."

The captain looked down at him again, annoyed. "Why?"

"Because I want to see him, that's why. My brother said you would show me what I wanted to see, and I want to see his horse." Petrah folded his arms. It wasn't that he wanted to see the horse as much as he wanted to see if he and his companions could escape on horseback when the time came.

Verek flexed his muscled jaw. He led them to the stables.

The stable hands stopped their work as the pair strode toward them. The stench of hay and manure became overbearing the closer they came. An older woman with riding leathers walked up to them. She bowed her head and pressed her fingers firmly to her forehead.

"Lord Verek, what can I do for you?" Her Glesh was clipped as if she'd come here from a faraway place.

"This is the Grand Marshall's younger brother. He wishes to see the Great Stallion."

Surprise etched wrinkles around her eyes. "Of course." She gave Petrah an appraising look. "I'm Milana, stable master. This way."

Milana guided them to a locked stall separate from the rest, near the end of the stables, by a large hayloft. The stall had metal bars and a gate, behind which stood Aman's monstrous destrier, black as coal. There was a manger mounted to a feed rack and straw scattered on the ground. The warhorse snorted and shook his mane. Petrah felt the rhythmic beating of his powerful heart, a beat that throbbed in his mind. This was a mighty steed.

"He only allows one rider," Milana said proudly. "At nineteen-and-a-half hands, he's the largest of all our horses, and we have close to a thousand."

"He's beautiful," Petrah said, and he meant it. *And dangerous. No wonder my brother had claimed him for his own.* He stepped toward the bars.

"I wouldn't get too close, not if you want to keep your fingers." Petrah ignored her. "Suit yourself."

The stallion looked at Petrah with one of his black eyes. Petrah's old horse, Pepper, was a dwarf compared to this exceptional specimen, whose shoulders and flanks rippled with toned muscles. He snorted, then roared, and Petrah noticed how he pinned his ears back and pawed the ground with a shod hoof.

"He doesn't like you," Milana said. Then, in a lower voice, almost to herself, she added, "He doesn't like anyone, really."

"It's all right," Petrah said. "He's just curious."

"If that's what you believe. Don't say I didn't warn you."

Petrah stood in front of the bars, allowing the heartbeat of the horse to flow through his chest, like the thump of a fist. He gazed deeply into the stallion's eyes. The ears slowly went neutral, and the snorting changed to grunting and then nickering.

"That's it," Petrah whispered, gingerly reaching up with his hand. It was like being back in the desert, facing the krell under the full moon—that same tension and peril, coupled with the excitement of discovery.

He stuck his fist through the bars, knuckles down. The horse sniffed and exhaled his hot breath against Petrah's skin, then whickered. "It's all right."

There was a long moment where the stallion continued to sniff his hand as if deciding what to do. Then the horse pushed up against the bottom of Petrah's clenched fist, unfurling the digits with a wet nose before bowing his head and nuzzling Petrah's palm with the bridge of his nose. Petrah rubbed gently, letting his fingers brush up and down before easing his fingertips beneath the black hairs of the steed's forehead, where it was warm. This was an exquisite creature in every sense of the word, brawny and built for battle.

If you were mine, we'd thunder across the plains for all to see. I'd bard you in bright colors. We'd go to Montabijon and show Mokan-lee how magnificent you are. He'd have no choice but to let Mina ride with me. We'd ride all day too. We'd take our time at Montabijon, then we'd stride through the streets of Hōvar and race back to the estate with the wind in our faces and Mina's hands wrapped around me. That's how we'd do it. It would be glorious.

"Well, I'll be," Milana said. "No one's ever done that before, except for his master, of course."

"What's his name?" Petrah asked as the stallion continued to nicker. The horse's heartbeat pumped in his chest, one with him now. It was as soothing as it was intoxicating.

"Shadowbringer."

"Shadowbringer," Petrah repeated, letting the syllables roll off his tongue. In a whisper to the animal, he said, "You're no longer a dream."

Night fell, and Petrah sat in his apartment, anxiously bobbing his knee.

Now that he had gotten a tour of the grounds, including the keep and the stables, ideas percolated to the surface, ideas of escape. It couldn't happen tonight, though, not before his friends arrived. So what was he going to do in the meantime?

Petrah closed his eyes and concentrated on the hallway outside. Someone was walking, but nowhere close to his door. He snuck out and made for the lower levels of the keep.

"Hi, Petrah," Sametha said cheerily as he eased her cell door open.

"Hi, Sam. I told you I'd come back."

"I knew you would." She clapped, happy, as if sitting in a room where there was no stink, no fetters, no threat of getting caught or punished.

Petrah saw welts on her arms. "He did this to you?"

Her cheerfulness disappeared. She didn't say so, but Petrah knew it was his brother's doing.

He crouched by her side. "I'm sorry, but it makes me angry seeing what he does to you." He softened his tone. "I'm still working on a way to get you out of here. Lord Verek took me around the castle grounds this afternoon. I even got to see the stables. I think I've figured out a plan for us once I break through this." He tapped the chain shackled to her foot.

"I already told you, you don't have to worry about me." Then she added, "I don't like Lord Verek. I don't like the way he looks at me . . . or smells."

"I don't like him either, but he proved his usefulness today. What I can't figure out is how to get out of the castle without going through the gatehouse. There's a postern gate, but it's sealed and guarded. Your master mentioned a secret passage. Do you know of it?"

She looked down, as if frightened to tell him.

"Sam?"

"It's on the lowest level. There's a tunnel leading to a dead end, but it's not a dead end if you know what to look for."

"How do I get there?"

She shared the details.

"Good, good," he said, his mind sprinting. "That's how we'll get out of here together. We'll secure horses and be gone from this place."

Sametha shook her head. "He'll know."

"We'll be long gone by the time he finds out, trust me."

"I trust you, but"—she held her tongue for a breath—"I don't trust him. He's too clever, and he knows things. Believe me when I say he *knows* things." Her breathing quickened as if she were running away.

"It'll be all right," Petrah said, trying to ease her apprehension. "I'm afraid too, but we can use the fear we feel to motivate us to do things we would normally never consider. Otherwise, I'd still be in my room, and we wouldn't be talking." He forced a smile.

The smile had little effect on Sametha. "Petrah, I need to talk to you about something important, more important than me leaving here. It might be the last time we talk." She gave it some consideration. "No, it *will* be our last time."

"Don't say that. What can be more important than getting you out of here?"

"You still don't understand. My master won't let you take me away. I'm his." The way she said "his" made him think of the way a hawk hooked its talons into its prey.

"You're not his. I won't allow it. As you said, I'm changing your future." *We're changing both our futures.*

Her gray eyes became sad. "You're not strong enough." She said it with such sincerity and sorrow that it took the wind out of him.

Was she telling him the same thing Kruush had: that Petrah wasn't ready? That his training as a mage journeyman was lacking, and that he didn't have enough command of the dark arts to face his brother?

"I *am* strong enough," Petrah said. But was he trying to convince Sam or himself? What was missing? His brother had an aura that radiated nether power. Was that the missing piece? *I need to command the dark, to make it mine.* The advice was familiar.

When Master Joriah had taken Petrah to visit the Seer, Baaka, at the grand temple in Elmar, Petrah had met with the Seer in private. During their conversation, Baaka had imparted sage wisdom that he called the Trillian of Darkness—three tenets that clerics training to be priests adhered to. To become a master of the dark arts, one had to bind with the dark, the Seer had told him. Aman certainly had. *Then I must too.*

"Petrah—" Sam started.

"Didn't you hear me? I know what I must do. I know the answer to the riddle that's been plaguing me. The answer lies in the dark. All I have to do is—"

"Petrah!"

He looked at her. There was something in her stormy eyes that told him to stop talking.

"I need you to listen, Petrah. Will you do that?"

He remained quiet, watching her compose her words with the grace of someone much older.

"Your brother has plans for you. I've seen it in my mind's eye, images mostly, but you were there, and so was he, and . . . I was there too." She shuddered, letting out a long, weary breath. Petrah thought of the hilltop in his dream, where his brother had killed him. Was she referring to that? But there was no such place, was there? "Do you know why you're here?"

"To lead my brother to Acia," Petrah said.

"No. You've already done that."

Already done that?

"Your purpose isn't to open the gateway between worlds." The sadness on her face deepened. "He's going to give you to your father. You're to serve the dark god. That's your purpose."

Aman's spiteful voice filled his mind. *Father has a special place for you.*

"But I'm the Key," Petrah said, like a child pleading with his mother. "Why would he give me to my father? What would I do? What purpose would I serve?"

"Do you know the end-times prophecy?"

He had read the text with his friend, Ajoon, but there wasn't any mention of him, only the Great One. "My brother is to conquer the world, according to the scriptures."

"And you?"

"There's nothing about me in there, although the Watcher said I'm the Key, whatever that really means."

"You *are* the Key, Petrah, but not in the way you think, or the way you've been told." She wrapped her delicate fingers over her metal shackle and looked at it thoughtfully. Her voice changed, turning deeper, more mature, as if someone else spoke through her. "You're the chosen son, Petrah. The chosen son sits at the left hand of darkness. Your father is darkness, an outcast of Heaven, struck down by his brother, Jovah, in the Great War, the war that divided dark from light. Even though your father rules the Netherworld with all the power of a god, he is a prisoner there, along with the angels who fought alongside him. They are all evil, and they hate the ones who cast them down. They want retribution."

Sametha's stormy eyes probed the shackle as if she was reading from it, as if the words were engraved into the metal. How did she know these things? Was someone else channeling themselves through her? Or was she channeling it herself?

"What kind of retribution?" Petrah asked.

"To reclaim Heaven for their own. They want to wage a second Great War, the Final War. But they are powerless to do so and have been since they were cast down. Until their champion was born." She let go of the metal cuff and looked up. "Their champion is you."

A gasp caught in Petrah's throat. "Me?"

"Yes."

"But why me? What do I have to offer?"

"More than you can ever imagine," Sametha said. Her voice remained deep and distant. She was too young to look at him with the sadness of an adult, too much of a child to speak like a wizened old oracle. "I'm afraid for you, Petrah. The Netherworld wants its chosen son. No one knows your secret, but the Father knows it. It's the secret of secrets, known only to him. It's a terrible power, unlike anything in the cosmos. If any of his angels knew what you possessed, any of them at all, they might try to possess it for themselves. It's not safe for you to have it, but you have no choice." She spoke as if he were cursed, truly cursed. It weighed down like a pile of boulders on his shoulders.

Petrah clutched the fabric along the neckline of his robe and pulled it away from his skin, as if it was suffocating him. "But you know my secret."

"Yes. I wish I didn't, but I do." Tears formed at the corners of her eyes. Sametha rubbed her thumb against a dirty fingernail. "You might not be able to control yourself if you learn to use your power. It will be too much for you. It's locked away—there." She pointed at his head.

Petrah was almost too afraid to ask. "What is it?"

She looked upon him with pity, as if he were more doomed than she was, shackled to her rod of iron. "The Word of God, the Word of Jovah himself." Sametha wiped the tears with her knuckles. "No one but Jovah is supposed to use it. It's his secret."

"Then how did I get it, and why do I have it?"

"I don't know, Petrah. But you mustn't use it. Not ever! It has the power to destroy worlds, perhaps everything. If your father gains control over such power, he could take Heaven from his brother. It would be the end of all good things. You can't allow your father to have this power, just as you can't allow your brother to deliver you to him."

"But how?" Escaping the castle was paramount now, more than ever. As soon as his friends arrived in the morning, he'd work with them to get far away from here. "How do I prevent this from happening?"

Sametha looked away, reluctant to say another word.

"Sam?"

She combed a hand through her hair, then stopped and looked at him like she was about to tell him the worst news in the world. "You must die a true death."

"A true death," he echoed, finding the words unfamiliar on his lips.

"It's the only way."

Petrah didn't want to die, just as he didn't want Sametha to suffer. "That's not acceptable."

"I've seen your future. It always leads to the same end. True death is the only way out, the only way to keep your father from having you. In order for you to die a true death, your soul must be parted from your body and destroyed. Otherwise, you'll come back, as you did after your mother killed you."

The way Sametha so bluntly stated what his mother had done was like a hammer to his skull.

Petrah glanced furtively over his shoulder at the open doorway. "I can flee. I can hide, so my brother never finds me."

"You can't hide. He'll find you."

"Not if I leave this world." *Not if I locate a portal and then destroy it from the other side!* "How much time do I have before he gives me to my father?"

"A couple of days at the most," Sametha said. "The visions are coming to me more often, which means your time is almost up."

Petrah calculated what he needed to do to give them a head start. "We'll leave tomorrow, after dark. Unless I can get us out of here sooner."

"Petrah, you're not listening to me: it's too late. I've already given my life."

"What do you mean?" He stood. "What do you mean, Sam?"

"I mean, these are my last words. You've changed my future, but I'm not upset. In fact, I want to be released." Her voice was frayed, like tatters in the wind. "I want it more than anything." She smiled through her tears. "Thank you, Petrah. Thank you for coming here. I'm glad to have met you, and I'm happy we got to share our time together."

"Don't say that."

"I'm sorry, Petrah, but it's true."

He couldn't accept that. He was responsible for Sametha, responsible for saving her. "There has to be another way. What do I do, Sam? Tell me!"

She blinked away the tears. "There's only one way to escape, to truly escape, but it's for you, not me." She parted her lips, but the words were delayed. "I can't tell you what to do. I'm scared for you, Petrah. Scared that he's too strong. That he'll torture you. That he'll send you to your father. I don't want to see him hurt you!" She cried in earnest.

Petrah hated to see her cry. He was already fighting down his own tears. He had to think, to really think. The only thing that came to mind was what Kruush had told him on their journey into Darkforth: that he wasn't ready. His skills as a mage journeyman were nothing compared to the strength Aman possessed.

"How do I kill him? There must be a way."

"The same as with you: a true death."

The only way to do as she suggested was to gain the skills of a mage warrior. No, not only a mage warrior, but someone who had mastery over life and death, someone with knowledge of divine secrets, like the Watcher possessed.

The Malaji, the legendary mage lords Petrah and Ajoon had studied, supposedly had that knowledge, perhaps even the know-how to bring out the secret Sametha swore Petrah possessed. *She said I must never use it, not ever.* But the Malaji could teach him other things. He and Ajoon had discussed it at length and had even speculated whether the Malaji still lived in the City of Night after their defeat at the hands of the Mighty One in Terjurmeh. But Petrah was a world away from Acia. He hadn't even made it out of this castle.

I might never make it out.

He crushed the thought.

One foot in front of the other, Antelle would say.

The first step was to regroup with his friends. Then he'd free Sametha and ferry them all to safety.

Somehow, someway.

"I'm not leaving you here," Petrah said, unwavering in his declaration. "And that's final."

Chapter 11
Sacrifice

PETRAH COULDN'T SLEEP. WHENEVER his eyes closed on their own, he'd wake up, breathing fast with an intense pounding in his chest. It would take several minutes before his heart slowed and he could try again. His mind was stuck on his quandary, on his vow to Sam, and on the time limit he faced.

Sam had revealed to Petrah the appalling truth: that he was doomed, and she along with him.

But I can free her. I know I can!

As for himself, he still reserved a sliver of doubt. Maybe his fate was sealed; maybe it wasn't.

There's only one way to find out.

Aman sent for him at first light. The hulking Lord Verek stood outside his door, breathing heavily like Petrah imagined a dragon might. Verek was so tall, the only part of his face visible beneath the stone lintel was his chin. Yet his distinct odor filled the space of Petrah's apartment, as if he'd killed a thousand men and hid their decaying corpses on his person.

For a moment, Petrah considered making a run for it.

Verek was outfitted in full plate armor. How fast could he move his legs with all that weight, anyway? Petrah could flee through the castle's corridors and easily outpace the titan. But what would that achieve? There were guards and plenty of opportunities to be caught.

But if Petrah eased his way over to the window and dropped to the courtyard below . . .

A jump would be foolish. He'd break his bones. A more intelligent solution was called for. Petrah had learned the power of levitation in school, but if he had intended to use it, he should have done so before the knock on the door.

Now it's too late.

That seemed to be the theme of his existence.

Verek dipped his head below the lintel and fixed Petrah with a brutal gaze. "Let's go."

A cold sweat clung to the back of Petrah's neck. Had Sametha misjudged when Aman would deliver him to his father? Was that to be today?

"Now," Verek said, making it clear that he would not ask again.

Petrah followed Verek as he led them to wherever they were going. The giant man's great sword, set into a scabbard strapped across his back, swayed like someone wagging their finger.

Another reminder that Petrah shouldn't try to flee.

By the time they reached the bottom floor, they were joined by two more soldiers, also in full armor. They took up position behind Petrah, marching lockstep with their captain as they left the confines of the castle walls.

Surrounded by a retinue of armed men and women, Aman waited in a muscled, black cuirass and blood-red cape beneath clouds frozen into puddles of gray, ash, and slate. A horse-drawn cart filled with soldiers was just pulling up to the flat, barren ground outside the portcullis.

Petrah's eyes widened when he saw Kruush and Tan disembark. His excitement sank to the pit of his stomach when he noticed their faces, pale and distraught, as if they'd seen a specter. Scarlet cloths covered their wrists.

Immediately, Petrah knew what had happened to them.

He marched right up to Aman, who seemed unconcerned. "Why did you order them branded? I thought you said they would come here safely!"

The accusation had no effect on Aman's composure. He replied calmly, in that disgustingly confident way he always expressed himself. "They offered themselves to their god. If they didn't want to be branded, they could have refused. But they didn't, did they?"

"And if they had refused? What then?"

Aman stared hard at him, blue eyes smoldering. "Ask them yourself." He left Petrah and walked toward the gate, where he conferred with the towering captain of his guard. Verek followed the Grand Marshall into the castle, leaving Petrah behind with his friends.

No words were exchanged. Petrah simply embraced them, thankful they were alive. He suppressed his inclination to lock forearms with them, seeing the condition of their wrists.

This is all my fault.

A soldier with bright-red ribbons on his shoulders escorted them up to Petrah's apartment. Once they were by themselves, Petrah beckoned his friends to sit while he fetched a water jug. They drank their fill and settled onto the couches. The mood was bleak.

"Are you hungry?" Petrah asked. "I can call for someone to bring food." A braided pull hung beside the headboard to his bed, which would ring a servant bell somewhere below.

Neither of his friends was interested in food.

"I'm too disgusted to be hungry," Kruush said. Petrah's eyes traveled to Tan's bound wrist, then Kruush's. Kruush held his up. "Yesterday was a day of days. A day of piss and misery. Look at what they did to us."

He untied the cloth and let it drop to the floor. The skin on his wrists was pink and inflamed, raised to form the pattern of the encircled serpent of the Marked.

"Kruush, I'm so sorry. I should have—"

Kruush stopped him. "There's nothing you could have done, lad. We were damned the moment we found out that vile brother of yours left without us. This"—he shook his branded wrist—"is worse than when they tattooed our ankles as slaves. It's purgatory. What will Ahleen think when I go to caress her face and she finds this curse upon my skin?"

"She will love you just the same," Petrah said, his throat tight with shame for having left his friends behind.

Kruush gave a long, wistful nod. "She's forgiving, for sure, and compassionate. I couldn't ask for a better wife, in this world or ours." He gestured with his chin at Tan, who was more tight-lipped than usual, although Petrah could see a maelstrom churning beneath the surface. "I've never seen a braver soul than this one. He didn't make a sound. But me . . ." Kruush let out a halfhearted laugh. "I screamed like a little girl."

"You were just as brave," Tan said. Then, with the tiniest of smirks, he added, "And, yes, you screamed like a girl."

"I'll say this, and you're both witnesses to my declaration," Kruush said, waving a finger. "San is no longer my god. I renounce him with all my heart and all my soul. If you hear me say his name, you'll be damned sure I'm cursing it."

Tan nodded his agreement. "I'll second that. Sorry, Petrah, I know he's your father and all."

Petrah cringed at the reminder. "No need to apologize. I suppose you can always pray to Jah."

Kruush harrumphed. "I wouldn't go that far. It's not like Jah has shed his grace on us. Not yet at least. But enough about religion and which god matters." He looked around the spacious room. "What's been going on with you in our absence?"

Petrah felt a presence without the apartment, a sentry most likely, making sure they stayed put. The heartbeat was calm and steady. "We're not alone," Petrah said, gesturing to the door. He kept his voice low. "I'll fill you in on events."

Petrah started at the beginning, telling them of his first meeting with Aman in the Iron City, followed by their abbreviated travel to the village, his impression of the fanaticism of Aman's followers, and the fulfillment of his lifelong wish to find his mother. He was about to get to the part about Sametha when Kruush interrupted him.

"Why didn't you say something about your mother, to begin with? This is big news. No, humongous!"

Petrah smiled for only a fraction, before losing out to a pensive sadness regarding his mother. "It was too short a visit," he admitted, saddened further by the fact it might be his *only* visit. "I told her about you two, of course, and Ahleen. I told her about my life in Acia, my throttled pursuit of magehood, our adventures into Darkforth, and"—Petrah truly smiled now—"Mina."

Kruush grinned slyly. "Of course you did. And how did she take it?"

"Better than I could ever imagine."

"There's no closer bond than a son to his mother," Kruush said. "If I had a chance to see mine again, I would gladly let your bastard brother brand my other wrist."

Tan shot him a dark look.

Petrah led the conversation in the direction most needed: their escape. He expressed a sense of urgency as he filled them in on Sametha, but he left out any mention of her prophetic vision.

"I have a plan for getting us out of here," Petrah said. "It's a long shot, but I think it'll work." He told them about freeing Sam and escaping through the secret passage.

Tan spoke after Petrah finished. "That's nigh impossible. You realize that, don't you?"

"We'll have Sam," Petrah said. "She can see things we can't."

Tan wasn't convinced. "Having visions isn't the same as knowing where to go. We'll be on the run, with potentially an entire army at our backs. And what about your brother's ability to pop up anywhere? If what you said is true, he can cover any distance in the blink of an eye."

Petrah hadn't factored that into his escape plan, but he assumed Aman's ability to "pop up" was predicated on knowing where Petrah and his friends were—something Petrah was counting on not happening. "We'll make sure we have a healthy lead."

"We had one when those people in the city blew their whistles," Tan said. "That didn't stop the horsemen from cornering us, remember?"

"We'll get our own horses from the stables. Then we can flee to the mountains. The Peshte are sworn enemies of the Marked. I can barter with them. I'll trade information regarding the secret entrance into the castle for safe harbor. That'll be worth more to them than all our lives put together."

"*If* they'll listen, and *if* we can get to them."

And if they don't kill us first, Petrah wanted to add. "We'll divide our efforts into two. I'll get you to the secret passage, where you'll wait for me and Sam. Once I've freed her, we'll meet up with you. Then we'll head outside, sneak into the stables, and round up three horses. From there, we ride hard and fast to the mountains."

"I think you left out one detail," Tan said. "Two, actually. Our friend standing guard outside—and the girl."

"I can handle the guard."

Tan arched a brow.

"You forget I know a thing or two," Petrah said, holding out his palms. When Tan didn't get it, he said, "My arcane abilities, remember? Once the guard's neutralized, I'll grab his sword and use it to free Sam." He folded his arms, proud of his solution.

"I'll bet you ten currah," Kruush said, "that even the best sword won't work on a chain like the one you described. A falchion maybe, but a run-of-the-mill sword, even with the finest steel? It'll break the blade. But on bone, that's a different story. It can cleave the joints quite nicely."

Petrah frowned. "I'm not cutting off her foot."

"Then get ready to have your head lopped off instead because no sword I've seen these fools carry can measure up to the task."

"And I'll bet two kanta, I'll sever that chain and set her free. That's two dozen currah, my friend."

Kruush harrumphed like the big oaf he was. "I'll see your two kanta and raise you a gold till that you're wrong. Considering you're going to make us wait for this miracle to happen, unarmed in a tunnel by ourselves, no less, you might as well tell the guard standing outside to go to the armory and fetch you a dozen swords . . . and a purse filled with coins."

"Make it two tills," Petrah said, caught up in the wager.

Kruush spat on his hand. "Fine. You'll be cleaning gonatan dung for a year to pay off your debt."

They shook on it.

Kruush sat back on the couch and tutted woefully. "All I have to say is, I hope you know what you're doing."

"I do," Petrah said, knowing full well he didn't.

"So, when do we put your harebrained scheme into action?"

Petrah had already given it considerable thought. Leaving in the day-time was out of the question. Leaving after supper, while Aman was occupied with guests, was tempting, but too risky. Even after everyone bedded down for the night was too soon. It had to be late, when there was minimal security.

"Midnight."

A SERVANT BROUGHT FOOD and drink for supper. Tan, Kruush, and Petrah shared a meal of fried flatbread and chicken that had been sautéed in a fragrant cream sauce.

When the tolling bell struck eight, Petrah detected the arrival of a second person outside their door. He picked up on the vibrations of their conversation. They were simply switching shifts. They discussed the status of the occupants in Petrah's apartment and the fact the Grand Marshall had ordered an around-the-clock watch. The first guard left, and the second took his place. It was exactly as Petrah had hoped for.

The bell struck midnight, the last toll until six in the morning. That meant no further disturbances.

As agreed, Petrah and his companions would wait about fifteen minutes before instituting their plan. From there, time was of the essence.

Around a quarter past the hour, Petrah had Kruush knock on the door while he stood in front and Tan off to the side. There was a click of the lock, and the guard pushed the door open. He was thick-bodied and had an annoyed look on his ugly face. He gripped the pommel of the sword sheathed on his belt.

"*What do you—*" he started.

Petrah thrust his palm out and intoned a word of power, sending the guard flying into the stone wall. The blow shook the guard but didn't down him. His torso was plated front and back in armor. A second word sent him shooting up into the paneled ceiling headfirst. Although he wore a helm, it wasn't enough to shield his skull. There was an agonizing split of wood. Then he fell a dozen feet to the terracotta tile, limp.

"Gods," Kruush swore. "Remind me never to get on your bad side."

"Grab his sword," Petrah said. "See if he's . . ." He didn't want to say the word.

Kruush felt along the soldier's neck. "He's alive." He unsheathed the sword. It was short, not quite what Petrah had hoped for. Kruush held it up by its pommel, letting it dangle between his fingertips. "Right—a chain breaker."

"Give that to Tan," Petrah said, not happy with the fact that Kruush's assessment of the weapon was probably correct. It wasn't like they had any other options. "Gag the guard, and I'll bind his wrists."

Petrah used a length of roped cord he had cut earlier from the curtains covering the courtyard window to tie the soldier's wrists and then a second length of cord to tie his ankles. Kruush used strips of bedsheet as a gag.

"There," Petrah said, giving his knot a tug. "Let's go."

They shut the apartment door and followed Petrah as he ran quietly along the corridor. He'd know who was ahead of him before they'd know he was there.

Petrah led them down a flight of stairs and hurried along a hallway lit by torches in brackets. When they came across a long gallery with niches and old tapestries, Petrah sensed the approach of someone from the far end. They ducked into an arched recess with a pew and altar and crammed into the corners to hide.

Petrah's heart thumped in his throat as sabatons clanked against the stone floor, the heel beat of a soldier in plate armor. The man whistled to himself. When he got to their hiding spot, Petrah caught a glimpse of his cape and long hair from behind. The man stopped, the clang of his armored boots ringing out. Petrah didn't move, didn't breathe. What was the soldier doing standing there? The soldier turned his head, and Petrah pulled back, praying the man didn't see him. Seconds later, the soldier recommenced his walk and his whistling, and continued on his way.

"That was close," Tan whispered, visibly shaken.

Petrah's heart was still pumping hard from the scare. "Let's go."

He resumed his lead and rushed along the remaining stretch of the gallery, pausing by an intersection of hallways, then turning right. From there, it was a quick twenty paces to a stairwell with flights of stairs running up and down. Petrah motioned for his friends to wait. He sensed two sets of heartbeats on an upper level near the staircase. A peek up, and he saw an armored man leaning against a stone rail, face hidden, speaking in hushed tones to the second individual.

Petrah placed a finger to his lips to let his friends know to be quiet, then pointed down the stairs for them to follow.

The trio descended with nary a sound, then continued to the lowest level, where the air was dank and stale. Petrah grabbed a torch from the wall and counted off turns in his head as they moved toward the secret passage. Sure enough, a roughly hewn tunnel appeared, leading a hundred paces to a dead end.

"Remember," Petrah said, exchanging his torch for the sword Tan held, "one of you needs to post guard at the mouth of the tunnel, the other at its rear. I'll whistle like a scarlet crescent to signal you." He mimicked the trill of the bird he'd heard outside his dorm in Elmar on many a hot morning. "Give me an hour at the most. If I'm not here by then, leave without me. If someone comes, get out. We'll rendezvous at the south end of the city, past the main road. If I'm not there by dawn, head for the mountains."

Kruush put a brotherly hand on his shoulder. "Make haste."

Petrah ran off, using his nocturnal sight to guide him.

H E WAS RELIEVED TO find Sametha in her cell. He had been worried that Aman had moved her to a different part of the keep. Her face fell when she saw the sword.

"It's all right." Petrah set the weapon on top of the hay bale for a moment. "I'm going to use it to get you out."

"No, Petrah, don't do it. My master knows you came here last night. He was very mad." She had bruising on her face from where the animal had struck her. Petrah quelled his rage. Now wasn't the time to let his anger overwhelm him.

Aman will get his turn.

Petrah squatted beside her. "Sam, I'm getting you out of here. I don't care what your master said, do you understand? Now, hold still. I'm going to break the chain."

He positioned her ankle away from the stake and searched the chain for the right link to sever. They were roughly the same thickness. The ones in the middle were the best option. They were flat against the floor, while the others were suspended by the stake or too close to Sametha's fetter.

Petrah practiced arcing the sword slowly to the center links. He needed to make sure it struck straight and true, not askew.

"Here it goes," he said.

The clang of metal on metal rang out, and a shudder ran up his arm. Sametha covered her ears. He examined the link he struck. There was barely a scratch. The blade of his sword had a decent nick, though.

"Are you all right?"

She nodded.

"Stay perfectly still. I'm going to try a little differently this time."

He grasped the hilt with two hands and swung as if chopping with an axe. Again, the blow rang out terribly. The sword twisted from the impact, and his hand with it. There was a second nick in the blade, even deeper than the first. He cursed his poor fortune. Sametha pulled into herself like a spider.

Third's the charm.

He struck again with every ounce of strength he could muster. The blade struck hard and true and . . .

Broke!

The top part of the blade went skittering into a clod of hay while he drove the bottom half into the floor, the crossguard hitting violently, sending a painful vibration up his forearm.

No, no, no, no, no!

Petrah stared at the pieces, then the unbroken link of chain. Sametha remained tethered to the stake. How could he have messed up so badly?

"I'm so sorry, Sam. I tried. I—" He didn't know what to say. He couldn't admit defeat. This was a stumbling block, a minor obstacle. "I'm going to fix this, Sam." He nodded his head. "I am, I swear it."

"I'm scared," she whispered.

"Me too." He looked around the cell. "There has to be a way to break this chain."

"You tried, Petrah. You can't break it."

"I can. I must! Let me think for a moment." He wished Kruush and Tan were here.

"Petrah, leave me. I'll be fine. You did the best you could."

"Fine?" Aman had beaten her. The next punishment would be ten times worse, perhaps fatal. "No, it's not fine. Not at all. I need to get you out of here!" Desperation screeched out of his mouth.

He examined the broken blade. It was in bad shape. He was left with the lower two-thirds of the sword. The new tip formed a sharp wedge on one side; the other ran flat, crosswise to the blade's edge. The links of the chain, however, were nearly unscathed. What use was the sword now? He needed a different tack to free her.

Think, damn it!

The rod embedded in the stone floor was about an inch thick with a loop at the top where the chain was secured to. What if he could find a rock big enough to pound the stake loose?

He searched the cell, but there wasn't anything of use. If he went out into the corridor, he might find a stone in the wall where the mortar was cracked or a piece that had fallen to the ground, something he could use to bash the metal . . .

"I've got an idea," he said. "I'll be right back."

A look of terror washed over her. "Oh, no. He's coming, Petrah. He's coming!"

Petrah could see it in her eyes: it was too late.

There was a scraping sound behind him, past the bend in the corridor, like metal raking over stone. He turned toward it. A foul draft of air momentarily guttered the torch mounted to the wall but didn't snuff it. The light shrank away as it had when Aman murdered the Peshte.

Petrah's legs became weak, his breathing raspy. His first instinct was to back away, to cower and cover his ears.

No, a voice in his mind told him. *Don't you dare let her down.*

Petrah steeled his resolve.

The presence was massively dense, like a mountain compressed into human form. It radiated spite and malice. As it grew, the twisting stain of hate consumed the walls, the ground, and the ceiling in darkness, darkness even Petrah's night eyes couldn't penetrate.

Sametha trembled, hiding her face in her hands.

Petrah stood between her and the door. "I won't let him hurt you." But as he set his feet apart in a magi warrior stance and tried to determine a Kantaka battle pose, a chill coursed his neck. His knees wobbled. His upper body shook. Tremors racked his entire body. Why couldn't he control the shaking, stop it?

The shadow expanded, eating the wall.

A voice, sharp and terrifying, hissed out of the darkness. "Sametha . . ."

She pitched forward and pressed her cupped face into the straw by her feet. "Please, Master, don't be mad. I didn't mean to disobey you."

Petrah replanted his feet and locked his knees. He positioned the sword pommel close to his body with the tip facing out, ready to lunge with the broken blade.

The presence grew nearer.

Twenty feet and closing.

Darkness spread like ink across all surfaces. Petrah pivoted his weight to spring forward.

Ten feet.

The black consumed everything in its path; ate the walls alive; swelled like poison in the blood.

Five feet.

A phosphorescent glimmer appeared in the inky void in the shape of a man.

San-Jahad. His brother.

The umbra reached the cell, drinking the flickering light. It stabbed out the torchlight and threw the cell into impermeable blackness.

Petrah could hear only his breathing. Then a fluttering sound followed by scratching from all directions, like claws on rock.

"Show yourself!" he demanded.

The darkness vanished, and he was momentarily blinded by torch-light.

Aman stood in the doorway, dressed in a black robe. Trails of crimson fire shifted across its surface. His eyes danced madly with a red glow, twin furnaces no longer bright blue.

The Grand Marshall stepped into the cell.

Petrah pointed his broken sword at him, quivering, gripping it tightly. "Don't come any closer."

Aman bent down and picked up the shard from Petrah's sword, about eight inches of steel from the foible to the point of the blade. He wrapped his fingers over the metal as if it were a dagger.

"I've dreamed of this moment. I know you have as well, except we were on a hilltop, and you were wounded, felled by an arrow, and surrounded by mountaineers."

Aman held up the shard and examined it as if looking at his reflection in the steel.

"You weren't just standing among them," he continued, "you were *with* them. And then they fell, one by one, until it was you and one other survivor." Aman shifted his gaze to Sametha, who cowered behind Petrah's legs. "Do you remember, Immael?"

Petrah's hands were slick, damp with perspiration. The sword felt unwieldy in his grip. "It was just a dream."

Aman pointed the shard at Petrah. "You see, it wasn't just a dream. If it were, you wouldn't have betrayed me by coming here."

Petrah kept his eye on the broken tip aimed at him. "Call it what you want, but I won't let you harm Sam anymore."

Aman took another step toward Petrah. He was well within striking distance. Petrah gave him a second warning. "What did I say about getting any closer?"

Aman scoffed at him. "Go ahead. Strike me with your sword. Kill your own brother."

Petrah barely kept his slippery hold on the sword. His hand wouldn't quit shaking. "You're no brother of mine. You never were."

Aman's aura expanded behind him, growing like wings of shadow, darkening the cell. "I should never have taken you to see your mother. She poisoned your mind."

"No," Petrah said, making sure Sametha was safely behind him. "I'd made up my mind long before that. You've done terrible things, Aman. I won't let you harm anyone else. This ends tonight."

The scorn on his brother's face intensified. "See, that's why you can't be allowed to follow the paths in your dreams. They're misguided paths, the muddling of light mixed with dark. But I'm here to change that, Immael. I'm here to set things right." He took another step forward.

Petrah drew back his sword, level and ready to thrust forth, elbow bent tight. "I'm warning you, I'll do it."

"Then do it!"

Petrah stabbed the tip of his sword toward the midline of Aman's chest. Instead of striking his brother, it rebounded harmlessly off something invisible and hard, deflecting him wide. He recovered his balance and wheeled about. He went for another thrust, but Aman acted first with a simple flick of the wrist.

An invisible force struck Petrah and flung him against the opposite wall. Sametha shrieked. Petrah struck his shoulder. A shock of pain flooded his body. He dropped his weapon and folded to the ground.

Aman reached down and yanked Sametha by the hair, making her cry out. "See what happens, brother? See what happens to the children?" He set the edge of the broken blade tip to her throat. "They seem innocent enough, so young, so sweet. You think you can trust them, trust their naivety. But this one, she's not so innocent, is she?"

Petrah pushed himself into a seated position. He coughed and sucked in air. Bits of hay fell from his cheek. He reached out entreatingly with his hand. "Please, Aman, don't hurt her. I'm begging you."

"See what you did?" The red in Aman's eyes burned hotly. "*You* did this!"

"Petrah?" Sam said weakly. Tears ran down her face.

Aman shook her like a branch. "No, you don't get to say anything. You were my prophet, my sweet Sametha, now turned traitor. Shall we show Immael what we do to traitors? Shall we show him how fate really works?"

Petrah focused inwardly, shutting out the pain.

The only way to stop Aman was to retaliate in kind, not through physical force, but with channeled energy. Petrah thrust his hand out and issued a word of power. The air rippled. What was meant to strike his brother dissolved into nothing.

Petrah stared, stricken with disbelief.

"Your skills are lacking," Aman said, twisting his mouth into a virulent smile. "Father will remedy that. He'll dig into that mind of yours and bring out your true potential. He'll show you the way through fire and pain, won't he, little one?" Aman pinched Sametha's chin and pulled up hard, exposing her pale throat.

"Please, Aman. Don't hurt her. Do what you want with me, but let her go. I'll do anything you want. Anything!"

"It's too late for that," Aman said. "I don't need her anymore. She's shown me all I needed to see about my future." He bent down and whispered into her ear. "Say goodbye, little one."

"Aman, please—"

He slit her throat.

Petrah screamed. "No!"

He lunged forward to tackle his brother. But his movement was awkward, and he tripped over Sametha's chain and landed painfully on his knees. She dangled above him, suspended like an angel, bleeding out, flecking his face with droplets of blood. Her gray eyes caught his for a fleeting moment, wide and terrified. He couldn't save her. He couldn't do anything but watch her die.

Her chin drooped. Then she shuddered her last breath.

The quiet lasted seconds, but it might as well have been an eternity.

Petrah was numb, unable to breathe.

Aman let Sam's lifeless body fall to the ground. Her head lolled to the side and went still, eyes frozen wide, frightfully beautiful in the repose of her death.

Petrah couldn't stand to look at her. He clawed the ground, scraping together straw with his fingers.

He cried insufferably, racking sobs and snot draining from his nose.

He had failed her. If he had stayed away, she'd still be alive. Why couldn't he have stayed away?

Petrah waited for his brother to kill him; *hoped* Aman would take the broken sword tip and drive it through his neck. That's what he deserved.

That's what he needed.

Do it! Please!

But Aman wasn't through with him. Not yet. Not tonight.

"And now, little brother," Aman said, standing above him, voice dripping with venom, "you're all mine."

Chapter 12
Altered Path

K RUUSH WAITED IMPATIENTLY AT the end of the stone tunnel that led out of the castle through an ingeniously concealed door.

He and Tan found the pressure plates Petrah had told them about. The first set was cleverly camouflaged in the ashlar, hidden behind a pair of stones on opposite walls that, when pushed in simultaneously, swiveled a section of the wall inward. The second set of pressure plates was found in a well on the external side, which ran up to a trapdoor via a winding stone staircase.

They waited for what seemed like hours for Petrah to show up with the girl. No semblance of time existed down here. Since the tolling bell was silenced until dawn, there was no way to know how long they had been waiting.

To keep from going mad, Kruush made a list in his mind of all the supplies he and Tan would need when they left Mokan-lee's estate with their workers for Terjurmeh. The idea soured halfway through when he realized Joriah would have his head should Kruush step foot in Elmar again. He had reneged on his deal with the mage. Kruush wasn't one to double-cross anyone, least of all a powerful party official like Joriah.

Damn that boy. And damn me for getting involved!

He pictured Ahleen shaking her head at him with hands planted on her hips as he pulled into the docks at Hōvar, smiling like a buffoon.

"Ah, my love, it's come to this, hasn't it?" He raised a hand poetically while squatting in the dark corner of the dreadfully chilly tunnel. He rubbed his arms, wishing he was with his wife, not stuck in this god-awful place.

Tan came toward him with his torch lifted high and a trail of smoldering pitch in his wake. He was supposed to remain stationed at the mouth of the tunnel, serving as their lookout . . . unless, of course, something happened.

Kruush got to his feet and massaged his cramped thighs. "Well?"

Tan shook his head. "Nothing."

Kruush grimaced. "You came all the way over here to tell me *that*?"

"Not just that. We're way past the hour mark. Petrah told us to wait an hour at the most. My torch is about to extinguish. We have to go with the backup plan."

"Donkey balls, I knew we shouldn't have split up. Now look at us!" Kruush had every intention of giving Petrah a kick to the rear when he saw him again. "So, what do you suggest we do?"

"Let's secure the horses. Worst case, we meet him and the girl at the rendezvous point."

Kruush ran through the scenario in his mind. If they waited much longer, someone was bound to discover the guard in Petrah's apartment. Once that happened, the castle would be on lockdown, and that damned brother of Petrah's would send out a bloody search party. It would only be a matter of time before they were caught. "Right, backup plan it is. Let's get out of here."

They shut the hidden door behind them and climbed the spiral stairwell to the top. Kruush depressed a lever, and the trapdoor fell inward, along with an avalanche of loose hay that had been used to conceal it from above. Tan's dimming torch revealed the inside of a silo. Bales of hay were stacked around them. The smell of dried grass was strong.

"I'm going to peek out the door. Get that torch belowground, so it's out of sight and away from all this tinder."

Tan dipped his head below the trapdoor opening, along with his torch.

Kruush eased the silo door ajar and peeked outside. A gust of damp, chilled air stung his face. It was dark in the immediate vicinity. The silo was in a field about fifty feet from the castle's north curtain wall. He could make out the shape of the stables a quarter mile to the south and a corral where several steeds huddled together.

He surveyed the castle's battlements but didn't see any heads sticking above the parapets, nor any faces poking through the crenellations. That didn't mean there wasn't anyone on watch or patrol. There was a light coming from each of the three towers along the wall, one on either corner and one in the center, just beyond the stables. The light was sufficient to illuminate the area beneath, but not enough to light up the environs.

Kruush shut the door and whistled to Tan, who popped his head aboveground. Kruush relayed what he had seen outside.

Tan got rid of the torch and closed the trapdoor beneath him. "What's the plan?"

"We make a straight line for the north side of the stables. Petrah said there's a barn with a tack room over there. We'll steal two horses from the stables for us—coursers preferably, not rounceys—then go around the corral, north at first, then east until we come to the trail that winds from the castle to the outskirts of the city. We'll want to stick to the shadows wherever possible. The tricky part is crossing the main road that goes from the gatehouse into the village."

"And stealing a couple of horses from under their noses isn't?"

Kruush frowned. "Just get ready to run like a jackal."

They ran across the field, over stumps of wild grass and clods of earth kicked up by hooves that had trampled the ground many times over. The scent of hay gave way to barnyard odors, heavy with dung. They slowed as they got near the backside of the stables, which formed one contiguous run of timbers and clapboards, barely discernible in the absence of light.

The stables made up the longest building Kruush had ever seen, easily large enough to house several hundred horses.

Kruush and Tan hugged the wood fence along the outside wall of the stables, using the darkness to their advantage, and moved toward the farthermost point, where there was a break in the buildings. They slipped between wood runners and walked as softly as possible up to the barn with the tack room, steps from the stables.

Tan posted as a lookout while Kruush fumbled for the latch. It squealed a little. Kruush mumbled curses as he opened it in fractions. With just enough of it gaping to stick his head through, he peered inside.

A young girl with cropped blonde hair slept atop a bed of freshly pitched hay next to a lamp with a low flame. A burlap sack covered her as a blanket. There were plenty of saddles, halters, reins, and other tack hanging from the wood walls or stacked around the barn.

The girl stirred as a breeze swept the bangs across her forehead. Kruush held his breath as she made a face and absently wiped the hair away. She settled back into her slumber, and Kruush silently spoke a prayer of thanks. He forced the door open enough to squeeze his body through. He kept one eye on the sleeping girl, the other on the equipment as he worked his way about. Any wrong step or loud noise, and the girl would awaken and sound the alarm.

A couple of minutes later, he had what they needed. Tan helped him set the equipment by the fence while Kruush carefully shut the barn door.

"Here, take this." Kruush handed Tan the girl's lamp. He had turned it down even lower, lighting up only their faces and bodies.

Tan bobbed his head. "Good thinking. We'll have to work fast, though. There's a patrol on horseback driving west."

"Coming here?"

"Couldn't tell. They're just south of the corral, six riders. Probably armed. They're carrying torches."

"Right. In and out with the horses then."

"Grab the halters and reins," Tan said as he wrapped his fingers over the handle of the barn door.

When Kruush had the items in his possession, Tan tugged at the door. It slid easily on oiled rollers, unlike the barn door Kruush had fought with. The heady odor of horses, hay, and dung floated out. It was dark inside, save for the flicker of a lit lantern about halfway down. Someone might be awake.

They worked diligently, quietly going stall to stall in search of cooperative equestrian candidates. Some horses stuck their heads over the stall doors, some snorted or withdrew, and others plainly ignored them.

A chestnut stallion about ten stalls in acted friendly enough, as did a jet-black steed with a splash of white across his withers. Both seemed able-bodied and swift. Kruush and Tan tacked up the horses and led them outside, where they saddled them.

Tan pushed on a gate, not twenty paces away, leading out of the corral. He headed toward his horse while Kruush began to mount the chestnut stallion. As Kruush's foot slipped into the stirrup, the barn door squealed open. It was the girl who had been sleeping. She was barely visible in the lamplight, a teenager with a small, bony physique and a not-at-all-happy look on her face. She started speaking rapidly in Glesh, gesturing at them with her hands, then her lamp, then their horses.

"Not so loud!" Kruush said, stepping down. He couldn't understand a word she said. He tried to shush her, but the more he tried, the louder she got.

"Seat your horse," Tan urged, coming around. "We have to go!"

The door to the stables opened, and an older man with a short sword and lantern stepped outside. He froze when he saw them. Tan acted quickly, catching the wrist of his sword arm and knocking the lantern out of his other hand. The glass shattered, but the flame didn't go out. He and Tan struggled as Kruush hung back, not sure what to do.

The girl let out an ululating cry.

"Shut her up!" Tan yelled, driving the older man back against the stable wall.

Kruush seized the girl, clamping one hand over her mouth, the other around her waist. She thrashed like a possessed creature and tried to bite him. It took every bit of strength to keep her from squirming out from under his grasp.

Tan knocked the sword free from the older man. He then spun about, elbow first, and cracked the man's jaw, dropping him to the ground. Kruush had seen his partner fight before, but even this surprised him.

A young man rounded the corner—a farmhand, judging from his dungarees and linen nightshirt—armed with a bow and arrow and carrying a quiver over his shoulder. He nocked his arrow and drew his bowstring, yelling at Tan, motioning for him to lower his weapon.

Tan held out his sword neutrally, but didn't lower it. The young man kept yelling, using his drawn bow to motion downward, stepping closer and stamping his foot threateningly. Tan made it like he was going to surrender the weapon, dipping to the ground. With his free hand, he swept the broken lantern up at the farmhand with blinding speed. The young man moved defensively to the side. An instant later, Tan impaled him in the gut. The bowstring twanged as the young man shrieked. Tan pulled the bloodied blade out, and the man dropped to the ground, rolling to his side and clutching his wound.

"Are you mad?" Kruush asked while struggling to keep the girl still. Tan grabbed the farmhand's bow and quiver.

"He gave me no choice!"

The girl fought ferociously against Kruush. She bit into his palm. He yelped and let her go. She ran over to the fallen young man and spoke urgently to him.

Tan mounted his jet stallion. He secured the sword in a loop in the saddle and placed the quiver over his back. "Get up there!"

Startled as Kruush was, he did as he was told. The girl was crying now, cradling the young man's head in her lap.

Tan spurred his horse through the gate. "Go, go, go!"

Kruush cursed and sent his horse galloping after Tan.

They rode north, away from the corral. The ground was uneven, and it was pitch-black for the first frightening minute. Kruush's eyes adjusted, and he could see his surroundings in various shades of black and deep brown. The land dipped sharply at one point, then rose. Kruush had forgotten how much he hated riding horseback, especially the way it racked his pelvis and knees.

Tan slowed his horse to a canter and veered east. Kruush matched pace, thankful for the reprieve on his body, but sickened all the same by what they had done.

"See the torches?" Tan pointed toward the stables behind them. Kruush saw several lit torches where they had been only minutes earlier. "Riders on horseback. We'll head east to lose them. Ready?"

Kruush started to say something, but Tan had already sped his steed to a full gallop. Grudgingly, Kruush followed suit, praying his horse wouldn't trip and kill him.

The horsemen's torches tracked along their path, then grew fainter eventually. Tan slowed once again, this time to a trot, and guided them southeast toward the main road leading from the castle. The city proper was east of the fortification, a shadowy collection of stone and adobe buildings. The castle loomed on the west side, an impenetrable fortress, staining the sky black.

"Are you all right?" Tan asked.

"Am I all right?" Kruush squeezed his reins with knotted fists. "That boy is probably dead, thanks to you. That's on top of the fact we just killed Petrah's only chance of meeting up with us. And you're asking if I'm *all right*?"

"What was I supposed to do," Tan retorted, "take an arrow in the throat?"

Kruush had several responses, each one cruder and meaner than the last. He bit down on his words and let the fumes dissipate.

"I'm sorry, Kruush, but I did what needed to be done," Tan called over his shoulder.

Kruush held his tongue. He was worried about Petrah. He and Tan could fend for themselves, but the boy . . .

He'll make it. I know he will. That boy is as smart as he is stubborn.

When they arrived at the edge of the city, Tan made them stop. He pointed at the castle. "Something's going on over there." The portcullis was raised. Foot soldiers bearing torches led a cortege of about a dozen priests wearing chains crisscrossed over their robes. The priests chanted as they made their way onto the main road. Behind them, a horseman pulled a cart carrying the body of a young girl.

It didn't make sense to Kruush. "A funeral procession at this late hour?"

"We need to wait them out before we cross the road. Let's get closer," Tan said.

They dismounted in the shadow of a large building on the corner of a quiet street and tied off their horses. Kruush squatted while Tan stood above him, and together, they peeked around the building's edge.

Several people had gathered along the main road to observe the procession, which turned out to be longer than Kruush thought. The girl in the cart was just crossing out of view. She was barefoot, dressed in a tattered tunic, and had her hands crossed over her chest. A trail of soldiers followed, along with a giant of a man in plate armor, more priests, and a second cart, this one carrying a young man Kruush recognized immediately.

"San save us!" He made the sign of the holy delta.

"Is that . . .?" Tan shook his head. "It can't be!"

"It's him, I'm sure of it. Is he alive? The girl's dead, but is he . . .?" Kruush didn't dare say it. He *couldn't* say it. "Tan, tell me he's alive!"

"Yes—no. Wait," Tan said. "Maybe. I don't know." His voice quavered. "What do we do, Kruush?"

Kruush gripped the rough stone edge of the building. Everything was falling apart. His wits were all he had, wits that had saved his life in the past, wits he needed now, more than anything else. He tamped down the wave of panic and let the sensible part of his brain take over.

"We follow them." With anger filtering into his voice, he added, "And then we kill the bastard who did this to him."

Chapter 13
Conjuring

THE FIRST THING PETRAH saw when he opened his eyes was the domed ceiling above, and then he heard chanting, a mix of bass and contralto voices. The heavy scent of incense, like tree resin mixed with beeswax, burned his nostrils. His head and back rested against a slab of cold stone recessed into a rectangular block of black granite. He ran his hand along the left edge and felt an etched pattern that flowed along the length—an inscription, perhaps. Korinians used stone sarcophagi like this for the dead.

Am I dead?

Smoke rose from a brass urn at the foot of the block, as hazy as his vision. He sat up, woozy and nauseated. It took several breaths of thick, incensed air to resolve the blurry shapes around him into their actual form. He was in a large rotunda. Runes were engraved into the polished granite floor, radiating outward in a spiral pattern from where he sat. Huge marble statues ringed the circumference of the chamber, each climbing a good fifty feet.

Angels, he thought.

Not like the Watcher, but like those he had read about in the Scriptures, proud and beautiful.

They were naked and genderless, lidless stone eyes gazing upward into the recesses of the dome, expressions on smooth faces teetering between majestic and terrifying. They bore great wings folded behind their backs and carried swords aloft, pointing to the heavens. Petrah followed their sword tips toward the shadowed apex.

Chanting, hooded figures stood around the outer perimeter of runes—about twenty total—holding metal-shod staves with looped ends and chains in x-patterns across the fronts of their thick, black robes.

Watchers?

No, these were clearly human: men and women priests of Aman's dark order. Their hymn was guttural and unholy, intoned in a fell language bitter to Petrah's ears. It made him think of the stories of San's angels, whose wingtips were often described as dipped in blood from celestial battles and whose eyes shunned the light. Sametha had called them "fallen angels."

One of the priests walked slowly along the runed perimeter, swinging a burning brass censer that hung from a short chain. He flicked the censer to the cadence of the chanting. Bells jostled with each shake, and a small puff of smoke exited the thurible like a dragon belching steamed breath, leaving a cloudy trail behind. The train of exhaled smoke moved as if a breeze were blowing, but it wasn't a breeze at all. Something incorporeal filtered through its wake.

Not ten feet away, Petrah caught a shimmer, a halo that blended into a darkened blur the shape of a man who had his back to him. Then he felt it—frigid, dense, sharp—Aman's hateful aura. A shiver coursed through Petrah's body. Aman was positioned past the incense urn, wearing his fire-emblazoned robe and flanked by a pair of priests in garnet robes, one with a decorative dagger sheathed on the belt, the other carrying a long metal staff. When Aman turned his head toward one of the priests, Petrah saw his eye color was back to its brilliant blue, no longer the scintillating red from when he—

Sametha!

The grogginess left Petrah, flushed out by the agonizing memory of her death. Those final moments of watching her haunting pale gray eyes as she bled out.

I'm sorry, Sam. I'm so, so sorry.

She was dead because of him, yet Petrah was alive. Why hadn't Aman finished him off? Why had he let Petrah live? Was it to serve the purpose Sametha portended?

He cleared the chalkiness from his throat and addressed his brother. "What is this place?"

Aman turned to Petrah, no surprise on his face, no reaction. "The Hall of Angels, our holiest sanctum." He spread his arms. "You see the likeness of the twelve greatest around you. This hall pays homage to them. They guard the way to the Netherworld and protect us from their spiteful brethren above. Our father's angels are listening right now. Can't you tell? Listening to our prayers and channeling our communion, so Father might hear us."

"You're summoning him." It was as Petrah feared. The wheel of fate was coming full circle. He wouldn't be able to escape the finale. *You're not strong enough*, Sametha had warned. Kruush had warned it, too.

"You were planning on giving me to Father all along." *But I had been too blinded to see it.* Another lesson involving Qufah and Qufay, the blind and the blinded. Petrah thought himself too clever to fall into Qufay's path. How wrong he was!

My mother knew. Sametha knew. Everyone knew but me!

"If you get rid of me," Petrah said, "how are you going to cross into Acia? The Watcher might open the gateway, but you still need a key to unlock it." Anger welled up, but Petrah's words carried an overtone of desperation. "You need me!"

Aman smiled, not the deceitful or spiteful kind as he had displayed in their previous meeting, but more of a fraternal kind, one sibling to another. "I still do, Immael. But the way is clear now, thanks to you. It's only a matter of time."

Petrah swung his bare feet over the edge of the stone block and tried to stand, taking a moment to steady himself. His head was still fighting a battle against vertigo. "What does that mean?"

"It means destiny is calling, and I'm answering her call. By entering Dagoth, you unlocked the door between worlds. For that, I am grateful."

"No, that's not possible. You need me to go with you. I've seen it in my dreams. I must open the doorway back to Acia."

"I saw the dreams too, but they're merely symbolic. In truth, you have done your job. When the time comes, I will march my army into Acia."

The Watcher had tricked him! Petrah didn't want to believe it, but that's exactly what had happened. "When?"

"When the time is right, just like everything else." Aman cupped his hands. "Have pride in knowing I will miss having you by my side. You have spirit, little brother. I have no doubt you could have become a great warrior in our fight among mortal kind. But your fight lies elsewhere now."

Petrah started to say something to his brother when he spotted another sarcophagus behind where he had lain. Resting upon it was Sametha's still form.

Petrah caught his breath as he looked at Sametha.

Brass torchiers on either side cast flickering shadows across her slender body. Someone had replaced her rags with a simple ivory dress. Her skin was free of grime, carrying a slight sheen as if washed and oiled in an ablution. Her hands were folded peacefully over her bosom, and her hair was combed straight, fanned out neatly behind her atop the granite, a swath of white. A veil of sheer fabric obscured her face, stitched into a diadem with a dull-black gemstone in the center.

Wake up, Sam. You're just asleep.

Aman walked over to her. "Our little Sametha, sweet as honeyed milk, even in death's embrace. The angels weep for her."

Petrah balled his fists as bits of rage came flooding back. He started after his brother, but a strong set of hands stopped him. One of the garnet-robed priests shook his head at Petrah.

Aman stepped slowly around the stone coffin. "Sametha," he called lightly. "Sametha, can you hear me?"

Outrage carried in Petrah's voice. "What are you doing?"

"Watch," Aman said. He called to Sametha again. "Come back to me, little one. Your master needs you."

The veil sucked in against Sametha's lips as if she drew breath. Petrah's hand flew over his mouth. It had to be an illusion, a trick.

"Yes, that's it. Come back to me."

She coughed weakly and gasped. The veil fluttered upward and over her forehead, revealing her pale face. All the color was drained from her complexion and lips, and her gray eyes stared corpselike into the abyss above, unblinking.

How? Petrah wanted to say, but the word caught in his throat.

"That's it," Aman said, encouraging her with a smile. "Come back to me. I still have a purpose for you."

She spoke in a raspy voice that scraped against Petrah's ears like nails. "No," she whimpered, but no tears came.

"This is wrong!" Petrah shouted.

"I'm bringing her back for the sacrifice." Aman gently coaxed her to sit upright. The veil flopped over her face, sparing Petrah from her vacuous stare. "That's it, little one. Stay with me."

"What sacrifice?" Petrah said. "You have me. Isn't that enough?"

"The demons want a virgin of the purest heart."

"Then let them take me."

"You might be a virgin, dear brother, but your heart is not pure. I will give them what they ask for. I will give them what they crave." Aman held up a hand, and the chanting ceased. "Listen."

It was frightfully quiet at first. Petrah heard a murmuring—a breeze fluttering the candles, followed by a buzzing sound, faint, then multiplying like flies gathering above a pile of stink. The air grew foul, the burning resin overpowered by the stench of death.

"They hunger, Immael. They gnash their teeth and beat their wings, hungering in the dark, desperate for an innocent soul to tear to shreds and sate the insatiable. In exchange, they open the way for us. Can you feel the shift? Can you feel the change around us?"

Petrah noticed a slight distortion in the surrounding air, the way the stuffiness dissipated, replaced by a draft. Except it wasn't a draft. It was more like a "loosening" of the air. A sharp sucking sound followed, and a whoosh echoed loudly in the hall.

"Father's coming," Aman said. The declaration sent chills up Petrah's neck. Aman turned back to Sametha. "Come, little one. Take my hand."

Petrah started for Aman again. This time, he dodged the garnet-robed man's grasp, but a robed woman close to them contacted Petrah's arm with her staff. Petrah convulsed as if struck by lightning. His muscles seized and joints locked. He fell heavily to one knee and stiffened in place as if held by unseen hands. It kept him from speaking or moving his head. He could only breathe . . .

. . . and watch.

T AN AND KRUUSH MOVED swiftly through the arched corridor of the shrine, dressed in leather jerkins, helms, and cloaks stolen from a pair of guards Tan had felled with two well-placed arrows. Kruush gripped a mace he'd taken from one of the downed guards, opting for it over the bloodied sword Tan had used on the young man at the stables. Tan stuck to his bow. There was no plan other than to get to Petrah.

Voices sounded ahead. Three men talking among themselves, at least one in heavy armor.

Tan signaled to Kruush to hide. Kruush and Tan split up and hid behind support columns on either side of the corridor. Tan pointed at his bow, tapped his chest, and then pointed a finger toward the voices to let Kruush know he was going to fire at whoever was coming toward them. He held out a palm, then tapped his chest again, which Kruush took as an indication to wait and not do anything. Tan drew three arrows from his quiver. He nocked one and waited.

Kruush breathed in and out—short, controlled breaths. He'd never used a mace before, and the helm was heavy. What if he froze? What if he seized up at the last second? *Swing. That's all you have to do.*

The clanking grew louder, an unnervingly heavy cadence mixing with the sound of the men's voices. They spoke in Glesh, unintelligible to Kruush's ears.

Tan glanced at Kruush and nodded once. Before Kruush could interpret what his friend meant, Tan stepped out with his drawn bow and let loose. A man's voice cried out. Kruush peeked to see a man in a robe crumble to the ground, clutching an arrow protruding from his chest. Another robed man shouted while a soldier in full plate armor unsheathed his sword and lumbered toward Tan. Tan, fast and efficient, nocked a second arrow and fired it at the shouting, unarmed man. It pierced his belly, sending him flailing to the ground.

The brute in armor came after Tan, but not before Tan had a third arrow ready. Tan retreated, keeping pace with the advancing soldier, falling back.

Kruush didn't think. He acted.

As the lumbering soldier came into view, Kruush jumped out, swing-ing. He aimed for the soldier's breastplate, but his untested swing was too wild, striking the left shoulder instead. The blow hit just inside the pauldron with enough force to knock the soldier off balance. Kruush caught himself from falling while the soldier teetered, then steadied himself, bringing up his sword arm. The blade was plenty long, plenty deadly. Kruush backed away, out of range.

The armored man had no helm, exposing an ugly face with greasy hair. He growled something in his tongue while the colleague with the arrow in the chest wheezed and the other clutched his stomach, cursing in pain.

With Kruush on one side and Tan on the other, the soldier looked back and forth between the men, perhaps deciding who was the bigger threat and whom he would go after.

Kruush, either bold or stupid, stepped within the circle of the man's sword range. The soldier pivoted to strike. A thwack sounded. Bug-eyed, the soldier dropped his sword and clutched the fletching of the arrow sticking out of his neck. He turned his head toward Tan, then landed backward, crashing noisily to the floor.

Tan snatched his quiver and sprinted past Kruush. "Hurry!"

Kruush glanced at the carnage, swore to himself, and ran after Tan.

P ETRAH COULDN'T MOVE. HE was forced to watch as Aman helped Sametha down from the stone slab. His brother took her hand.

"That's it, little one," Aman said. "Come with me." Together, they walked toward the center of the rune spiral, to its genesis. Aman let go of her and stepped back.

Small bursts of air struck Petrah in the chest, the face, and the back.

Demons.

Even though he couldn't move, he could feel their icy touch, like strips of nether metal nipping at his flesh. They gusted in a tight circle, a vortex of ethereal predators spinning toward their prey. In a minute, they'd encircle Sametha and rip her soul to shreds.

Move, Sam!

He couldn't warn her.

Frustration turned to anger.

Anger turned to fury.

I must stop him.

Aman was the fulcrum that would tip the balance against mankind. He needed to be neutralized, here and now. Even if Petrah sacrificed his own life, Aman would finish what he started without him. The gateway to Acia was open, Aman claimed. The Watcher's assertion that Petrah was the Key was a farce. Sametha had tried to tell him.

No, I must kill him.

He had asked Sametha if there was a way. Only a true death would suffice, she had told him. The utter destruction of the soul, and nothing less. But none of that could happen, frozen here like a twisted statue. Petrah had to break free.

How, damn it?

Petrah recited Copper Still and dropped into a meditative trance. He cleared his thoughts and sent his mind in search of a solution.

A question Master Nole once posed came to him. The mage had asked the class how they might snuff the flames of a burning cask of oil. *How would you extinguish the fire?*

Petrah's classmates had given a variety of answers, but only Petrah gave the one that resonated with the mage. He had glossed over its simplicity, but as his instructors said repeatedly, the best solution was often the simplest one.

I would will the fire away.

Strength filled his hollow cavities. It gave him clarity and control. Petrah willed his left leg to move, and it moved.

He focused on his right leg, and it bent at the knee.

His arms released next. Then his hips, shoulders, and the rest of him.

Placing his palms flat on the floor, he pushed away. He shifted into a crouch and rose to his feet. He was free.

The garnet-robed priestess recoiled with a gasp. Her staff, a symbol of control a moment earlier, wavered in her grip. Her astonishment turned to a scowl, darkening her face. She stepped back, shifted her weight, and angled the staff as a weapon. With a swift, practiced motion, she swung at Petrah.

Petrah reacted instinctively, deflecting the blow with pure thought. Before the woman could take a second swing, Petrah gripped the metal shaft with his mind and brought it crashing down on her face. Bone cracked, blood spurted from her nose, and she shrieked. She reeled, lost her footing, and fell to the floor, blood streaming down her chin.

The robed man beside her drew his dagger. He swiped once, fast, across Petrah's midsection. Petrah could barely throw up an invisible barrier in time to stave the blow.

He sensed the weapon and jerked the handle from the man's grasp. The handle flew into his palm. A word of power sent the priest flying backward into the urn with the burning incense. Urn and man toppled, striking the floor in a tangle of hot coals that sent him flopping madly.

Petrah's heart raced, and his hands shook. His eyes darted left and right, scanning for danger.

His sharpened senses picked up the swell of his brother's aura, the cold storm of malevolence. He turned to see Aman standing calmly within his churning field of dark power, fierce, blue eyes fixed on Petrah. Beckoning, daring. An unspoken challenge.

Petrah hefted the dagger. Although heavy, the leather-wrapped handle molded just right to his hand. The substance, the feel of it, steadied his nerves and subdued the panic fighting to overtake him.

With a firm grip on the weapon, he stepped toward his brother.

T AN AND KRUUSH HID behind the feet of a giant winged statue. At any moment, guards would come bursting through the sanctum door and find them. Surely someone would stumble upon the dead guards outside the shrine or find the litter of bodies leading to the sanctum.

A mace and arrows were no match against a detachment of heavily armed soldiers.

Kruush thanked the stars Petrah yet lived, but something was wrong with the lad. He and Tan had arrived to find Petrah on his knees, in an awkward, frozen position, as if he were paralyzed. Was it the chanting from the priests that kept the boy from moving? Or was it his brother? When Kruush saw the Grand Marshall in his midnight black robe, he swore to himself. Something was off with the man's raiment, as it seemed to come alive with contrails of flame writhing over its surface. Or maybe it was the light and the suffocating fumigation of incense.

Tan whispered to Kruush, "I have five arrows left. I'm going for Aman first. Then I'll use the rest to buy you time to get to Petrah. Be ready to move."

Kruush squeezed the haft of his mace. "I'll bash anyone who gets in my way. Just make sure you hit what you're aiming at."

Tan took a knee and edged himself to the inside arch of the statue's foot. He nocked an arrow.

As Kruush anticipated Tan's first shot, the chanting stopped.

The silence lasted only a moment. Then a buzzing started, accompanied by a stench reminiscent of feces burning in a field. The flames flickered madly on the torchiers. A chill seeped into Kruush, driving into his bones and stirring up primal fear.

A loud hiss carried through the air.

It prickled Kruush's skin as if a river beast were crouched behind him, exhaling slowly on his neck, poised for the kill. Kruush's round face was taut, his eyes wide with fright.

Gods, what's happening in this cursed place?

It was at that moment Kruush saw Petrah's body twist into a grotesque bend and go rigid. It lasted maybe five seconds before Petrah freed himself of it. Petrah dispatched one garnet-robed priest, then the other, finally turning on Aman, dagger in hand.

Tan drew his bowstring. There was a single target in the chamber that counted, and he trained his arrow on him.

Kruush readied himself to spring into action.

P ETRAH STEPPED TOWARD HIS brother, armed with his dagger and the hope he might break the spell over Sametha long enough that her soul could be put to rest.

I won't fail you a second time, Sam.

Aman didn't move or back away, nor did he exhibit any concern. "I underestimated you. You *are* a killer."

Petrah came closer. The air around Sametha stirred. She had seconds before the demon vortex had her.

Aman pointed at the dagger. "What do you think you're going to do with that?"

"What I need to do. I won't miss again."

Aman scoffed. The dark river current of his aura contracted, tightening into a razor-sharp band of black. "This is the end. Father will have to stitch you back together by the time I'm finished—"

Aman staggered forward. He looked down, dumbfounded at the arrowhead sticking through his right shoulder. His aura warped, distended, and billowed, losing its cohesive shape. He turned just as another arrow skewered his left clavicle.

Petrah looked to the source. An archer, perched behind the foot of one of the stone angels, had loosed his bowstring. He drew a third arrow from his quiver just as the door behind burst open. Soldiers rushed in, seizing him and another man. The giant form of Lord Verek towered above all of them.

Aman screamed at his soldiers. "Bring them to me!"

Petrah saw his chance.

He moved stealthily while Aman had his back turned.

The soldiers dragged the would-be assassins onto the floor and ripped off their helms. Petrah's eyes met Tan's, and he froze in place, but only for a second.

Aman wheeled toward Petrah. Madness boiled in his fire-hot eyes. It morphed into surprise as Petrah lunged. A shroud of blackness fell upon Aman, but it wasn't enough to save him.

Petrah jabbed lightning-quick, as Taka had taught him. No preamble, no warning—just raw speed and ferocity. Into the dark the blade went, swiftly and accurately. It found its mark, striking flesh, then bone. Petrah withdrew the blade equally fast, and the cloak of darkness vanished. Aman stumbled backward, howling and clawing at the bloodied cavity where his left eye had been.

The whirlwind of demons scattered, slicing the air haphazardly.

Petrah wasted no time.

He ran over to Sametha, who stood still as stone, gray pupils looking nowhere. He shook her shoulders. "Sam!"

Her vacant eyes turned upward toward him. "Petrah?" Her voice was hollow and eerily distant.

"I'm here. Look at me." She did. She was saintly, even in death, with pristine gray eyes, unblemished skin, and long, white hair. Just a child. The idea of it knifed Petrah's heart. She had been deprived of a full life, a life that could have been whole and virtuous. Death was the only answer now. "You're free, Sam. Do you hear me? You're free!"

She mouthed a frail *thank you* and collapsed.

Petrah knelt and took her lifeless hand. "I'm so sorry." He kissed the cold skin and placed her hand against her chest. She could be at rest now, Aman's unearthly claim over her vanquished.

A percussive *whoosh* rocked the chamber, shaking the walls to the foundation with a resonating *boom*. The priests all dropped to their knees, prostrating in unison. The soldiers stood where they were, but bowed their heads. Lord Verek forced Tan and Kruush to kneel.

The hairs rose on the back of Petrah's neck.

What he saw didn't seem real. The two stone angels opposite the entrance appeared to move away from each other as if making room. On the wall between them, a black stain spread from the center, pushing outward into an oval void.

San was coming through.

The Father.

His father.

The void was like a lake of pitch, ready to ignite with the smallest spark. Petrah didn't notice the cold bands wrapping around his torso until it was too late.

Something icy seized him from behind.

It knocked his feet from under him and dragged him toward the sarcophagus he had awoken on. It pinned him against the stone side. He fought, but couldn't grab what was holding him.

Aman came toward him, twin arrows embedded in his body in opposite directions, his injured eye unrecognizable beneath a swell of ruptured tissue. Rivulets of blood ran from the gash to his chin.

But he was no longer a livid beast. Aman was disturbingly calm and in control. He held the bloodied dagger that had impaled his left eye in his hand.

The space around Aman grew dark as he stepped closer, curving at the edges, turning into an amorphous haze. From within the shroud, Aman spoke, his voice amplified, as if speaking directly in Petrah's ear.

"Father's almost here," he said in a caustically steady tone. "He asked that I bring you to him alive, whole, and unspoiled. I think the circumstances have changed, don't you?"

Aman's good eye narrowed, and his tone grew stronger.

"The only thing you had to do, brother, was wait for Father. But you had to meddle with that girl, then attack me—your own brother. Everything's changed now." Blood trickled from his chin.

"I took you in as family," Aman said. "I treated you as my kind. I thought we were the same, bound by the ichor flowing through our veins. I was wrong."

Aman pressed the dagger's tip against Petrah's ribs. It poked through his shirt, pushing into his skin. The frigid, invisible bands kept Petrah immobilized.

"Every Unbeliever," Aman said viciously, "every Jovah-lover will suffer. I promise you, a million Samethas will die, every one of them screaming, and their mothers will have *you* to blame. I will whisper your name into the ear of every one of them, and they will cry out and curse your name and beg Jovah to come down and smite you."

Aman twisted the tip of the blade, cutting into the skin. Petrah bit down on the pain. "And that pathetic world of yours, the people you cared about but left behind so eagerly? I will rip fire from the ground and make them cower in fear. I will show them the way to Truth. And they will curse the name 'Immael,' the coward who betrayed them."

Petrah couldn't speak, couldn't breathe. The demon's freezing hold robbed the breath from him.

Aman gripped the dagger's handle with both hands and pushed. The blade slowly penetrated Petrah's flesh. Petrah thrashed and yowled as the metal cut through his skin, fascia, and muscle. Aman put his weight on the dagger's pommel and shoved the blade through in a single stroke, skewering Petrah's lung.

Petrah tried to scream but coughed up blood instead.

Aman spoke into his ear as his collapsing lung filled with fluid. "Father told you to do the right thing. He told you to help me. Now look at yourself. You die in agony. And for what?"

Aman ruthlessly yanked the dagger from Petrah's ribs in a gush of blood and flung it across the floor with a loud clatter.

He spoke in a fell tongue, and the spirit restraining Petrah slammed Petrah onto his back. Petrah coughed and sputtered as his body was dragged across the stone by invisible hands and deposited beside the void.

Chapter 14
Sum of all Fears

PETRAH CLUNG TO THE world of the living. He rasped and fought to inhale. Each breath became more difficult, each one ending in a blood-soaked wheeze. The demon kept him pinned to the stone floor, hissing in his ear, whispering vile words in its fell tongue. Beside Petrah, the void tugged at him, beckoning. Though he was weak and dizzy, he sensed its nether energy, the freezing cold of its rippling surface. How long before his body gave out? How long before the demon could claim his soul and drag him through the void? How long before he ended up a prisoner of his father's domain?

A sweet sound filled his ears, distracting him from his bitter thoughts. The harmony, soft at first, grew louder, rising, rising. It wasn't quite music, but—

A song.

A chorus of mellifluous voices weaving together like silk in a symphony that filled him with rapture.

He scanned the heights for the source of the singing. The song came from above, beyond the domed ceiling. Angels?

Yes, he thought. *Angels. Jah's angels.*

He coughed violently, spat blood, and wheezed another breath. A tremor shot through his body. The demon cackled a sharp, ravenous hiss.

Petrah shook his head. He couldn't allow this evil thing to take him to the Netherworld. If only the angels could see him, hear him . . .

Take me, he pleaded, searching above. *Please!*

He couldn't find the voice, couldn't muster the strength to call out to them. His thoughts were dimming, his vision growing darker.

If they could just hear me.

He closed his eyes, unable to keep them open. But the song of angels stayed with him. He drifted off to their sweet, soothing song.

T HE ANGELS OF THE Above abided by the Oath. Since time immemorial, the Oath forbade them from entering the mortal plane unbidden. Only if summoned could a celestial enter the realm of mankind, and even then, the celestial risked Judgment.

But one angel dared to pierce the ethereal bounds of Heaven and enter the firmament of his own will. He alone dared to break the Oath. Had the dying young man not begged to be taken? Was the fate of the cosmos not at stake? How could the Fallen be allowed to take this child of doom to the Netherworld?

A trumpet blast heralded the angel's arrival. He sped faster than thought on wings of white and entered the great Hall of Angels from above. Through the apex of the domed chamber, a shaft of holy light bathed the still form of a man teetering between life and death. An ill spirit kept the young man captive, claws dug into his flesh, fangs gripping the nape of his soul.

"Begone!" the angel cried, and the demon fled before his holy light.

The way was clear.

Reaching down, the angel pursed his lips against the young man's and blew life into his good lung.

The mortal opened his eyes.

The angel floated above him, encasing the young man in a golden light. "Sleep," whispered the angel. "Beyond the Oath, I dare to intervene and snatch you away from this place. Be at peace. The end has come for you, son of man."

The young man sputtered his words. "Please! Give me a true death." A tear welled up in his left eye and dribbled down his cheek.

The angel's warm words filled his ears in the language of his kind, the tongue of the Above. "*Sollien inna enninia.*" *Rest eternally.*

With those words, the angel waved a hand over the mortal's face. The young man closed his eyes and exhaled his last breath. The angel reached with his hand and grasped the soul.

A thunderous boom sounded. The angel's grasp wavered.

The young man's eyes flicked open. "No, no, no, please, no!"

Unholy fire swept out of the dark, and the smell of brimstone filled the air. The angel put up a shield of light, but it wasn't enough to withstand the assault.

"*I will not allow this!*" exclaimed a voice in angelic tongue, like the cascade of an avalanche.

The walls trembled before the might of a god.

The Master had arrived.

From the void, darkness spilled forth.

The void that consumed his inchoate form curved and shimmered. His shadow spread to either side of the void, ragged and terrible, a penumbra taking the shape of wings. San sundered the angel's shield, sending a great shudder throughout the hall.

"*You dare come here?*" San said. "*Jah will not save you, Yagonel.*"

"*Nor you, King of Perdition,*" replied the angel.

The air hissed and grated. "*He's mine. Mine!*"

A fell command rent the shaft of light shining down on the chamber floor, and it disappeared. Then, without mercy, San grappled with the angel.

Their struggle was furious, dark pitted against light.

The angel was mighty, his fortitude great, but not as great as his adversary's. No blessing, no amount of divine virtue was enough to stem the inevitability of his fall. San wrested his willpower, sapping the remaining light until it was no more.

The angel shrieked.

Then the darkness closed in, and the angel was gone.

H E WASN'T SUPPOSED TO be alive.

Hadn't the angel promised him eternal peace, true death? That promise was forsaken.

Petrah had felt his spirit pulled away for the briefest moment, releasing him from pain and worldly concerns, lifting the chill, and bathing him in warmth. Not the heat of a campfire, but a cloak of comfort, like a babe might feel nestled against his mother's bosom.

Now he was trapped among the living, injured, and cold, about to be transported to the Netherworld.

I can't go. I won't go!

Petrah lay mere feet from the void through which the Father had entered.

A father, he realized, whose only connection to him was through divine seed. Not the paternal sort who might have heard his first words, helped him walk, protected him from strangers, molded his view of the world, and seen him grow from boy to man. He was none of these things, yet he claimed Petrah as his. Like property. Like what a slave owner touted as his own. Petrah had endured four torturous years of slavery.

The Draadi had beaten him, whipped him, and used him for their foul needs.

The black gateway hung on the wall as an empty portrait with concave edges, as if drawing the surrounding light inward.

Get up!

Petrah wasn't dead yet. It hurt to breathe, but he wasn't coughing up blood as before. If nothing else, maybe he could cause enough of a distraction so his friends could escape.

Petrah craned his head.

A nebulous swirl hovered over Aman's kneeling form. It might have been an angel, save for the deep red aura that projected unquestionable dread. Even with his blurry vision, Petrah knew who this was.

San.

Sag-ahn.

Shay-tan.

Lightstealer.

Darkwreather.

He had many names, but he was, without question, the God of Darkness.

The swirling presence bathed Petrah like a blanket of ice crystals as it focused on Aman, who spoke entreatingly to his father. The priests and soldiers around them were still as night, heads not daring to lift. Tan and Kruush too. His friends were positioned in front of Lord Verek, like a pair of pebbles before a mountain.

Petrah concentrated on Kruush.

See me.

Kruush turned his head up. He caught Petrah's eyes with an astonished look. Petrah nodded to him, and Tan as well. *Ready yourselves.*

San's response to his favored son sounded like a peal of thunder. Aman was flattened instantly against the ground. A horrible mewling followed. Petrah hoped San would crush the life from him, but he knew his brother would be spared. San would only be preoccupied with Aman for so long.

Petrah needed to act now.

He tried to move his hand.

His skin was cold, almost devoid of feeling, yet he curled his fingertips.

Don't stop. Keep trying.

He wiggled his fingers next. Then his feet. Each breath was painful, but he'd endure ten times the pain if it meant saving his friends.

But go where?

The void on the wall drew his attention. It tugged on his numb mind. It was as if something were coming through the black, like music.

No, not music.

Singing.

Perhaps an angel, or . . .

Mina!

He heard her voice, or maybe he imagined it—soprano and sweet, singing to him the words of a Con-jurahn lullaby.

It's not her. It's not real.

But what if it was? What if she was there, just on the other side, waiting—

Could the inky window take him to her?

Could it take him home?

It wasn't just a void.

It was a portal!

If it could usher the Father into the mortal realm, it could lead elsewhere. Perhaps Heaven. Perhaps the Netherworld. Or maybe—

Petrah coughed up blood.

Don't die yet.

The last time he died, he was reborn in Acia. But if his friends died—

Then save them!

He calmed his painful breathing to a steady wheeze. He calmed the chaos in his mind and let his raging thoughts settle. He heard the voice of a child, a sweet, innocent white-haired girl who told him the raw truth of who he was and what he was capable of.

You're the chosen son, Petrah.

He could learn from the Con-jurahn magi, maybe even the mythical Malaji. He could learn to shape his abilities into something that could stop his brother. Or he could dig deeper, deeper into his mind and unearth the secret Sametha said was buried inside—an equalizer with the power of a god.

Her voice shouted to him: *You mustn't use it, not ever!*

She was right. He needed to find another way to stop his brother.

Master Maglo had taught him that souls were nothing more than vibrations of pure energy tethered to the flesh throughout life. They could be released, however, and not just through death. To reach one's deepest potential as a mage, one had to set the mind free from the body.

Shut out the wind. Quiet the storm. Be an island unto yourself.

Petrah closed himself off to the shooting pain in his chest. He quieted his gasping and the smother of dread and imminent death. He flushed the extraneous thoughts and hushed his mind.

Time slowed around him.

He felt outward.

There was the stone floor beneath him, with all the tiny pits in its imperfect surface, and the puddle of coagulating blood under his body.

Farther.

He detected the void and the way its edges lapped at the mortal world like a tidal pool. He sensed the obedient soldiers, raked with fear, and the prostrated priests, dutifully praying for their salvation.

Farther.

He wrapped giant, invisible hands around the bodies of the towering stone angels, testing their weight and weaknesses. One, in particular, the one nearest the door, had a stress fracture running up from the foot to the calf to the sculpted hamstring.

Farther.

The hemispherical dome stretched above, culminating at its oculus. Stone voussoirs ran between vaulted ribs, creating compression on the circular wall and rotunda below.

Petrah felt along the stone cornice blocks. There were metal tie rods embedded in masonry channels, loosened with age.

Push.

He bent his willpower to the task. He pushed on a tie rod.

It resisted at first.

He reapplied the force as Master Nole had shown his students, adjusting the angle of attack to take advantage of the most vulnerable point. This time, the mortar encasing the rod cracked, and the metal shoved through. The cornice fractured but held.

He repeated the process on the next rod. The cornice split horizontally, then part of it broke off. Pieces fell to the floor below. One soldier looked up and scratched his head. A second one rubbed his chin, equally baffled.

Petrah ignored them and worked faster.

He detected multiple rods and used his invisible fingers to push on the ends of the most susceptible ones. They inched through their masonry channels, destabilizing not only the cornice but one of the stone ribs above the spot where the soldiers were concentrated. Spidery fissures shot through the stonework.

Petrah blocked out the burn in his throat, the bile-like taste in his mouth. He shut out Aman's beseeching with his father and the coalescing of the shadowed shape of San into human form.

He projected an image of falling stones to Kruush, in the hope his friend would take heed and prompt Tan to prepare to run. He then projected an image of the void, the gateway that would ferry them away, either to safety or their own demise.

Twist.

He mentally pushed on the voussoirs adjoining the weakened stone rib while pulling on the rib, creating torsion. Silt showered the chamber floor. Soldiers and priests looked up. A few exchanged glances or headshakes. Petrah grabbed a second rib with his thoughts, wrapping unseeable tendrils around the base of the arch, using it as an anchor.

Now pull!

Petrah pulled on the damaged rib. He strained with his mind, letting out an audible groan.

The rib cracked, and the arch buckled, releasing a tapered stone, then another, then a shower of them, relieving the integrity of an entire arched section of the dome.

Cries and shouts of dismay rose as the waterfall of blocks hammered those below in a merciless torrent, sending up a cloud of dust. The adjoining sections broke loose, sending a second wave of stones plummeting.

By the time Petrah looked down from the storm of ruin, the entire hall was in chaos.

K RUUSH SAW THE CEILING collapse in his mind a minute before it happened. It was a startling image, giving him momentary lightheadedness, followed by a close-up of the black ellipse hovering just above the floor, across the rotunda.

Kruush caught Petrah looking at him, a man as close to death as any could be. *He's warning me.*

A glance at Tan, and Tan nodded. He'd seen Petrah too.

The first pieces of ceiling fell, and Kruush signaled Tan with a couple of rapid blinks.

Not yet.

He tensed and listened for the sound of sundering stone.

The towering captain of the guard stood behind him, breathing on the back of his head like a belching furnace. Several more soldiers flanked him and Tan. If Kruush tried to escape them too early, they would cut him down.

There was a loud crack. He blinked again.

Now!

He and Tan jumped to their feet and sprinted toward Petrah. A shuffle of movement sounded behind them, but it was drowned out a moment later by the deafening downpour of debris. He didn't look at Aman or the swirling darkness of San.

Kruush and Tan skidded to a halt beside Petrah's prostrate form.

"Petrah!" Kruush called. He shielded Petrah with his body as the dust cloud from the collapse caught up to them. It coated everything in a thin film of white while a haze of dust remained all around.

Petrah looked up as Kruush swatted the air to keep the white powder from settling on his face. The lad was a mess, his shirt soaked through with blood, and more blood pooled beneath him. He tried to speak, but coughed weakly instead. He stopped his coughing long enough to mouth one word: *portal.*

"Tan, help me," Kruush said. He spat chalky paste from the dust that had mixed with his saliva. They each scooped an arm under their injured friend's armpit and hauled him up. Petrah wheezed. He dangled limply in their arms.

The black void hovered about ten feet away, wobbling along the surface, like the rippling of water on a lake. Everything in Kruush's mind warned him to stay away, but Petrah had made it abundantly clear their only way out of here was through that thing.

Krell dung and piss!

He nodded to Tan, and together they dragged their poor friend toward what might very well be their end.

PETRAH BREATHED ONE AGONIZING diaphragm contraction at a time.

The tendons in his neck strained to keep his head upright as his friends dragged him. His heart palpitated in his chest. His lower body was leaden, pure deadweight. He focused on the void. How could he get it to take them to Acia instead of the Netherworld?

Aman's voice carried over the echo of the stone pileup as the surge of crashing material tapered off. "Stop!"

Only a few feet from the void.

Keep going!

Kruush and Tan carried Petrah another step or two before Petrah was yanked backward from their grasp by unseen means and landed on his back with a painful shudder.

From his inverted view, Petrah saw Aman standing caked in grayish-white powder and reaching out toward him with his hand. Their father stood behind Aman, no longer winged or wreathed in shadow. San was fully formed now, unmarred by the pulverized stone that coated everything around him. He was not too unlike the stone angels still intact among the rubble of the collapsed dome: fair-faced and naked, with skin that took on an ebony glimmer, black hair that flowed as if stirred by a breeze, eyes of obsidian that seemed to stretch as the nighttime sky, dotted with stars. The god's lips parted like a bath of oozing tar to utter a single word in the angelic tongue.

"*Son.*"

It reverberated in the ruined hall, a hammer upon the anvil.

Petrah's body dragged helplessly along the floor toward Aman's outstretched hand. He clawed the ground, but the invisible tether was too strong. In seconds, he would be at his brother's feet, a bloodied heap for his father's taking.

No!

Petrah hadn't lost Sametha so he could hand over whatever secret power lurked in the depths of his sleeping mind. He wasn't just a cog in the wheel of fate. He was a shaper of his own destiny, the captain of his own ship.

Jayeem had taught him how to command a vessel. To unfurl, hoist, and sheet the sails. To perform tacking maneuvers to change position. To feel the wind and know instinctively how best to steer the boat.

What if the portal was like a ship? What if you stepped through to board your craft, and from there, guided your ship? You would have to direct it if you wanted to reach a particular destination. Otherwise, it would go wherever the cosmic wind blew. Sailors used the sun and the stars to guide them, charts and landmarks to let them know they were on course, and their instincts to make sure they arrived safely at journey's end. The cosmos was full of landmarks, each unique from one another. Was Acia any different from Dagoth? Terjurmeh from Meerjurmeh? Elmar from Hōvar?

They're all different, all unique.

Oceans that became rivers and then ports.

Each port a destination. Each destination distinctive.

A mariner could discern one from the other and guide his ship home.

The void tugged at Petrah as he scraped across the floor, like water lapping at his feet along the shoreline, beckoning. A vast sea awaited him beneath its surface, ready to be sailed across. It just required a helmsman to take charge.

But how could he get there?

The answer lies in the dark.

It was the epiphany he'd had while talking to Sametha, stemming from a memory of his private audience with the Seer, Baaka, as a mage apprentice.

You must bind with the dark, Baaka had told him during their meeting all those months ago. *You must glean the secrets of angels, borrow the stealth of demons, and tap into the unfathomable well of providence from the Father. You must become your most vulnerable self to become your most capable self.*

Petrah had shirked the dark, hated everything it stood for, and shied away from how it frightened him. Yet in it were the answers he sought. In it was the solution to his dilemma. To face his fear, he had to embrace it. To embrace his fear, he had to open himself up. To open himself up was to make himself vulnerable.

Become one with it.

He dove deep into his mind, into the black, into the nether reaches where fear festered and bloomed. He smothered himself in it, cloaked the terror about him like a blanket, and used it to stoke the furnace of his resolve.

Bind it!

With a strangulated cry, Petrah issued a word of power. It was different from any other he had uttered—sharper, jagged, and black as night.

Aman blew backward.

The sudden movement caused him to lose his hold on Petrah.

Petrah was free!

Without the invisible tether to hinder him, Petrah reached out to the void. He grasped either side with his mind and pulled. The void stretched out toward him, tugging, tugging . . .

Petrah imagined himself compressing like a spring. He pictured his body as a missile cupped in the bucket of a catapult, waiting for the restraining rope to be cut.

He severed the cord in his mind . . .

. . . and shot forward.

The momentum sent his stomach into his throat as his body was propelled toward the hovering bullseye. He whipped past his friends before he could take in their astonished faces.

Like diving into a lake, he plunged into swirling black and decelerated immediately, flipping overhead in ether. The space carried no sound and emitted no light. Nor did it give off any scent or heat. It was thoroughly empty.

Two more bodies plunged in after him. He let go of his mental hold that tied him to the portal and pulled the edges of the gateway toward him. They resisted at first, wobbling in a sinuous motion, holding their form a moment longer. Then the aperture of the void burst like a bubble, leaving no trace of the Hall of Angels or the world of his birth.

He was left floating in a vat of perfect stillness, drifting, drifting . . .

"NO, NO, NO!" AMAN cried as he came to his feet.

He clenched his fists, knuckles turning white, skin surging with nether power. He struggled to contain the raging storm within him. How could Immael have escaped? How could that worm have gotten away from him?

The shadows whispered to him, but they offered no answers, no solace for his failure.

The hot plume of rage pulsing in his face morphed into a seething ball of cold that settled in his core. With it came the daunting revelation that he'd not only failed himself, but his father.

The dark god drenched him from behind with his frigid, sweeping shadow.

Aman's fists went flaccid—his power gone, his hands turned feeble, weak, and trembling. It was as if he was standing at the edge of a cliff, overhanging an endless chasm with the full weight of a mountain behind him, pressing down.

Slowly, he turned. He looked up with his one good eye at the writhing mass that was his father. Sag-ahn enveloped him with a pitch-blackness that foretold pain and punishment. The unyielding shadow squeezed him from all sides, tightening him in its noose. No magic, no power, could save him now.

"*Father*," he begged in the tongue of the fallen. "*Let me redeem myself.*"

The darkness gripped him by the throat. A second later, it ripped him from the mortal plane and carried him into the depthless black of the Netherworld.

Chapter 15
Back from the Dead

Tʜᴇ ᴀɪʀ ʙᴀᴋᴇᴅ ᴡɪᴛʜ a familiar warmth, laden with the scent of honeysuckle and burning clove incense.

Petrah felt a cool palm press against his forehead. He looked up to see Ahleen's face looking down on his, with concern at first, then delight. She had her long, brown hair braided, and her cheeks were fuller than he remembered. Or perhaps he'd seen so many gaunt faces recently, he'd failed to notice a healthy one. Or perhaps she wasn't real at all.

Can the dead smell honeysuckle? he wondered. Did they fill with gaiety and the sudden desire to laugh out loud? Did they have the urge to cry, because of how beautiful the living were to them? Did they feel anything at all?

Petrah felt all of these things.

He wanted to sing and shout and act silly as a child. He wanted to embrace the young woman standing over him—one of his closest friends and forever a sister to him. But mostly, he wanted to savor this moment as if it were his first.

"Ahleen." His voice was croaky. He tasted mint from the salve on his lips. He was lying flat on perhaps the softest bed of his life, or maybe it just seemed like he was floating on a heavenly cushion. Was this the afterlife?

He reached for the necklace his mother had given him, the leather cord with the glass matia, the all-seeing eye.

"How long—?" A tickle in his throat made him cough.

"Three days," she said, adjusting the strap of her cream-colored dress. The freckles on her delicate nose were darker than when he last saw her, and her skin was a healthy bronze. "Here, let me get you some water."

Ahleen helped him upright and placed a pair of down-stuffed pillows between his back and the headboard. His ribs ached from the movement. They should have felt more sore, and his breathing should have been more painful. How could he draw a clean breath without wheezing, without hurting, after having been impaled in a lung? He looked down to see a dressing wrapped over his bare chest. Had he undergone surgery? Or had that angel done more than keep him alive?

Ahleen poured water from a pitcher into a hollowed alabaster cup and handed it to him. He took a long drink. It hurt to swallow, but the water refreshed him and cleared the mist from his mind. At least he wasn't cold anymore.

"How do you feel?" she asked.

"How do I feel?" How did anyone who was given a second chance feel? How did a toddler feel when his mother smiled at him?

Dark memories from his encounter with his brother came flooding back, squeezing the contentment away. He looked at the bed poster to the right of his feet, Ahleen's question forgotten. In his mind, he saw the small hands of a brave young girl with storm-gray eyes grasping the wood, waiting to talk to him.

Oh, Sam, I wish we had more time. I wish—

"Petrah?"

He turned back to Ahleen, slack-faced.

"Is something wrong?"

"Not at all." He lifted the corners of his lips in an attempt to put up a good front. "I'm fine, really." Then he added, "You have to stop taking care of me every time I'm injured. It's embarrassing."

Ahleen smiled radiantly for a moment before her expression changed to concern. "*You* should take better care of yourself then."

"I should."

Petrah looked around the room. "Kruush, Tan, are they all right?"

Ahleen knitted her brows. A flicker of unease reflected in her eyes. She cupped her belly protectively, as if Petrah's question had jabbed her in the gut.

"Well enough, but skinny, like you. My husband was a stick when he showed up, and Tan was even worse. You, though—" She shook her head. "You're the skinniest by far. Just skin and bones." She took a seat on the side of his bed.

"But you're sure they're all right?"

"Yes. You were the only one who needed mending."

He was relieved to hear that. "Are they here?"

"They're here." She exhaled heavily. "They're with Mokan-lee at the moment, still ironing out the wrinkles from your extended"—she cleared her throat—"*disappearance*, I'm sure. Mokan was far from pleased about everything that's transpired since your departure."

Petrah could only imagine poor Kruush and Tan having to explain themselves. "It's my fault. If I hadn't insisted on going east, they wouldn't have felt compelled to accompany me. They were worried I'd get myself killed."

"But you're not dead. And neither are they. I, of course, was at my wits' end worrying about the three of you. I knew right away something was off when I received my husband's letter after I came back from Tuur. The whole story about accompanying you on official Green Flame business sounded phony, concocted. Do you know how many nights I cried myself to sleep?" Her hand went to her belly again. She rubbed it clockwise as if to soothe herself. "I subjected poor Lila to my endless worrying. And then the lot of you shows up at the front gates of Montabijon, soaking wet as if you had come crawling out from the Tangeen like muddied salamanders."

Petrah chuckled, but not intentionally, and certainly not to mock her. Her description of their bedraggled state explained the hazy memory of hitting the water.

She narrowed her eyes at him.

"Sorry," he said. "I was just picturing Kruush trying to explain himself, smiling like a donkey—and beet red, no doubt."

Her face relaxed. "That about sums it up. On a more positive note, he's been the sweetest he's ever been. No, 'sweetest' isn't the right word. I think 'fawning like a teenager' is a better way of saying it. It's almost too much." She gave a sly smirk. "Almost."

Petrah asked the question that had been on his mind since he'd opened his eyes. "Is Mina all right? I mean, after what happened in Tuur, when we sent her back home." He had hoped Mina would be here, but it was too much to ask, considering what he'd put her through.

"She's well and good. Well enough, I should say. She cried on the way home, thanks to you. That girl has a lot of growing up to do. Her father wasn't happy with her."

"Nor with me, I would imagine."

Ahleen didn't answer him, but she didn't have to. Mokan-lee hadn't liked Petrah since the beginning. The fiasco in Tuur probably cemented his opinion of Petrah.

Petrah's mother had offered him sage advice: to not give up on Mina, but rather find a way to prove his worth.

A pang of sadness lanced his heart. Not only was Mina not here—which told him she'd been ordered to stay away—but he wouldn't be able to see his mother again either. He desperately tried to hold on to the memory of her voice . . . and those last moments together.

Petrah pinched the inside corners of his eyes, hoping the sudden need to cry would pass.

"Petrah, what's wrong?"

He withdrew his fingers. A tear fell to his lip. He wiped it away. "How much did Kruush tell you about what happened to us?"

"He spared the details, but I know you ended up in Darkforth. I know a lot of bad things happened to you all."

"Did he tell you I found my mother?"

"He did."

Another tear worked its way down his face. "I shouldn't have left her. I should have made her—" He couldn't finish the words. He was too ashamed of himself.

Ahleen placed a warm hand of comfort on his arm. "Oh, Petrah. I'm so sorry. You'll get to see her again."

His mother was trapped in Dagoth, literally a world away. "Maybe in my dreams," he said wistfully.

Ahleen patted his leg. "Come. I know what'll cheer you."

PETRAH HUGGED HIS FRIENDS, careful to protect his still-tender ribcage. Kruush gave him a gentle clap on the back, and Tan locked forearms with enthusiasm. They were gathered in a posh salon in Bokania, alone. Although his friends were dressed in silk robes, they looked as if they'd fallen off a mountain, with purpling bruises and scratches on their faces and arms.

Still, they looked miles better than the last time he'd seen them. Their hair was cut and clean. Kruush's beard was trimmed, and Tan was clean-shaven. Petrah imagined himself looking like a wild man with his knotted hair and scraggly face as if he'd taken up residence with the Idarian hillmen.

One of Mokan-lee's servants brought chilled leek and potato soup with a serving of freshly baked bread. Petrah thought it to be perhaps the most wonderful soup he had ever smelled or tasted. It even had ground peppercorns on top, a true treat, considering how almost every meal in the past month had been tasteless or eaten under duress. Petrah slurped loudly, remembering his Meerjurmehan manners.

"You're going to need a hundred more of those to fatten you up," Kruush said, flashing the rascally smile of a buccaneer. "Not that *we're* faring much better." He slapped the slight hump of his belly, which had been far bigger in the past.

"At least the three of us made it," Tan said. "As they say, three is a very fortunate number."

"There were four of us at one point," Petrah said, remembering their dour guide. "Five, if you count Choola. Do you think he and Sooka made it?"

"If the gray bastard didn't kill them or torture them or send them back to the An-jurah, then maybe," Kruush said. "Sooka had a knack for surviving. Choola was, well, what can we say about him? But if they didn't make it, let's hope they met a quick ending. They were good men, and shan't be forgotten."

Kruush pointed at Petrah's nibbled-on heel of bread. "If you don't eat, you'll be counted among the losses, too."

"Have you patched things up with our gracious host," Petrah asked, "or are we to be on our way?"

The frown lines on Kruush's forehead bunched together. "I admit, Mokan was a tad unhappy with us."

"More like incensed," Tan amended.

"Yes, that," Kruush agreed. "Given the fact our men had been holed up on his grounds, eating his food, sleeping in his beds, with no remuneration, did sour the initial welcoming upon our return. Not to mention that we looked—and smelled, mind you—like wet bandits when we arrived."

Petrah smiled. "I heard about that."

The joviality vanished from Kruush's face. "You were a stone's throw from leaving us for good, lad. The veins on your neck stuck out, and your face had turned an unholy shade of blue. The healer thought your time was up. She had to stick a tube into your chest to re-inflate your lung. A few more minutes, she said, and . . ." He shook his round head. "Thank Jah you survived."

Petrah tented an eyebrow. "Jah, huh?"

"As opposed to . . . ?" Kruush let the thought go unfinished. He changed back to the primary subject, which Petrah appreciated. "As I was saying, we had some mending to do with our good friend and host. I think we've worked it out, wouldn't you say, Tan?"

"I'd say it's a work in progress," Tan said. "Good thing Mokan likes us."

"The point is," Kruush continued, "we're not getting kicked out on our rumps; and that, my friend, is a good thing."

Petrah wanted to ask about Mina. He was eager to see her. Did she feel the same? Or was she avoiding him? Or, worse, had she been told to avoid him, as he'd feared when he and Ahleen had spoken? Instead, he asked, "What happens from here?"

"An excellent question, my boy. Excellent indeed." Kruush rubbed his hands together, a moneymaker gleam in his eyes. "We're thinking about taking our trade business in a different direction. No more import-export with Terjurmeh, especially after, ahem, you know . . ."

"He's talking about trading with the Northern Kingdom, namely," Tan said. "Liquor, furs, woodcrafts, art, things the Meerjurmehan elite might appreciate. In exchange for dusk, of course."

"Not to point out that Terjurmeh has closed its borders to all outsiders," Kruush added. "There are rumors of a coup, with the Temple installing its own government. A unified Terjurmeh, I surmise, will become a dangerous Terjurmeh."

"When did this all happen?" The news concerned Petrah. It reminded him of Terjurmeh's secret alliance with the An-jurah. The promise of war with the Con-jurah threatened to become a reality.

"Right after we left," Kruush said. "Mokan said all caravans from Meerjurmeh have been turned away and any goods confiscated or destroyed. Just imagine if we had traveled back to Elmar, flush with wares. It's caused quite a hullabaloo on the international trade front, I'll tell you. That, and economic turmoil for exports. Hence a good reason to reinvent ourselves while we can. Although, our partnership with the White Hand will be no more—which is a shame really, and a burden on our debt. Still, we have Mokan's dusk we can sell. Tan and I have big business in mind. We hear the Korinian aristocrats in Gōsh have acquired a taste for it, including the Prallite nobility. The question is, do we head north or south?"

Petrah wanted Kruush to talk more about the coup, but his friend was all about business. "Why are we talking about trade? We should be talking about saving Meerjurmeh. It's only a matter of time before the Ter-jurah and An-jurah join forces and attack this country. Why aren't you talking to Mokan-lee about *that*?"

"We have," Kruush said, growing equally irate. "You think we've been sitting idly, eating and drinking and laughing like the old days? That man has priorities: first his family, then his business, and after that, his ties to the leadership of this country. He's a big-picture man stuck with a small-picture view of the world. He doesn't grasp the possible fight ahead, and how enormously complex the situation is. And, again, we are still in the same position as we were in Tuur after you showed me how dangerous the future looked: we're the only ones who know about it. But it begs the question: did we do enough?"

"Enough?" Petrah found the word odd, as if the Glesh equivalent might be better suited. "We've shut Aman out, but for how long? He's not dead. Injured maybe, but very much alive."

"I even got him with two arrows," Tan said. "And then you with that dagger. His survivability is quite impressive, I must say."

Petrah frowned. "Not impressive enough. San will heal him. After that, he will resume his preparation to leave Dagoth. I've already opened the way." *And I can't close the door*, he wanted to add. "We need someone who will listen. We need someone who won't shut us out. Mokan-lee has connections with the Senate and with the leadership of this country. If we can convince him of the threat this country is facing, he can reach the right people, and they can do something about it."

Kruush looked at Tan, then back at Petrah. "That's a bigger mountain to climb than either of the Eastern Gates."

"A mountain worth climbing."

"It's too soon to talk to Mokan," Kruush said. "We need to repair our reputation. We need to heal our bodies and spirits and earn the required respect to be heard. If Mokan-lee won't listen after that, we'll find someone who will. Just think: you've stood before the face of evil, fought it, and lived to see another day. How many can say that? Our sitting here right now is a miracle—one that shouldn't be overlooked, dismissed, or forgotten."

"Believe me," Petrah said, "I keep wanting to slap myself to make sure I'm alive and not interred in a sand dune."

"Indeed," Kruush said. "We owe our lives to you. If not for that trick at the end with the portal, we'd be prisoners in Dagoth—or worse."

Petrah's friends had put themselves at risk to come to the Hall of Angels and save him. "We owe each other our lives. I think it's fair to say we're even." He attempted a smile, but then, in seriousness, he added, "Thank you. You too, Tan."

Tan smiled. "I accept payment in women. By my tally, I'd say you owe me at least three."

Kruush shook his head at Tan. He reached over and gave Petrah a friendly shake of the shoulder. "The tales we'll be telling our children, eh?"

Petrah rolled his tongue around his mouth, tasting the oniony flavor of leeks. "I certainly hope I get the chance." He thought of Mina again, and his chest tightened.

Kruush raised a brow. "You're not getting all sappy on me, are you?"

"I was just thinking of someone, that's all."

Kruush sighed, nodding. "Aye, your dearly beloved. I shouldn't be telling you this because of how your head will swell."

"Tell me what?"

"Your lady's been sneaking around, trying to see you, much to her father's delight. It's quite comical."

Petrah drew a deep, hopeful breath, as if breathing for the first time in his life. "She has?"

"Now don't turn all to mush just because I've mentioned it," Kruush said. "You're not exactly in anyone's favorable graces, if you recall."

Petrah ignored his friend's attempt to dash his hopes. "Can I see her?"

"Are you just thickheaded, boy, or am I talking to you in a different language? You can't see your little inamorata now, nor this evening, tomorrow, or even in the foreseeable future. Got it?"

"But you said she was looking for me."

Kruush rolled his eyes and turned to Tan, who seemed to get a kick out of the exchange. "Am I speaking Jurmehan or—what is that blasted tongue?"

"Glesh," Tan said.

"I don't think I need to remind you of how delicate things are," Kruush said to Petrah. "You know that, don't you?"

Petrah gave a resigned nod of the head. He had a singular thought, and it had nothing to do with his native tongue. Suddenly, all the dark talk about the end of the world didn't matter anymore. He was as nearsighted as Kruush said of Mokan-lee, focused on the smaller view of things—although, to Petrah, Mina's affection was anything but small.

"You look like you've fallen off the side of a mountain," Kruush said. "Cheer up, lad. At least she hasn't forgotten you."

"At least that," Petrah echoed dully. Perhaps his friend was right: beneath the tarnish of silver, there was a shine. He should consider the positives, not the negatives.

"Right," Kruush said, standing. He took a whiff and shriveled a nose. "Let's find you a bath," he said to Petrah. "You stink like a donkey's ass."

Petrah agreed a bath needed to be first and foremost. He very well couldn't run into Mina looking like a mendicant. Now that he thought of it, a shave and haircut were in order too. He was determined to look his best, despite being underweight and freshly revived from the dead. The notion of a bath lifted his spirits.

The three headed out. Before Petrah took two steps past the salon doors, Tan pulled him aside. Petrah expected something serious, but Tan had mirth written over his face.

"What is it?"

"You know he's going to be a father, don't you?"

So the fullness of Ahleen's face wasn't just his imagination! No wonder she was rubbing her belly. "I didn't," Petrah said, already thinking of himself as an uncle. "But it's the gladdest news I've heard this year."

Chapter 16
Bittersweet

AFTER TAKING A HOT mineral bath in the bathhouse next to the manor, Petrah declared himself "truly revived" from the dead.

More like reborn, he thought, feeling invigorated.

He had been careful to scrub the grime away and not get the dressing on his chest wet, although, with the humidity in the chamber with the sunk-in pool, it got damp anyway.

Afterward, Ahleen combed what she could of his tangled hair and cut off the clumps and runaway strands with a pair of scissors she'd borrowed from one of the household staff. She used a razor to give him a clean shave and rubbed oil to smooth his skin. Petrah tried not to sneak too many glances at her belly, still flat, as she stepped around his chair. He thought of the life growing within her and how grateful he was that Kruush had come home safely to her. No wonder she had been at her wits' end. She was with child, a child who would need a father.

Kruush will make a fine father. And I'll be an uncle!

When Petrah looked in the small mirror Ahleen held up for him, he didn't recognize the civilized young man staring back. A young man who appeared older than his sixteen years of age. A young man, he hoped, who would someday start a family of his own.

P ETRAH SLEPT LIKE A babe that night. He woke, not remembering if he had dreamed or not, and he laughed at how wonderful a mystery that was. There would be plenty of dreams ahead. The question was, how many would be good ones?

He met briefly with Kruush and Tan over a hot breakfast of porridge, blueberries, and sweet cream. After, he went in search of a place to meditate. He wandered Bokania, seeking a quiet, outdoor spot, perhaps a place with a view of the grounds and a pleasant breeze. He remembered one on the third floor, with a good vantage point of the sloping gardens. After several wrong turns, he ended up on the terracotta balcony.

Petrah was perspiring, not yet used to the heat. His chest ached from his still-healing stab wound, and he found himself woefully short of breath. He'd meditate for an hour, he decided, before the day got too hot.

Petrah leaned against the alabaster railing and closed his eyes, allowing his breath to return and the ache to subside. He listened to the songbirds among the fruit trees as they sang to each other with their staccato rhythms. He homed in on a bluetail that trilled in dulcet ascending and descending scales. He whistled to match the song, then listened and repeated his call.

Another trill close by made him open his eyes.

When he did, he saw Mina standing on the balcony, dressed in a silk tunic with a pattern of purple j'boun flowers running down and across her waist in a sweeping flow. Her hair was in a double braid with lavender ribbons.

Petrah's heart skipped a beat.

She was even more beautiful than the last time he'd seen her.

Her large brown eyes caught his, and his heart skipped another beat. Then she frowned at him.

"Well, are you going to at least say hi?"

Petrah laughed. The laughter hurt his ribs, and he stopped abruptly.

"That's not supposed to be funny," she said, crossing her arms in mock anger. The furrows in her brow eased up. "I've been worried sick about you."

"I've heard."

He took a step toward her and drew in a warm breath of fragrant air as if greeting Mina for the first time in his life. He was hesitant to reach out and touch her. He certainly didn't have the courage to embrace her. He expected to say something foolish, but she saved him the trouble and spoke.

"I thought you were gone forever," she said. "I shouldn't have fretted so, but I did. I drove my handmaiden Julette to her wits' end, blathering about it. The gods know what rumors have circulated because of her whisperings to the other servants. I can't say I blame her. I was definitely out of character." She looked at him with the intensity of the blinding sun. "You could have died, Petrah. It's not very nice, you know."

He breathed in the floral scent of her hair. "I know." He was maybe a foot away, impossibly close.

She surprised him by placing an appraising hand on his arm. She squeezed, sending shivers racing up to his neck.

"You look like you've wasted away." She gave his chin a delicate push, turning his face sideways. "Yes, quite emaciated." She clucked her tongue softly. "But still handsome."

He took her hand and examined it. He was afraid she might resist or pull back, but she didn't. Her skin was warm and supple, just the way he remembered it. "I'd be remiss if I didn't say you were the most beautiful woman in the world."

She rolled her eyes but didn't let go of his hands. "Now you sound like one of my suitors, groveling at my feet."

He blurted it out before he could even put a governor on his words. "You have a suitor?"

She pulled her hand from his grasp. "Not *a* suitor. *Suitors*." She emphasized the last word, looking at him dead serious before lapsing into a tumble of giggles. "Don't worry, silly. They're mostly ugly or boring. Well, not Liamme. He's quite fetching, actually." Before Petrah could stumble over more of his words, she clasped his hands again, subduing the welling panic in his gut. "The thing is, I don't care about them. They've not stolen the moon and given it to me."

"Stolen the moon? Who stole the moon?"

She shook her head. "You really are quite empty up there when it comes to matters of the heart." She playfully tapped his temple. "What I'm saying, Petrah, is I still care about you, despite . . ." She left the words unspoken.

Petrah knew what she meant. "Despite your father's misgivings." He reluctantly dropped his hand to his side. He wished his mother were here. "Kruush reminded me."

"He did?"

"Yes, painfully so. He said I need to learn my place. I'm of a different pedigree than you."

"What does that mean?"

"It means I'm on the wrong rung of the social pecking order. It means your father will ban me from his estate if he finds us together. It means I need to keep a respectful distance, for now, even though my heart doesn't want to."

A hurt look crossed her face. "So, that's it? You're giving up so easily? You're going to let the others win?"

He saw the heartbroken look on Mina's face. If he kept at it, he'd push her away completely. "No, I don't want to give up. And I certainly don't want anyone else to 'win.' But I have to find a way to earn a seat at the table, as they say."

"Is that so?"

"Yes. To do that, I must earn your father's approval. No easy task. And to earn his approval, I have to prove myself worthy."

"How, pray tell, will you accomplish that?"

A smile slipped out, more at the way she phrased her question than what he had simmering in his head. Still, he ran with it. "I have a plan."

She arched a brow. "Do tell."

He shook his head. "I can't. But you have to trust me. This isn't an overnight plan either. It's going to take some time."

"As long as I'm not an old crone by the time it comes to fruition."

"Absolutely not!" He was surprised by the strength of his reaction. Mina seemed equally surprised. He toned it down. "All I'm saying is that I want the chance to be the one. If I must compete with these—" He couldn't find the will to say it.

"Suitors?"

"Yes, them. If I must compete with these *gentlemen*, I shall. I'll do whatever it takes. Will you at least allow me to do that?"

She looked up at him, the top of her head barely up to his chin. He stared into her brown eyes, hopelessly love-struck.

She nodded delicately, affirming her trust. "Yes. But you must agree that we not hide from my father when we talk. If you are to gain equal footing, you must start off on level ground. Let me handle Papa's overreactions. Do we have a deal?"

He smiled down at her, a smile he would gladly do for the rest of his life. "It's a deal."

She clapped emphatically. An affectionate smile graced her lips. "Will you walk with me? It's too beautiful a morning to stay put. If you're up for it, of course, considering . . ."

He gently prodded his ribcage. It was tender, but he'd endure a climb up a pyramid if it meant having Mina's company. "I'll be all right."

The breeze was blowing stronger now, cooling the air to a sublime temperature. A perfect morning for a stroll. "Where would you like to go?" he asked.

"You decide."

He knew just the place. It stirred up fond memories of a bumbling journeyman captured by the spell of a young lady. A spell that still captivated him. "How about the garden where you first told me your name? I think that would be an excellent destination."

She gave it a moment's consideration, tilting her head thoughtfully. Her braids followed. "Fair enough." A rapscallion's smile crept onto her face, making the browns in her eyes twinkle like a faerie's. "Under one condition. You tell me a story."

"A story?"

"Yes, something adventurous. Something filled with bravado. Perhaps with magic or swashbuckling, but with plenty of danger." Her smile was in full bloom now. "Tell me a tale from your journey. A tale of Petrah the Brave. Surely, you have dozens."

"I could tell you about how we got captured by Machoo and then escaped while being chased by wild dogs."

"Ooh, I think I'd like that."

"Or how I tumbled over a waterfall and then stumbled upon a giant pyramid in the middle of the jungle?"

Mina smirked. "Now you're just teasing me."

"Or maybe," Petrah said, gathering the courage, "I can tell you about how a son traveled across worlds to finally find his mother."

Mina placed a gentle hand on his arm. It felt just right pressed against him. "A story about your mother?" She rubbed his skin with her thumb. "I think I would like that best of all."

He nodded, fighting down the emotions caught in his throat. He blew the hair out of his face, released a long breath, and said, "But first, I'd like to recite a poem Kruush made me memorize before we entered the wilds of Darkforth. And not just any poem, but one penned under the dark of night. A very special one, written from the heart, and for a very special someone." He inhaled sharply. "But only if you want to hear it."

She lifted off her tip-toes. Her eyes grew large with wonder. "A poem just for me?"

"Just for you," he said.

She twirled the tip of a braid with her finger, twisting the hair ever so lightly. Petrah could spend the remainder of the day watching the gentle change of expressions on her face, and the rest of the time just being in her company.

"I would very much like to hear it," she said at last, regaling him with a smile that was pure joy to behold.

Petrah smiled to match. "Excellent, my lady. Shall we?" He presented the open doorway at the end of the balcony with a sweep of his hand and offered her his arm.

She hooked arms and clutched him tight. "I think we shall," she said, and let him lead the way.

Poem for Mina

This is the poem Petrah started on for Mina in Chapter 7, which he completed after returning home. He was inspired by the rain and thunder while in the tower overlooking the Iron City in Dagoth.

Though the skies are dark
Though the clouds weep
I can't help but
Cherish the tears they cast

For they remind me of you
And you remind me of us
We can weather any storm
No matter how strong

Listen to the rain with me
Hear the plink of its song
The patter of its melody
Let us soak in it together

And laugh like the thunder
And splash through the puddles
And dance like the trees sway
Just you and me, forever

Preview of the next book in the series

K EEP READING FOR A sneak peek of **Book 4**, *The Dark that Usurps*

Fireborn

GRAND MARSHALL AMAN ENTERED the temple at the base of the snow-fringed mountain, black cape flowing behind him. He left the setting sun to spill the last of its blood-red light upon the frozen valley. He had only just returned to Dagoth. Soon, he would leave this dying world. But first, he had the most important duty of his life to perform.

Aman passed kneeling priests in ruddy burnooses. They lined an ancient, candlelit corridor of vaulted stone with their heads bowed, chanting in the fell tongue of their forebears. Such sweet music. Aman had missed the sound of mortals during his time in the Netherworld.

He'd paid a hefty price for failing his father. He still bore the scars from where the demons had peeled back his skin with their frozen, knifelike teeth and claws and scorched his skin with infernal flame.

Such pain. Such necessary pain.

His skin would heal, the scars would fade. But the memory of his punishment—*that* he would keep. How else could he learn from his mistakes?

I will not fail you again, Father.

The temple dug deep into the mountain, a forgotten tribute to his god. Aman followed the sloping, spiraling corridor until he reached the granite sanctum that was once a prayer chamber. The head of his priest order was waiting for him, an old man with withered skin and twin chains of devotion crisscrossed over his chest.

"It is ready, Your Greatness," the old man said, inclining his head, eyes averted from the scars on Aman's face.

"Seal the chamber."

Aman moved past him. The brazen door clanged shut from behind.

He strode past centuries-old marble statues, up a dusty aisle and set of broken steps, to the high wall in the back. Torches set into sconces illuminated a large, grooved circle in the wall's bedrock. Twelve chiseled runes marked the circle's edge.

Aman placed a hand against the cool stone. He dipped his chin and whispered.

"Father?"

The torches flickered as if a breeze had stirred.

Son, said a voice in his mind.

"Fill me with your immortal strength," Aman said. "Guide me."

Speak the words.

Aman recited the *Words of Ingress* in the tongue of demons. The north rune grated within the rock, turning clockwise. The east, west, and south runes followed. Then all twelve. They went through three full revolutions before stopping. The torches guttered and went out. The runes and circle glowed in the dark, the pleasing hue of firelight.

The bare rock within the circle turned gray, then silver. Aman saw a dull reflection of himself. He examined his blind left eye. It had healed, grown back after being stabbed out by his brother, that craven scourge who had escaped into the abyss, escaped from him, and most contemptibly, escaped their father. Except for the slight imperfection in the iris, the new eye matched his good one, down to the stark-blue coloration.

The mirror changed to opaque gray, and the surface swirled. Aman saw clouds as if he flew above them.

Forward.

Aman touched the wall with his fingers. The surface rippled like a pond. It had the feel of water. He tested the boundary, and his right hand passed through. The mist of clouds clung to his skin. Beyond, he sensed the thrum of the earth—the foreign land of Acia—and people gathered. He felt as if he were a raptor floating on a current of wind, looking down upon the land.

Closer.

He used the pull of the earth to draw his view toward it.

Clouds parted to show a desolate landscape, rocky and pitted. A mountain climbed from the center, its peak torn open to reveal the fuming, boiling red womb of the earth. Aman reached to draw himself closer. He was met with intense heat and an unexpected shock of pain.

He channeled nether energy to dull the pain, and he probed the lava. Within the folds of molten rock, he found what he was seeking: his Dragon—a being of pure fire, coiled in the shape of a nautilus, slumbering. A babe waiting to be born, waiting to be unleashed upon Acia, to cast it under an umbra of shadow and eternal flame.

"My child," Aman whispered, feeling a swelling in his chest, a paternal pride. His eyes stung from the searing heat, his fingertips blistered. The agony would come later, after he was done, after the nether energy dissipated. But first . . .

First, he would finish his task.

This was the moment he'd waited for his entire life. The moment he set destiny into motion.

Aman's father beckoned.

Now.

Aman held his breath . . .

. . . and plunged his hand into the fiery heart of the mountain.

R AIN PELTED THE GROUND. Steam rose from the mouth of the
volcano, and the smell of sulfur filled the air with poisonous
fumes. Atop a crag overlooking a hewn escarpment scattered with scoria,
a shrine loomed, darkened above by clouds and illuminated below by
reddish light from boiling lava.

The Fire Sect's High Priest of the An-jurahn Temple stood at the edge
of a black granite ramp spanning the bubbling flow. A gust of noisome
wind whipped the ponytail back from his red-stained scalp as rainwater
spattered his face. With both hands firmly gripped, he circled the tip of
his iron-shod staff above him. The clouds swirled in the same direction,
the ones in the center faster.

The priest pitched his head back. His eyes rolled up, exposing the
whites. He chanted in a throaty voice, uttering the guttural tongue of
his ancestors. The words reverberated off the surrounding stone. Lava
spewed and dropped into the seething pool, only to spray upward in even
higher spurts.

Without warning, the rain ceased, and the billowing clouds of steam
evaporated into nothingness.

Thunder pealed and lightning skated across the malevolent sky. The
priest withdrew his staff, but the clouds continued their circular motion.
He squinted and scanned above. At first, there was nothing. Then, he
saw it: shapes among the clouds. They flitted in and out, running in
concentric chains. The sky darkened as the shadows multiplied.

Another priest, garbed in a robe of the deepest red, came out from the
tunnel bridging the inner and outer sides of the volcano.

"High One," he said. "The people are anxious. They await your blessing."

The high priest kept his eyes fixed above.

"High One?"

"Look at them, Suvius," the high priest said. "They heed my call, yet
they won't open the way for San-Jahad."

Suvius glanced up and said, "What about the blessing?"

"Forget the blessing. Don't you see? We must appease the demons. They hunger. Quick, go to the people. Find a virgin—young, but not too young—and return to me. We must have a sacrifice to open the way."

"Your will, High One."

S UVIUS WENT THROUGH THE tunnel to the other side of the mountain. Below, on a rocky slope plunging into a barren valley, hundreds of men, women, and children gathered. Some had faces painted the holy colors of red and black; others bore the consecrated blood-and-oil markings of Sercula on their foreheads. They packed in body to body, praying, separated only by boulders and steaming fissures.

"Come with me," Suvius said to a soldier posting guard at the tunnel entrance.

Together, they picked their way through the congregation. When Suvius spotted a boy with the holy delta painted upon his brow, he stopped.

"San calls upon your family," he told the boy's father. "We need a youngling. Is your son pure and untainted?"

"He is," the father said without hesitation.

The man's son, a thin boy with worried eyes, grabbed his father's hand, but the man pulled free and pushed his son forward.

"Papa," the boy pleaded, "I don't want to go."

"Behave yourself," the father told him. "Don't disgrace us." Then, to the priest, he said, "He is ready, High One."

"Your service is well received," Suvius told him. "I assure you, your son will be taken care of. Come, child."

The boy looked at his father, who nudged him forward. Suvius took the boy by the hand and escorted him to the inside of the volcano, where the high priest waited.

"Come here, little one," the high priest said.

The boy padded over to him. Fearful eyes gazed down at the simmer of liquid rock below.

"You are in San's favor this day," the high priest told the boy. "Keep still for a moment. Don't be afraid. This is necessary."

The high priest unclasped a small, spiked thimble from a necklace resting against his robe and fit it over the top of his right thumb. While holding the boy's chin firmly with his left hand, he used the thimble's spike to trace over the holy delta on the boy's forehead. Blood dribbled and streamed, and the boy's left eye became awash in it. He shook a little, but didn't cry.

"That's it, child," the high priest said. Then, in a stronger voice, he said, "With this holy delta, I anoint thee. Follow me."

The two navigated the narrow expanse of the stone ramp until they came to the edge. There was no guardrail to protect them. Below, the lava writhed. The boy's eyes watered. He covered his nose and mouth from the fumes.

The high priest slipped a dagger from the sash of his robe. He tilted his head back and spoke aloud. "I give you a virgin. With this blood I take, I release his soul. Open the way for us, San-Jahad!"

He cupped one hand over the boy's chin, and with the other, he slit his throat. The boy panicked and struggled as the blood gushed, but the high priest held him tight. He went limp in the priest's arms shortly after. The priest released the boy, and he tumbled into the fiery chasm below, consumed.

The priests watched the skies and waited. The demon-infused clouds continued to churn, unaffected.

"They refuse the offering!" the high priest said. "How could they refuse the offering?"

"Perhaps one is not enough, High One. Perhaps we must offer another."

"Not enough? How many virgins must we sacrifice?" The high priest shook his staff at the sky. "How many, damn you?"

A great peal of thunder responded.

Flitting shapes came together, funneling downward into a vortex, sucking the cloud mass with them. The conduit rotated until it became a column of black. The wind picked up, and soon the priests fought to keep their robes from flipping them about.

The mountain trembled, a deep groan of volcanic rock and the shaking of stone. Sediment sifted from the shrine above onto the ramp, but the priests stood fast. With an updraft of superheated air, the funnel rent the clouds apart. Shafts of crimson light burst through as if the sky were bleeding. Down the vortex spiraled, whistling as it sharpened into a point. It would reach the volcano's rim in a matter of seconds.

"What is happening?" Suvius shouted.

"The demons open the way," cried the high priest.

"They're going to bring down the mountain! High One, we must leave. We must get everybody off the slopes."

Suvius turned to go, but the high priest grabbed his robe and spun him around. "No, Suvius, we can't. They want their sacrifice, and not just another virgin."

"Then who?"

"Everyone."

Suvius saw the red flicker against the high priest's face. It revealed eyes that knew the end had come.

Another quake shook the mountain, this one stronger than the last. The pillars of the shrine buckled, cracked, and crumbled. A large section crashed into the ramp, breaking off a huge segment. Suvius held his balance on the remaining, jutting span of stone for a fleeting breath. Then the rock splintered and gave way.

And he plummeted to the lava below.

FROM A HIGH CLIFF bordering the An-jurahn city of Symorrah, the Watcher witnessed the eruption. Pulverized rock ejected into the air, swelling into a titanic plume of molten debris that came down violently. Lava and scalding ash descended in a radius of inescapable destruction, instantly erasing hundreds of lives. The Watcher gripped his staff as the pyroclastic flow killed every living thing in its path.

"It is the beginning of the end," he said to the scarlet-robed man and woman standing next to him, the Articulates Septamo and Nisheppeh from the Temple in Terjurmeh. "The Great One has plucked his child from the mother, and the child is hungry. Soon, the child will feast on those who don't believe."

Septamo gestured at the smoking mountain. "How long before San-Jahad arrives?"

"A few months hence, when the moon is of blood and the Dragon takes flight from this very place."

Nisheppeh, the more eager of the two Articulates, slavered as if drunk with power lust. "The Dragon's shadow will grow and spread. The godless and Unbelievers alike will cower beneath skies of fire. The Dragon will purify them. They will either commit themselves to the one true god or be burned to cinders. San-Jahad will make it so."

"Behold the birth of a new era," the Watcher said, holding his staff aloft. "Take word of it home to your Temple. Prepare yourselves. Unify your people. Inspire their hearts and souls. Ready them for the fight ahead, for it will be the most important one in the history of this world. This is a new dawn. We must do our part if we are to win."

Septamo inclined his head. "We will, Gatekeeper."

The lava would cool and harden, the smoke would clear, and Symor-rah would birth an army of the peoples of Darkforth—the An-jurah, Idarians, and Machoo—eventually to be joined by the mighty forces of the Great One and the Ter-jurah in the west. They would coalesce into the largest single army the world had ever seen and descend upon the Unbelievers, slaves of the false god.

Samath, the priests called this new age, *Armageddon* in the Jurmehan tongue.

It would be the end for those who prayed to the God of Light. For them, their souls would be harvested and cast into the fiery pits of the Netherworld, to be gorged upon by the demonic children of San's an-gels. For them, there was only one outcome.

Apocalypse.

The trio watched the destruction in silence.

Dusk

P ETRAH AWOKE TANGLED IN his sheets, soaked through to his straw-stuffed mattress, back slick with sweat from another night of uneasy slumber. Outside the guesthouse that belonged to affluent Meerjurmehan businessman, Mokan-lee, roosters crowed in the cool predawn. The sweet scent of grain filtered in through the open window above Petrah's bed, reminding him he was awake.

Yet the nightmares linger.

The dreams ravaged him like the bite from a red-nosed viper, slowly dissolving his insides with venomous fire shooting through his veins. The one from this morning was the worst, filled with disembodied chanting and a girl crying out of the darkness for help. A girl with silver-white hair.

I couldn't free you in time. I'm so sorry, Sam.

Petrah roused himself from his bed and shed the wet sheet that clung to his skin. He tried to rid himself of the awful dream. He fluffed the sheet and stuffed the straw that had fallen out back into his lopsided mattress, but he couldn't stop thinking of Sametha. She had been but a child, an innocent Peshten girl kept captive in Aman's dungeon for her second sight. Why couldn't Aman have let her live?

Because he was selfish. He wanted to sacrifice me to my father. But I freed you in the end, Sam. At least that.

Kneeling, Petrah pushed down on a lump of wadded straw that formed a small hill on the mattress top. As he tilted his head, he noticed more hills. He thumped them with the flat of his hand as if he could stamp out his guilt over Sametha's death. As if he could erase the mem-ories, his mistakes, the things he'd seen.

Not just with Sametha, but his encounter with his brother in the Hall of Angels. And his father.

Petrah shivered, despite the sweat. His father was a sight to make any mortal's blood run cold. San was nothing like Petrah had imagined. His eyes—

His eyes!

Eyes as black as the night sky, like an entire cosmos littered with stars, and deep as time itself.

Petrah shook off the image and donned his camel-hued saba. He need-ed to clear his mind of the dark thoughts, perhaps drink a cup of cha and eat something. He sniffed the air and swore he could smell sulfur, like he had in Darkforth when the Watcher took him to Symorrah to witness the volcano Vanya in labor, the unborn Dragon churning in her molten womb.

Dragons should be the stuff of fairy tales. They shouldn't be real.

Petrah sat on his bed and laced up his sandals. Tan snored on the other side of the bamboo privacy divider that separated their tiny sleeping quarters. At least one of them slumbered well. He doubted Tan ever had a bad dream. The man always awoke with a smile.

Petrah checked to make sure the knots on his laces were nice and tight before he left to fetch a kettle of water for tea. As he leaned forward, his necklace slipped out of his saba. The glass pendant dangled from the cord around his neck, twisting back and forth. His mother's necklace. It was one of two things she had given him. The other was his trueborn name.

Immael.

Petrah mouthed his birth name as another rooster crowed in defiance to the gloaming's first light. He was Petrah of Acia now, not Immael of Dagoth. Dagoth was a dying world, ruled by the Marked.

Yet my mother named me Immael. She did it out of love.

Petrah ran a finger over the pendant—the smooth glass bead of the matia, the all-seeing eye the Dagothans used as a good-luck charm.

Mama, I miss you. I should have never left you over there.

The pang of losing her washed over Petrah, clenching his chest in a vise. Only a month had come and gone since he saw her, but it seemed like years.

Petrah lifted the leather cord over his head and gazed at the blue-and-white matia, at the thumbnail-sized disk of hand-blown glass. He rubbed the glass with his thumb, gave it a kiss, and placed it over his head again.

You'll be with me forever, Mama, I promise.

Whispers drew Petrah's attention.

He peered around the bamboo barrier. Tan still snoozed on his cot. The whispers were coming from the main room, where Ahleen sat on a chair in a simple bodice and skirt. She smiled down at Kruush, who kneeled beside her, dressed in breeches, field boots, and a linen shirt, one hand on her belly, the other on the arm of her chair. He looked up at her adoringly and spoke softly while holding on to the growing life within her.

Petrah stood fast, daring not to speak or breathe for fear of interrupting them.

Ahleen's freckled face was filling out from her pregnancy. Soon, she'd show in the belly. In a little over half a year, she'd give birth. Kruush wanted a son, Ahleen a daughter. Petrah was happy with either outcome. He'd be an uncle to their child.

I'll spoil that baby too. Wait and see.

Kruush disrupted his thoughts. "Are you planning on standing there all morning like a peeping dove?"

"I was going to fetch water for tea and put a pot on the hearth for us, maybe even grab a basket of biscuits from the manor," Petrah said. "Or

I could continue to peep." He smiled. "Actually, I was taking a moment to enjoy the beauty of your love."

"It's true love, don't you forget it," Kruush said. "Not like the arranged love they sell among the elite of this country." He kissed Ahleen's hand. "Isn't that right, darling?"

"Mokan-lee and Lila seem happy enough," Ahleen said. "Theirs was an arranged marriage, wasn't it?"

Kruush raised a finger. "Arranged, yes. But are they happy as we are? 'Happy enough' and 'blissfully happy' are two different things. I prefer the latter. Love should draw people together, not come about because they're stuck together. I think Petrah would agree with that."

"I do," Petrah said. He liked what Kruush and Ahleen had, simple as it was.

Kruush got to his feet. He winced as he did so. "Gods, I'm getting old."

Ahleen patted his gut. It was almost as large as it was before they'd set out to Darkforth. Unlike Petrah, Kruush had regained most of his weight. "Or just growing," she said.

"Aye, that too. Keep feeding me the way you do, and I'll give birth myself. Petrah, I believe you said something about fetching biscuits."

"And water for tea," Petrah said.

"I suspect the stars will burn out by the time you get to it."

Ahleen smacked Kruush on the hand. "Be nice, husband."

Kruush smiled dutifully. "Yes, darling. See, Petrah, you need a wife to keep you in line. An honest woman, mind you, someone with vigor and a good heart. Makes a man of you."

"I'm working on it," Petrah said.

Kruush sighed. "Aye, so it seems."

It was no secret how much Petrah pined for Mina, Mokan-lee's only daughter. And it was no secret how foolish that endeavor was, with Petrah having no title, no land, and no mastership in any trade. A Terjurmehan mage journeyman was nothing in Meerjurmehan society, frowned upon worse than a street urchin. Any practitioner of channeling from the enemy country was considered a menace.

Terjurmehan magi were masters of the arcane, drawing power from the unseen world but also drawing upon darkness, rather than light. To practice these arts in Meerjurmeh was not only forbidden, but subject to the immediate arrest of the offender and imprisonment, possibly death.

Petrah had renounced his ties to Terjurmeh, but he was still Terjurmehan in the eyes of the Con-jurah. It hampered many opportunities, including one Petrah wanted more than anything: to attend the University of Akan and join their magi apprenticeship program.

They wouldn't allow me to attend, not in a million years.

It seemed strange to Petrah that an open-minded society like Meerjurmeh would be home to one of the greatest learning centers in the world—the University of Akan, located right here in the capital city of Hōvar, where scholars and students flocked to and where divine practices were taught—but condemn students who learned their craft abroad.

Petrah had already inquired as to whether the University might accept a student like him, a journeyman willing to undergo retraining. The answer in no uncertain terms: absolutely not. Once taught the dark arts, there was no retraining. The Acadium in Korin offered an antiquated program on the arcane arts, and the College of Andora, farther south, was even less suited to the mystical teachings of the arts. That left Terjurmeh, but it was too dangerous for Petrah to return. There was too great a chance someone might find out he was alive and back in Acia.

Master Joriah must never know. Nor Masters Maglo or Ecclesias or even Ajoon.

It troubled Petrah deeply that he'd never be able to talk to his friend Ajoon again. That path was forever out of reach. Going back to Maseah, where he'd been a student, would mean coming face-to-face with his masters—and those who had the means to deliver him to the Watcher—and his brother.

Then I must remain here, away from—

"Are you listening to me, boy, or are you off in your own world again?"

Petrah looked blankly at Kruush. Kruush's face was scrunched like an unhappy krell's. "Sorry?"

"I was saying we should head out to the oplia fields early. The harvest is due, and we need to have it counted. If you're going to fetch biscuits and water for tea, you better do it now." Kruush cocked his head toward the room divider, where Tan was still snoring. "And wake Sir Sleepyhead while you're at it. We have a busy day ahead of us."

BAREFOOTED FARMHANDS DRESSED IN simple sabas occupied the oplia fields in droves, harvesting the bulbs from the dried plants whose stalks resembled thistles. Woven reed hats shielded their heads from the scorching late-morning sun. They deposited the bulbs in baskets.

Mokan-lee's soldiers patrolled the fields and watched the workers closely. They were dressed in tunics belted about the waist and armed with short swords or bows and arrows, here to ensure no one stole a single bulb. Petrah heard stories of soldiers hacking off the hands of thieves.

Kruush and his workers, Summi and Julan, tabulated the bushels on a clay tablet while Tan counted the bulbs aloud. One hundred twenty-five bulbs per bushel. Petrah noted how similar the Con-jurah and Ter-jurah appeared to each other, thanks to their An-jurahn roots and common lineage: squat builds and sandy complexions, dark-brown hair and rounded cheeks.

Petrah had been told many times he looked like a Prallite from the Northern Kingdom: fairer in skin, more angular in the jaw, and more sinewy, like a Prallite huntsman. No one knew he was from Dagoth, an entirely different world. All they knew was he was different, especially his eyes—blue as the sky.

Mina likes different, he thought. She liked a lot of things about Petrah, and she didn't care that he was a baseborn foreigner. *She likes me for me.*

Milio, Mokan-lee's eldest son of eighteen years, sidled up to where Petrah stood observing the transference of the baskets to a large cart hitched to a donkey. Kruush had assigned Petrah the job of monitoring the tabulation to make sure the numbers agreed between him and his workers. It was tedious and boring, but Kruush insisted Petrah learn the importance of inventory since he'd offered to take Petrah under his wing as a merchant apprentice.

"You look distracted," Milio said.

Petrah pretended it wasn't the case, feigning deep concentration with the furrow of his brow. "Just doing a recount in my head."

"You'll get lost if you do that. This will be our largest yield yet, not something you keep track of in your head. You should be using a tablet."

Petrah frowned, irritated that Milio was right. "Now you made me lose count."

"Did I? How many bushels are we up to?"

Wasn't it thirty-eight or thirty-nine? No, it had to be at least forty. Tan had stopped counting, so Petrah couldn't be sure. Tan was looking over what Julan had written on his tablet while Kruush and Summi conferred among themselves.

"You don't know, do you?" Milio smirked. Petrah hated it when he smirked, because Milio always looked down on him. He hadn't liked Petrah since the day they met, considering him beneath him—a lowborn peasant from another country. "If you hadn't been daydreaming about my sister, you'd know."

Petrah colored in the face. "I was *not* thinking about her." But he was. How did Milio know? *Because I was probably smiling.* Mina always made him smile. "And the answer to your question is forty-one bushels."

"It's forty-four, actually. Do you know how I know?"

"You don't have a tablet, so how could you possibly know?"

"Because the cart is at capacity. Forty-four bushels." Milio tutted.

He looked out of place in his impeccably clean, pressed saba. Everyone else had dust on theirs, small rips or tears, and wear marks on the cloth, Petrah's included.

"At least I've been paying attention," Milio said. "But this is your first harvest, isn't it? It's all new to you."

"The first of many, I hope," Petrah said, trying to sound upbeat and change the tone of their conversation. "I will strive to improve my methods."

Milio flexed his square jaw. His long face and amber skin were just like his father's, although his crescent-tapered eyes were clearly his mother's. "Do you even know what we do with the oplia bulbs?"

"I know you take the bulbs to a storehouse, where they will season further, and that they eventually turn the sap into dusk."

Milio laughed, but it wasn't friendly. "And they say grass turns into hay too, by some miraculous process."

Petrah refused to show his annoyance. Milio obviously believed he was a fool. Well, he would change that.

"Fine, you want to know; I'll tell you. The bulbs sit on wooden racks where they dry. Once they crack open, the sap leeches onto the wood. After it's dried, it's ready. You scrape it off the wood, mill it to a fine powder, and package it in fire-glazed pots that get stoppered, sealed in wax, and stamped with the signet of your house, then inspected by a government official, who grades it." As Petrah spoke, Milio's smugness faded until his lip formed a tight line. But Petrah wasn't finished.

"At that point, the dusk is ready for sale. But it's not legal to sell it in this country, even with the government grade, which is a paradox. You have to sell it on the black market, but you also use it to bribe those same government officials, so they look the other way. With demand being high among the rich, and dusk of the highest grade, like yours, coming at a premium, you make a hefty profit, and everyone is happy. Should I go on?"

Milio kept quiet for a beat, then conceded a nod. "Kruush taught you well." He placed a hand on Petrah's shoulder and leaned in, lowering his voice. "A little advice. Stick to the mercantile disposition of a trader. It suits you well enough. As for dabbling in the affairs of aristocrats, I'd steer clear of any aspirations. But Petrah." He spoke into his ear. "Stop daydreaming about my sister. She's not yours, and she'll never be yours." Milio gave Petrah a pat on the arm and left.

Petrah rubbed his arm as if Milio had punched it. *He's protecting Mina, that's all. It's what brothers do.* But Mikano, the youngest of the three siblings, liked Petrah, and always had, so it wasn't simply Milio's brotherly, protective nature causing him to be an insufferable ass to Petrah.

She'll never be yours.

Petrah fumed, unraveling as Milio's declaration sank in. He wouldn't be surprised if steam came off his skin.

Kruush called to Petrah. He was standing with Tan as Summi and Julan finished checking the baskets on the cart. "Oy, Petrah, come here." Petrah walked over to them. "What was that all about?"

"Milio was testing me on the process of turning oplia into dusk," Petrah said.

"He was doing it more for his own edification than yours, I assure you," Kruush said. "He likes to feel important."

"That the dapper gentleman does," Tan said with a nobleman's flourish of the hand. "Did he ask why we were off by one bushel? We found it behind the cart, in case you were wondering."

Petrah wasn't aware of the miscount. The donkey brayed as if the animal knew Petrah had failed to do his job. "No, but he was full of advice."

Kruush harrumphed. "I'm sure he was. He's taking a liking to you. Don't let his words sting you. He enjoys tormenting you. That one would have you dine with the crows, but only because you don't let sleeping dogs lie."

I can't help how I feel about his sister. Petrah decided against saying it, only because Kruush and Tan had heard it more times than they cared.

Kruush clapped Summi on the back to get the cart of oplia bulbs over to the storehouse. He turned to Tan and Petrah. "Let's take a walk."

The sweet smell of oplia permeated the air as the trio strolled. Petrah ran his hands through the straw-like stalks that jutted from the dry earth, where the bulbous tops had been scythed clean. It reminded him of the field he'd awakened in half a decade ago when he was new to Acia.

"This is the gift of the gods," Kruush said, breathing deeply. "We're lucky to be alive, gents, and lucky to be here. Can you believe, just weeks ago, we were in that godforsaken, frigid wasteland, fighting for our lives? And before that, sweltering in the jungle, one breath away from—well, we know what might have happened to us."

"I still have dreams about those places," Tan said, eyes set on the horizon as if Dagoth loomed beyond. "I wake up in the middle of the night in a cold sweat sometimes." He shivered, as if reliving the experience. "But then I realize I'm in Hōvar, not Darkforth or Dagoth, and my friends are here with me. Unharmed, in good health, and working together." He smiled at Petrah. "It's a good thing, eh?"

Petrah laid a hand on Tan's shoulder. "A very good thing." He took a deep breath of his own. The exhale released the tension from his talk with Milio, easing the knot in his chest and pressure in his shoulders.

He'd assumed Tan had somehow found a secret place in his mind to bury the events of their journey and then locked the memories behind an ironclad gate. But Tan wasn't as infallible as Petrah had gathered. Tan's admission about his troubled sleep heartened Petrah—not that he wanted his friend to suffer, but that Petrah knew he wasn't alone in his struggle to deal with the aftermath.

"I think we can nix those horrid places from our list of travel destinations and instead focus on what's next," Petrah said.

"Aye," Kruush said. "We have a fine harvest. Mokan-lee would be content with selling his dusk to the upper crust of this country, but I see greater potential. We need to expand internationally."

"Terjurmeh closed its borders," Petrah said, navigating the narrow path between oplia stalks. "I suppose there's Korin. Their nobles enjoy the finer indulgences in life, so I've heard."

Kruush grinned, showing his teeth. "So you *have* been paying attention. Shall we set our sights on Korin, then? Travel to Kasâh, the heart of the empire, and make a deal with the imperials? What do you think, lad?"

Petrah whiffed the sugared air. A few oplia blooms had burst open prematurely, releasing their sappy perfume. Some said dusk could be made into an apéritif when mixed with water, liqueur, and exotic botanicals. Others claimed it was best sampled as a powder, sniffed through a silver straw. Then there were those who swore dusk's potential was best realized when set directly on the tongue, where it would dissolve and invoke euphoria, invigoration, and a taste of the afterlife. When Petrah had asked Kruush if Milio or Mokan-lee had partaken in the spice, Kruush simply answered, "They're no fools." Which meant they had abstained, and rightfully so. Its addictive properties were said to rob wealth from the wealthy and turn them into grovelers, destitute and raving mad, and left wanting for the craving. The decoction of sprushah Petrah and his fellow slaves were forced to drink in Kanmar as slaves had destroyed many a mind, so he didn't doubt the downside of a spice as potent as dusk.

"I think we should trade this craft in for a more honorable one," Petrah said.

Kruush laughed in a grating manner. "More honorable, you say? That's poor man's talk."

"Call it what you will," Petrah said, "but nothing good can come of a stimulant like the one you propose to sell. It ruins minds."

Tan put in his worth. "We're in debt, Petrah. If we don't produce, we're done for. Where's the honor in that? Besides, with no way to return to Terjurmeh, we're cut off from the White Hand. We really are on our own. It's true dusk ruins the mind, just like sprushah. And like sprushah, the more you take, the worse the damage. That doesn't stop the Draadi from making the slaves drink their tea. Why should we deprive the rich of overindulging? If not dusk, another vice would consume them. We might as well part coin from purse from those willing to pay. As they say, if one nobleman goes mad, another will gladly take their place."

Petrah didn't want to argue the point with his friends. They'd sell dusk as a nostrum, a cure-all for everything from palsy to impotency, anything the rich wanted to believe. In the end, it would give its user exactly what they craved: an escape from the ordinary. Isn't that what all the bored, wealthy elitists wanted anyway?

"You're right," Petrah said, setting aside his misgivings. "You have debts to pay. Korin is an obvious trade candidate, but several Meerjurmehan merchants have trade routes already established, don't they?"

"They do," Tan said. "That doesn't mean there isn't room for more."

A warm breeze kicked up bits of torn stalks and the syrupy sweet aroma of oplia. "North is where I'd go," Petrah said. "To Prall. The

Northerners are plain people, I've heard, but I believe their nobility would indulge if given the option."

"You've always fancied the North," Kruush said. "You've been drawn there like a lodestone since we left Tuur. Prallites are stubborn, there's no denying it. There are two classes of people up in the highlands: nobility and regular folk. Regular folk have no use for fancy indulgences, nor can they afford it. But the ruling class . . ."

Petrah nodded. "You decided to go there long ago, didn't you?"

Kruush smiled in all his glory. His heavy cheeks bunched cheerily, as full as oplia blooms. "The Con-jurah are afraid to take the risk, but we Terjurmehan businessmen . . ." Kruush's smile broadened. "Why, we like to take chances, don't we?"

"We sent a homing pigeon to the capital city of Durenbeck," Tan said. "The pigeon carried a simple note, along with a sample."

Petrah frowned. "I thought only the Korinians used homing pigeons."

Tan chuckled. "They use hawksters, not pigeons. Same purpose, though. The birds deliver their messages and then return home. A clever way to communicate. Not as good as—what do magi call them?"

"Mind links," Petrah said. It had been ages since Petrah had mind linked anyone, the last person being his former master, Joriah.

"Not as good as those, but good enough," Tan said. "In fact, we received a message just yesterday from Durenbeck. Care to guess what the response was to our included sample and proposal to do business up North?" Tan beamed, Kruush too.

"A favorable one, I take it," Petrah said.

"More than favorable," Tan said. "'Enthusiastic,' I'd say. They want a full shipment. We're going to deliver it. It's an exclusive deal. Mokan-lee is excited too."

"When do you leave?"

Kruush gave him a queer look. "When do *we* leave, you mean? How many times have I told you that you're one of us now, boy? *We* includes *you*. Did you think you were staying here to keep Milio company?"

"Not particularly," Petrah said.

"Then what? Try for the University? See if you can get arrested while you're at it?" Kruush narrowed his eyes. "I'll say this again, just because I know how much wax you have in those ears. Your days of becoming a mage are over. You're with us now, lad."

Before Petrah could reply, Kruush said, "Do you want to prove to be someone worthy of Mina? Or do you want to let her go? Which is it?"

The mention of Mina's name thrust a lump in Petrah's throat. "You know my intention."

"Then listen up, boy, and listen up well. As Jah is my witness, there are only two routes for you to take if you want the slightest chance of currying her father's favor: gain land and title or become a prominent businessman. Seeing you can't pay for a pair of sandals, let alone a patch of dirt, your only option is business. That, as I've said a thousand times, is my forte, which means if you don't want to look like a gonatan, you need to stick with me. So, what do you say, lad? Tend to the pigs or become wealthy enough to purchase your own ranch? The choice is yours."

Petrah looked north, where the sun was near its zenith. The hot disc bathed him in unyielding heat, as if Jah himself were mocking him. Heading north meant months of being away from Meerjurmeh.

And away from Mina.

She's not yours, remember that.

Mina was sixteen, like him. She had several suitors after her, thanks to her father, but that didn't dash Petrah's hopes entirely. As long as he was here, he could divert attention from her suitors.

But if he were to go away for a length of time . . .

"I know," Kruush said, reading his face. "We all do what we must, but we don't always do what we want. Sometimes, it's better that way. Sometimes, it's the *only* way."

Petrah gave his friend a long, conciliatory nod. "North, it is. How soon do we leave?"

"Three weeks from today. Now don't go mucking things up for us, you hear?"

Visit https://www.stevepantazis.com/lod4 to get ***The Dark That Usurps***, **Book 4** in the series, or scan the following QR code.

Appendix A – Reference Guide

1. Overview

This reference guide provides background material for the fictional world of Acia in the Epic Fantasy series, ***The Light of Darkness***. It includes cultural, historical, and geographical references to the societies in **Acia**. It also includes information about the connected world of **Dagoth**. This guide is by no means a full account of the history of these lands, for that would require a book on its own. Instead, this guide gives you an introduction to the people, culture, customs, government, commerce, beliefs, and magic used in these worlds.

2. Acia

For all intents and purposes, Acia and our world are almost identical. There are four seasons, cold and hot climates, similar animal and plant life, and other aspects you'd find familiar. Acia, however, comprises a single populated continent of the same namesake. The civilization is on par with our notion of ancient Egypt and Rome, with influences from Medieval Europe. Except for some variations in wildlife, the flora and fauna match ours. The same goes for the lunar cycles and the number of days in the year. There are no elves or dwarves or mythical races in Acia, only humans. However, there is magic. And we all love magic in a fantasy world.

3. Domains

You can think of a domain as a major geographical region. Six domains in Acia divide the continent. Some domains, like Terjurmeh and Meerjurmeh, are also countries. Others, like Darkforth, are a mix of territories and wilderness.

Domains of Acia:

- **Terjurmeh** is a desert nation, located in the western desert of the Northern Hemisphere. Its populace is a mix of nomadic tribesmen and city dwellers. A single political party controls most secular affairs but is held in check by competing parties. Terjurmeh is also considered a theocracy, where the Temple imposes influence upon the parties and oversees its own militia.

- **Meerjurmeh** is a desert nation as well, located east of Terjurmeh. Except for the city of Canuush-met, its population congregates along the fertile riverbanks of the country. Meerjurmeh is a republic, but like Terjurmeh, the Church greatly influences daily life and uses temporal power as a theocratic umbrella over the country.

- The **Northern Kingdom** is a sovereign nation located in the forests north of Terjurmeh. It's the youngest of the cultured civilizations in Acia, only six hundred years old, compared to Terjurmeh and Meerjurmeh, whose roots go back three thousand years. Its government is a monarchy.

- **Korin** is an empire geographically separated from Terjurmeh and Meerjurmeh by a mountain range. Its reach spans the greatest of any nation on the continent. The empire has a dynastic system like ancient Egypt. The nation comprises twelve major principalities and the loosely annexed Provinces of the South.

- The **Provinces of the South** is a federated set of territories south of the Empire of Korin. The Provinces receive the empire's protection in exchange for goods and services. Each province has its own governorship and governmental system but is part of the federation's council, where participating members collaborate on interprovincial policy and interaction with the empire. Korin prevents one territory's subjugation of another through the presence of an occupational force.

- **Darkforth** encompasses the forested regions to the east of Meerjurmeh and Korin, including the Green Unknown. It's the least understood domain and seldom traveled by westerners. Three dominant cultures coexist and span its length and breadth in disparate clans and tribes. The An-jurah, who maintain close ties with the Ter-jurah at the leadership level, dominate Darkforth.

We'll take a deeper dive into these fascinating domains later in this guide.

4. Time and place

The **story** begins in the year **3387**. All calendars of the world use the **Year One** as the major boundary between modern and ancient epochs. The demarcation point is similar to how we divide CE (Common Era) from BCE (Before Common Era) in our calendar system. In Acian history, the Year One marks the first year following the Great War.

The Light of Darkness takes place across various domains, starting with Terjurmeh in Book 1, then venturing on to Meerjurmeh, Darkforth, Prall (the Northern Kingdom), and Korin in subsequent books.

5. Important historical events in Acia

5.1 Origin of humanity

Acia is a world filled with deeply religious peoples. The notion of creationism is the only accepted ideology of how humans came to be, and each culture has its own story to tell. According to the **Watcher**, **Azazel**, as he relates the story to our protagonist, Petrah, the first people of Acia were created by Jah the Creator from the bones of the Chosen at the behest of his angels. The purpose of this celestial act was to give humanity a second chance to prove their worth in the eyes of the Maker following the corruption in mankind's original world of Dagoth. But, as the Watcher points out, humans are easily corrupted, and their second legacy is no better than their first.

5.2 The Great War

The Great War is the equivalent of our World War I. It took place over three millennia before the start of the story. Its duration spanned forty years. Prior to the war, the **An-jurah** were the dominant people of the north. Sectarian differences led to civil war and division among the An-jurah. Those who believed in the god, **San**, remained An-jurah. Those who believed in the god, **Jah**, called themselves **Con-jurah**. Both sides recruited pagan armies from different parts of the world for their campaign. The **Battle of Jedahn**, which took place in modern-day Meerjurmeh, ended the conflict, driving half the An-jurah to the west where they would settle and later become known as the **Ter-jurah**, and the other half to the east where they would disappear into the wilds of Darkforth and never resurface again. The conclusion of the war signified the end of one era and the beginning of another. The **Year One** is the first year in the official Acian calendar and the first year following the Great War.

5.3 Settlement of Terjurmeh

After the An-jurah splintered into tribes at the end of the Great War, half journeyed to Darkforth while the other half traveled to the western desert of modern-day Terjurmeh. The westerners settled in the Kesel River region in the northeastern part of the country, establishing several communities along the Kesel. The largest of these settlements became the city of **Ekmed** in the latter part of the first century, Terjurmeh's first capital. Upon the establishment of an official government at the beginning of the second century, the nation was officially given the name of Terjurmeh, and its people became known as the Ter-jurah.

During a three-hundred-year transformation, settlers spread throughout the south and west, where they established communities along the fertile riverbanks, and later, the major modern-day cities of Kanmar, Fangmordah, and Elmar. Elmar became the capital of Terjurmeh after Ekmed was destroyed by Con-jurahn invaders in the fourth century. During this same period, the Temple was formed, and the **Codex**, the layman's law of the land, was written. To this day, the Ter-jurah remain nomadic and the system of government is still factional, made up of over three hundred parties.

5.4 Settlement of Meerjurmeh

Sectarian strife among the An-jurah during the years preceding the Great War of Acia gave rise to the Con-jurahn sect, a people dedicated to the worship of Jah, the Creator. After defeating and driving out the fragmented An-jurah, the Con-jurah settled in the **Hōvar Region** in modern-day **Meerjurmeh**. Unlike their nomadic ancestors, the Con-ju-rahn tribes gave up their migrant ways and settled heavily along the riverbanks throughout the country, establishing well-formed city-state governments. Intercity waterway commerce boosted local economies and led to rapid growth in the second century. During this time, the Con-jurah established an oligarchy of governors that ruled for half a century. Meerjurmeh wasn't recognized as a nation until the third century, when the city-states formed a senate and unified under a single leader, backed by the newly formed Church. Modern-day Meerjurmeh is a republic.

6. Terjurmeh

6.1 Geography and climate

Mountains border the landlocked desert nation of Terjurmeh on three sides. The country receives almost no rain during the year. Cities and villages occupy the fertile river regions bisecting the land. The **Juum River** traverses the country west-to-east, fed by the **Fural Mountains**, splitting off into the **Kesel** and **South Kesel** Rivers. Hostile desert surrounds the populated areas. There is an invisible border between Terjurmeh and Meerjurmeh, marked by the end of the **Bunai Desert** to the west and the **Agobo Desert** to the east. Summers are brutally hot and dry in Terjurmeh, and winters are mild.

Three cities occupy the country: **Kanmar**, **Fangmordah**, and **Elmar**, the capital. Kanmar is the largest, but Elmar is the most populous. High walls border Kanmar and Elmar while Fangmordah is open. The **Shrine of San**, located west of the South Kesel, is the equivalent of Rome's Vatican and houses the leadership of the **Temple**. Oases dot the deserts of the country and are temporary homes to nomadic tribesmen. Of importance are **Bea-tet**, in the south Bunai Desert, for its strategic position as a trading post, and **Mingèl**, in the **Wastelands of Derel**, for its salt mining operations.

6.2 People

The people of the country are referred to as **Ter-jurah**. A person from this country may be called **Terjurmehan** (of the country) or **Ter-jurahn** (of the people). The Ter-jurah divide themselves between city and village dwellers and nomadic tribesmen who travel the great wastes from oasis to oasis. Nomads journey the deserts during the cooler months, leaving the cities after the summer-end holiday of Hah'xallah and returning at the end of spring. The cooler weather in the deserts allows them to spread far and wide and engage in commerce in villages scattered throughout the country. Nomads often travel as tribes of extended family members. The more established tribes have **Teradi** as patriarchs, versed in the arcane arts, which help protect their tribes from bandits and cutthroats.

The Ter-jurah descend from the An-jurah, the first non-pagan civilization in the world. They are squat and amber-skinned, like their An-jurahn ancestors, and speak **Jurmehan**, the common tongue of the Northern Hemisphere. The people of Terjurmeh are bitter enemies with their neighbors to the east, the Con-jurah, and have a history of conflict dating back to the Year One. According to the ***Book of Prophecy*** in the

Holy Scriptures, the Ter-jurah are prophesized to rise up one day and destroy the followers of the enemy god, Jah, including the Con-jurah. At the beginning of ***The Light of Darkness***, an uneasy truce stands between Terjurmeh and Meerjurmeh.

The **Mumooni** tribespeople make up a tiny segment of the Ter-jurmehan population and are nomadic by nature. Originally from the **Fural Mountains**, they settled in West Terjurmeh after Kanmar became a major port city. Darker skinned than the Ter-jurah, with complexions that run copper and honey, the Mumooni have stuck to their roots over the centuries, rarely mixing with the Ter-jurah. Women often wear colored beads wrapped around their throats. The beads symbolize the experiences in the women's lives—their joys, struggles, and seminal moments. The youngest wear white beads to show off their virtue. The men often scarify their faces with intricate patterns, similar to the **Machoo Indians**, adding patterns to their faces over their lives to tell their stories. While not directly related to the Machoo, some believe the tribespeople migrated west from Darkforth thousands of years earlier, crossing the Northern Range to the Fural Mountains and then on to the Permal Sea. Pockets of Mumooni remain among the Furals. They trade with the Ter-jurah during the summer months while visiting the cities, and have even accepted Sanism as their religion. Mumooni can be seen as far east as Fangmordah.

6.3 Government

Terjurmeh is a party-ruled government. The **Temple**, the religious authority in the land, defers control of layman affairs to a secular body of parties or factions. The term **faction** can be used interchangeably with **party** because the Temple acknowledges only one party system in Terjurmeh, the "secular" party system, while the laymen consider any organization with a unique charter as its own party. Over time, the distinction between faction and party has blurred to where both terms might be used by clergy and laymen alike, although "**party**" is the preferred term, used extensively throughout *The Light of Darkness*.

Over three hundred parties exist at the beginning of the story, with five major ones in control of the country. Each party runs as a mini-government, with officials, laws, and even troops. The major parties own large tracts of land, and the most powerful rule over entire cities or systems of trade (slave, commerce, and waterways). A secular set of laws, known as the **Codex**, dictates policy for the country. A single ruling party holds the executive power to effect policy and wage war. At the start of *The Light of Darkness*, the **Fist** is the ruling party. The popular vote at the **Great Council**, an annual three-day gathering of faction leaders, affluent society members, and tribal heads (known as **Teradi**), determines whether the ruling party stays in power. Although the Temple keeps out of most layman's affairs, it has the authority to intervene in the affairs of citizens. A devout following ensures the Temple's power remains unchecked.

Despite Terjurmeh's multi-party system, the Fist governs from the country's capitol, **Den Gajjal**, located at the pinnacle of the hilly city of Elmar. The massive black granite complex serves as the center of lawmaking and governance, in accordance with the Codex. The capitol building sits across from the **Dome of San**, the main temple of Elmar, where the city Seer **Baaka** presides.

6.4 Major parties

There are five major parties in Terjurmeh at the start of the series:

- **Fist**. The ruling party in the country. Their dominance is often seen as tyrannical, although their focus on suppressing the people of Meerjurmeh has been received with wide-sweeping support in the past. Support, however, is dwindling as economic suffering and over-taxation take their toll on the population. The Fist has majority control of the cities of **Elmar** and **Fangmordah**.

- Leader's title: **Iron Fist**

- Party colors: **crimson and black**

- Device: a **clenched fist**

- **Black Arrow**. Second-most dominant party, with a stranglehold on the slave trade and control of the **Slave Guild**. The Black Arrow has exclusive control of the city of **Kanmar**.

  - Party leader: **Manis-cor;** goes by the title, **Dark Arrow**

  - Official party colors: **black and gray**

  - Device: **twin black arrows** crossed with their barbed arrowheads pointing up and away

- **Silver Blade**. Until a recently botched government campaign with devastating economic impact, the party held the number two spot in the country and control of Fangmordah. Their support has slipped and threatens to unravel them, but they still have ownership of the **Commerce Guild**, which provides financial strength and grounding for the troubled party.

  - Party leader: **Mras-Leebum**

  - Official party colors: **silver and black**

  - Device: **spear blade**

- **Green Flame**. The most controversial of the major parties. It is a brotherhood of magi, the secular equivalents of Temple priests. Until recent years, it was an obscure party with little support. That changed when **Uhtah-Pei**, Fifth Articulate of the Temple, took over. He is the first clergyman to assume a non-clergy leadership post in over a century. The Green Flame is the main constituent of the **Magi Guild**, the non-partisan association dedicated to magi and Teradi, the mage tribal leaders.

- Party leader: **Uhtah-Pei**

- Official party colors: **green and black**

- Device: **green flame**

• **White Hand**. An unconventional consortium of merchants and traders with a focus on commerce, particularly trade with Meerjurmeh. The party is under continuous pressure to sever ties with Meerjurmeh, particularly from the Fist, but an undercurrent of economic prosperity keeps the party among the top five.

- Party leader: **Degas Sau**

- Official party colors: **white and off-white**

- Device: **hand with palm facing out** and fingers extended

Another party called the **Copper Shield** has made inroads with the country's leadership. They control shipping and the major ports along the Juum, Kesel, and South Kesel rivers and have a standing alliance with the **Silver Blade** on commerce.

6.5 Religion

The Ter-jurah are a deeply religious people. They pray to the god, **San**, and put him first above all else in their lives. Their primary religion is **Sanism**, and those who believe in San are called **Sanists**. The **Temple** is the governing body that sets forth religious doctrine based on the canonical writings of the ***Holy Scriptures***, a thirty-six-volume series.

According to the writings, only San and his host of angels may be prayed to. Iconography is strictly forbidden and punishable by death.

6.6 San

Also known as the **Father** or **Father of Truth**, **San** is considered the "one true god" by the Ter-jurah and is famously known as the **God of Darkness**. It is said he and his angels left Heaven and took Truth with them, leaving only lies. Although the Ter-jurah believe **Jah** (the Creator) exists, Jah has fallen from grace (the opposite viewpoint of the Con-jurah, who believe San has fallen from grace).

6.7 Serak

This is the holy device represented by an equilateral triangle with an all-seeing eye in the center. The delta shape coincides with the sacred number three. The eye is thought to be the eye of San or the eye of Truth. Seraks are found in shrines, homes, and places of business. Only priests may wear the device as jewelry, often as amulets hanging from necklaces. Priests of higher rank typically wear larger amulets to denote their greater relationship with San.

The Holy Scriptures have a passage that speaks of its genesis: "And San saw fit to consecrate his angelic hosts, three times three. And thus the holy delta came to be, for he saw it was right and pure and true. To his angels, he bestowed his blessing thrice. And he bound his all-seeing eye within the blessed device cast in his name. And they praised him, for he is the Father of Truth, and there shall be no other."

6.8 The Temple

This is the religious organization of Terjurmeh. The **Temple** comprises clergy and has its own militia, about a third of the total number of soldiers in the country. A strict hierarchy governs the Temple, ranging from **acolytes** at the low end, to **clerics** and **priests** in the middle tier, and ending with the **Sacred Nine** at the top. **Red and black** are the official colors of the Temple.

6.9 End-times prophecy

The Ter-jurah believe in an end-times scenario where the devout followers of San, known as the **Truthful** in the scriptures, shall rise up and consume their enemies in an Armageddon-like fashion. The last book of their canon, the ***Book of Prophecy***, outlines this outcome in great detail, as well as the reclamation of Heaven by San. A mighty son of San, named **San-Jahad**, or the **Great One**, will be the one to set the end of days into motion. He is the **Savior** in Sanism, born of a mortal woman, but deified as a demigod through the seed of his father, San. The Great One is to reach from his world to Acia and call forth the **Beast**, also known as the **Dragon**, a being of smoke and fire born from a volcano. The Beast's purpose is to snuff the hope of the **Faithful**, the followers of Jah. The scriptures do not specify when the end times will occur. Believers always think the time is nigh.

6.10 The Sacred Nine

No individuals are more revered in Terjurmeh than the **Sacred Nine**. They are the leadership of the Temple and are considered the divine vessels of San. No layman may oppose their will. Their titles are capitalized.

Constituents of the **Sacred Nine**:

- The **Mighty One**. Considered San's physical representation in Acia, he is the head of the Temple. As such, he is an extension of San's will, forsaking his birth name and shedding his human past. When the Mighty One passes on, the Seers select one of the five Articulates as the successor. Favor is traditionally given to the First Articulate, who often has the ear of the Mighty One. The Mighty One is addressed as **Your Most Holiness**.

- Five **Articulates**. As the theocratic policymakers of the Temple and executers of the Mighty One's will, they are the true power of the Temple. Each Articulate is numbered according to their seat, in order of ascension. The First Articulate is considered the most senior and handles much of the correspondence with the

Mighty One. When an Articulate passes on, their replacement becomes the Fifth Articulate, and the others move up. The Articulates of the Temple at the start of the series are:

- **Septamo**, First Articulate

- **Efta-lah**, Second Articulate

- **Nisheppeh**, Third Articulate

- **Refteron**, Fourth Articulate

- **Uhtah-Pei**, Fifth Articulate

- Three **Seers**. As top-level Temple officials in charge of the religious affairs of their respective cities, they are chosen among the Temple's oracles for their gift of second sight and the ability to predict the future. Some of the greatest Seers in Terjurmehan history are revered as prophets. The Seers of the Temple at the start of the series are:

  - **Baaka**, Seer of Elmar

  - **Quoor**, Seer of Fangmordah

  - **Kalresh**, Seer of Kanmar

During ceremonies or prayer gatherings, crowds prostrate, touching forehead to ground, as is customary in the presence of a high-ranking priest.

6.11 From creation to end times

The Ter-jurah believe Jah is the Creator, but do not worship him. According to the ***Book of Creation*** in the ***Holy Scriptures***, **Jah** was made from the **Great Void** and gave substance to the Great Void. **Kattra** was the first word ever spoken, the Word of Creation. Its utterance divided the void from nothingness and the Heavens from the firmament. Kattra is also referred to as the **Divine Awakening**.

Following the Divine Awakening, Jah begot a brother, **San**, in which he instilled **Truth**. He then begot the first archangels, **Mika, Gabra,** and **Rapham**, to be his messengers and executors of his will. Then he begot the rest of the angels of Heaven and organized them into celestial orders.

Not content, he created man in his likeness, made a world for man to worship him, and gave man immortality through procreation. The angels saw that man was held above them, and this created the **Great Rift**. Jealousy and dissension abounded in Heaven, and San urged his brother to remove the light from Heaven, for he believed the light blinded the Creator's judgment.

According to the ***Great Transfiguration of the Father*** in the first book of the canon, war raged in Heaven between the hosts of Jah and San. Jah eventually cast his brother out of Heaven, and the truth with it. In the darkness, termed the **"color of no color,"** San awaits the day when, according to the ***Book of Prophecy***, he shall reclaim Glory in the **Final War**, where he will defeat Jah with his mighty hosts and secure Heaven as the victor.

6.12 The Great Act

The **Great Act** is a sanctioned assassination of a layperson by a clergyman. There is no higher honor among the clergy than to be given this task. It begins as an order from high up the Temple hierarchy. Senior clergy select a worthy acolyte to carry out the act. A cleric prepares the acolyte by painting the face, hands, and feet red and black, the holy colors of the Temple, and specifically: right foot red, left foot black, left hand red, right hand black, face black with the holy delta painted in red. The red symbolizes bloodshed and sacrifice, and the black faith and devotion. They form six holy colorations upon their body in a crisscrossed pattern, acting as poles of heat and cold that draw in spiritual energy from the

Netherworld. The acolyte carries out the mission in plain sight. It is forbidden for anyone to interfere with the act. To do so warrants death with the promise of eternally excruciating punishment in the Netherworld.

6.13 Divine power: the arcane arts

Divine power sits at the core of the magic system in *The Light of Darkness*. Only a person gifted with the ability to harness spiritual energy may use it. The power manifests itself through vocalization and will power, and can be witnessed through a person's ability to control the elements and manipulate the surrounding environment without the use of hands or mechanical devices. The individual uses the soul as the conduit and the mind as the controller of spiritual energy. Meditation and prayer are key components in the development of this power.

Mastery of divine power is seen both in secular and religious circles in Terjurmehan society. On the secular end, the **mage** stands atop the hierarchy as master of the arcane. The mage goes through apprentice, journeyman, and master stages—a seven-year process—to receive the title. Society views magi with the utmost respect. The respect extends to the tribe, in which the tribal leader, the **Terad**, must become a mage before assuming the top tribal position. On the opposite end, the Temple requires all its members to obtain mastery before becoming ordained priests. The priest, also called a **Terad-mara**, invokes spiritual power directly from the Netherworld and uses it mainly during religious ceremonies and sacred rites.

Channeling is the arcane art form employed to use divine power. The body serves as the vessel, the mind as the manipulator, and the soul as the conduit. The three work in tandem to draw power from the ethereal realm of the Netherworld. This trinity concept is termed **unity**, and its purpose is to create a union between matter and energy. Subvocalization aids in focusing the divine energy, although channeling is primarily performed using the mind in a prepared state. **Magi, Teradi, and Terad-mari** are all channelers.

Words of power are the vocalization of channeled energy. They can be used for a variety of tasks, often when a focused burst of energy is required to carry out the task, such as the levitation of a stone. The word of power might propel the stone into the air; channeling keeps it aloft.

Kantaka is a combat art form of channeling that uses the hands to shape energy and direct it at an opponent. Different poses create different energies, almost all offensive and designed for warfare. The **Guild of Magi** forbids Kantaka from being used outside the battlefield since it's such a deadly art. **Kantaka-irri** is full-contact combat, the unrestricted use of all three hundred poses. A learned channeler will choose from an array of offensive and defensive poses to overwhelm an enemy.

In Kantaka, tanga is everything. **Tanga** is the well of power the caster draws from, used to accumulate and shape energy. It's temporarily, often in the action of catch-and-release, to prevent the energy from harming the caster.

Defensive Kantaka poses used throughout the series:

- **ai-dem** – "iron cross;" heels of the palms come together, with one palm out, the other down

- **duhm-ga**, "smolder's breath;" upraised fist to dissipate attack

- **ebbu-da** – "the bubble;" diagonal smack of the hands together creates a protective bubble around the defender, lasting just a few seconds, enough to deflect an attack

- **habeen** – "link breaker;" quick chop of the dominant hand; used to cut off smothering attacks

- **iqquoi** – "flying eagle;" hands curled away from each other like wings

- **nok-na** – "the wedge;" flat palm pointed toward the enemy, thumb angled up, wrist against the sternum

- **sekka-sinsu** – "saucer mirror;" cupping of the hands; reflects energy

Offensive Kantaka poses used throughout the series:
- **atsek** – "hammer's spike;" quick drawing down of a fist

- **engama** – "dancing fire;" a small pyrotechnic offensive pose meant to heat the air in the opponent's space

- **ermi-na** – "gooseneck pose;" arm hooks at the top into the shape of a gooseneck

- **gadzu** – "the mountain;" hands by the side, followed by circling the arms above the head, then crashing the hands down; used to collapse an object with downward force

- **ja-ben** – "tiger claw;" claw-like curling of the fingers to concentrate energy for a lethal blow against an opponent

- **ju-dem** – "crab strike;" fingers are formed into the shape of claws; useful for close quarters with multiple targets

- **lailee** – "silent noose;" forefinger and thumb touching to form a slipknot; by moving the thumb, the slipknot tightens, smothering the intended victim

- **mallek-na** – "wasp sting;" the channeler fires needles of energy at the opponent

- **tsi-tsa** – "spider's grasp;" a smothering technique

- **turami** – "killing blow;" index finger is pointed at an opponent

- **ubbakesh** – "stone thrust;" hooked thumbs and palms face out; useful as a Murrati pose to multiply damage, with the force of throwing a stone pillar

- **voon-sai** – "flapping wings;" palms are spread like wings; creates a light gust of energy

Even more advanced than Kantaka is **Murrati**, or shared combat, where magi attack an enemy in concert to multiply their offensive. The skill is taught to journeymen in the final stages of their training to achieve mastership as magi. It's a notoriously difficult skill, as all wielders must work together. A single variance can cause the entire offense to fall apart, leaving the channelers open to attack.

A lesser-known discipline is **Doktori**, the summoning arts, also referred to as the "forbidden arts." It's a dangerous form of magecraft because the channeler attempts to summon spirits for his or her bidding. To do so, they must reach into the Netherworld, always a perilous affair, because death is but a mistake away for the caster.

One of the side effects of channeling, particularly for the newly initiated, is **surati**, "dreams of a higher power." The dreams are vivid and sometimes violent. It occurs when the soul outpaces the mind in its attempt to extend from the body into the spirit world. The physical self tries to compensate, and the victim ends up with anything from nightmares to convulsions to even death, sometimes setting their beds aflame in the night and burning themselves. To remedy the issue, a technique called **divine norming** is applied to bring the soul and body into balance with each other.

Elementalism is another forbidden art form, used only in secret and for achieving mastery over the primal elements in nature, such as fire, water, lightning, and earth. An **elementalist** uses a practice called the **absence of mind** to separate the waking and sleeping minds from each other and harness the power of the sleeping mind to control the elements. Some consider elementalism the most powerful of all arcane arts because it mirrors the spirit world by combining astral and ethereal elements to take on godlike qualities within the wielder. Examples of elementalism include the transmutation of stone, conducting lightning, and creating storm systems.

6.14 Prayer at meals

It is common for the senior-most person at a table to give thanks to San. The **holy delta** is a gesture done with the hand, similar to the holy cross practiced by Christians. You press your thumb, index finger, and middle finger together and dab the air counterclockwise from the top in the shape of a triangle. Depending on the situation, it might be accompanied by the phrase, **"blood to spirit,"** similar to how Christians say "amen" at the end of a prayer or the giving of thanks before the start of a meal.

6.15 San-mahadi

The San-mahadi were an order of priests sanctioned during the second millennium to suppress heresy. The priests, considered enforcers of faith, traveled mostly in threes and had the jurisdiction to enter any secular establishment and condemn heretics on the spot. While decommissioned, the Mighty One reserves the right under canon law to restore the order.

6.16 The number three

The number three is sacred among the Ter-jurah. It represents a holy trinity of god (San), human, and spirit. Any combination of three is considered a blessing in society: the father, the mother, and the child; the land, the rivers, and the sky; the three cities in Terjurmeh. Terjurmeh itself is called a "Desert Peninsula" because mountains border the nation on three sides. Multiples of three are also considered a blessing, such as in the **Sacred Nine** of the Temple or when soldiers form units of six. The number four is often frowned upon because it is one past the sacred number three. It's the reason slaves are housed together four at a time.

6.17 Holidays

There are several national holidays in Terjurmeh. Three carry significance:

- **San-tel-moor**. The biggest holiday of the year and also the start of the New Year. It's a three-day celebration often filled with jubilation and intense periods of prayer. Clergy mark the foreheads of citizens with **Sercula**, a sacrament of holy oil and blood. It is considered blasphemous to remove the dried, triangular marking from the forehead during the three days.

- **Hah'xallah** (a.k.a. Feast of the Hammer). A national holiday marking the end of summer and celebrating the victory at the **Battle of Andelah**, where the Ter-jurah defeated the Con-jurah in retribution for the destruction of the first capital city of Ekmed. The Ter-jurah commemorate the victory by sacrificing Con-jurahn captives in front of crowds and bludgeoning their skulls with war hammers. A feast always follows the sacrifice, which is why the holiday is sometimes referred to as the **Feast of the Hammer**.

- **Majana**. Takes place on the ninth day of the ninth month. It is one of the holiest days of the year. The country comes to a standstill on Majana, as businesses are required to close and people to attend Temple to receive the holy Sercula. Tribes often flock to the cities for the occasion before heading back out to the desert. A Ter-jurahn is expected to make the holy pilgrimage of **Kevath** at least once in their life during the holiday to the Shrine of San. The devout take the pilgrimage to the extreme, walking the entire distance on foot as a display of their devotion, fasting in the daytime, and eating a single meal at night.

6.18 Customs and traditions

Ter-jurah hold **San's Day** sacred. It marks the end of the seven-day week, similar to our notion of Sunday, and is a day often dedicated to rest and reflection. Citizens are encouraged to attend Temple and pray in the evening to renew their devotion to their god and faith. It is also a day of community, where neighbors come together to share meals in the daytime.

Men have traditionally held a dominant position in society, although times are changing. What was once the domain of man, religion, politics, business, and the military have begun to slowly transition to accept women. In tribal settings, the patriarch is the leader, although the matriarch is revered for her wisdom and respected as the hub of the family. Historically, a small percentage of women have been ordained by the Temple. Nisheppeh, Third Articulate of the Temple, is the highest-ranking member of the clergy at the start of the series, and is both respected and feared by those who serve beneath her.

6.19 Greetings and salutations

A priest is called **Holy One** when addressed or **His Holiness** or **Her Holiness** when referred to in the third person.

A party leader of high station is called **Your Greatness** when addressed or **His Greatness** or **Her Greatness** when referred to in the third person. The Great One also receives this honorific.

Soldiers often salute each other by pressing a fist to the chest. The gesture is also used in a ceremonial greeting or parting.

When two individuals meet, they typically bow their heads as a form of respect. The deeper the bow, the more respectful. Men who engage in conversation will typically lock their forearms first, the equivalent of shaking hands. Locking forearms is accomplished by grasping each other's forearm just shy of the elbow.

6.20 Military

Terjurmeh maintains an active military force to enforce civil order in the cities and to protect its lands from foreign invaders. The controlling party of each city is responsible for feeding, training, arming, and housing the troops garrisoned there. At the beginning of the story, the Black Arrow manages the garrisons in Kanmar while the Fist manages those in Fangmordah and the capital city of Elmar. In a time of war, all city troops fall under the authority of the ruling party, the party chosen to execute the will of the people.

6.21 Slavery

Slavery is a major part of life in Terjurmeh. The parties and Temple both support slavery. Slaves are private or public property, depending on the owner. In the public case, the city owns the slaves and houses them in common quarters. They are typically marked on their left ankles with tattoos designating ownership.

City slaves commonly wear linen outfits and color-coded rope belts. Red signifies a common slave and black a **Jabahn**, a slave with privileges.

To induce control, the city requires publicly owned slaves to drink a tea called **sprushah**, a stimulant that provides energy and staves hunger. Sprushah is addictive and has damaging long-term effects on the mind, resulting in memory loss and eventual catatonia, which is why the typical life expectancy of a slave is five to ten years.

City slaves often engage in public works projects and the basic manufacturing needs of the government, helping reduce labor costs. In Kanmar, the center of the slave trade for the nation, the slaves sleep in an extensive set of underground cells in what is termed the **pits**. They sleep four to a cell and work in pairs to remind themselves that they are not worthy of San's holy blessing, which is signified by the number three. It is forbidden for a publicly owned slave to shave or cut his or her hair.

Draadi, or slave masters, control the daily lives of publicly owned slaves. Through a chain of command, ending at the top with the **Draad-lord**, they dictate regimens and mete out punishment. The Black Arrow party runs the slave trade and Slave Guild, which sets policy on ownership and manages the slave market.

It is a capital crime for a slave to look directly into the eyes of a clergyman.

6.22 Diet

The Ter-jurah are a nomadic people. They eat dense foodstuffs available to them for their long journeys, such as nuts, flatbreads, dried fruits, and cheeses. When able, they hunt desert game or fish the river causeways bisecting the country or herd when living close to the fertile banks or within the oases occupying the desert regions. Some of the population is static, living in the cities yearlong instead of venturing with their tribes. Their diets have more variety, as they have access to local markets, ranches, and farms. They consume grains and leafy greens and enjoy a rich diet of fish, poultry, and fowl. Adults enjoy a variety of beverages, including ale, wine, and spirits.

6.23 Clothing

The hot clime of Terjurmeh limits clothing material to cotton or linen. **Tunics** are worn as everyday garments. Footwear is mostly in the form of sandals and the occasional boot for soldiers. Headdresses are common to protect people from the scathing sun.

Nomads wear variations of the tunic. The men prefer the loose-fitting **gebban**, an ankle-length garment made of cotton or sheep's wool that covers the arms and legs to protect the body from the desert sun. Gebba can be earth-toned and plain, striped, or stitched with intricate Jurmehan script that tells of their family heritage as stories that run around their hems and sleeves. The women prefer cotton headscarves and **gebbettes**, which contain embroidered front panels and billowing backs. To protect their faces from the merciless sun, men and women both wear headdresses called **bukara**, shaped like the coffin head of a cobra, with flaring cotton on either side of the face that trails behind their necks in a variety of colors and patterns, held in place by a circlet of reedwood or leather strap.

Draadi often wear tunics with heavy leather belts and red sashes laid diagonally across the chest or triangular epaulets upon the shoulders to denote rank. A double sash as an "x" is typically reserved for the highest-ranking Draad in a group, such as an element leader. The Draadlord also wears the double sash, but the second sash is gold to denote his rank.

Terjurmehan soldiers rarely wear armor. Those in Kanmar wear leather over tunics and linen headdresses wrapped over helms when out in the sun. Squad leaders and higher wear triangular epaulets on the shoulders. The typical soldier is armed with a short sword. Shields and bows are uncommon, except in warfare. Soldiers in other cities, like Fangmordah, dress similarly to those in Kanmar, but sometimes substitute burnooses for headdresses.

Magi wear black robes while priests wear red robes.

Robe colors worn by magi from apprentice to master:

- Junior apprentice: white

- Senior apprentice: green

- Journeyman: gray

- Mage (master): black

An **apprentice** is called a **White Robe** or **Green Robe**, depending on experience. A **journeyman** is called a **Gray Robe** and a **mage** a **Black Robe**.

Robe colors worn by clergy from junior (acolyte) to senior (priest):

- Acolyte: off-white

- Cleric: gray

- Priest: red

Besides their robe, priests may wear a serak as jewelry, often an amulet hanging from a necklace worn prominently over their robes. As tradition goes, the higher the priest's rank, the larger the device, although there is no law written in the canon to support the use or wear of seraks.

6.24 Allies and enemies

Modern-day Acia divides itself primarily along religious boundaries between Sanists, followers of San, and Jahnists, followers of Jah. Although a country such as Terjurmeh might trade with the Northern Kingdom, the two are trade partners, not allies. The Northerners believe in Jah while the Ter-jurah believe in San. Conversely, the Northern Kingdom and Meerjurmeh consider themselves allies because of their common belief in Jah. Korin allies itself with these countries as well, although there are pockets of Korin still entrenched in the old pagan beliefs.

The enmity between Terjurmeh and Meerjurmeh precedes either country's founding. The Temple perpetuates the Sanists' prejudice toward Jahnists. According to the Holy Scriptures of the Ter-jurah, the enemies of San are considered inferior and shall be put down when the appointed time comes. Because the peoples of the rest of the world have mostly converted to Jahism, an uneasy truce exists between domains favoring Sanism or Jahnism. The top seats of their respective religions reinforce the division, adding to the tension between countries through endless campaigns of religious hatemongering.

The Ter-jurah support their An-jurahn roots by maintaining ties with the An-jurah, who dwell among the tribal states east of Meerjurmeh, in Darkforth. At the start of the series, these ties have strengthened into a formal alliance between the two. Terjurmeh has pledged support to help the An-jurah annex their states under a cohesive leadership among warring territories in Darkforth. With increased control over the native populations of Machoo Indians and Idarian hillmen, the An-jurah are becoming a unified and formidable power onto their own . . . and a force to be reckoned with.

6.25 Commerce

Waterways speed up the transportation of goods and materials. They serve as the primary mechanism of intercity trade. Terjurmeh has an entire fleet of river-going vessels, from barges to slave galleys, to commute people and products.

The summer months represent the height of waterway travel because the nomadic tribesmen, who encompass about half the population, live in the cities during this time. Many tribes use barter or services in exchange for goods.

While Terjurmeh supports isolationism, it entertains limited trade between countries out of necessity and to boost the economy. Terjurmeh exports salt and textiles and imports exotic spices and liqueurs from Meerjurmeh and lumber from the Northern Kingdom.

At the beginning of the story, Terjurmeh's economy is in turmoil, with parties pointing fingers at one another for overspending, trade deficits, and failed government projects. Much of the blame is directed at the Silver Blade, which has lost popularity among the more prominent tribes for a failed infrastructure project that's resulted in increased taxes.

6.26 Currency

While Terjurmeh still engages in the barter of goods, most transactions are monetary. The Ter-jurah use coin for currency, ascribing greater value to precious metals like gold and electrum. Because other countries use similar metals, the exchange rate depends on the net weight of the coin and the perceived value of the currency internationally.

Denominations (lowest to highest) and shape of each coin:

- **Ruh** – copper – round

- **Currah** – silver – delta

- **Kant** – electrum – square

- **Till** – gold – round

Monetary conversion (lowest to highest):
- 20 copper ruh = 1 silver currah

- 12 silver currah = 1 electrum kant

- 3 electrum kanta = 1 gold till

1 till = 3 kanta = 36 currah = 720 ruh

6.27 Trillian of Darkness

The **Trillian of Darkness** is a set of tenets taught to clerics before they become priests. An elder priest sequesters a cleric underground for three days to remove the distraction of light and reveal the Trillian in total darkness.

Three pillars comprise the Trillian:

- The dark that binds

- The dark that usurps

- The dark that rules

Each one serves as a stage in the metamorphosis of cleric to priest. The goal is for the cleric to become vulnerable so they can liberate their mind and soul. Darkness is the key to all practitioners of the arcane arts, whether mage, Terad, or Terad-mara (priest), because it is the color of no color, and only when blind in the dark can one truly see.

Stage one of the metamorphosis is to bind with the dark by embracing it and using it as a cloak. This is achieved by uncovering secrets used by divine vessels like fallen angels, demons, and San.

Stage two is to usurp the dark by taking its secrets by force of will. This is the stage where a cleric is the most vulnerable to the dark forces of the Netherworld. It is the cocoon stage where one is defenseless in their attempt to absorb the dark's true potential. Only the most vulnerable self can lead to the most capable self. By doing so, one separates their spirit from their body, exiting their cocoon and physical being to enter the third and final stage, where they can rule the dark. If the cleric cannot break free of their cocoon, they will either resurface a failure and be forced out of the clergy or succumb to dark forces and perish.

Stage three is where the initiate becomes the master, able to harness the full potential of their craft. The well of power they tap into is limitless, and so they become like their angels and god as practitioners (and rulers) of the dark arts.

6.28 Prophetic Scriptures of the Ter-jurah

The ***Book of Prophecy*** is the last book in the **Holy Scriptures**, the cannon of the Terjurmehan Temple. Two key excerpts delve into end-days prophecy, also called the **Great Reckoning**. The Great Reckoning serves as a demarcation point in the history of mankind, followed by the prophesied **Age of Shadow**, a new era where the followers of San reign supreme over Acia.

The first excerpt that follows speaks of the transformation of the Father into the Son, where the Father is the god San, and the Son is his favored child, San-Jahad, also known as the Great One.

The second excerpt speaks of two wars. The first, waged by man, is **Samath**, which translates to the word Armageddon. The second, waged by San and his angels against Jah and his angels in Heaven, is the **Final War**.

Interestingly, Samath speaks of the second coming of the Great One. This coincides with the Korinian account of the Great War, where An-ta, the Sun God (Jah), bestowed upon the Emperor Exantecor, the first emperor of Korin, a weapon of Heaven called Korillion, also known as the Godkiller.

In the first coming of the Great One, Korinian lore tells of Emperor Exantecor going up against Da-amad, the Korinian Lesser God of Spite, which some theologians believe to be the incarnation of the Great One during his first attempt to destroy the believers of Jah. During the battle, Exantecor slayed Da-amad. He also slayed Kosmos, a fabled beast portended to bring ruin upon the world. Kosmos draws a comparison to the

Dragon (Beast) of Terjurmehan lore. This means the Great One and his Beast attempted to overtake Acia once, only to be defeated, thus ushering in the Year One, and prophesied to return to fulfill Samath and bring darkness, the color of no color, to Acia.

Here are the two excerpts from the *Book of Prophecy*.

1. The Great Transfiguration of the Father

Jah, Creator, and First of Heaven, begot a brother to share his domain. His brother, the seed of Truth, of which there is no color, was named San. Then Jah begot Mika, Gabra, and Rapham to be his messengers and executors of his will. They were the first angels. Such was the Beginning.

Jah begot the multitudes in the realm of Heaven and they became his chosen, and there was peace, and all was well. But Jah was not content with his creation, and so he spawned man. When man came to be, there was given unto him an essence of the Creator, and Jah called it the soul of man. But man was imperfect, for he had not the essence of Truth within him.

And so Jah sent his messengers to speak his Word to man, and the angels, once favored above all, were cast aside, made to serve his will and nothing more. San, who was the First, brother to Jah and Seed of Truth, saw that all was not well and that disparity divided the cosmos. He heard the Word of the Maker, and in it, he heard the Great Lie.

And San, who was the Truth, spoke, and his brothers listened, but not all, and there was a great war in Heaven. The Heavens opened up and Jah cast out the Truth, and Heaven became devoid of it, for San and those who believed in the Truth left. Thus, Heaven came to be imperfect and stained. San begot his own kingdom, the color of no color, and named it the Netherworld. And he made his brethren, the excluded angels of Heaven, princes unto their own domains, and so the Great Rift came to be, and San became the Father of this domain and to all who followed his word, and a god unto his own.

So was the Great Transfiguration of the Father.

2. The Account of the Final War

San, the Father, who was the First and above all, came to beget a son. Of a mortal woman, this son was born. And it was said that he would have hair of black, face of a god, and eyes of sky, and in it, all would see the Truth of the Father.

And the Father announced to his angels, "This son I bear shall be great. And so shall he be named Great One and inherit the world." Born was he, Great One, unto the world of men, blood of a virgin, blood of a god.

But the Father said, "And he shall toil among the world of men, rise in power, and fall. Such will be the fate of his first coming. Those who choose the Truth will be at his side and will be marked so as to be invisible to the eye. And those who will rise against him will be the faithful of Jah, purveyor of the Lie. So, too, shall rise a great Beast of fire and smoke to shake the resolve of Jah's Faithful, and it, too, shall fail. Such will be the first coming, and the year of man shall be marked Year One."

And there came a time when the angels asked, "Father, when shall the Great Reckoning come to be?" Of which, the Father replied, "When my son, the Great One of man, is born of another land in the second coming, so shall the Great Reckoning begin. Upon his sixteenth birthday, the time of his choosing, shall he come to me, and I shall teach him anew. And the Great One shall rise above all others of his land and teach the Truth, of which I am its seed. Upon his thirty-sixth birthday, he shall ascend in greatness and reach across the cosmos to this world and stir the great Beast, a Dragon of fire and smoke from the Mother, the Womb of the Earth.

"The Mother shall give birth to the Dragon, and he will smother the light with smoke and fire and drive fear into the hearts of the Unbelievers. From the Dragon's birth will come Samath, the cycle that ends all things, and the Great One shall draw strength from the Dragon's shadow and unite the peoples of the world with the might of the Father, and those who oppose his might will despair and falter.

"My angel of this new world, my Gatekeeper and Watcher, shall open the way for him, and the Great One shall become my Sword. With the aid of the vast armies of the Marked, man shall succumb to the Truth in the time of Samath, and this world shall become the color of no color, and all who resist will fall before the Sword.

"And a great war shall ensue and the Marked shall prevail and the Great One shall return. So will be the fate of man."

And the Father spoke of the Great Reckoning. "And a time shall come when the Great One does battle among the world of men, and at that time, another child, begotten of my seed shall open Heaven for us, and we shall come to the Great Reckoning. Of him, I will name 'Chosen One,' for he will be chosen to open the way. And I will speak the Truth and all the hosts of Heaven shall listen, but not all will rally to us.

"There will be a Final War, a war to end all wars. Jah, purveyor of the Lie, shall know the Truth again and give way to its seed. He shall hear the terrible silence and all the color blinding those who cannot see the Truth shall be removed. You and your brethren shall become Kings of Heaven and rule for all eternity, and the marked of men shall become gods unto their own. This I promise, for it is the Truth."

So was the Account of the Final War.

7. Meerjurmeh

7.1 Geography and climate

Like Terjurmeh, Meerjurmeh is a desert country. Except for the **Muu-na Flats** to the north, which are great plains of sandstone and limestone, the rest of the desert is sandy, with the dunes of the **Agobo Desert** in the west reaching as high as a hundred feet. The desert is also known for its treacherous sandstorms, called **vaellra**.

The rivers sustain life and provide for its people. The **Tangeen River** flows from the southern end of the Eastern Gates, the mountains bordering Darkforth, to the east, and travels to the west, branching off to the **Estuary River** and the **River Nomad**. Cataracts along the eastern end of the Tangeen make upriver travel impossible. The same holds for the River Nomad, which swells where water fed from the Tangeen converges with water fed from the Gōsh Mountains. The northern wastes of Meerjurmeh are inhospitable and rarely traveled.

The **Gōsh Mountains** border Meerjurmeh on the south side and the **Northern Range Mountains** on the north side. The forestland of **Darkforth** borders the east side. Summers are extremely hot, with temperatures reaching as high as 140 degrees Fahrenheit in the Muuna Flats and Agobo Desert. Winters are cooler than those in Terjurmeh, with nighttime temperatures dropping as low as forty degrees.

Hōvar serves as the capital of Meerjurmeh and the nation's center for trade. It is also a holy city, as it is the center of the Jahn Church for all of Acia and a destination for missionaries across the world. The sprawling metropolis is set strategically at the intersection of three river systems—The River Nomad, Estuary River, and Tangeen River—nestled in a fertile river valley, surrounded by plantations, farms, and vineyards. The city is known for its beauty and bounty of floral displays that spill over the tall walls that serve as a defensive perimeter against invaders.

Key attractions within the city include **Potter's Square**, the statue-lined **Avenue of Saints**, **Barrow's End**, the **Cathedral of the Blessed**, the famed **University of Akan**, and the **Copper District**, where most government buildings are located, including the **Holy Court of the Ascended** (justice hall and highest court in the land), the **Ponia Tapa** (senate building) and **Vellum** (headquarters building).

The city is filled with colorful terraces, pastel-hued homes, monuments, paved streets, parks, and churches, built upon one another with crooked causeways among larger avenues. The wealthy own estates outside the city walls, along the fertile river delta as well as in the **Lion's Quarter**, an elite neighborhood. While there are few slums, there is

Louse's End, which attracts the poor. The **Bandolin Canal**, an offshoot of the Estuary River, divides the city center from the rest of Hōvar, crossable by three bridges, including the famous **Tiplet Bridge**, also known as "Lover's Lane" for its scenic setting for couples.

Sushtâh lies northwest of **Hōvar** along the Estuary River. The city is known for its nut farms, clayware, silk growers, and silk weavers, who make some of the most desirable clothing of all the domains, with most of their fabric shipped to Korin, where gossamer skirts of sheer silk are all the rage among the nobles. Their parchments and inks are also renowned and sold abroad. Sushtâh is known for its mead, which is only available to visitors; no exports are allowed.

Geographically speaking, Sushtâh is a small, crowded city. White-washed plaster buildings cluster among a maze of walls. Several interesting architectural wonders include a church with a pyramidal crown; the seven-sided **Library of Ilion**; the hypostyle court of **Saint Karmus Square**, with its thirty-six columns positioned precisely to cast shadows in honor of the spring and fall equinoxes; the palm-shaped clerks and records offices that give the illusion of a long, sweeping front; many votive chapels; and the three-thousand-year-old ruins of **Parpet**, a crumbling complex of columned structures rife with mysterious hieroglyphs that give the appearance of Korinian origin.

Vergahl is the northernmost city of Meerjurmeh, a port city like Sushtâh, located on the Estuary River. Here, farmers tend to ju-man groves, the most famous crop of the region. When distilled, the fruit from the ju-man produces a ruby-colored liqueur called **ju-ju**, a major export and source of income. The pricey, sought-after liqueur gives off the aroma of cherries and cardamom and tastes of tart cherries and spice.

One of the whimsical tourist attractions of the city is the goat trees, which are nut trees with low-hanging branches goats can climb. A tree laden with nuts will also be laden with goats—quite the sight for visitors. Farmers capitalize on this strange arrangement between animal and tree, taking the seeds from goat dung to make luxury cosmetics exported abroad to wealthy consumers.

Tuur is the easternmost city of Meerjurmeh, a lot smaller, drabber, and less populated than the capital. The port city is located on the fertile bank of the Tangeen River. Locals dislike visitors from the west and are wary of foreigners. The city's claim to fame is its catacombs, an extensive network of ancient tunnels running beneath the city, where the dead were once interred. It attracts tourists who pay guides to lead them underground. Skulls and skeletons occupy the myriad cubbyholes dug into the bedrock, untouched for centuries. To disturb the dead is to be cursed, and the message is echoed by superstitious tour guides. Tuur locals prefer simple attire. Men favor the **saba**, a body-length shirt.

7.2 People

The people of the country are referred to as **Con-jurah**. A person from this country may be called **Meerjurmehan** (of the country) or **Con-jurahn** (of the people). The Con-jurah are city dwellers mostly (unlike the Ter-jurah, who are a mix of city dwellers and nomads). They live along the fertile riverbanks of the country and have one settlement (**Canuush-met**) in the south part of the Hōvar Region. The people descend from the An-jurah and have a long history dating back to the Year One. They are squat and amber-skinned, like the Ter-jurah, and speak **Jurmehan**, the common tongue of the Northern Hemisphere.

7.3 Government

Meerjurmeh is a republic. The senate effects all policymaking in the country. The public is supposed to elect its senators, but only the wealthy are eligible to become senators and only the influential are eligible to vote. The office of the **Lesser Light** is the highest secular post in the land and is held by one person. The Lesser Light serves as the country's head of state and has both executive and judicial power, arbitrates any disputes in the Senate, and has the final say in all affairs. The Lesser Light holds the post for life. When the position is vacated, a new leader is appointed by the Senate through majority rule. You can consider the position as the "Julius Caesar" of the Senate. **Kōs** is the present Lesser Light.

Because of the Church's dominant role in the lives of the Con-ju-rah, its leader, called the **Prime Manifest** or **Greater Light**, has authority over layman affairs and can override any political decision if it is in the best interest of the Church, including decisions made by the Lesser Light.

The **Judicial Council** ensures crimes are measured and justice is served. Elected **magisters** arbitrate and render judgments, officially titled **Adjudicators of the Holy Court**. They wear wigs and white robes, along with silver clasps with holy disks that signify their role as judiciaries. During legal proceedings, a magister is often accompanied by a **Registrar of the Holy Court**. The registrar administers the court record. Magisters are addressed as **Your Eminence**.

7.4 Religion

Jahism (also called **Jahnism**) is the approved religion of the Con-jurah. It places Jah, the Creator, at its center, and the **Jahn Church** as its authority. The **Greater Light** (the **Prime Manifest**) serves as the head of the **Church** and relates the word of Jah to the masses. Jah's word is sacrosanct and may not be refuted. Think of the Greater Light as the equivalent of the pope during the height of the Catholic Church.

The **Jahn Church** is an extensive organization whose center is in the **Holy City of Hōvar**. Pilgrims from all over the world flock to the city each year to receive blessings from the Greater Light. The clergy comprises **archons** at the high end, then **priests, clerics,** and **acolytes**. There are **six archons** and they hold a position equivalent to the Articulates of Terjurmeh. They execute canon law and take on the additional duty as magistrates for the Senate, when needed.

The **Archon Guard** serves as a protective detail for the archons. They wear helms with white horsehair and cloaks with silver star-shaped fibulas. The **Prime Guard**, fewer in number, protects the Prime Manifest. They wear helms with red horsehair and white cloaks with gold fibulas.

Priests wear devices over their robes in the shape of the **holy disk**, a circlet often made of gold to distinguish them from the silver disks of government officials (although they wear other metals, such as iron, on the open road). Priests belong to **numbered orders** (e.g., the Ninth Order), headed up by senior priests.

In countries where the Jahn Church is the center of faith, a **Prefect** is ordained to lead the regional church for the respective nation. The **Northern Kingdom** has the **Prefect of Prall, Korin** has the **Prefect of Korin** and the **Provinces of the South** have the **Prefect of Andora**. The Greater Light serves as the **Prefect of Meerjurmeh**. A Prefect is addressed as **Your Most Holy Reverence**.

Unlike the Ter-jurahn Temple, which bans **idolization**, the Church sanctifies and encourages it. The Church canonizes **saints** and even has a street dedicated to them (**Avenue of Saints** in Hōvar), lined with statues depicting men and women with halos overhead. The most famous of all saints is **Saint Karmus**, who has a square in **Sushtâh** dedicated in his honor. Karmus was an archon who became the Greater Light in the year 1024 and handled the expansion of the Church's influence in Korin over its native polytheism. He increased the power of the Prefects in their respective domains. Karmus served as Greater Light for thirty-eight years and was loved for his tireless devotion to the Church, which canonized him as a saint shortly after his death. To achieve sainthood, an archon must first nominate a candidate. If all six archons agree on the selection, the four Prefects of Acia will vote, including the Prime Manifest. A unanimous vote of yea results in the candidate's canonization.

7.5 Holidays

The Con-jurah celebrate **fetes**, religious festivals that honor the archangels of Jah. There are three fetes during the year:

- Fete of Mika

- Fete of Gabra

- Fete of Rapham

There are four additional holidays:

- Rite of the Summer Solstice

- Rite of the Winter Solstice

- Festival of the Spring Equinox

- Festival of the Autumn Equinox

The Greater Light presides over these holidays, with religious services given on the adjoining Jah's Day. In other domains, such as the Northern Kingdom, the domain's Prefect is in charge.

7.6 Customs and traditions

The Con-jurah are a spiritual people who attend church in the morning on Jah's Day and then spend the remainder of the day with family. Marriage starts with the Church and the blessing of a priest, as the religious aspect of matrimony sets the tone of spirituality for the rest of the newlyweds' lives.

One tradition that honors the soon-to-be-married couple is the **Dinner of Unity**, a tribute to good fortune for a life of happiness and fulfillment celebrated the night before the wedding. The father of the groom arranges and pays for this event. Guests include close family and friends. Those of means throw lavish banquets, but even the poor rejoice with the best meal they can afford. More important is the significance of the occasion: a loving gathering on the eve of a blessed event.

On the day of the wedding, it's tradition for the guests from the Dinner of Unity to wear the same outfits to carry forward the celebration from feast to ceremony. Only the bride and groom dress differently.

During the officiation, the bride and groom wear wooden reed diadems, tethered to each other by a cord to signify the bond of matrimony.

7.7 Greetings and salutations

Unlike Terjurmeh, where it's customary to lock forearms, Con-jurahn men place hands on each other's shoulders as a sign of friendly greeting and parting or touch fist to breast under more formal settings, such as with the Meerjurmehan senators. Women often hold each other's hands in greeting one another.

7.8 Food and drink

The diet of the Con-jurah is like those of the Ter-jurah. Many staples include flatbread, nuts, cheese, and a variety of fruits like prots. They slaughter chickens, hogs, and cattle for meals, but also enjoy fish from the various rivers bordering the major cities.

The Con-jurah are big tea drinkers. Their favorite is **cha**, a tea with an Earl Grey quality. Slurping is a form of respect to let a host know that the tea is above par. Even if it isn't, it's just a matter of common courtesy.

7.9 Clothing

Because of the hot desert clime, clothing is limited to lighter wear (tunics and sandals), similar to that of Terjurmeh. Priests and magi wear robes. In the eastern part of the country, a body-length garment called the **saba** is popular.

Senators dress in off-white wool tunics cinched about the waist with leather belts. Bright-red-and-gold striped sashes run crosswise over their torsos, secured by ornamental brass buttons at the hip and breast.

7.10 Allies and enemies

Meerjurmeh holds a unique position in the west as the center for Jahism. The Empire of Korin, once a pagan nation, has almost completely converted to Jahism, and recognizes the Church's authority in Hōvar, as do the Northern Kingdom and Provinces of the South. As such, Meerjurmeh is the center of an unofficial alliance between western Jahn nations. From a military standpoint, Meerjurmeh hasn't had to call on its allies in over five centuries. Terjurmeh, Meerjurmeh's archenemy, is aware of Meerjurmeh's loose alliance but doesn't officially recognize it.

Meerjurmeh has long been at war with Terjurmeh, but a threat along its eastern and northern borders continues to cause the country major problems. Marauding Idarians often attack travelers near the city of **Tuur**. In centuries past, the Idarians would attack the city outright. Because of this, Meerjurmeh's navy lends military support when needed.

7.11 Commerce

Intercity trade is managed via the waterways bisecting the country and via caravan for those settlements not accessible by water. Meerjurmeh flourishes through a combination of intercity commerce and international trade with the Empire of Korin and the Northern Kingdom. Trade with the Northerners is a tricky business because of Terjurmeh, which tries to control the trade of lumber. Exports include liqueur, spices, and silk clothing. Imports include iron ore, salt, and glassware.

One export considered controversial is the psychedelic, **dusk**. Enjoyed by the wealthy for its hallucinogenic and euphoria-inducing properties, the spice is heavily regulated and considered illegal, not just in Meerjurmeh but in other countries. That doesn't stop plantation owners from producing the product and paying off government officials to look the other way.

The production of dusk is a painstaking, time-intensive process. The spice comes from the oplia plant, which grows selectively in Hōvar (and nowhere else in the world), and only in the spring and summer. It's ready for harvest come early fall after the bulbs have fully grown. Farmers deprive the plants of water, drying them out. Oplia plants comprise a thistle-like stalk and bulb at the top the size of a fist. Harvesters separate out the bulbs from the stalks, then place the bulbs onto wooden drying racks in storehouses, where the bulbs season. Once the bulbs crack open, sap leeches out onto the wood where it will dry completely. A worker will then carefully scrape off the dried sap, where it will be milled to produce a deep amber spice that gets weighed, apportioned, and stored in stoppered clay jugs or glass jars for mass storage or into smaller vessels for distribution. Government inspectors grade the spice, and then a wax seal is applied with the signet of the house, along with the grade. A higher grade demands a higher price. While the concept of government inspection seems contrary to the legality of the product, the law states that production in itself is not illegal, but the distribution and sale are.

7.12 Currency

Like Terjurmeh, Meerjurmeh relies heavily on its currency for commerce. All coins are circular with square notches in the center that makes them easy to string together. Parents often hang a coin by a cord to gift to their children as a seed for future prosperity. Each coin is stamped with a flower on one side and a wise Jurmehan saying on the other. The flowers reflect the natural beauty that abounds in Meerjurmeh's fertile river valley. The larger the denomination, the larger the physical size of the coin, which makes gold coins the rarest of all. It's interesting to note that the singular and plural form of each currency is the same (e.g., one urat or ten urat).

Denominations (lowest to highest) and the flowers stamped on the front:

- **Desh** – copper – naprot

- **Urat** – bronze – desert poppy

- **Loon** – silver – j'boun

- **Tak** – gold – water lily

Monetary conversion (lowest to highest):
- 10 copper desh = 1 bronze urat

- 5 bronze urat = 1 silver loon

- 10 silver loon = 1 gold tak

1 tak = 10 loon = 50 urat = 500 desh

7.13 Arcane arts

Meerjurmeh boasts many magi and priests proficient in the arcane arts. Like their Terjurmehan neighbors, they use **channeling** practices to channel divine energy. They also use **vocali**, words of binding that serve as a method of intonations and vibrational notes that harmonize with the frequency of the soul. It's like **divine norming**, but more effective, and used to help the magus control their power. Other channeling techniques include **Leventi**, the bending of light, where the practitioner draws upon a light source to wield its power. Fire is one source, but the most significant and effective is the sun.

All magi belong to the **Sacred Mage Order of Meerjurmeh**, the association that governs the regulations and policies of magi and the use of the arcane arts in Meerjurmeh. A mage titled **Magus Exetor** leads the order while also serving double duty as the head of the **University of Akan**.

Students of magecraft attend formal training, exclusively through a program at the University of Akan. Unlike Terjurmehan Magi, who wear black robes, Meerjurmehan magi wear white.

8. Northern Kingdom

8.1 Geography and climate

The Northern Kingdom sits in the northwestern end of the continent, separated from its closest neighbor to the south, Terjurmeh, by the **Prall Hills**, and Meerjurmeh, in the Southeast, by the **Northern Range**. Grasslands and forests make up most of the country. Soil rich in minerals provides for excellent harvests, and much of the land is devoted to farmland. Summer days are hot and humid, but nights are moderate, while winters are cold and sometimes brutal, with snowfall in the higher elevations and along the **Northern Range** and **Errant's Pass** to the south.

Six **Valudoms** carve up the kingdom, each run by a nobleman of **Valudin** rank. You can think of a Valudom as a duchy or state.

- **Luxony** – the seat of power, home to the capital city of **Durenbeck** and port city of **Markania**; accessible to travelers by **Errant's Pass**, which sits between the **Prall Hills** and the **Northern Range**

- **Prall** – largest of the territories, mostly plains; located farthest north, stretching to the sea and east to **Darkforth**, where the forest forms a natural border

- **Julesland** – northwestern territory, mostly forest and plateau

- **Lenferd** – westernmost territory, set among the **Prall Hills** and forested lands along the sea

- **Billany** – landlocked territory bordered by **Luxony**, **Prall**, and **Kenton**

- **Kenton** – southeastern territory set on the **Prall Plateau**, butted up against the Northern Range Mountains

Errant's Pass serves as the primary passage between the Northern Kingdom and the lower domains of Acia. Other passages through the Northern Range exist but are nigh impossible to venture across in the winter. In warmer weather, caravans travel the well-worn natural roadway of Errant's Pass, but in the winter, access is often cut off by snow and ice. Guarding the road on the north side is **Errant's Keep**, a strategic fortification overlooking the pass, built on a promontory of granite that gives it a tactical advantage against potential invaders. The Tissel family handles the safety of travelers across the pass, helmed by Quellen Tissel, Warden of the South.

Durenbeck is a bustling capital. Think Victorian-era London, and you'll get the picture. The downtown area is broken up into districts, each with its own theme, often in the name: the **Art District**, **Garment District**, and **Rose District**, to name a few. Durenbeck straddles the northeast bank of **Lake Dess**, a large lake that offers picturesque views and respite from the busyness of the city. The capital hosts two major landmarks: **Dennington Palace** and **Windmoor Castle**, both seats of power for the monarchy. Durenbeck is famous for its clothiers, haberdashers, lively eateries, and taverns.

Markania, the Northern Kingdom's second-largest city, is known as the fashion capital of the kingdom, but also for its clockmaking—the best in the world. They sell their timepieces for outrageous prices to foreigners. To own a watch or clock from Markania is a statement of status . . . and the talk of the town.

8.2 People

The people of the kingdom are referred to formally as **Prallites** and informally as **Northerners**. There are two classes of citizens in the country: commoners and nobles. A middle class exists, but it accounts for such a narrow segment of the population that only those engaged in international trade fit into this class. Because agriculture is such an important part of the economy, most of the common class engages in farming and ranching.

Prallites are related to Idarians and have similar physical characteristics. Idarian hillmen settled in the Northwest over a thousand years ago. Clan chiefs became landowners and then nobles over the four hundred years that followed. Husbandry advances led to a more settled lifestyle and, subsequently, the growth of community and economy; and finally, the creation of a cohesive government structure. An ambitious clan chief named **Markania the Great** subjugated his neighboring states and united the country under sovereign rule in 2738. King Markania's reign as monarch lasted twenty-six years and accounted for much of the nobility system that exists today.

The Prallites are the first people of Acia to adopt full names—that is, forenames with surnames. Most have two names (e.g., Chamfor Rengle), although it's not uncommon for aristocrats to give their children three or even four names as a sign of social status.

8.3 Government

The Northern Kingdom (often called **Prall**) is a monarchy. It's the youngest country in Acia, at just under 640 years. The monarch governs the land and gains title through hereditary right. Nobles, typically relatives of the king or queen, hold title to vast tracts of land which the common class cultivates in exchange for food and housing. The highest-ranking nobles, the **Valudin** (considered on par with Britain's Dukes in terms of nobility hierarchy) control the largest territories in the kingdom, called **Valudoms**.

The kingdom adopted a feudal system that comprises a hierarchy of nobles, vassals, and serfs. Because the kingdom is so young and continues to expand, mainly eastward, generational border and title changes have created a state of flux in the country. The primary culprit is the division of territory to support new minor lords, which creates additional vassalages and overtaxes the feudal system.

The **High Office of the Steward**, located in Durenbeck, serves the Crown on international affairs. The **Steward** acts in the capacity of both ambassador and liaison and oversees representatives with expertise in foreign affairs, called **Vice Stewards**. Each Vice Steward represents the Northern Kingdom to a single foreign power under their purview.

The kingdom has a variety of laws, but a well-known one is the **Law of Prohibition**, which forbids the practice of magecraft. Interestingly, priests are allowed to train and use the arcane arts, as it is considered a "godly practice among the worthy."

The **Royal Bureau of Alchemy** is an odd duck among the organs of government, consisting of alchemists charged with the chemical sciences for the kingdom. Many believe these alchemists as charlatans, performing cheap tricks and illusions, but they've been part of the government for well over a century, dedicated to the advancement of compounds and control of pharmaceuticals and therapeutics from the stance of legality and use. The Bureau falls under the governance of the High Office of the Steward.

8.4 Nobility class

Nobles rule throughout the Northern Kingdom and are servants of the Crown—the king and queen. The nobility class follows a rigid hierarchy. The monarch may bestow or revoke title, rank, and land, which makes the Crown all-powerful.

Here are the nobility ranks, from highest to lowest, and how they equate to the ones of our world:

- **King** and **queen** – monarchs; the king is also titled Knight's General of the Army

- **Valudin** – equivalent of Duke

  - Six Valudin hold this title in the Northern Kingdom

  - Each governs a major territory

  - Most are related to the Crown by blood

- **Pernal** – equivalent of Marquess

  - Their respective sub-territory is called a Pernaldom

- **Quellen** – equivalent of Earl

- **Devant/Devantess** – equivalent of Viscount

- **Saquetier** – equivalent of Baron

Valudin of the Northern Kingdom:

- Luxony: Arnot Rengle, Regent to the Crown and brother to the king

- Prall: Arin Moreau, no ancestral ties to the Crown

- Kenton: Chaif Enure, second cousin to the king

- Billany: Anette Ador, first cousin to the king

- Lenferd: Gibbs Moraine, distant cousin to the king

- Julesland: Hender Bixury, first cousin to the king

The **king** and **queen** are addressed as **Your Majesty**, the **Valudin** as **Your Grace**, and all other nobles as **My Lord** or **My Lady**.

8.5 Houses (families)

The great houses of the Northern Kingdom make up the country's ruling class. Some houses go back to the country's founding.

Oldest among the houses is House Rengle, whose most prominent members include King Amure Rengle, Queen Elissa Rengle, and the king's brother, Valudin Arnot Rengle. The Moreaus represent the second-oldest house and one of great power in the realm. A centuries-old animosity exists between the Rengles and Moreaus, which causes unrelenting tension at the highest levels of the monarchy. The phrase, 'beware the Moreaus' speaks volumes as to the Rengles' take on their archnemesis. With a Moreau holding the top post in the Jahn Church as the Prefect of Prall, the Rengles must be careful how they balance their secular power against the Church's widespread influence over the people of the Northern Kingdom.

Houses of note:

- **Rengle**

  - Crest: rearing black horse surrounded by a motif of woven leaves

  - King's colors: red and gold

  - Queen's colors: green and gold

- **Moreau**

  - Colors: black and gold

- **Tissel**

  - Colors: beige and copper

- **Moraine**

  - Colors: gray and white

- **Ador**

  - Colors: amethyst and white

- **Enure**

  - Colors: crème and forest green

- **Bixury**

  - Colors: brown and pearl

8.6 The Crown

Dennington Palace is the three-story estate of the king and queen of the Northern Kingdom. It is the Buckingham Palace of Acia, with its splendor and storied history. A cellar equal in size to the structure above contains a secret tunnel that bridges the palace to **Windmoor Castle,** the Crown's fortification in Durenbeck.

Famous rooms:

- Gilded Room

- Green Room

- Blue Room

- Red Room

- Grand Ballroom

The following positions represent the household staff:

- **Grand Marshal of the Household** – heads all staff

- **Chamberlain** – attends to personal matters for the Crown

- **Master** or **Mistress of Larder** – manages the supply and storage of food and drink

- **Master** or **Mistress of Tablecloth** – manages dining affairs

- **Master** or **Mistress of Kitchen** – oversees cook staff

- **Master** or **Mistress of Cellar** – manages the supply and storage of wine and spirits

- **Master** or **Mistress of Horse and Mews** – manages the royal stables

- **Master** or **Mistress of Artisanal Desserts** (formerly of Pastry) – responsible for baked goods

- **Master** or **Mistress of Dress** – responsible for royal garb and fabrics

- **Master of Arms** – head of palace security and lead inquisitor into breaches of safety

Male staff are outfitted in liveries of starched black and white. Female staff wear conservative dresses, also black and white. Palace guards wear gleaming helms and breastplates over doublets.

8.7 Religion

Pagans for millennia, the Idarian-descended Prallites are mostly converted to Jahism. Missionaries from Vergahl in Meerjurmeh traveled to the kingdom near the end of Markania's rule and set up the first church in the capital city of **Durenbeck**. Today, the Church holds significant influence over the daily lives of Prallites. Like the Korinians, pilgrims often journey annually to Hōvar to receive blessings from the Greater Light.

The center of Jahnism in the Northern Kingdom can be found at the **Cathedral of Archangels**, in Durenbeck. The cathedral is the seat of power for the **Prefect of Prall**. It was built by King Joram in 2875, a century after the country's founding.

8.8 Holidays

Because the people of the Northern Kingdom are Jahnists, they've adopted the fetes from the Con-jurah that celebrate Jah's trio of famous archangels, Mika, Gabra, and Rapham. The festivals bring together commoners and nobles, who celebrate the occasions with food, music, and merriment. The Prefect of Prall presides over the religious ceremony that gives thanks to the angels for their protection over the people of the Northern Kingdom.

8.9 Customs and traditions

Fashion is big in the Northern Kingdom, boasting a thriving textile industry and many clothiers. Women and men equally drive trends in garb, with things like short capes, wide skirts, and fanciful doublets being all the rage. Markania is oft considered the home to fashion in the kingdom, which also includes footwear, hats, jewelry, hairstyles, and the use of makeup. Clothing choices distinguish classes of citizens and serve as social statuses for the wealthy and privileged. With fierce competition among the nobility, staying up on the latest fashion is often a differentiator at court and means of gaining favor . . . or losing face.

Sports are geared toward having fun and pitting wits. The game of **thieves' ball** is a popular sport, where mallets and brightly colored balls are used. Two teams of two, each divided into different sides of a narrow fairway, compete against each other. One player hits a ball toward the flag on the opposite end, while his opponent attempts to knock the ball out of the way, stealing the position. **Jousting** is another popular sport, albeit a costly one, relegated to tournaments sponsored by the wealthy.

Marriage among Prallites is a time-honored tradition dating back to the country's Idarian roots, where the parents of the bride would offer beaded necklaces as an act of well-wishing and fertility so their daughters might mother lots of children. As Prall became a kingdom and prospered, these matrimonial gifts expanded to include heirloom pieces of pottery, jewelry, and essential oils, along with land for the newly married. To consecrate a wedding, a priest must offer a blessing before the public so the marriage might be witnessed in the sight of Jah. For prosperous families, a goose is cooked and served at dinner following the wedding, along with a bounty of fruits, cheeses, and baked goods to demonstrate generosity and good fortune for the newlyweds. Families who can't afford a goose settle for roast chicken or meat pies.

With honoring the deceased, the Prallites inter their dead in burial mounds, called **barrows**. Nobles and royals dedicate large tracts of land to these auspicious bounds of raised earth, containing multiple chambers for family members. They connect the barrows through a network of tunnels belowground. The chambers contain niches for offerings, such as flowers, jars of wine, and vials of scented oils. Stones and earth are used as building materials. The entrances are often aligned to let light in during solstices as a way of allowing the light of Jah to bless those who have passed from the world. Workers called barrow keepers attend to the service and safekeeping of these tombs for the dead.

8.10 Greetings and salutations

The **bow** and **curtsy** are courteous forms of greetings. They're signifiers of respect in Prall culture and an art form all unto their own. For the ladies, there are three curtsies; for the gentlemen, seven bows. While the curtsies have names (e.g., half curtsy), the bows are numbered one through seven.

Curtsies:

1. Full curtsy

- Use: formal curtsy often aimed at one of a higher station or when full-blown respect is required

- Technique: a full bend in the front knee while the back leg pushes out and the entire body lowers while keeping the torso upright

2. Half curtsy

- Use: semiformal greeting or parting

- Technique: less exaggerated form of the full curtsy with barely a bend at the knees

3. The nudge

- Use: informal acknowledgment of the other party, sometimes used as a reflection of a bow made by the opposite sex

- Technique: a graceful but simple dip of the head with no bend at the knees

Bows:

1. Bow number one
- Nickname: the greeting

- Use: a semiformal method of greeting someone, such as an acquaintance, peer, or friend (when at a formal function)

- Technique: a medium-paced dip forward of the torso

2. Bow number two
- Nickname: the parting bow

- Use: similar to bow number one, but to say goodbye

- Technique: a quick dip forward of the torso

3. Bow number three
- Nickname: the flatterer's drape

- Use: to flatter or pay respect to a woman, often intending to show affection without coming across as flirtation

- Technique: a low bow

4. Bow number four
- Nickname: the gallant bow

- Use: a flamboyant bow used to express delight or affection without being flirtatious

- Technique: a low sweep with the hand, followed by the bend in the torso, where the back of the hand appears to brush the ground, then sweep away like a flourish of a quill on parchment

5. Bow number five
- Nickname: the humble sweep

- Use: when a gentleman wants to instill his full respect upon a lady in his company or upon his betters

- Technique: similar to the gallant bow, but with a more dignified and slower sweep of the hand

6. Bow number six

- Nickname: bow of reverence

- Use: to display the very highest form of respect, often to one above your station

- Technique: a slow, deep bow at the waist, with one hand over the belly, the other over the lower back

7. Bow number seven

- Nickname: the nod

- Use: the least formal of the bows; more of an acknowledgment than anything else; similar to the curtsy form of "the nudge"

- Technique: a dip of just the head with the barest forward movement of the torso

8.11 Food and drink

Prallites claim to have the finest **mead** in Acia, and many believe it to be true. The secret is in the form of natural additives, namely pepperleaf and avala bark, which enhance the intrinsic notes of clove and nutmeg. **Pepperleaf** imparts spicy notes while avala bark mellows the sugars in the beverages to create a smooth finish. **Gingerberry** adds a tangy, almost citrusy profile, which creates the most sought-after mead in the realm (and, some say, the world).

A variety of comfort foods sate the hearty appetites of the Northerners, whose harsh climes demand lighter meals in the summer and heavier ones in the winter. Everything from stews to roasts enrich suppers during the cold season. With Durenbeck's cosmopolitan culture, fine dining abounds among the upper class, pushing up the demand for pricey wines and liqueurs imported from the southern domains. For those with simpler tastes, hearty foods offer satisfaction. Such items include things like **crispies** (fried breakfast cakes) and **halos** (eggs scrambled inside nests of shredded potatoes).

8.12 Clothing

Prallites dress similarly to Europeans from the Middle Ages. Their garb is simple, especially the commoners, which include such apparel as pants, breeches, boots, and cloaks. The nobility uses more expensive materials and designs, with flaring dresses and doublets, often in the colors of their respective houses. Soldiers wear chain mail over their clothing. During ceremonies or official events, they also wear tabards. The country's crest depicts a rearing black horse surrounded by a motif of woven leaves, which is also the crest of House Rengle.

8.13 Allies and enemies

The Northern Kingdom, through the influence of the Church, has loose ties with Meerjurmeh. Trade with Terjurmeh has caused a conflict of interest among secular communities dependent on lumber exports, particularly in the country's southern region. To date, the kingdom has yet to decree an official stance with its neighboring countries, although Meerjurmeh came militarily to the country's aid early in its history when Idarian invaders attacked its eastern borders and threatened to sack the newly formed settlements and even the capital.

8.14 Commerce

Agriculture is the primary economic driver in the country as far as intracountry commerce goes. Terjurmeh's demand for wood has created a boom in the lumber trade over the last century, changing the dynamics of wealth distribution for the southern nobles, whose coffers quite possibly have grown to exceed the monarchy's. The kingdom's reliance on steel for manufacturing weapons and use in construction has boosted ore imports from Terjurmeh and spawned a considerable number of new mining operations along the recently founded settlements bordering the west end of the Serpent's Belt. Overall, the country prospers from economic expansion, even though the last few decades have proven nearly disastrous for the agriculture industry, which has seen hard winters nearly wipe out many of the late-harvest crops.

8.15 Currency

The currency of the Northern Kingdom comprises three denominations, divided neatly into units of copper, silver, and gold. All coins are round.

Denominations (lowest to highest) and stamps on the obverse:

- **Sovereign** – gold – pronged crown with six points, one for each Valudom, and a hexagonal gemstone in the center representing the monarchy governing the realm

- **Warren** – silver – rearing horse bearing a knight in plate armor holding a flaming sword aloft, surrounded by a wreath of woven leaves

- **Shim** – copper – falcon with wings back and talons extended as if about to snap up its prey, superimposed over a heraldic shield

Monetary conversion (lowest to highest):

- 50 copper shims = 1 silver warren

- 10 silver warrens = 1 gold sovereign

1 sovereign = 10 warrens = 500 shims

9. Korin

9.1 Geography and climate

Korin takes up the largest geographical area of any individual country. Its capital sits just below Acia's equatorial axis. The lands to the north are arid, composed of desert plains and wastelands. The lands to the south and the east are mostly plains and grasslands. Low rainfall makes for poor cultivation in these regions, despite the suitability of the soil. Korin is bordered by a variety of natural barriers, including the **Gōsh Mountains** to the north, **South Furals** to the west, and the forests of the **Green Unknown** to the east. The largest river in the world, **The River Life**, stretches almost a thousand miles, traversing the nation longitudinally, fed by **Lake Gōsh** to the north. Summers along the equator are hot and dry, with temperatures reaching upward of 120 degrees Fahrenheit. Winters are fairly warm, with temperatures rarely falling below seventy. The climate changes in the south and east where higher humidity provides a milder clime.

9.2 People

The people of the country are referred to as **Korinians**. Korinians are a diverse people whose aristocracy and regal bloodlines can be traced back thousands of years. The primary language of Korin is Korinian. Jurmehan is spoken as a secondary language, although those of means are encouraged to learn it both in verbal and written form. The history of Korin is rich and the country's culture is best described as a cross between ancient Egypt and the Roman Empire.

9.3 Government

Korin is a dynastic empire, comprised of **twelve principalities** and the loosely annexed **Provinces of the** South. The emperor is considered divine, a son of Jah, and is treated as a divine entity. The current ruler, **Xantecor**, is the third emperor of the twenty-fifth dynasty. The dynasty can be compared with the Roman Empire of the first and second centuries with its broad reach and military strength, although the strain of maintaining such breadth has caused fracturing and dissension, particularly in the outer territories, where the capital's influence wanes.

The emperor's seat of power is the **Pearl Palace** in the capital city of **Kasâh**. His court contains a mix of relatives and political appointees. A

steward runs the court in the emperor's absence. The post is the highest layman position in the capital. The **chancellor** is the top diplomat on the international front and manages a cadre of ambassadors to different nations and territories. The chancellor's job is to direct interaction with heads of state of foreign countries on behalf of the empire.

Korin has an extensive, geographically disbursed military. The military falls under two departments, Army and Navy, led by **General Niak** and **Admiral Pulchak**, respectively. Both report directly to the emperor. Naval components are split between The River Life and the seaport of Kanteron on the East Coast of the continent, with the naval center at the nation's capital. Kanteron's naval presence is nascent and not a priority of the current dynasty. Spread throughout the empire are imperial garrisons. **Legions** form the basic strategic unit of the empire and comprise six thousand troops. They fall under a governor's rule during peacetime and imperial rule during wartime.

The official imperial colors are **gold and white**. White is typically used as the background for gold insignia. The nation's crest is a gold disc, which represents the sun and Jah, with a dozen spearheads, one for each major city, radiating out of the center, but not touching the disc itself. The detachment symbolizes the closeness of the people to Jah, with the lack of contact denoting a separation between mortals and the divine.

9.4 Principalities

There are twelve major cities in Korin. Each city is the capital of its eponymously named **principality**. The empire tasks governors with the management of commerce, security, and the interests of the empire in their respective principalities, and support for the empire abroad. All governors are required to have blood ties to the royal family.

9.5 Religion

Jahnism is the official religion of Korin, although there are sects that still pay tribute to the old gods. The post-Great War missionaries of Meerjurmeh converted the Korinians to Jahn in the third century.

Jahnism became the official religion in the ninth century, but because of resistance among emperors who proclaimed themselves as living gods, monotheism didn't supplant polytheism until the fifteenth century. Even then, the self-proclamation continues in modern-day Korin.

Necromancy is an important part of Korin's religious history, and it is still practiced today, and protected by the emperor. Many want the practice abolished, but the **Imperial Sect of the Necromantic Order**, which is headquartered in the **Great Necropolis** near the capital, maintains a stranglehold on the imperial elite and has done so for the better part of the past four thousand years.

The **necromancer** is the most powerful religious figure in the imperial religious hierarchy. A **shaman** is a practicing priest, a step down in the pecking order. Both practice Jahnism, but only necromancers are ordained to commune with the dead.

9.6 The old gods

Before Jahnism came along, Korinians were pagans who worshipped and paid homage to multiple gods. Their pantheon has **twenty-four gods**, twelve greater and twelve lesser.

Greater gods:

1. **An-ta** – god of the sun and father to all gods (considered by modern-day Korinians to be the original incarnation of Jah)

2. **Nuna** – goddess of the moon and mother to all gods

3. **Monos** – god of war

4. **Heroon** – goddess of the rivers and seas

5. **Topak** – god of the skies

6. **Hura** – goddess of fertility

7. **Atos** – god of night

8. **Chakna** – god of death

9. **Petuk** – god protector of souls

10. **Rakussan** – god of fire

11. **Thuth** – goddess of wisdom, laws, and judgment, and arbiter to the gods

12. **Kilios** – god of chaos and Unmaker of the cosmos

Lesser gods:

1. **Da-amad** – god of spite

2. **Endura** – goddess of wine and spirits

3. **Ibis** – god patron to the lara and ferryman of the deadlands

4. **Cannuset** – goddess protector of women and the unborn

5. **Bek** – goddess protector of children

6. **Ernasek** – god of mischief, pestilence, and disease

7. **Manutef** – goddess of tongues and knower of all languages

8. **Aktamonnen** – god of agriculture

9. **Kululeh** – goddess of luck, fortune, and prosperity

10. **Annor** – god of statecraft and commerce

11. **Lilinet** – goddess of love, marriage, and beauty

12. **Holos** – god of music, poetry, and song

The **lara** serve the gods as their undead servants.

9.7 Holidays

As with the Prallites, Korinians share in the fetes, rites, and festivals observed by the Jahn Church. Other holidays predate these and are still celebrated:

- **Eye of the Sun** – a New Year's celebration that honors the sun god (An-ta originally; Jah in modern times)

- **Nunamon** – a festival begun by Isos, first emperor of the second dynasty, to honor Nuna, goddess of the moon, and the blessings of mothers to their children; celebrated during the first full moon of the year

- **Feast of Life** – a festival that pays homage to the bounty provided by The River Life, which takes place on the first Jah's Day following the autumn harvest

9.8 Customs and traditions

Because death was such an important part of ancient Korinian tradition, when citizens prayed to the old gods and the emperors were considered divine representatives on the mortal plane, many traditions honor the old ways. Korinians believe the dead should be interred on the west side of The River Life because the sun sets in the west. Many still bury loved ones in the desert or in crypts carved into sandstone on the west side of the river. While mummification was an integral part of the preparation process for the newly deceased, its practice died off when Jahnism took over as the primary religion of Korin, although people in less populated areas still tend to the practice today.

As important as death is symbolically, so is life. It's not uncommon for a father to make an offering of food and drink to an old god to request good health for the upcoming birth of a child. Hura, the goddess of fertility, still comes up in votives for this purpose, as does Bek, goddess protector of children.

Not all is serious among Korinians. They enjoy their fun too. One such outlet is the game of **khet**, the oldest board game in the world. It's a two-person game, much the way chess and backgammon are. The goal is to move pieces strategically along the board to topple the dynasty of the other player. The first to succeed wins. The game relies on subtlety as much as it requires strength and posturing. Players make use of feints, bluffs, and misdirection to outmaneuver and trick opponents into overprotecting their pieces or luring pieces out into the open. It's said the game mirrors political posturing.

Khet has gained such popularity among the Con-jurah that entire cafés have sprung up in Meerjurmeh for patrons to challenge one another to a game of khet while drinking tea and smoking djap. The popularity has also spilled over to the Provinces of the South. International tournaments allow friendly competition among neighboring countries, but the rivalry is fierce, with nationalism at the heart of these contests.

9.9 Greetings and salutations

Korinians are a proud people who respect their lineage. A person is referred to by their name and their relation to their parents when spoken of. For instance, someone named Mikah, whose father's name is Heliot, would be referred to as Mikah, son of Heliot, in speech or writing.

Soldiers and officers greet each other with a salutation of a fist over their chest.

Imperials are greeted reverently by commoners. An official greeting also requires the commoner to kneel before an imperial.

9.10 Food and drink

Korinians love their food. The elite are known for casting lavish banquets, none more extravagant than the emperor, who might throw a twenty-course dinner party on the whim for a hundred guests at a time. Exotic dishes like roast tongue of quail and braised mussels imported from the Permal Sea can fetch exorbitant prices. Aristocrats use exotic foods as a demonstration of social status and a means for gaining political favor.

While Korin boasts fine mead, ale, and wine, they also produce beer, which everyday citizens enjoy, some over water, especially in regions where clean water is scarce. Korinian beer dates back to the early dynasties, but many believe its origin heralds from the province of Boronio to the south, where shamans praying to the spirits of the mountain-fed waters of West Lake would brew the beer as an offering to ward off evil sprites.

9.11 Clothing

The vast reach of the empire encompasses many cultures, and different clothing styles have been adopted by the people spread throughout the country. The hot desert clime in the central part of the country creates an environment for minimal loose-fitted clothing, such as the wear of **kilts** among men and simple cotton dresses among women. **Raks** are popular attire among the upper class, gossamer-and-cotton kimono-like outfits. Men and children often forgo tops during the hotter months. Jewelry is common among all classes of people. Men and women wear collarbone necklaces and earrings made of copper, silver, or gold. Korinians love color, which is why jewelry often includes the use of faience beads, glass, jewels, and gemstones.

Foot soldiers wear sandals and breastplates over tunics. Their outerwear is typically white with the country's official crest. Imperial palace guards wear white-lacquered breastplates and golden helms bearing the feathered plume of the icarus, a beautiful songbird of pure white, and long capes draped off their shoulders. Breastplates and capes bear the imperial insignia.

9.12 Allies and enemies

Korin has an old-standing alliance with Meerjurmeh, which is drawn along religious lines. There are talks in place to strengthen old ties, in particular, because of recent aggression from Terjurmeh, but neither

Korin nor Meerjurmeh has called upon each other militarily for centuries. Korin regards Terjurmeh neutrally and has a truce in place to protect its mining interests in the Gōsh Mountains.

9.13 Commerce

Because of the extensive highway system built between the twenty-first and twenty-third centuries, trade between principalities across the empire is efficient and flourishing. Kasâh, the capital, and the cities of Finth and Scoriah are the major commerce hubs of the empire, with all roads leading to Kasâh. Korinian engineers are said to be the best at building roads that endure the test of time. One technique used is a method of crushing sedimentary rock into gravel, which is mixed with a bonding agent. Giant rollers drawn by pack animals press the surface flat.

The River Life provides an expedient means for travel and inter-hub commerce over a thousand-mile stretch of imperial territory. The empire is rich in spices and spins some of the most sought-after silks. Vast gold and silver reserves, along with ore mining operations in the South Furals and Gōsh Mountains, provide financial backing for trade. Marble, granite, porcelain, and rare gems are exported to the forest-rich Provinces of the South in exchange for lumbar and crystal. International trade is limited in the northern hemisphere because of desert and mountainous barriers and the isolationist policies of Terjurmeh and Meerjurmeh. Korin is currently exploring the use of sea travel to extend its reach to the southernmost provinces and transport highly sought-after pearls from Shell Bay on the West Coast to the cities of the East Coast. There are seaports in the eastern cities of Kanteron, Atanah, and Dezīah, and a new one is being constructed in the western city of Pentegeiah.

9.14 Currency

Korin and the Provinces of the South use the same Korinian currency.

Denominations (lowest to highest) and symbols stamped onto each coin:

- **Tet** – copper – wheat stalk and spike

- **Koff** – bronze – coursing river

- **Emblem** – silver – cycles of the moon

- **Imperial** – gold coin – pyramid

- **Double imperial** (solar) – gold coin – sunburst

Monetary conversion (lowest to highest):

- 5 copper tet = 1 bronze koff

- 4 bronze koff = 1 silver emblem

- 10 silver emblems = 1 gold imperial

- 2 gold imperials = 1 double imperial

1 double imperial (solar) = 2 imperials = 20 emblems = 80 koff = 400 teff

9.15 The number twelve

Twelve is a sacred number in Korinian culture, dating back to the empire's founding. There are twelve major cities, twelve principalities, and twelve **Grand Pyramids**. Twelve spearheads form the insignia of the imperial standard. The number's significance heralds from the pantheon of ancient gods: twelve greater and twelve lesser gods. In modern-day Korin, it represents the divine number of Jah and is believed to bring good fortune.

10. Provinces of the South

10.1 Geography and climate

The topography of the **Provinces of the South** varies from grassland to hills to woods. Many rivers occupy the countryside, the larger ones fed by lakes and mountains to the north. The climate is temperate most of the year, allowing farmers and ranchers to work the land all year long. Three large bodies of water surround the Provinces: the Permal Sea in the west, the Eastern Ocean in the east, and the Asyran Ocean in the south.

10.2 People

The Provinces of the South—often referred to as just the **Provinces**—contain **twenty-three distinct provinces**. The people are as varied in skin tone as they are in heritage, many with roots that pre-date the formation of the Korinian Empire to the north. Many believe provincials are of Idarian descent, the result of migratory hillmen pioneering the southwest in the search for a new home.

Korinian is the official language, although many speak their own dialects. With the advent of Jahnism, Jurmehan has increased in popularity over the centuries. One can easily speak three or more languages, especially among those who trade with the empire, Meerjurmeh, and other provinces. Most provincials live a simple life, occupying farmsteads, ranches, hamlets, villages, towns, and seaside settlements or migrating with herds of cattle and horses across open plains.

10.3 Government

The Provinces of the South form a **federation** under Korinian rule. Each province has its own set of laws and government, superseded by imperial law when the empire's interest is at stake. A persistent occupational force from Korin maintains order in the Provinces much the way the Romans did in North Africa during their height of power. The **Federation Council**, located in the port city of **Kurth**, which the empire recognizes as the official capital, dictates interprovince relations and acts as the liaison between the Provinces and the empire. Each of the **twenty-three provinces** is represented by a voting council member of equal stature, called a **consul**. A Korinian-approved **proconsul** governs the respective province. While the Provinces adhere to a federated system of governance, a few progressive provinces like Kurth and Visdon use a democratic approach of electing officials by way of the people's vote.

10.4 Religion

Jahism is the official religion of the Provinces of the South. Necromancy, once pervasive because of the empire's influence, has died out, and paganism, which was widespread up to the middle of the last millennium, is nonexistent, with many of the old temples destroyed and most traces of worshipping the old god eradicated by followers of the Jahn Church. Like Korinians and Prallites, the more devout followers make an annual pilgrimage to Hōvar in Meerjurmeh to receive a blessing from the Greater Light. Provincials who practice Jahnism often partake in the holidays and celebrations sanctioned by the Church, which are shared among Con-jurah and Prallites.

10.5 Commerce

With seafaring vessels and a willingness to overcome agelong superstitions of venturing into open waters, shipping has become big business. The Provinces boast the best shipwrights in the world. Many rivers and seaports provide accelerated means of moving goods between provinces and Korin. Kurth, the largest port in the world, sits on the East Coast. Travel from the treacherous waters of the **Eastern Ocean** to **Shell Bay** on the West Coast wasn't possible three centuries earlier. Advances in hull, mast, and sail design have made long journeys feasible. Since then, waterway commerce has exploded, providing prosperous opportunities for a select number of provinces and a new means of taxation for the empire.

Traders barter wares, furs, and livestock among neighboring provinces, with the more urbane trading goods with the empire. Currency is used sparingly but growing in popularity as provincials become more cosmopolitan, especially those engaged in shipping and seafaring. The Provinces don't mint their own coins, using imperial currency instead.

10.6 Arcane practices

The peoples of the Provinces dabble in channeling but lack the skills of magi and priests of Terjurmeh and Meerjurmeh. There are no formal schools that teach the arcane arts, but the Kurthans have developed an art form called **Kashpet**. It allows for the manipulation of the wind and the taming of the sea in open water, which helps sailors manage treacherous conditions out at sea. Kashpet is manifested through vocalization and communing with the elements, namely air and water.

11. Darkforth

11.1 Geography and climate

The domain of Darkforth divides east from west on the continent. From a Western perspective, little is known of the wilds of this domain. Dense forestland creates a natural border, ranging from the **Green Unknown** forest in the south, which borders Korin, to the main forest in the north, which borders Meerjurmeh. Jungles, rainforests, swamplands, mountains, and wastelands make travel inland a logistical nightmare for the uninitiated. The forests and mountains have a cooler clime than the rest of the domain, with snowfall in the higher elevations during wintertime. Swampland and jungles are perpetually hot and occupy the central and eastern portions of Darkforth. A large stretch of volcanic wasteland takes up the northern area of the domain in the **Âhn** region. This inhospitable territory has one defining landmark visible from miles in all directions: a volcano named **Vanya**, translated as "mother" in Old Jurmehan. It is the only active volcano in Acia.

11.2 People

The peoples of Darkforth are diverse. There are three distinct races:

- **An-jurah**. The dominant segment of the Darkforth population. Originally from modern-day Meerjurmeh, the An-jurah entered the wilds of Darkforth just after the Year One and slowly spread over the domain, separating into disparate states ruled by warlords.

- **Idarians**. Native to the forests and lower elevations, these wild "hillmen" continue to live in clans as nomads, not only in Darkforth but across the Serpent's Belt Mountains and parts of Mendegōsh. Westerners consider them barbarians.

- **Machoo**. Relatively unknown to the rest of the world, the Machoo are indigenous to the warmer regions of Darkforth and are the most primitive of civilized cultures. Machoo villages are spread throughout Darkforth. The people, mostly converted to Sanism, live peacefully within the An-ju-rahn-run states.

The following goes into more detail regarding these peoples.

11.3 An-jurah

The An-jurah have lived in Darkforth for over three millennia. After their defeat in the Great War, they splintered into two groups, half settling in modern-day Terjurmeh and the other half heading east across the Meerjurmehan countryside, until they entered the forests of Darkforth. Since then, they have spread across the domain and prospered. The An-jurah maintain ties with their geographically separated Ter-jurahn descendants through the leadership of the An-jurahn Temple. Other than this relationship, the rest of Western civilization knows little of the An-jurah, except what the history books say. The An-jurah speak Jurmehan as their primary language and **An-jek**, or low tongue, secondarily. Like their Ter-jurah cousins, they are short and squat.

11.4 Military

Warriors wear horned helms and armor, including emblazoned breastplates, shin, and forearm guards. Black and red are favored colors, the black symbolizing the dark power of their god, San, and the red the spilled blood of their enemies. They fight with swords and spears at close range and use longbows to assail opponents from a distance.

Horn colors signify the warrior's hierarchy within the military ranks. A white-horn is the equivalent of a lieutenant, a red-horn a captain, a gray-horn a major, and a black-horn a general.

11.5 Government

The An-jurah are deeply territorial. Over the centuries, settlements and villages turned into states with distinct but shifting borders. Chieftains became warlords, and territorial disputes arose, ending in bloodshed and the transfer of power, and change in borders. Although the Temple remained a central part of An-jurahn daily life, it never took on a secular role, and therefore, the fighting continued . . . until three centuries ago. Âhn, the center of the An-jurahn Temple, has slowly become the most powerful state in Darkforth. Its capital city, **Symorrah**, is now considered the capital of all An-jurah and, many say, Darkforth. A tribal council controls secular affairs with the role of warlord supplanted by a War Chief, the most powerful layman position among the people.

The tribal council's current initiative, backed by the Temple, is the unification of all states. Many of the northern states fall under the council's control, with warlords as participating members. Annexing the southern states is slow. The Southerners are less cultured than their Northern counterparts and are fiercely opposed to cooperative governing.

11.6 Religion

The **An-jurahn Temple**, or "Temple" in the vernacular, varies from the Terjurmehan Temple. Much of the Temple is local to the An-jurahn states and exists in a more primitive form than its Terjurmehan sister organization. Only within the last few centuries has the Temple taken on a more centralized role, accumulating power within Âhn, where the main temple is located.

Six **high priests** lead the Temple—the equivalents of Articulates of Terjurmeh—with one holding the role of **grand high priest**, currently the **High Priest of the Blood Sect**. The role carries tremendous power, but not on the same scale as the Mighty One, the Ter-jurahn incarnate of San in Acia, because of disparate leadership of the people, split among warring states.

Each high priest heads up a different order, called a sect. There are **six sects** in the An-jurahn Temple:

- Blood

- Moon

- Death

- Fire

- Shadow

- Warrior (Su-yi)

Like the Ter-jurah, priests make up the bulk of the clergy, followed by clerics and acolytes in the hierarchy.

Priests often shave their heads as a display of status, leaving just a ponytail. They stain their scalps in dark-red discs as a pledge of fealty to their god and tattoo the inner circumference of the circles with sharp-edged runes needled in black ink. Like their Terjurmehan brethren, they wear seraks hanging from necklaces. One addresses an An-jurahn priest as **High One** and refers to them in the third person as **His** or **Her Holiness**.

Most fanatical and feared among the Temple is an order of priests called the **Su-yi (Warrior Sect)**. Su-yi are warrior priests used by the Temple to enforce canon law and put down secular uprisings. They are vicious in their methods. The ruthless priests take down warlords when the need arises. To display their loyalty to their religion and god, they tattoo the crowns of their shaved heads with the holy delta in solid black, saving a small circle of hair they grow long into a ponytail. They never cut their hair, a sign of their never-ending devotion to their cause.

Su-yi blood-let in service of their god, letting droplets of blood dribble into an iron cup of offering, heated over hot coals. The iron in the cup is the key to **Azul-nahg**, the **Rite of Binding**. The unholy properties of the metal allow it to bind the blood onto itself, fusing the body to the vessel to prepare the host to receive a demon from the Netherworld. The demon, tempted by the blood, invades the vessel, only to bind to it, trapping itself in the process and becoming a servant to its wielder. Once bound, the trinity of demon, vessel, and priest enter an unholy contract, allowing the host to wield the demon's nether power as his own. Only death can release the bond.

11.7 Holidays

The An-jurah observe most of the same holidays as the Ter-jurah. Some sects practice offerings in special ceremonies held during different phases of the moon or times of the year. Lunar and solar eclipses play a large part in the timing of sacrifices and offerings for certain sects.

11.8 Allies and enemies

The An-jurah maintain a symbiotic peacefulness with their indigenous neighbors. Conversion to Sanism has made Idarians and Machoo allies in the wild. Of strategic importance is the alliance with the Ter-jurah, who also believe in an end-days scenario where the followers of San will rise up against the followers of Jah and raze their enemies and unite the world under one faith. While the An-jurah have traditionally warred among themselves, they hold enmity with any who enter their domain and have encouraged their barbaric allies to wage war on those races near their borders. It is for this reason no outsiders enter Darkforth and live to tell the tale.

11.9 Commerce

Barter is still the key form of commerce among the An-jurah, although the more developed states have established a monetary system. Trade is isolated to intrastate trade and occasionally interstate commerce. International relations are nonexistent, nor is it a consideration.

11.10 Idarians

Tall and lithe, these Darkforth natives live in clans ruled by chieftains. They're avid hunters and warriors and territorial by nature. **Idarians** are often called **"hillmen"** by westerners for the belief they live only in the hills. They are in fact a nomadic people who travel far and wide across a myriad of terrains and territories. Idarians occupy the greatest geographic span on the planet, living in hills, plains, forests, and even jungles. Idarians who settled in the Northwest became modern-day Prallites, and those in the Southwest became citizens of the Provinces of the South over the centuries. Many westerners label Idarians as savages and consider their continuous encroachment on the more civilized nations to be barbaric and threatening. They do this mostly out of ignorance and fear, forgetting their genesis, which often resulted because of migration.

Idarians hunt, forage and trap game to survive. They speak various dialects of their own guttural tongue, but the more educated clansmen speak Jurmehan or An-jek. One of the oddest (and least understood) traits is how they greet foreigners. They whiff the air whenever they encounter a stranger. If the scent displeases them, they make a face, which can bring about aggression toward the stranger, even an arrow to the throat.

Idarians vary in skin tone from reddish-brown to deep copper like the Machoo. They distinguish themselves among clans using feathers, piercings, tattoos, animal hides, and brightly colored jewelry. They often keep their hair long, which they manage with leather headbands or circlets of metal, particularly when on horseback, on the hunt, or on patrol. Facial decorations include piercings of the nose, cheeks, and ears, and beaded necklaces or dangling trinkets of stone or bone, coarse outfits with colorful feathers or patches of hide, tribal-patterned tattoos on their faces, necks, or arms. Warriors like to paint black lines in geometric, jagged patterns across the face to intimidate rivals.

Idarians are excellent warriors, using javelins or bows and arrows to fell prey and navigate the wilds upon their steeds. They typically fashion their arrowheads with bone, horn, or stone, although recent An-jurahn influence has better armed them with iron broadheads used for hunting and warfare, and equipped them with superior longbows for firing missiles at a distance. Men and women are equally formidable warriors, often forming hunting parties of mixed sexes. They're also capable horsemen, navigating difficult terrains upon the backs of their steeds.

The Idarians refer to San as the "night god." Like the An-jurah, they prey to San and give thanks for his blessing.

11.11 Machoo

Also called **Machoo Indians**, the **Machoo** are typically found in the warmer climes of Darkforth. They are short and skinny by nature and dress and live as primitives, confined to small villages spread throughout Darkforth. Machoo, like Idarians, believe in San and recognize the An-jurahn Temple as the official religious organization in the domain. They speak their own tongue, which sounds remarkably similar to the Idarian language, although the two are as different as Jurmehan and Korinian.

The height of their civilization lasted between 1100 and 1300, although it's a rough estimate, as their history was carved into stone relics and monuments, many eroded over time by the persistent rains. At their peak, the Machoo built pyramids and had kings who ruled over chiefdoms in West Darkforth. They used the pyramids for rituals and sacrifice, but also as cultural and spiritual centers. The pyramids honored the old gods who had dominion over wind, water, thunder, war, birth, death, and fertility. Members of the royal family exhibited strength through barbaric acts, such as bloodletting of their own bodies after numbing themselves first by smoking leaves from the rare tíka tree.

Machoo are a short people with copper skin that borders on nut-brown. Their noses are flat and wide like spades and their hair is dark brown. Some tribes trim their hair into bowl cuts. Because of the warmer climates of the jungle the Machoo often inhabit, their garb is limited to simple loincloths made of dried grass and reeds. For decoration and individuality, they add colored feathers they drape from their hips. They also string bits of bone, wood, and stone to form long earrings that cause their ears to droop. It's not uncommon for the tribespeople to pierce their noses with bones, wear lip plates to distend their lower lips, and scarify their faces and chests in unique, bumpy patterns to showcase their beauty and strength. Males over the age of thirteen will undergo scarification as a rite of passage from boy to man, choosing patterns they hope will attract females. Women rarely cover their breasts, showcasing their serried patterns of decorative scars. Children may wear decorations such as black squiggles, dots, and dashes painted onto their faces and bodies.

Machoo hunt with spears, bows and arrows, and use machetes and other rudimentary bladed weapons. They use the cover of their natural surroundings to aid in the element of surprise, ambushing enemies and game alike. They engage in limited husbandry to grow grains for milling into flour for unleavened bread, a staple in their diet, although they often harvest starchy tubers, which they dry and mill for a variety of foodstuffs.

The Machoo live in small villages that comprise a single tribe, mostly in clearings or along a river's edge. They live in huts with thatched roofs and use the wood of their forests as building materials. They construct shrines of stone in the forests to pay homage to their god and ancestors.

High priests offer their people a channel to the divine. The priests wear headdresses of bright plumage and carry staves that symbolize their connection to San. One addresses a Machoon priest as **High One**.

12. Kushan

Although technically not a domain in Acia, **Kushan** is unique because it belongs to no country, nor is it claimed. Also referred to as the **City of Night**, Kushan has a long-standing history dating back almost 4,000 years. It's long been assumed to be a ruined ancient city—cursed and feared—but in fact, it is very much alive and well. The citizens call themselves Kushites.

Great walls rise from the desert sand to surround this fortress of a city. Fed by an underground river from the Northern Range to the north and nestled at the mouth of the most massive subterranean cavern in the world, the city is self-sustaining. The cavern connects a tunnel system that runs clear to the mountains. What makes the city unique is that it's hidden by a curtain of darkness that appears to be a vaellra suspended in place with sand drifting upward from the desert floor. This curtain is called the **Rift**, a magical barrier created after the city was originally destroyed by invaders. Like a vaellra, the motionless sandstorm is violent and capable of killing trespassers.

Kushites live as isolationists in the middle of the desert, thanks to the underground river that supplies fresh water from the mountains in the north. An aquifer supplies well water to the citizens. The **Cavern of Dei**, with its fertile stone terraces and entry to the life-giving water source, allows the Kushites to grow the foodstuffs they need, tend to cattle, and nourish the population without importing anything. The self-sufficient nature of the population provides ample opportunity for creativity and ingenuity. Smithers make their own armaments, tools, and armor. Clothiers make textiles and clothing. Coopers, tanners, tinkers, and a host of other craftsmen use their skills to ensure the city remains autonomous.

Unfortunately, the Kushites live under a veil of fear. The **Malaji**, their rulers, govern ruthlessly. They comprise ten wizened men thousands of years old, once prominent An-jurahn magi. They forsook their souls for power and, in doing so, trapped themselves for eternity. Their master is

Gadreel, one of the fallen angels known as the **Watchers**, who holds the city captive under his fell power, including the Malaji. At one time, Gadreel lived among the Watchers in Aerth (Dagoth), only to be punished by Jah in the end and put in chains.

The story goes that San freed the Watchers, but not Gadreel. Gadreel eventually tricked one of his brethren into breaking his bond and destroyed the angel. He fled through a portal to Acia, where he wandered the great deserts until coming upon Kushan. It was there that he gave the An-jurahn magi immortality for their souls, binding their spirits to him and making himself a god to them and all who lived in Kushan. To prevent their escape, and to ensure no one could enter the fabled city, Gadreel constructed the Rift. The Malaji, unable to die, have grown decrepit in their old age, but the angelic power drawn from their master sustains them. It's a miserable existence for all because the Malaji cannot die, the citizens cannot leave, and Gadreel, the renegade angel of Heaven, is afraid of both San and Jah and can find refuge only within his own prison.

Gadreel is named the **Prince of Vanity**, appearing as a comely young man in human form. His servants address him as **Exalted One** to appease him and prey to him as the **God of Kushan**. Gadreel is ever wanting, ever needing praise to maintain his tortured existence among mortal kind.

The **Malajus Exetor** is the title given to the lead Malajus. In 1207, a Malajus Exetor named Mallavant the Cold began a century-long war against Terjurmeh. According to Terjurmeh's history, the conflict ended in a duel between Mallavant and the reigning Mighty One of Terjurmeh. The Mighty One purportedly killed Mallavant and imprisoned his soul in black diamond in the Shrine of San. The remaining Malaji were branded heretics and executed by the Temple. The second day of San-tel-moor commemorates their victory. However, the deaths of the

Malaji are not corroborated, nor are the Malaji proven to be gone for the world. Some believe they still rule in Kushan.

13. Dagoth

Dagoth is the origin world of mankind. It was originally called **Aerth**, the "land of plenty," created by **Jovah** (**Jah**, the Creator). According to the Watcher, Azazel, Jah spawned man from dust, where the rains mixed with the earth, and the mud took shape. It dried, cracked, and out came the first man. Jovah saw that man was good, and he begot woman, and mankind multiplied and prospered. But man became wicked, for in his heart he harbored lust, greed, hate, vanity, and jealousy. Jovah selected a handful of good people—the **Chosen**—to survive the **Great Flood** that destroyed the wicked. The offspring of the Chosen gave rise to a second generation of man, which became corrupt in the Creator's eyes. Because Jovah vowed never to flood the world again, he created mankind anew, this time in Acia, using the ashes of the Chosen's bones in the hope his third attempt would rectify the failings of his first two creations.

It was during the time of the Great Flood that the **Watchers**—angels sent to watch over mankind—were punished in Dagoth for their corrupting influence over humans and for mating and begetting children, giants like themselves (estimated at around seven feet in height). They were set in chains as punishment to watch their children die along with the rest of the wicked people of the world. **Sag-ahn** (**San**) freed the Watchers, bringing the fallen angels under his fold to do his bidding.

At the height of their civilization, the peoples of Dagoth prospered and built great metropolises that flourished. During Petrah's visit to Dagoth, he comes upon his birthplace, the **Iron City**, a former architectural marvel, now in decay, scavenged by the locals for its rich supply of building materials. Great towers of steel and glass once crowded the busy avenues, now in ruin and disarray, a shadow of their former glory. They speak of the great engineering feats of the past, lost to the inheritors of this savaged world.

A great pestilence affects Dagoth. Along with the perpetual winter, disease has ravaged the world, which now dies a slow but inevitable death. Pasturelands and forests are in decline; food is scarce; life is brutal. City dwellers use creative farming practices to keep crops warm by sheltering them from the elements by growing produce and other foodstuffs within the skeletons of tall buildings. Ranchers also use the city, herding livestock into sheltered spaces away from the elements.

Dagothans abide by **the Law**. The Law creates order among the denizens. Those who break the Law, face punishment. A magistrate presides over a court in a justice hall called a **Juditarium**, where they determine the guilt of the accused, along with sentencing. Magistrates are addressed as **Your Honorable**.

Dagothans speak many languages, but the common tongue is **Glesh**. The clergy and military know the priest's tongue, which is Jurmehan.

Greetings, especially ones of respect, involve touching one's fingers to the forehead with the left hand.

The disparate peoples of Dagoth are divided along religious lines: those who follow Jovah (**Jovahns**) and those who follow Sag-ahn (**Sag-ahnists**).

13.1 Jovahns

Jovahns believe in **Jovah**, the **God of Light** (**Jah** to the peoples of Acia). The **Peshte**, also referred to as mountaineers, are the primary constituent of Jovahns in Dagoth. They maintain strongholds in the mountains, harrying their enemies on foot and horseback. Jovahns are a fierce, free people, but also a disadvantaged people, as their enemies have decimated their kind over the centuries. Weakened, they stand fast against a growing darkness and face potential genocide at the hand of their enemy.

13.2 Sag-ahnists

Sag-ahnists are the sworn enemies of the Jovahns. Aman's rise to power in Dagoth has allowed him to unite several peoples of Dagoth, all followers of **Sag-ahn**, the **God of Darkness**, also called the **God of Shadows**, **All Father**, **Truthforger**, and **Darkwreather**. These Sag-ahnists include the **Angorians** from the forests, the **Novatoa** from the hills, the **Meslins** from the desert, the **Jaketh** from the prairie lands, and the **Ska'rites** from the sea. The Angorians control the Iron City, the Meslins the outlying desert lands, including the castle and city Aman uses as his stronghold.

Sag-ahnists display their devotion to Sag-ahn through the branding of their left wrists. The left is preferred over the right, as it represents the glory attributed to the "left hand of darkness." They refer to themselves as **the Marked**.

The **moodra** is the branded symbol of the Marked. It depicts a serpent wreathed in flame with a circle around it. The circle represents infinity and the undying devotion to Sag-ahn. The serpent's head starts left of center, with gaping jaws that project a lick of fire for a tongue. Its body spirals clockwise, terminating at the center of the spiral. The serpent is called the **nautilus serpent**, shaped like an inverted nautilus. It's said to be born of flame, reaching out from its genesis toward oblivion.

Another symbol is the **syriak**, the triangular device with the all-seeing eye in the center, similar to the serak of the Ter-jurah.

The **Shrine** is the religious body of Sag-ahnists as well as the name of the religious building where they gather. Devotees pledge their faith at shrines, the most devout wearing wooden masks over their faces to block out distractions as they pray. They often paint their masks gold to exhibit the value of their faith, the eyes holy black, with hollows over their mouths to let out the prayers and dribbles of red tears on the cheeks to symbolize the shedding of blood as a testament of faith. Bloodletting is also seen as a sign of faith, with droplets used on masks to show off the devotion to fellow Sag-ahnists. The **Great Shrine** is the largest shrine in Dagoth, a few days' march from the Iron City.

Enforcers are anointed servants of the Shrine whose duty is to enforce the faith. They are like the San-mahadi of the Terjurmehan Temple in their mission to capture heretics and bring them to justice.

13.3 Amerans

The **Amerans** were once a powerful people, gifted builders, and master craftspeople credited with many of the metropolises in Dagoth. Their demise is unknown, but their contributions live on with their many monuments and cities, deemed engineering marvels for their mastery over steel and glass, and the scale of their buildings.

Acknowledgments for The Light of Darkness series

T HIS SERIES HAS BEEN decades in the making and has taken on many forms, culminating with the book you just read and the other books in the series.

As many an author can attest, writing is a lonely pursuit, but bringing a work of fiction to life and making it the best it can be requires a team. For those who've helped me along the way, I am truly grateful. What follows is a list of extraordinary human beings who have lent their sharp eyes, astute minds, and brilliant suggestions to me during my journey with this series.

Because *The Light of Darkness* started many moons ago—back when I thought my nine-book series would be a duology; then, a trilogy; and finally, the nine books it has become—I need to acknowledge three talented editors: First, there's Michael Wolf, who made all his amazing edits using a red pen and printout of the manuscript. Then there's Joshua Essoe, who tackled the beginning of the story. And, finally, Jonathan Miller, my current editor, who went above and beyond with his masterful edits and thoughtful suggestions, and pushed me to take my story to the next level.

Then there are my alpha and beta readers, starting with those who helped with the earlier version of my work (in no particular order): Daniel Piangerelli, Roy Hamilton, Janis Flax, and Andrew Alberti. My alpha (first) reader for this latest version of the series, Leslie Bridgwater, who dove into uncharted waters and offered indispensable feedback. And the beta readers who volunteered to read and comment on my work: Karen Harrison, Jerry White, Kate Julicher, Candice Lisle, and John Parus. A many thanks to you all.

Of course, we mustn't forget the gorgeous cover art and interior artwork.

The covers would not have been close to where they are if not for the critical eye of my good friend, Wulf Moon—an author and artist in his own right—who helped me choose the best color palettes, action poses, and lighting, and advised me on "guiding the eye of the reader on a journey."

For the cover design and creation, I want to thank my cover artist, Les (Germancreative), who worked tirelessly to make the eBook and print covers for all nine novels and the prequel novella. She created a brand for the series that offers an engaging and consistent look and feel. No matter how many revisions I requested, Les rose to the challenge to produce her best work.

While I can claim credit for creating the maps of my fantasy world, my artist, Sam (Samsul Hidayat), turned them into masterpieces, each with an engraved look that's both classical and timeless. He also made the background art you see at the start of each chapter. Ten custom pieces of art, one per book, based on the book's theme.

Because of my long voyage at sea with this series, which began as a watercolor map I painted in 1992, there will be those who helped me but whose names have slipped through the cracks of my ship. Know that your kindness and generosity are not forgotten and that your contribution is forever bound to this enduring work.

About the Author

S TEVE PANTAZIS IS AN award-winning author of fantasy and science fiction. He won the prestigious Writers of the Future award and has published short stories in leading anthologies and magazines, including *Nature*, *Galaxy's Edge*, and *IGMS*. He is the author of *The Light of Darkness* epic fantasy series. When not writing (a rare occasion!), Steve creates extraordinary cuisine, exercises with vigor, and shares marvelous adventures with the love of his life. Originally from the Big Apple, he now calls Southern California home. You can learn more about him at www.StevePantazis.com.

Connect with Steve

G ET A **FREE eBook** just by signing up for Steve's newsletter: https://www.stevepantazis.com/subscribe

Support Steve at **Patreon** and receive early access to his short stories and novel chapters, along with cool swag: https://www.patreon.com/StevePantazis

To find out more about Steve and his happenings, check out these links:

Facebook page: http://facebook.com/SFFAuthor
Twitter: https://twitter.com/pantazis
Website: https://www.stevepantazis.com

Also by Steve Pantazis

Visit **HTTPS://WWW.STEVEPANTAZIS.COM/BOOKS** TO SEE Steve's current and forthcoming releases or scan the following QR code.

Short stories and novellas:

A Matter of Time

A World Without Flowers

Aliens Anonymous

Apostate

Before I Let You Go

Between a Rock and a Fireball

C'est la vie, Humans

Chameleon

Cold as Space

Curse of the Goddess of Kaanapali

Cursed Magic

Daddy's Girl

Daughter of Time

Decadent Deception

Earth for Sale (Sold!)

Eternity's Traveler

Gods of War

Hex

Honor Bound

Humanity's Last Hope

I Dream of Stars

Illusions

In a Blink

In Darkness Lies

Infernally Yours

It's Only Skin Deep, Darling

Light in the Shadow of Worlds

Magic in the Land of Oppression

Murder on Moonbase 9

Odin's Daughter

Out of Print

Race to the Relic

Purple Orchid Eater

Reset

Surrogate

Switch

The Abernacle

The Daughter You've Always Wanted

The Devil Walks into a Bar

The Hunt

The Legacy

The Longest Mile

The Old Man and the Sea Siren

The Prize

The Sacrifice

To Be Human

Universal Problem

Unlucky

Untamed

Boxed sets:

Alien Worlds

Dragons & Magic

Human 2.0

Miscreants & Mayhem

Modern Magic

Robot Dreams

Space & Time

The Alien Within

The Light of Darkness epic fantasy series:

Prequel: The Dark That Ignites

Book 1. The Dark That Begins

Book 2. The Dark That Creates

Book 3. The Dark That Binds

Book 4. The Dark That Usurps

Book 5. The Dark That Defies

Book 6. The Dark That Burns

Book 7. The Dark That Destroys

Book 8. The Dark That Rules
Book 9. The Dark That Ends

Science fiction novels:

Blackout
Godnet

www.ingramcontent.com/pod-product-compliance
Lightning Source LLC
Chambersburg PA
CBHW060744190726
48285CB00002B/295